# Praise for the [illegible]es



## YOU REALLY GOT ME

"Lovable characters and pulse-pounding chemistry make this one of my favorite reads of the year!"—Laura Kaye, *New York Times* Bestselling Author

"Sexy, lyrical and electric with hot, romantic tension." - NYT and USA Today Bestselling author Lauren Blakely

"This is an author to watch."—*RT Book Reviews*

## I WANT YOU TO WANT ME

Booklist calls I WANT YOU TO WANT ME "...steamy, hot, and totally engaging. The characters are realistic, and Kelly paints a vivid picture of what happens behind the scenes in the world of rock."

## TAKE ME HOME TONIGHT

All About Romance awards TAKE ME HOME TONIGHT a Desert Isle Keeper review. "All these (characters) are so authentically human they nearly walk off the page. If you like books where real people have real problems and find real love (while having really hot sex)? Pick up **Take Me Home Tonight** and enjoy the ride."

"TAKE ME HOME TONIGHT was simply put phenomenal. I loved the unusual plot, the amazing characters and the words that just seemed to flow seamlessly from beginning to end." - Guilty Pleasures Book Review

TAKE ME HOME TONIGHT "is emotional and tremendously sexy, with a large cast of characters that readers will adore — Kelly's rendering of Calix's grieving parents is particularly well-done — but it is Mimi's strength that will linger long after the finish." - Sarah MacLean, Washington Post

## Titles by Erika Kelly

YOU REALLY GOT ME
I WANT YOU TO WANT ME
TAKE ME HOME TONIGHT

# MINE FOR NOW

Erika Kelly

This book is a work of fiction. Names, characters, places, and incidents are used fictitiously or are a product of the author's imagination and any resemblance to actual persons, living or dead, business establishments, events, or locales is entirely coincidental.

ISBN-13:978-0-9859904-2-8 (ebook)
ISBN-13:978-0-9859904-3-5 (print)

Cover designed by Novak Illustration
Formatting by Polgarus Studio

This book is dedicated to Olivia for being my punkin pie sugar bean sweet pea love scone. Thank you for sharing this journey with me, angel. It's made it that much sweeter.

# ACKNOWLEDGMENTS

To Superman, my everything. Your patience, your generosity, your deep sense of honor…you're the best man I've ever known.

To Sharon, for always being there. Your friendship is what gets me through.

To Amy Patrick, for holding my hand. I couldn't have done this without you.

To Kristy DeBoer, for loving this book so hard you willed it out from under the bed and onto the shelves.

To Kevan Lyon, for your never-ending support and guidance.

None of this would be possible without the generous support of the romance writing community: readers like Kathy Page; bloggers and reviewers like Sharon Slick Reads and Reading in Pajamas; and the support from my friends in RWA chapters like COFW, CTRWA, WRW, and CoLoNY.

Keep reading for an excerpt from MINE FOR THE WEEK, the next in the Wild Love series by Erika Kelly

# CHAPTER ONE

**Bass pounded in the air, red plastic cups littered the** table, and a half dozen students played beer pong in the dining room. Party time in the Scholar House.

Dylan McCaffrey strode right past them, heading for his room.

"Dude." A guy lifted his cup, waving him in. "Play with me."

He didn't recognize him, but it was only the second day of school. Breezing by, Dylan gave him a chin nod. "Later." And then it struck him.

No one knew him here.

For the first time in his life he wasn't *That damn McCaffrey kid*. He wasn't Lorraine's son. No one would glare as he passed by or watch his hands when he walked through a store.

He had a fresh slate.

*Well, hell.* That tiny glint of freedom sent a pulse of energy through him. But just as he turned back around to join them, his phone vibrated.

Anxiety tripped down his spine. He thumbed the button to take the call. "Hey."

"We're here." His uncle sounded calm. *Good sign.*

"You just land?" Okay, forget beer pong. He had to deal with his family first. He had plenty of time to get to know these guys.

"A few minutes ago. We've only got carry-on, so this should be quick."

Dylan raced up the stairs, only to find the girl across the hall from him pounding on her door.

"Let me in, Caroline. This is my room, too." In her bright yellow dress and red high tops, the girl swiped bangs out of her eyes.

"What's going on?" his uncle asked. "Everything all right over there?"

"Yeah. Someone's locked out of her room."

"Lost her keys already?" He chuckled. "I remember those days. Listen, we're heading for the rental car place. Should we swing by on our way to the hotel?"

"No. "He lowered his voice so the girl wouldn't hear. "I have to go into town anyway, so I'll just meet you there."

"You're worried."

He really needed to work on his knee-jerk reactions. His mom had done great the past several months, going to her job and AA meetings. She'd mostly stayed clean this summer. Just one relapse at the beginning, but she'd pulled it together. Gotten back on track.

Besides, his uncle believed in her. He wouldn't be back in her life if she'd been messing up. So, she *could* come to the house. Since she didn't need cash for drugs and booze, he didn't have to worry about her stealing from his housemates.

Relief carved a path right through him, giving him breathing room for the first time in…well, ever. "Yeah. A little, I guess." Eighteen years of living with an addict had made him cautious.

"I understand, but she's been terrific. Best I've seen her in years."

Dylan hadn't realized how wound up he was until the tension in his neck and shoulders suddenly eased. His uncle was right. Even her sponsor had encouraged this visit.

"Caroline." The girl pummeled the door with both fists.

When he got off the phone, he'd ask the residential advisor to come up and let her in. "I have to fill out some job applications in town anyway. By the time I finish, you guys should be at the hotel. We can eat there."

Of course he'd bring her by the house—that was the reason for her visit, to see his new life in college—but maybe he'd wait until everyone was in class. He'd only been away from home three days. And it was the first time they'd been apart in eighteen years. Exposing her to all these new people—kids who mostly came from boarding and prep schools—might be too stressful. Better to ease her into it.

"Sounds good." His uncle paused. "I know you've never understood why we cut her off, but we're just damn glad she's pulled herself together."

"I know you're in there," the girl shouted. "I can hear you moaning. Come on, Caroline, you're not going to lock me out every time you want to get laid." Tilting her head back, she blew out a breath. She wore something weird in her hair—a big bow of some kind.

"Let me talk to you later. This girl's—"

"We're so damn proud of you, son." His uncle sighed. "I know how hard it was for you, choosing this school…but it was the best choice you could've made. We want you to do well. And now that she's thinking clearly, your mom does, too. I think seeing you in college will give her peace of mind. And it might just give her that extra incentive to stay clean."

Accepting a scholarship to a school two thousand miles from home had been the hardest decision Dylan had ever made. But how could he turn down a full ride to the best liberal arts school in the nation?

And having his family back in the picture would make it possible for him to stay. He'd done everything he could to set her up for success. Using his summer paychecks, he'd paid her bills for the next two months. He'd also marked the calendar when she needed to pay future ones. He'd even gotten her a job three towns over, where no one knew about her, just to give her a clear shot at reinventing herself.

Unlocking his door, he glanced over to find the girl jamming a metal nail file into the doorframe and jiggling the knob. He smiled at her perseverance.

"Is she there?" Dylan asked his uncle. "Can I talk to her?"

"She went to get us some water, but I'll bring the phone to her. Hang on a second."

He entered his room, checking for his roommate. Then, he caught himself. Shaking his head, he realized he'd done it again.

He didn't have to hide his conversations. He didn't have to *hide*. His mom was sober now. *This'll take some getting used to.*

"Dylan?" his mom said.

A rush of warmth spread through him at the sound of *this* voice. She sounded…well, like a normal mom.

That meant everything to him.

"Hey, Mom. How was the flight?"

"It's been so long since I've traveled anywhere, I guess I was nervous. But I'm so glad to be here. I wish…well, I wish I'd come with you. Helped you move in."

She'd told him she couldn't take the time off from work, but he suspected she'd wanted to punish him for choosing Wilmington over Boulder—or any school in Colorado. AA was working, if she could apologize and see past her own needs. "There wasn't much to move in, but I'm glad you're here now."

"I can't wait to see you." He heard voices in the background. "Oh, okay. We're getting on the shuttle to the rental car place. I'll see you soon, sweet boy."

Emotion flooded him so hard his fingertips tingled. He couldn't remember the last time she'd spoken to him with such pure kindness. Christ, she really *was* going to be all right.

He disconnected the call and hurled his backpack onto his bed. Glancing out the door, he saw the girl trying to unwind the wire of a coat hanger.

"Do I seriously have to take my keys with me every time I leave my room? This is ridiculous." The girl let out a growl. Then, fingers curling into fists, she threw her shoulder into the door.

"Hang on."

She looked up at him—the first time he'd actually seen her face—and he felt a jolt in his chest. The intensity in her hazel eyes made everything inside him go quiet.

He slipped his phone into his pocket. "You want me to get Chase up here?"

She tightened the bow in her hair, smoothing her hands down her sundress. "I learned something. I'm not the Hulk. The door doesn't yield to my supernatural strength." She flexed her biceps. "These guns? Not intimidating in the least."

He eyed the slight rise in her slender arms. "Surprising,

considering how impressive they are."

"Right?" And then she let out an exasperated breath, pushing the drooping bow out of her eyes. "This is the second night she's locked me out so she can fadoodle with a total stranger."

*Fadoodle?* He bit back a smile. "Yeah, well, how long can it take?"

"Really? Because I slept on the couch last night. And you know what? That is not gonna fly with me. This is my room. My only place on this whole freaking campus, and there's not a chance in hell I'm going to let some entitled heiress keep me out of it." She turned back to the door.

"Having fun in college yet?"

She had a mischievous smile and a warmth in her eyes that sent a surprising wash of heat up his neck. "Not yet, but I will. You can count on it."

"You need a hand?"

"And have you get sucked into the sexual vortex that is Caroline Thayer? No freaking way."

"All right, well, I'm gonna head into town."

"Enjoy. I'll be *in my room.* Planting my flag in the carpet." She gave him a dazzling smile, sticking her hand out. "I'm Nicole."

"Dylan." He needed to get going, but he knew Nicole wasn't getting into that room any time soon. And he also knew what it felt like to need a place for himself. "Let me see what I can do." He turned back and rooted around in his desk for his Swiss Army knife. Motioning for her to step aside, he quickly removed the screws that held the doorknob.

She pushed up behind him, her body brushing against his.

He stilled, aware of her heat and the scent of something sweet, clean. When her hair brushed over his arm, chill bumps burst out and spread along his skin.

He glanced at her over his shoulder, surprised at his reaction to her.

She gave him a warm smile. "I want to watch how you do it, so I can do it myself next time."

Didn't she notice how close she stood? Close enough to make his heart pound. He stepped back a little, giving her room to watch. Reaching into the hole, he removed the bolt that connected the knob to the strike plate and opened the door.

Light from the hallway spilled into the room, where he got a view of two people going at it on the bed. Caroline jerked up, hands covering her breasts. "Oh, my God, what're you *doing*?"

The room stank of pot, sex, and…

Nicole charged in. "You're eating my peanut butter."

…peanut butter. A locker sat open in front of the other bed, its contents spread all over the blanket.

Nicole grabbed her things and started tossing them into the trunk. "You can't just take my food."

"It's a few snacks. Get over yourself." Caroline reached for a silky robe, shoved her arms in it. "When the scarf's on the door, that's your cue to give me some privacy."

Well, that explained the droopy bow in Nicole's hair.

"Wrong. When you want to hook up with someone, you find a private place to do it. When you want to look jaunty, you wear the scarf."

Caroline narrowed her gaze to the bow. "Oh, my God, give that to me, freak." She made a grab for it, but Nicole ducked.

*Jaunty?* He smiled. Something about this chick. He couldn't figure her out. Caroline was easy to tag—hot, rich girl. Liked to party. But Nicole? She didn't look rich. Her hair—dark brown, no fancy highlights—looked choppy, as if she'd hacked it off herself. It had so many layers it shook and shimmied every time she moved. Her yellow sundress hid her shape, and the high tops did nothing to flatter her pale, slender legs. No manicure, no make-up, but a sparkle in her eyes that showed intelligence and a sense of humor.

But what hit him the most was her warmth. It got inside him. She wasn't his type at all—but then what was his type? He couldn't deny he'd stayed with Kelsi as long as he had because she knew his mom. His situation. And she'd handled it. Most girls wouldn't.

They shouldn't have to.

And then that wild sense of freedom whipped through him again. He had a fresh start here. That meant he could date whoever he wanted without his mom fucking it up.

The guy rolled out of bed and stepped into his cargo shorts. "I'm out of here."

Caroline got up, tying the robe's sash around her waist. She walked toward Dylan, not disguising her blatant interest. "Mr. Tall, Dark, and Dirty from across the hall. Finally, we meet."

Nicole closed the trunk and pushed it under the bed. "His name is Dylan, and he smells like clean clothes and cinnamon. So, yeah, not dirty at all."

Dylan smiled. He hadn't had cinnamon gum since that afternoon—funny now she'd noticed.

Caroline's eyes went hooded, and she smiled. "So glad to meet you."

"Oh, perfect." Nicole shot him a look. "Please don't be

the reason she locks me out tomorrow."

"Don't worry." Dylan never took his eyes off Caroline's. "Never gonna happen."

The blonde's smile spread wider. The look in her eyes said, *Sure it will.*

The guy smacked her bottom. "Catch you later, babe."

Dylan stepped aside so the guy could leave the room. Since Nicole was all set, he'd go.

"Slow down there, gorgeous." Caroline opened a drawer in her nightstand, pulled out a half pint bottle of vodka, and waved it at him. "Let's hang out."

"Oh, my God, what is wrong with you?" Nicole looked ready to rip her roommate a new one. "We signed a *contract.* No alcohol, no drugs. Do you want to get kicked out?"

Caroline gave him a look that said, *Can you believe I have to live with this?* "Wow, we are so not going to get along." She sat on her bed, letting the robe fall open enough to reveal her upper thighs.

"You do realize if Chase comes in here, I get in trouble, too, right? We share this room, so I'm implicated in your illegal activity."

"Um, okay. Uptight much?" Caroline held the bottle out to Dylan, then gave Nicole a careless wave. "Look, how about you give me and him some time to get to know each other, okay? Go find somewhere to study or something."

Dylan had had enough. He came up to Nicole. "Grab your things."

She looked at him, brow furrowed.

He leaned into her ear. "Crash in my room tonight. Talk to Chase tomorrow about switching rooms."

"Where would I sleep?"

"You want to stay here?"

"God, no."

"Then, let's go."

Nicole grabbed her toiletry bag, a pair of pajama shorts, and a T-shirt, and stuffed it all in her backpack. She unplugged her laptop and clutched it to her chest, ready to go.

Caroline watched them. "You're leaving with *her*?"

He ignored her, following Nicole out of the room.

"Wait a minute. You have to put my doorknob back on."

Dylan turned to her. "You gonna keep locking her out?"

"Are you kidding me? Like you aren't going to do the exact same thing when *you* want some privacy?"

"You know, I never was under the impression the world revolved around me so, no, I won't be locking my roommate out when I want to get laid." He joined Nicole in the hall, gesturing to his room. "You gonna be all right in here?"

"Sure. I'll just get ready for bed and read."

"Okay, then. I'm heading into town. If I'm not back before you go to sleep, just use my sleeping bag."

As he turned to go, a group of girls came sauntering down the hallway toward Caroline's room. Their diamond earrings, expensive watches and clothing…Jesus. Talk about temptation.

And there was that knee-jerk reaction again. His mom was in a great place. He didn't need to worry about her stealing things.

He let out a breath. He had to let all this shit go.

For the first time in his life, he was free.

******

Nicole sat on the floor at the side of Dylan's bed, checking out ratings of her professors on her laptop. Really, though, her mind was elsewhere. Like where she'd sleep. Taking up the limited floor space would only make it hard for the guys to get around. She didn't want to be an imposition. Maybe she'd just suck it up and go back to the heiress.

But she could see into her room, and Caroline still had a bunch of friends in there.

"Hey."

She looked up to find Dylan's roommate, the loner rocker boy, standing in the doorway. "Hi." While it was nice of Dylan to let her crash, she had no idea what his roommate thought of the idea. She started to get up, but he held up his hand.

"Stop. Dylan told me the situation. You can stay here. It's fine with me."

"Are you sure? I feel terrible about it. It'll just be for tonight. I'll talk to Chase in the morning and figure something out." As if the RA didn't have enough problems the first week of school.

"No worries." He dropped his backpack and knelt before her, extending a hand. "James Worthington."

"Nicole O'Donnell." The house roared with music and conversation, and she tilted her head with a smile. "I see you're the life of the party."

His eyebrow lifted, the piercing catching a glint of overhead light. "I don't see you dancing on any tables."

"Oh, honey, if there were a table, you can bet I'd be on it. Shaking my sassy ass."

He fought a smile. "And here I was worried about getting through the next nine months."

"You're not excited about college?"

"We're at *Wilmington*."

"What's that supposed to mean? It's a great school.

We're lucky to be here." She set aside her laptop.

"Twenty-four hundred students."

"So?"

"So, I like a little more selection. Not to mention anonymity." Sitting on the edge of his bed, he pulled off his polished black boots. He seemed overdressed for late August in upstate New York.

"Then you might want to quit with the tattoos, piercings, ripped jeans, and leather…" She gestured to all the bands on his wrists and chokers around his neck.

"Yeah, but if I take it all off, I'm just…"

"James Worthington?"

"Exactly."

Ah, so the outfit was his get-up. He wouldn't be James Worthington in cargo shorts and flip flops. She got it. "And that's not enough?"

"Well, I hadn't really thought about it until you brought it up, but I guess not. So…thanks for that."

"Hey, James Worthington must be pretty cool if he got into Wilmington. What's your glow?"

"My *glow*?" He stretched out on his bed, grabbing a couple of throw pillows and bunching them behind his back.

"You don't get in here 'cause of your GPA and test scores. Those are a given. To get in, you have to have something that makes you stand out. A specialty. What's your thing?"

"You seriously can't tell?" He made a sweeping motion over his body.

"Music."

He aimed a finger-gun at her. "Bingo. I got into the Blanchard School of Music."

The top-ranked music program in the country. "That's

so awesome. How many people do they accept?"

"Twenty each year."

"Holy cow. We're talking nuclear glow. Congratulations."

"Yeah, thanks. But I kind of dropped the ball in my Senior Year of Disgusting Decadence, so I have to work on getting my glow back. What's yours?"

"Well, that's just it. I have nothing." She held up a hand. "Don't take that the wrong way. My bulb lights up as well as everybody else's, obviously, or I wouldn't have gotten in, but I'm not the editor of the school paper or a jazz prodigy. I haven't won any science or math awards, and I didn't break any records vaulting with a pole." She shrugged. "I got no glow."

"You got so much glow I could wear you around my neck at a Kings of Leon concert. Five minutes talking to you, and I can see the glow. I bet you wrote a hilarious essay."

"I wrote about the Zombie Apocalypse and why I would survive."

"I would literally be the first to go. I'd get one look at those people-eaters and drop to the ground, curl into the fetal position, and piss my pants. Totally serious."

"You underestimate yourself."

He smiled. "So what're your survival skills?"

"I'm a mad cook."

He tilted his head, giving her a disbelieving look. "*That's* going to save you from the zombies?"

She smiled. "Think about it. We're all hiding out in caves, living in rusted-out cars. At some point, a couple months in, we're going to be jonesing for something other than raccoon meat or whatever. And then my food truck's going to drive by, and you're going to smell all my delectable desserts, and you'll come running. I'm going to become a national treasure."

"That's your survival skill?"

"You've never tasted my lavender cupcakes."

He growled. "Why does that sound so unbelievably good?"

"Because it is."

"One problem. Where're you going to find sugar and butter?"

"James, James, James, James, James. Have you never heard of honey? Agave? Stevia? Sugar is abundant in nature. Besides, I can always conjure up any ingredient I need."

"Can I be your sous chef?"

She shook her head. "Not if you're going to curl up at the first sign of crisis. What if I have a kitchen fire? A flat tire? Can I count on you or are you in the fetal position?"

"I revealed my weakness way too soon. How come you're not at the Culinary Institute or something like that?"

"Oh, I could never be a chef. I'm kind of particular about the food I eat." *Kind* of? *Ha.*

"Right, but you want to be a baker, so…?"

"I *love* baking. That's my Zen space. But I don't want to *be* a baker. I'm majoring in Food Science."

"Okay, um, what is that exactly?"

"It's about nutrition and sustainable agriculture, global food distribution." He looked a little confused, so she'd get to the heart of it. "Did you know forty-seven *million* Americans go hungry? Think about that. It's crazy. With all our advancements, with all the freaking technology, how can we let that happen? It kills me. I seriously can't stand to think of people going hungry."

"I didn't know it was that many people but, yeah, I get you. It's pretty outrageous."

"We think it's just third world countries, but it's right here. But I can't really get involved in the discussion if I don't know anything about it." Well, other than the hunger part.

"It's weird 'cause I'm from Atlanta," James said. "And I think of all the poor neighborhoods I've driven through, and I guess…I guess I thought of them as poor. Not *hungry*. You know? Like, they probably had Sunny Delight in their fridges, instead of actual orange juice. I honestly never thought beyond that."

"Exactly. It's so outside the realm of our understanding. So, I just want to do something." She *needed* to.

"I think that's really cool, Nicole. That you want to change that."

Heat climbed her neck, and she looked away. "No one should go to bed with an empty stomach." It hadn't occurred to her until just then how her housemates might make fun of her for the trunk of food she kept under her bed. But the moment she considered getting rid of it, she got that sick feeling in the pit of her stomach.

No, she'd keep it. Nothing wrong with having her favorite snacks around.

"So, does your family, like, own a restaurant or something? Is that how you got interested in food?"

"Ha. No. I'm the lone foodie in a herd of athletes. My oldest brother's entering the draft. He plays baseball for Mich U, and my other brother's the starting quarterback for Yale. Oh, and my dad was a wide receiver for Notre Dame back in the day."

"Wow. Fit in much?"

She smiled. "Exactly. I'm the outsider. On the other hand, there would be no Thanksgiving without me."

"So, do you get to bake in this Food Science program? Because no matter what words are coming out of your mouth, all I hear are *lavender cupcakes*."

"No, no baking, but I'll be doing some cooking. For the first time in the program's history, they've hired a chef to run one of the labs. But the super cool thing is that this chef? Henri Desmarais? He's going to choose twenty of us to launch the school's first ever Sustainable Culinary Arts minor."

"That is *awesome*. How do you become one of his students?"

"He'll choose us from the labs he's teaching. We have to present a dish for our final."

"Lavender cupcakes?"

"Not submitting a *cupcake*. Though I'm by no means modest. They are mouthwatering."

"So you *do* have glow. It's just the kind that won't dazzle until later in life. I'd rather glow later than burn out early like these guys." He motioned to Caroline and her friends, dancing to Rihanna across the hall. "You just need a little learnin' from Chef Henry, and then you'll surpass these glowhards by a mile."

She thought of Dylan. Could someone's glow be their striking good looks? Their hard muscles and perfect physique? "So, um, what do you think of your new roommate?" Where James's side of the room looked like a decorator had come in—he even had hammered metal shelves on his walls—Dylan's was stark. A duffle bag rested atop a thin blue comforter. No office supplies on his desk, unlike James who looked like he'd had a visit from Mr. Staples himself.

"Oh, good grief," James said. "Don't even go there."

"Go where?"

"Please. I see your expression. He's sexual heroin."

"Oh, I..." She would've liked to say he wasn't her type, but that would be lying. He was everyone's type. At first glance, he looked rough and rugged, a man who'd just come down off the mountain. But, really, that mess of shoulder-length hair? Silky, light brown with glints of blonde, like he'd spent the summer on the trails? Gorgeous. His hard, toned body looked like an athlete's, and he was so handsome it was hard to look at him for too long.

"You were saying?"

"Yeah, so not my type." But she said it with a smile.

"Right," James said. "Quit it right now. Mr. Brooding Bad Boy shows up for nine months of college with a duffle and a sleeping bag, won't look anyone in the eye, and totally keeps to himself? Seriously, he might as well have orange hazard cones around him."

"Believe me, I'm not interested in him like that. I don't want to get involved with anyone this year."

"Me neither. And I mean it more than you do."

"Senior Year of Disgusting Decadence?"

He nodded, looking pained.

"I'll bet your story's much more interesting than mine."

"You go first."

"Fine. You had your one year of drama? I had four. I dated the same guy for three and a half years in high school, and let me tell you, I am done with boy drama."

"You did not dump him before prom? You put in all that time and didn't even get any bang for your bucks?"

"I got lots of bangs."

James stared at her, as though trying to figure out if she meant what she'd actually said. When she cracked a smile, he burst out laughing. "So this whole sweet-lil-thang look you've got going on is just a cover for a very naughty girl. I like that. I like that a lot."

"I look like a prude?"

He shrugged.

"Why? 'Cause I don't advertise the goods? I'm not interested in snaring some guy with my body. I want him to want *me*."

"Not a Hooters girl. Noted. So, you stayed with him for the sex?"

"I stayed with him because we started out as best friends, and I kept believing our friendship would be the thing that pulled him back when he started going off the rails. It didn't." Even though she'd broken up with him eight months ago, the hurt still lived inside her. She'd never understand why he'd chosen partying over her. Especially when he'd taken the break-up so badly.

"Fine. You still should've waited until the day after prom to break up with him."

"I'm guessing prom was the highlight of your life?"

He tugged on a leather wristband. "No, but it was the turning point."

"I think this is where your story gets good."

He smiled. "I went to the prom with one person, hooked up with someone else in the bathroom, and went home with one of the hotel's wait staff."

"Ah."

He winced. "So, I'm on a self-imposed hiatus from relationships. I'm also on probation from partying, but that's father-imposed."

"Slut."

"Sassy face."

"That's it? That's your best shot?" She yawned. God, she was tired.

She took in the room, twin beds, matching nightstands and dressers—it left a small rectangle of floor space in the middle. Where would she sleep? "Well, I've got to get up early for my freshman seminar." She reached under Dylan's bed and pulled out the sleeping bag.

"Do you want to take my bed?" James rolled off, got to his feet.

"Oh, God, no." She untied the bag. "He said I could use this."

He made a face of displeasure. "On the *floor*?"

"Of course, I could always share with Dylan." She was only teasing, but the look of warning in James's eyes caught her out.

"Stay away from that one."

"I know." And yet her chest tightened at the thought of being held in Dylan's big, powerful arms.

For all those years of hell she'd endured trying to get through to her ex, she'd never once listened to her friends. It was like she'd been on some kind of mission to save him or something.

But her friends had been right. She couldn't save anyone.

This time, she'd listen.

She'd keep away from the guys with orange hazard cones around them.

# CHAPTER TWO

**A creak roused her from a fitful sleep, reminding her of** the hard floor beneath her. Just as she started to roll over, a big foot landed on her stomach.

"Oh, shit." James crashed onto the other side of her. "Are you okay? Oh, my God, I'm so sorry. I totally forgot you were there."

He hadn't put all his weight down, so it didn't hurt that badly. Just the shock of it had her a little shaky. "It's okay. I'm fine."

"Shit, Nicole. I can't believe I did that. Are you sure you're all right?"

And then big arms slid under her bottom, lifted her in the air, and deposited her on a mattress.

James stood there watching, as Dylan climbed over her and got into bed. He pulled back the covers, slid inside, and punched the pillow. Both James and Nicole stared at him. "What?"

"Nothing. Going to the bathroom." James hurried out of the room.

Well, holy moly. In bed with Dylan...she just...*God.* "You don't have to do this."

He turned, giving her his back. "Sleep. I have to get up early."

*Sleep?* Seriously? Sharing a tiny bed with this big, muscled, unbelievably hot guy? Heat radiated off him, and she could smell the clean scent of his sheets.

Should she go? No way could he be happy about sharing his twin bed with another person. A *stranger*. Yeah, she should go.

And yet, there was a part of her that...well, leaned into him. Wanted to wrap herself up in all that big, hardy strength. *I mean, come on.* The guy had taken apart her doorknob to get into her room. He'd given her a place to crash. He hadn't had to do any of that.

"Nicole." His voice sounded tight.

"Sorry. Sleeping." She closed her eyes.

After a moment, he turned to her. "No. You're not."

"You don't think this is awkward?"

A corner of his mouth started to lift. "If we're sleeping, we won't notice how awkward it is."

And there he was, right in her face. In the hall light pouring in from the open door, she could see the little scar at his temple, the cleft in his chin. Her nerves hummed. No way could she sleep. She started to get up. "You'll never sleep with a stranger in your bed."

His arm snugged around her, pinning her to his warm, very hard body.

*Oh, God.*

She chanced a tilt of her head to look into his eyes, and the intimacy trapped the breath in her throat. He was so freaking handsome. Strands of his long, silky hair fell across his cheek, and she had to tuck her hand to her collarbone to keep from smoothing them back behind his ear. He smelled delicious—like soap and fresh air and that hint of cinnamon.

But it was the look in his eyes—the vulnerability—that did her in. She could see the truth in those watchful eyes. Somehow she saw not the eighteen-year-old guarded man, but the sweet little boy who'd seen things no child should ever see.

She understood.

Giving him a soft smile, she sighed. "Good night, Dylan.

Deep into the night, the hard wall of heat against her twitched, jerked. Dylan gasped.

She remained still, waiting. He woke up, blinked, got his bearings. When he looked at her, she gave a gentling smile. She placed her hand over his heart. "It's all right."

He kept an eye on her. Perspiration beaded on his brow and over his lip. Gently, she dragged a finger across his skin, wiping away the moisture. He drew in a breath, closing his eyes.

"I have bad dreams sometimes, too," she said softly.

He didn't answer, didn't open his eyes. Carefully, she leaned in closer, aware of the rise and fall of his chest, and she set her head in the crook of his arm, stroking a strand of hair away that had fallen across his cheek. She tucked it behind his ear.

She knew just the moment he fell back asleep.

******

A vibration under his pillow snapped Dylan's head up. Startled awake, it took a moment to get his bearings. But not long to become aware of the warm, sweet-scented body jammed up to his.

Arousal hit him hard and fast, as he realized his hard dick

was pressed right up against her ass. Oh, shit. He inched back, his body screaming to reclaim the contact.

This girl had him so wound up he couldn't think straight.

The phone vibrated again. He reached for it and saw his uncle's name light up the screen.

Alarm rang through his body. *Fuck*. Four AM. "What's wrong?" He eased out of bed, careful not to shift her too much. His mind scrambled to recall exactly where he'd dropped his jeans, shirt, and boots.

His uncle let out a hesitant breath into the receiver.

*Shit.* "What happened?"

"She's gone. I got up to go to the bathroom." Another sigh. "She's not in her bed."

"I'll be right there." Reaching for his jeans, he jammed his legs into them, grabbed his boots, and left the room as quietly as possible.

*Breathe. Just fucking breathe.* Last night his uncle had called, told him not to come to the hotel. Said they'd see him in the morning.

Apparently, at the coffee place in town, his mom had overheard a bunch of women who'd just moved their kids into dorms talking about the empty nest, how they didn't know what to do with themselves without their kids at home. Lorraine had gotten agitated, so his uncle had called her sponsor and gotten her to bed early.

But just because she wasn't in the hotel room didn't mean she'd gotten loaded. This trip had to be hard for her—facing the reality that her son wasn't going to be there to take care of her. But that didn't mean she'd taken something. She could be walking around town.

She didn't have drug dealers out here. Besides, didn't bars close at two AM in Wilmington County?

It could be all right.

Heading down the stairs, he heard voices. A group talked quietly on the couch in the living room, and some others hung out in the kitchen. Hoping to slip by unnoticed, he opened the front door.

"Dylan?" a girl called from the sofa.

He paused, turning to her.

"Some woman came by looking for you."

*Christ.* "When?"

The girl looked to the others in the group. They seemed to be hiding their amusement. "Half hour ago?"

"We told her you were sleeping," another girl said.

"Why didn't you get me?"

Everyone looked away. One of the guys snickered. "She was wasted."

Disappointment slammed him so hard he reached for the doorframe. "So, you sent her away?" He closed his eyes—just for a moment—and he felt like he was floating.

*Oh, Mom.*

Fuck.

*Why?*

"Not exactly. She said she was hungry and, like, just walked right into the kitchen."

"Like she owned the place. She was crazy."

*She was crazy*. He hated hearing that about his mom.

Heaving off the crushing blow of his mom's set-back, Dylan forced himself to focus on the conversation. He had to find her, make sure she was okay.

"Garret and those guys were kind of mean to her. They kicked her out."

*Oh, shit.* "Why didn't anyone tell me?"

"She didn't seem like someone you'd know."

His mom could be anywhere by now. "Do you know what happened to her?"

"No, sorry. But you don't know anyone from around here, right? Aren't you from Colorado?"

He ignored them, walked out the door, and shut it hard behind him. He scrubbed his jaw, gazing up at the star-speckled sky.

Damn. They'd hurt her. And he knew his mom.

She'd hurt them right back.

Leaning over, he shoved his feet into his boots, then headed toward town.

Hurrying toward Main Street, he pulled out his phone and called her. If she wasn't too fucked up, she'd answer him. As it rang, he considered where she might have gone. In Gun Powder, he knew where to check. Set at the base of three mountains, where two rivers met, the town was small but heavy on tourist traffic. That meant lots of Wild West kitsch and Outfitter companies. And it was small enough that he knew just where to find the parties and dealers his mom frequented.

But he didn't know a damn thing about Wilmington. When her phone went to voicemail, he left a message in a calm, untroubled voice. "Hey, Mom. It's Dylan. Give me a call, okay?"

He hated that she was hurting. His uncle had thought seeing him in college would be an incentive for his mom, but what if it had the opposite reaction? What if it freaked her out to the point she relapsed?

*Jesus.* She couldn't blow this shot with her family. He needed their help in taking care of her.

As he reached the bridge, he looked around carefully. If he could get to her before she got too wasted, everything would be all right. A couple of beers wouldn't make his uncle disown her again.

A flash of red on the road caught his eye. Immediately, he thought of Garrett. His housemate had a red Ferrari. But why would Garrett drive into town at four in the morning?

He tensed at the idea that Garrett had his mom in the car. But, no, the girl had said he'd kicked her out of the house. They'd seen her leave. Garrett and his buddies wouldn't come after her. Would they?

Just as he headed across the grass to the gazebo, the roar of an engine caught his attention. The Ferrari raced across the bridge, going so fast the driver barely controlled it. Lynyrd Skynyrd blasted out the open windows.

Garrett wouldn't drive it like that. Dread rushed him so hard he felt sick to his stomach.

The car jerked, bouncing onto the curb, before slamming back down onto the street. Dylan took off at a run. Jesus, it couldn't be his mom, could it?

*Please tell me she didn't steal Garrett's car.*

Tires squealed as the driver wrenched the wheel, sending the Ferrari into a spin in the middle of the intersection. A familiar shriek split the night.

"Mom." He waved his arms as he ran into the intersection. "*Mom.* Jesus Christ, stop. Stop the fucking car."

As she pulled donuts on Main Street, her face lit up in flashes from the streetlights. He could hear her hysterical laughter over the pounding rhythm of the music.

"*Mom.*" He saw the moment she recognized him, her feral joy turning into shock. The car slammed to a stop, his mom flopping forward and back like a rag doll. Heavy silence filled the air, as the car stalled. And then she burst out laughing.

Anger tore through him, and he gripped the window, leaning in. "Get out of the car."

But his mom just reached for the stereo. "Turn it back on. I liked that song."

Nothing sickened him more than hearing her slur. "Can you please get out of the car?"

With glazed eyes, she smiled. "I don't want to. I'm having fun."

"Okay, then just move over and let me drive."

"Oh, hell no. This is *my* ride. But you can get in if you want. Come on, let's open this baby up, see what she can do." She was so wasted, he could hardly make out her words.

His body shook with fear and anxiety, but he kept his tone light. "Come on, Mom. Let me have a turn."

Gazing up at him, recognition softened her features. "Dylan."

"Yeah, Mom. I'm here."

"You're my boy." She looked at him with pure gratitude. "I don't know what I'd do without you."

"You'll never have to know."

"That's right. We stick together like..." She looked confused. "It's you and me, right? It's always been us against the world. You'll always take care of me, right, baby?"

"Always. Now, let me have a turn with this car, okay?"

"Okay, my boy. You can have a turn. But then I get it again, right?"

Headlights flashed, and fear sliced through him. He straightened to see over the roof of the car. "Move over. There's a car coming, and I need to get us out of the intersection." Oh, Christ. What if it was a cop? Between the music, the growling engine, and her laughter someone had to have heard or seen something. He couldn't afford trouble.

But instead of moving over, his mom looked up at him. "You're not trying to trick me, are you? I know you. You're always tricking me." She reached over to the passenger seat, bringing a bottle of vodka to her mouth.

"Mom, please. Move over." He opened the door, keeping watch of the headlights. But the car turned onto a street before the intersection. "We have to go."

The moment she climbed into the passenger seat, Dylan lunged inside, shutting the door. With any luck, Garrett had gone to sleep without noticing his keys missing. Before taking off, though, Dylan shot a quick text to his uncle.

*Found her. Give me fifteen to get her back to hotel.*

But what if Garrett *had* noticed? What if he'd called the police? Dylan was so used to dealing with his mom on his own, he hadn't even considered getting his uncle's help. But stealing a car? This was serious.

He texted again. *She borrowed a car.* Come on. Jesus, this was not the time to protect her. *A housemate's Ferrari. Meet you at the house?*

Hands shaking, he reached for the wheel, only to notice the leather Ferrari keychain. "Hey, Mom? How'd you steal his keys?"

"I didn't *steal* them. I borrowed them." She pulled a card out of her bra. "Borrowed this, too. But nothing's open in this shitty town, so I couldn't use it."

"You stole Garrett's *credit card*?"

Wanting to keep the car quiet, he eased into first gear then, quickly as possible, he shifted into second and then third. Five minutes, and he'd have it back at the house. "Tell me exactly where you found the keys."

"I don't know."

"Mom, listen to me. Right now I'm driving a stolen car,

and you're holding a stolen credit card. We could go to prison. This is serious, okay? But it's four in the morning, and I have a chance to put everything back before he finds out. Now, please tell me exactly where you found the keys."

"In the kitchen." She leaned over, nearly collapsing into him. Shoving him, she burst out laughing. "Here, sit up a little so I can pull the stick out of your ass." Her laughter hurt his ears, and all he could think about was not drawing attention. "Come on, Dylan. This is *fun*."

He hit the buttons to close the windows and turned onto his street. No one was out, but he couldn't see the Scholar House yet.

"These people suck. Do you know how they treated me?"

"They didn't know who you were."

"I told them I was looking for you."

"Yeah, but I hadn't introduced you. They thought you were some strange lady who walked into a house on campus."

"I was looking for my baby." She tried to stroke his hair, but she didn't seem to have the strength to reach that high. "I can't do this, Dylan. I can't. I don't want you to go to school here."

"I know that, Mom."

"Why do you want to live in New York anyway? You could go to CU. It's just as good. And you could be with your friends. You don't want to lose Kelsi, do you? She's going to move on if you don't come back for her."

He wanted Kelsi to move on. Very much. And he needed to get away from his friends. From that whole life. "I got a free ride to the top university in the country." But they'd been over it a hundred times. She'd never get it.

"Boulder's just as good. And then you could commute. We could get one of those new apartments off Brice. You know the ones with balconies?"

The university in Boulder was an hour and a half from Gun Powder. He wasn't commuting. Up ahead, he saw people on the lawn.

His pulse spiked, blood roaring in his ears. He was fucked. Part of him had known taking this opportunity could never work. He just hadn't imagined having it blow up on his second day of school and in such a blaze of glory.

As he edged the Ferrari to the curb, he saw a small crowd had gathered. His uncle stood talking to Garrett just off to the side.

"Oh, great. The fucksticks are out." She flicked on the stereo, and a Guns 'N Roses song came blaring out. She leaned out the window. "Woo hoo!"

"*Mom.* Don't say anything. Let Uncle Zach take care of this."

"Take care of what? I didn't do anything wrong."

"I need you to give me the credit card."

Her lips pinched, and he could tell she was about to go off. So, he leaned in close. "If he calls the police, we go to jail. Do you want me to go to jail? I can't take care of you if I'm in jail."

She blinked a few times, like she was trying to clear her head. It could go either way, depending on how fucked up she'd gotten. One thing he knew, it never had anything to do with his welfare. He had to threaten *hers.*

Finally, she blew out a breath and handed over the credit card. Tilting the bottle to her mouth, she drained the last of the vodka. Then, she got out of the car, the bottle clanking on the ground.

As Dylan got out his side, Garrett came rushing up to him.

"Motherfucker, you stole my car." Both hands thumped his chest, but Dylan didn't budge.

"Oh, my God, leave my son alone." His mom wavered, her words slurred. "He didn't do anything. What's your problem? I just borrowed it for a minute. Nothing happened."

"Mom. I need you to be quiet."

Uncle Zach made a quick assessment of the car. "Okay, let's all keep calm here. I don't see any damage."

Without a word, Dylan handed over the credit card.

Garrett's eyes went wide, and he punched the air in rapid succession. "She took my fucking credit card? Are you insane?"

"Oh, what do you care? I could buy a fuckin'…ostrich and your rich daddy wouldn't even notice the charge." She threw her head back, her laughter like a shriek. "*Ostrich.*"

Garrett looked at him like he was scum of the earth. "You are going down." He turned to his buddies. "Call the cops. Now."

"That's not necessary, is it?" his uncle said. "Everything's been returned, no harm done."

Garrett got right up in his face. "Are you fuckin' kidding me? They stole from me."

More people came out of the house, lights flicked on in other rooms, windows opened.

"My nephew recovered everything."

"You drive a fucking *Ferrari*." His mom's voice turned brittle. "What does it matter to you?"

Rage tensed Garrett's features. "Listen, you psycho—"

"Stop." Dylan shouted so loudly everyone froze and

stared at him. "Just stop." Motioning Garrett to follow him, he moved a few paces away. "Can I talk to you for a second?"

Garrett followed. "This is bullshit." His arms crossed over his chest, his whole body shaking with rage.

"Listen, I'm sorry about this. My mom's an addict." He fucking *hated* saying those words. "She doesn't know what she's doing. I get that you're pissed. I'd be, too. Believe me, no one understands better than I do." He had to convince him. "She's been clean all summer, so we thought…we thought she was good. I can promise you, if you let her go right now, you'll never see her again. My uncle will take her back to the airport, and she won't come out here again." He let out a shaky breath, hoping he could get through to this guy. "There's no harm done, so I'd appreciate it if you'd let her go. Can you do that for me?"

Garrett flexed his fingers, upper lip curling, exposing his teeth.

Dylan caught a quick glance at the crowd. The guy who'd wanted to partner with him for beer pong leaned against the porch column, hands dug deeply in his pockets. The group he'd talked to in the living room laughed quietly with each other.

And then he saw Caroline. Alert, focused. Like she was *invested* in the situation.

Fucking hell.

Finally, Garrett let out a breath. "Fine. Just get her out of here."

"Oh, my God." Caroline broke from the crowd in her tiny pajama shorts and tank top. "You're not letting them get away with this."

"Leave it alone." Garrett just looked tired.

"Are you kidding me? They stole your car." She stabbed a finger at Dylan. "He was driving. We all saw it. Call the police."

"The matter's been resolved." Uncle Zach clapped a hand on Dylan's shoulder, using pressure to turn him away from the others. "I'm sorry, son. I really am." And then he reached for Dylan's mom, giving Dylan a tight nod. "I'm taking her back to the hotel. We'll be on the first flight out this morning."

"The hell we will." His mom fought like a wild cat, but his uncle herded her away. Whatever he whispered in her ear seemed to work, because she settled down. She never looked back.

Dylan closed his eyes against the sharp pain in his heart.

"Well, I'm calling campus security," Caroline said. "There's not a chance in hell I'm living with a thief. He's right across the hall from me."

The weight of disappointment bore down so heavily, Dylan wanted to crash to his knees. But the McCaffrey shitshow was over, and he needed to put an end to the spectacle. He started for the house.

Caroline blocked his path.

He gave her his death glare, the one that never failed to make people back off.

She faltered. He could see the fear in her eyes, but she held her ground. She looked around to her friends. She must've seen something in their eyes because she turned back to him, narrowing her gaze. "You're not living in this house."

"What is the matter with you?" Nicole stormed down the porch steps. "It's over, okay? Let it go." She gestured to his uncle and Mom, slowly disappearing into the darkness. "She's gone."

Tension pounded so hard in his head he could barely think. He couldn't lose his housing. His scholarship covered the Scholar House, not dorms or off-housing apartments. And certainly not the twenty-six hundred dollar a semester meal plan.

"Oh, please," Caroline said. "What if he'd stolen from *you*? Nobody wants him here after a stunt like that."

As if they were old friends, Nicole wrapped her hand around Dylan's biceps. "*He* didn't steal anything. He's the one who brought everything back."

He hated that his life had been exposed to these people. Hated that his family had given his mom another chance and she'd blown it.

"Either he moves out or I call security." Caroline pulled a phone out of the waistband of her shorts.

Hated that someone like Nicole had to be exposed to this kind of ugliness.

"News flash, heiress, the tiara only sparkles on Park Avenue. It has no power out here." Nicole tugged on his arm. "Come on. Let's just go to bed."

But Dylan needed this to end. "No." He pulled his arm away. "I'm moving out."

Nicole swung around to him. "You don't have to do that." She looked to Caroline, then Garrett. "His mom is sick. She has a *disease*."

After everything that'd happened tonight, Dylan knew he couldn't live with these people. "Forget it. I'm gone."

"No. Everything will look different in the morning. Right, you guys?"

Only Garrett responded. "Yeah, sure."

"The hell it will," Caroline said. "I'm not living with white trash."

"Oh, my God, guess what? *You're* not special. Your parents might be rich—cool—but you're not." Nicole stepped back, appealing to the others who just stood on the lawn watching. "Come on, you guys. No one wants him to move out, right?" Nobody said a word. "You're just going to stand there? Oh, my God. What is the matter with you people? Dylan didn't do anything."

When no one said anything, she shook her head. "You people horrify me."

"Ha. We horrify *you*?" Caroline's voice rose. "That's hilarious coming from the freaky little food-hoarder."

All his own worries dropped away the moment he saw Nicole's look of utter anguish. He reached for her, grabbing her a little too roughly, but thinking only of getting her away from these assholes. He towed her through the crowd, aware she hadn't said a word in response.

When they hit the porch, James stepped forward. "What the hell was that?"

"I'm leaving," Nicole said, her voice a whisper.

"What?" James said.

Her spirit seemed to flow back into her. "I'm moving out."

"No, you're not." Dylan turned her to face him. "This is my problem, not yours."

"I'm not living with these people."

Holy shit. He hadn't even started his third day.

So much for his clean slate.

The moment Dylan came out of his freshman seminar, he found Nicole and James huddled together on the quad. He ignored the cut of jealousy at seeing the two so close. Whatever attraction he might've felt for her—this morning's bullshit had killed it.

He had enough on his plate anyway. Jesus, the scene on the lawn kept flashing in his mind. What the hell should he do? Should he go back home and take care of her? He'd like to think he could convince his family to give her a chance to pull out of this tailspin, but they'd given her too many chances over the years. She'd failed them every time.

Then again, she'd never been sober this long. Besides, hadn't her sponsor said she'd stumble a few times before gaining enough strength to maintain a lifetime of sobriety?

He was so bummed for his mom. In any event, he had shit to do, and hanging out with his former housemates wasn't on the list—no matter how pretty Nicole looked in a white sundress with a yellow sash. And those battered red sneakers.

They looked up and saw him, Nicole beaming one of her radiant smiles.

And just when it started to penetrate, when the heat of it sank in, he shook it off. Nope, not going there. There was one absolute truth in his life: anyone who got near him got the blowback from his mom.

And that shit was not touching Nicole. Not more than it already had, anyway.

He gave them a nod and walked right on by.

"Oh, so that's how it's gonna be," Nicole called after him.

"Where you going?" James fell into step beside him.

"Find a place in town."

"No need." James reached for him. "Hang on a sec, okay?"

Nicole came up on his other side. "We must've done great things in a former life, because karma is totally our bitch."

He didn’t want to ask what she meant. He really didn’t. He just wanted to find a room. But, damn, if she didn’t make him smile. So, he stopped, waited for her to go on.

“The Music Man here scored us spectacular new digs.”

He shifted his gaze to James. “You’re moving out, too?”

“He is now.” Nicole nodded to James. “Tell him.”

“This girl from my high school lives in a house right across the street from campus. She doesn’t really need rent money, so I figured she hadn’t looked too hard for roommates. I called her this morning.”

Nicole’s fingers brushed across his hand. “Turns out she hadn’t.”

Holy hell. Her simple touch lit him up inside. What *was* it about her?

“We’re heading there right now,” James said. “If you want to come.”

“Sounds great. Thanks for thinking of me, but I’m just going to find a room in town.” He broke away, giving them a nod.

He’d be better off on his own.

# CHAPTER THREE

**Nicole caught up with him. "Hang on."**

"It's that big white house right there. The colonial." James pointed to the end of the road. "With the blue shutters?"

He didn't bother looking. "Since I'm going to be working in town, it makes sense that I live there, too."

A hint of a breeze drew the fishy scent of the lake across campus. The hem of Nicole's white dress fluttered around her thighs, and he peered into hazel eyes that seemed to see right into the heart of him. She didn't look hurt or offended or even desperate to get her way. She just looked, well, sweet.

"Okay, but will you hear me out?"

Of course he would. This girl pretty much had him by the balls.

"You're not going to walk into town and find a place to live just like that. But we *might* find the perfect situation in that one. So, for the fifteen minutes it'll take, come with us and check it out. Nothing to lose, but something to gain."

These two had seen the whole thing go down with his mom, and they still wanted to room with him? That was a first. Still, he'd rather live off campus. "I'm just going to find something cheap. A room in some old lady's house or something."

"Sydney's charging us two hundred a month," James said. "Think you can do better than that?"

"Two hundred?" He couldn't beat that price anywhere. Unless he had to buy a meal plan. "Would we get to use the kitchen?"

Wait, why was he even asking?

"Of course," James said. "Hey, come on, it'll be fun. The three amigos. We'll have a blast together."

"Yeah, I don't think so." The image of his mom stumbling out of the Ferrari in front of his housemates flashed again.

"Wait, but I got us matching robes and everything." Nicole grabbed his arm and gave him a little shake. "Would you lighten up? We're talking about a place to live. We're not inviting you into our super-secret fraternity with the special handshake. Besides, we don't even like you that much."

She bit back her smile, and he wanted to do something—anything—that made her unleash it. He needed to feel that rush of happiness and heat she gave him.

"This is the perfect situation all around," James said. "You can't go wrong."

He pulled in a deep breath, gave them a half-smile. "I'm trying to save your asses from me."

"Do you actually think you're the only person in the world with crazy parents?" Nicole said. "Please. Now stop taking yourself so seriously and come with us to see our new digs."

In spite of his very best intentions to head into town and set himself up away from everyone on campus, everything changed when she reached for his hand—hers so delicate and soft—and clasped his like she had a lover's right.

Ignoring the warning bells clanging in his brain, he allowed himself to be towed by the sweet-scented girl in the white sundress.

******

Staring up at the ceiling, crowded against the wall thanks to the mother of all tanning beds, Nicole couldn't get Caroline's voice out of her head. *Freaky food-hoarder.*

Bringing a trunk to school hadn't seemed that odd. If anything, she'd figured people would assume it had clothes and school supplies in it. And, if they did find out about the food, she'd just tell them she was a finicky eater. Which, of course, she *was*.

Whatever. She wouldn't have to deal with Caroline again. And now she got to live in this unbelievably gorgeous house.

Dylan and James had taken the furnished bedroom right across the hall, while she had the room formerly used as a tanning salon. The furniture was on order, so she'd only have to crash on the floor a couple days. No problem, especially when she considered the house's huge, fully-stocked kitchen. It was to die for. She doubted the other students would use it for more than microwaving popcorn or storing cases of beer, so she'd pretty much have it to herself.

She was so glad Dylan had decided to move in with them. He didn't know about *her* mom, of course, so he couldn't know how well she understood the shame and distress of being raised by an alcoholic.

Dylan. She turned her face into the pillow. Last night, sleeping beside him…his body heat, the rhythmic rise and fall of his muscled chest…God. His strong arm had felt so freaking good around her. They'd shared a moment. A big moment—staring into each other's eyes, no words spoken, just raw, compelling emotion. *Connection.* Desire streamed through her, filling every nook and cranny, making her body come to life. She rolled onto her back.

But, really, forget her body's reaction to him. Those hazard cones screamed *Stay away.* He was completely closed off. And she absolutely wasn't getting involved with yet another guy who couldn't be hers. Maybe she was asking too much, but she needed someone who could love her with all his heart. Not someone battling serious demons.

And, boy, did Dylan have demons. Impossible not to with a mom like that. She could've turned out the same way, but she'd gotten out at a much younger age.

A sliver of yellow light cut across her small room. She froze. Not everyone knew she'd moved in here, so maybe someone wanted a quick tan before school started?

But then she recognized the hulking figure crouching before her, inhaled his fresh-air scent, cut through with cinnamon.

"I can't sleep knowing you're on the floor," Dylan said. "Come to my room?"

A flurry of emotion rendered her speechless. All she could do was nod.

Before she could even make a move to get up, he'd scooped her in his arms—sleeping bag and all—and carried her across the hall.

She could feel the rush of air over her skin as Dylan settled her on his mattress. But she had to look away, because, God, he'd brought her to his bed.

He wouldn't let her sleep on the floor.

She loved her dad and brothers, but they'd never—ever—treated her with such care. They'd never put her needs first. Mostly because they didn't know them. They'd never asked. She just wanted them to hang out with her—be relaxed around her. Instead, ever since she'd come back to them, they didn't know what to make of her. So, they'd just left her alone.

He leaned close to her ear, and she glanced over to make sure they weren't disturbing James. "You can have the bed and I'll take the floor."

She shook her head. "We managed it last night. We can do it again. I mean, if you don't mind."

Heart thundering, she watched him unzip her bag and motion for her to get out. She crawled out of it and stood beside him as he tossed it on the floor, pulled back the covers of his bed, and got in. He didn't even look at her. No patting of the mattress to indicate she should get in. He just folded an arm under his head and closed his eyes.

In her whole life, she'd never been so touched, so…exhilarated. She got in, and he pulled the blanket up over them. His body heat seeped into her, his cinnamon scent filled her senses. She wanted to snuggle into him, talk about school, his classes, his life back home—did he miss it? Or anyone in particular? But she knew he didn't want that. He was offering her a mattress until she got one of her own. And that was it. She couldn't read more into it.

Seconds stretched into the longest minutes of her life, until she couldn't take it anymore. She knew he was awake. His damn phone kept buzzing under his pillow. Didn't it wake James up? She glanced over to her friend's bed again, saw him curled up like a pill bug. He snored softly.

Finally, she rolled over to face Dylan. "Don't you want

to see who's texting?" She kept her voice to a whisper.

"I know who it is."

"Shouldn't you answer?"

He looked like he was in pain. She wanted to touch him so badly, reach out and stroke his arm. Just let him know she was there, and that he'd be all right.

"Where'd you go tonight?" Even in the darkness, she noticed the strong lines of his jaw, the sensuous mouth, and guarded look in his eyes.

He didn't shift his head to talk to her, just looked down at her from an awkward angle. "Gym. After that, I went into town."

"Oh." Did he go to a bar or something? He didn't smell like booze. Just of toothpaste and his familiar scent.

"Applied for jobs."

"I've been thinking about that all night."

"Yeah?" Was that a hint of a smile?

"I was thinking what I'd do outside of school. Like maybe start a baking club or something. And then I thought why not make money doing it, you know? Get some extra spending money."

She checked to see if he was interested. Maybe he just wanted to go to sleep. But she had his full attention, which was...nice. "And I was thinking about how, when my oldest brother went off to college, I was bummed that I didn't get to make him a cake on his birthday anymore. I tried to find a bakery around his campus that would make one and deliver it to his dorm, but no one did that."

"Okay?"

She smiled. "So, *I* bake. And I was thinking we—you, me, and James—could start a business, making cakes and cupcakes for students. You know, for birthdays and stuff."

He opened his eyes. The distrust in them jarred her. Did he think it was a terrible idea? Or did he think she'd come up with a business idea so she could *get* with him?

Either way, she didn't like the way it made her feel. "Whatever. We can talk about it in the morning." She didn't need him to launch her business. James would totally want to do it with her. She tried to turn over—okay, she flounced, she wasn't proud of it—but he rolled onto his side and caught her with his arm, holding her firmly in place.

"I'm listening."

"Forget it. Let's just go to sleep."

"Don't be like that. Just tell me your idea."

"Well, Dylan, I don't really want to tell you my idea when I see that look in your eyes."

He actually seemed offended. "What look?"

"Uh, the one that says, What exactly does she want from me?"

"If I have a look, it's because I have a hell of a lot on my mind. It's been a long damn day and I want to get to sleep."

Of course she knew that. He hadn't slept in twenty-four hours. "I know. We can talk tomorrow." But they didn't close their eyes, and the tension between them grew, becoming a force-field around them.

He watched her thoughtfully. "I have to make money *now*. I don't have time to build a business."

Of course. That was dumb of her "Well, you could get a job while we grow it."

"Not sure I'll have time for that."

"It's just baking and delivering cakes."

He still didn't seem interested.

"Whatever. It's just an idea." She tried to turn away from him—she was *not* sleeping in the crook of his arm—but he still held her in place, and it was starting to make her a little crazy. "*What?*"

He looked a little crazy, too. She could feel the restraint in his arm that banded just beneath her breasts, feel the intense heat from his gaze. Desire raged up from her core. God, what did he want from her? It wasn't her imagination—he was giving her very mixed signals.

But then the moment passed. He exhaled. "Maybe there's a bakery in town."

"I'll find out tomorrow."

"Not sure how much money there is in making birthday cakes."

"It doesn't have to be just birthdays. It can be for faculty events. Maybe professors would order them for their dinner parties. I don't know. Who doesn't want cupcakes? And, you know, my stuff isn't all that common."

"She makes lavender cupcakes." James's voice sounded gruff and sleepy.

"Oh, my God, I'm so sorry." She craned her neck to see him over her shoulder. It occurred to her just then that her position thrust her chest out. Her breasts were covered in a thin cotton tank top. She turned back around to find Dylan's gaze riveted to them. She slumped forward, not wanting to give him the wrong impression, but the freaking heat in his eyes sent her up in flames. God, what was going on between them? Her legs shifted, her knees bumping into his thighs.

"I think it's a great idea. I'm all in." James sighed. "I'm also going back to sleep."

"I'm so sorry I woke you up. I thought I was so quiet."

"I'm not sleeping." James sighed.

"You were so sleeping. I heard you."

"You can't *hear* someone sleep."

"You snore. Loudly."

"Take it back." He sounded more awake now. "Take it back right now. I do no such thing."

"You're getting yourself all worked up. Now go back to sleep."

"*Fuck*," James said, voice filled with frustration. "I can't sleep. I'm completely freaking out."

"About what?" The moment she started to roll out of bed to go to him, Dylan's arm tightened on her. She turned back to him, and they shared a heart-stopping gaze so filled with desire and want and need that she literally couldn't take a breath.

"Maybe my dad was right," James said.

She broke away from Dylan. "What're you talking about?"

"Maybe I should've waited a year."

"James," she said softly. "What're you worried about?"

"Maybe I'm the best jazz keyboardist Roger Miller High has ever seen, but what if I'm, like, the pity player here? What if I suck compared to these guys?"

"Well..." She gave it some thought. "First of all, I'm going to guess that to get into this program, which is the best in the country, you had to audition."

He nodded, hands folded under his head, staring up at the ceiling.

"And you *were* selected, so I'm going to guess it wasn't because they felt sorry for you. But, secondly, even if you're not as good as some of the others, you *are* in the best program in the country, so you'll have the best teachers to help you get where you need to be. So, really, it's win-win, no matter how you look at it."

Dylan's hand squeezed her waist hard, causing her to

turn back in his direction. She expected him to be pissed or something, but he was staring at her mouth. The heat rolling off him made her want to throw off her clothes.

"You're right. You're totally right." James sighed, then rolled over. "You're better than Xanax any day. I feel so much better. G'night."

She couldn't tear her gaze away from Dylan. What would it feel like to kiss that sensuous mouth? A jolt of lust struck hard, as she imagined kissing Dylan McCaffrey. Him wanting her as badly as she wanted him. Oh, man. Dumb, dumb, dumb.

She had to stop thinking like that. Just focus on business. Leaning closer, she whispered, "So, what do you think?"

"About your business?"

She nodded.

"I don't cook. What would I do?"

"I don't know. It's a business, so there'd be a lot more than baking. Marketing, delivering, accounting. It's just…it makes sense for all of us. I'm going to be baking anyway and for you, with school and all, fitting a regular job into your schedule will be tough. This job'll let you make your own hours."

"What'll you get out of it?"

"I'm not going to just go to classes and study. I don't party, and I'm not joining a sorority. I have to do something. I can't just have a resume that says I went to school. Why not start our own business?"

"Hell, yeah," James said.

"I'm practically mouthing the words, James. You can't possibly hear me."

"It'll take a while until we make any real money," Dylan said.

She gave him a soft smile, wishing he'd stop fighting her. She could totally make out with him right then. "Probably. But if it works, it'll be pretty awesome. So, are you in?"

He didn't answer, just studied her.

"Just say yes and let's all get to sleep," James said.

"Say yes," she whispered.

"I'll think about it."

What could possibly hold him back? It was a great idea. "Whatever. You're in James, right?"

"Totally. Love it. Don't worry about Dylan. Make a batch of your cupcakes tomorrow. He'll be your slave for life."

"How do you know?" Dylan asked. "You've never tasted them."

"Did you not hear me say *lavender* cupcakes?"

Dylan let out a slow breath and kept silent. After several long moments, as James started snoring again, she turned within his arms. He grabbed the comforter, drew it up to their chins and tucked it in tightly around them. "You smell like honeysuckle."

"I make those cupcakes, too."

He made a grumbling noise deep in his throat.

# CHAPTER FOUR

**Dylan woke up with the most painful hard-on of his life.** Immediately, he thought of Nicole and jerked his hips back. But when he opened his eyes he realized he had nothing to worry about.

She was gone.

And the disappointment slamming him just pissed him off. What the hell had he been thinking bringing her into his bed last night anyway? Yeah, he felt bad that she had to sleep on the floor. But he could've given her the bed. He didn't care where he slept.

Whatever. He'd already shared his bed with her the night before, so what did it matter? It wasn't like he'd act on his attraction. And if he needed a reminder why, he just needed to pick up the phone vibrating under his pillow.

Whipping through the messages, he could see his mom had been texting him all night. Which meant she was either lit or apologetic. He'd find out soon enough.

Knowing how upset she was, it had killed him not to respond to her, but he also knew if he didn't set up boundaries, she'd be calling him night and day until he went home for Thanksgiving. He couldn't let that happen. Not only for his own sanity, but because she needed to build her own life.

He hit her speed dial, and she answered right away. "Dylan." She sounded sober.

"Hey, Mom. What's up?"

"You just...you won't talk to me. I can't stand that you're mad at me."

What could he say to that? He *was* angry with her.

"I'm sorry." She sounded tired. "I fucked up."

Pushing off the covers, he sat back against the wall. "Why?" She'd gotten her family back in her life, and she'd blown it. "What happened?"

"I don't know. I guess...you're really gone, you know? It's always been you and me, and now...you're gone."

"I'm not gone. I'm in school. And I'll be home for Thanksgiving, Christmas, spring break, and then three months in the summer."

She laughed softly. "Well, when you put it like that."

"Mom..."

"I *know.* I fell off the wagon. But I'm back. I swear to you, I'm back. I'll even start going to meetings again."

"You stopped?"

"I was doing great, and I hate hanging around all those fucked up people. It's so depressing."

"Jesus, Mom—" But he shut his mouth before he leveled an accusation or reprimand. Beating her up about past crimes only drove her to act out. He needed her strong. He needed to encourage her.

"Yeah, yeah, I know. I'm one of them. I get it." She blew out a breath. "I fucked up." At least she sounded ashamed. That meant something. "But don't worry. I'm back, and I won't miss any more meetings. I see what happens when I do."

"Well, I'm glad to hear it. You've got this, you know. You'll be fine."

"Yeah, I guess so."

"Is there anything I can do?"

"You can keep your phone on. You know how I get when you don't answer. I need to know you're there for me."

"I won't have it on during class, and I'll have it on silent at night so I can sleep. Other than that, I'll have it on, okay?"

"When you don't answer, I worry about you. What if you're run over or something? How will I know? I'm just…I'm going to need you to get back to me. It helps me, just knowing you're there."

"I have to focus, Mom. I need a three-point-five to keep my scholarship. But I'll do the best I can."

"I want you to do good. You know I do. You're the best thing in my whole life."

This line of thinking got him riled up. If she wanted him to do well, she shouldn't have asked him to steal his aunt's car to get her booze. Or go on drug runs for her.

*Stop.* He couldn't go there. Didn't help anything. Best to change the subject.

"You better get some sleep. You've got work in a few hours."

"Oh, I'm not going to make it in today. I'm too tired."

"You have to make it. Get a few hours of sleep, and then make yourself some coffee. I left a brand new canister on top of the refrigerator for you. But you can't miss work. You can't lose this job."

"I won't lose my job if I take a day off here or there."

*Oh, Christ.* She'd never kept a job in her life. This time, though, she had to. "Yes, Mom, you will." How did he get through to her? "But you can't let that happen because I have no more money to give you. All the money I made this summer went to pay your rent. And I don't have a job here yet, so I can't send you anything for a couple of weeks at least."

"I didn't sleep at all last night. You know what it's like right after you quit drinking."

He gripped the back of his neck and squeezed. "You have to do this, Mom. I'm in school. I can't…" He caught sight of something in his peripheral vision and snapped upright. James stood in the doorway, towel wrapped around his waist, looking apologetic.

*I'm sorry*, his roommate mouthed. *Want me to go?*

Shit. How long had he stood there? What had he heard? "I have to go."

"Already?" his mom said. "I miss you, baby."

"I miss you, too." He hated to say this in front of his roommate, but it had to be said. "You have to go to work, okay? I don't have any money coming in, so you have to keep this job. Just…tell me you understand."

After a long moment, she finally let out a huff of breath. "I understand."

He ended the call, tossed his phone onto his pillow, and then brushed past James and headed for the bathroom.

The house smelled like flowers.

Dylan came downstairs, wanting to avoid everyone and just get to the gym. He hated that James had heard that conversation. He'd have to be more careful in the future.

But one glance into the kitchen and his heart kicked hard in his chest.

In a pretty yellow tank top, Nicole leaned over the

counter, her hair pulled up in a ponytail. But since it was cut so choppily, bits and pieces spilled everywhere. A bunch of guys hovered around her, stuffing their faces with muffins. Two guys stood behind her—one of them rocked his hips back and forth, his hands fisted, arms pumping in the gesture of fucking, while the other laughed, covering his mouth with the back of a hand.

*Assholes.*

He trampled down the stairs and charged into the kitchen. Coming up behind her, he pushed the guys aside.

"Dude." One of them gripped the counter to keep from falling over.

"Don't ever disrespect her again." He said it low so only they could hear.

Both guys looked stunned, mouths open.

Adrenaline spiked through him, making his facial muscles twitch. "Do you understand me?"

"Chill, dude, what's the big deal?"

He felt a gentle hand on his back and turned to find Nicole watching the scene in confusion.

"Here." James shoved a muffin in his hand. The only reason Dylan wasn't giving *him* shit was because he'd been at the oven with his back to the scene.

"No, thanks. I'm going to work out." But he didn't take his eyes off the jerks, not until their stances showed they'd backed down and understood him.

"Have one," James insisted.

Nicole uselessly pushed locks of hair out of her eyes and smiled at him. "Please?"

"She made them for you." James pushed a pale purple-frosted cupcake into his hand. Not a muffin after all.

Right. She'd made the lavender cupcakes for breakfast.

Everything she did—just fucking *looking* at her—pulled at his heart. He dropped his backpack on the floor and peeled the paper away. He hesitated, thought about telling them he didn't eat sugar, but one look at her hopeful expression killed that thought.

One bite wouldn't hurt. But before he sank his teeth into it, the scent wafted up to his nostrils, and he couldn't help breathing it in. It was unbelievable. He shoved half of it in his mouth, and the flavor hit him full force.

When he opened his eyes—he didn't even realize he'd closed them—he found James smiling at him like he'd just won an argument.

"Good?" James asked.

He shoved the rest of the cupcake in his mouth and closed his eyes to experience it.

"He's in," James said to Nicole.

When Dylan opened his eyes, he found Nicole smiling at him, looking pleased.

He had to stop being so damn happy when he pleased her.

******

Chef Desmarais faced the class, checking out each student that entered the lab. Was he sizing them up to see who he could cut? What did a worthy student look like to him anyway?

"Bonjour." His voice boomed, silencing the chatter. "Welcome to your first food science lab. Please take a seat, silence your phones, and stop fidgeting."

Nicole had chosen to sit in the first row, center. She wanted him to see her interest, her dedication. She wanted him to choose her.

"You will notice there are twenty chairs in this..." He made a dismissive gesture to the room, set up for lab experiments, not cooking. "Laboratory. No more, no less. And that is because exactly twenty of you will work with me for the next four years in Wilmington University's first Sustainable Culinary Arts minor. We will, of course, have an actual kitchen by next semester."

Someone's phone rang, and Chef's expression turned harsh, his gaze cutting to the source. "I won't tell you again. Shut off your phone or leave my kitchen."

The guy scrambled to get his phone out of his backpack.

"As you know, Wilmington is known for the rapport between its students and professors. The professors take them to lunch, welcome them into their homes." He paused. "I, however, am not a professor. I am a chef. I will not take you to lunch, nor will I answer the door if you ring the bell at my house."

He picked up a stack of papers and slowly made his way from student to student, handing them out. "I am teaching six labs of twenty students each. At the end of this semester, twenty of you will be invited into the program. You are wondering how in the world I will be able to cull twenty out of one hundred and twenty potential chefs, but you are mistaken. It will be difficult to *find* twenty. Many of you will drop out before the October fifth drop deadline and switch to a different lab." He stopped, eyeing them again. "No need to suffer guilt or embarrassment. You are welcome to leave at any time."

He dropped a packet onto Nicole's desk. *Food Science Syllabus*.

"Read the very simple and basic rules of this lab before showing up to the next one. I offer no office hours. I take no excuses whatsoever. If your dog dies or your best friend is run over by a bus, you are not welcome to come talk to me about it. In case of an emergency, you will see your freshman advisor. If he determines there is something to say to me, I will listen. My *only* interest is your performance in this lab. Grading is based exclusively on attendance, participation, and performance. It is black and white. No exceptions for anyone."

A chair scraped back, and a student muttered, "This is bullshit," as she threw the door open and bolted from the room.

Nicole swung her gaze back to see Chef's reaction.

He smiled with glee. "One hundred nineteen. Excellent." He looked around the room. "Anyone else?"

******

The house smelled so good his mouth watered. Now what was she making? As Dylan came down the stairs, he found even more of his roommates in the kitchen. Some crowded around the island, others sat around the table.

"I made scones," Nicole called out to him, just as he hit the bottom of the stairs.

Grabbing a warm scone off the baking sheet, he brought it to his mouth, but before he could take a bite, he closed his eyes and inhaled. He couldn't get into the habit of eating shit like this—

"Dude." Harry Cohen thumped him on the back, nearly dislodging the scone from his hand. "Rush starts tonight."

"Okay."

"You're coming, right?" Harry was a nicer version of Garrett. He wore a diamond-encrusted watch, parked his BMW on the lawn so it wouldn't get hit on the narrow street, and talked about his family *compounds*. He wasn't a bad guy, but Dylan had nothing in common with him.

Weirdly enough, the only place Dylan wanted to be right in that moment was inside Nicole's scone. He smelled nutmeg, cinnamon, and apples.

"We're having a party tonight. I'll bring you. Introduce you around. Cool?"

Dylan opened his eyes and gave him the death glare. Usually, it made people scatter.

Not this guy. Harry just shoved half a scone into his mouth, chewed twice, and then swallowed. What was he, a German shepherd? Did the guy not appreciate the amazing flavors in his mouth?

"Thanks, but I'm not rushing."

"Dude. You're totally joining Sigma Phi."

"Sorry. Can't afford it."

"I'll sponsor you, man. You're joining."

*Sponsor* him? "No, thanks." He turned away to enjoy his damn scone.

"Dude, you're a freshman. You don't know. Come by tonight, you'll get it."

"What's he going to get?" Sydney, the homeowner, came in and eyed the baking sheets.

"Scone?" Nicole said.

Sydney looked tormented. "I wish."

"It's not like you'll get fat from eating one scone. You *can* eat breakfast, you know. One scone and a glass of juice won't make you fat. Besides, these scones are like the five food groups in one tasty morsel."

Dylan snickered. Morsel. She cracked him up. But she was wrong—the sugar from the juice and the scone? Not good for the metabolism.

Once the calorie discussion got underway, he leaned against the wall and took that first bite. His teeth broke through the crunchy outer layer and sank into the crumbly, wildly flavorful, goodness. Holy mother of God. What did she put into these things? Yeah, he tasted apple and spices, but there was something more—a tang—no, a twist. Something lemon. Shit, it was like standing in the middle of an orchard on a hot summer day.

"Good?"

He opened his eyes to find Nicole gazing up at him with those warm hazel eyes. No make-up, straight, shiny hair falling around her beautiful face. The scone tasted unbelievably good, but then to wrap her voice around the flavors—desire burned through his dick, and he got a semi right there in the kitchen.

"It's all right." He shrugged, giving her a half-smile.

She beamed, and he loved that he could do that to her.

"I gotta jet." Harry insinuated himself in their conversation as if there were no place on earth he wasn't welcome. "We'll head over tonight around nine. Cool?"

Dylan had had enough. He wanted two minutes alone with his scone and Nicole. He wouldn't see her again for the rest of his day, and the last thing he wanted to talk about was joining some club that put him in the same room with Garrett and Caroline. "Seriously, man. I'm not interested in joining a frat."

"Well, we're interested in you. You're like hot chick bait. But, seriously, man, what's not to be interested in? You'll love it. You'll see."

"Look, my dad isn't friends with Trump, I don't summer in the Hamptons, and I don't drive last year's model Ferrari that my dad got tired of. Sorry, but I'm just not your kind of people."

The buzz of activity in the kitchen died. He turned to

find all eyes on him. Some looked embarrassed, while others looked enthralled, like they were watching reality TV.

Harry took off his diamond-encrusted platinum watch and handed it to him. "Here. Now you fit in. See? No one gives a shit. We're in college, man. We're here to have fun. You just gotta relax." He shrugged. "Besides, you gotta think about the future. These're the guys that're gonna hook you up with jobs when you graduate. It's a lifetime of connections you get to score right now. Get it?"

Dylan had to concede the point. Couldn't deny the valuc of connections. "I'll think about it."

"Cool. See you at nine." Harry grabbed another scone, shoved most of it in his mouth, and headed off.

Too many eyes on him, too many people knowing his shit. He had to get out.

A hand fell on his shoulder, and he whipped around to find another of his housemates, Tatiana. "I'm a Theta, and I'm telling you, you're going to love Sigma Phi. You'll be very popular, if you know what I mean."

He shot a look to Nicole, wondering if this conversation made her uncomfortable.

And then Sydney flashed her pure white smile and said, "Seriously, Dylan, it doesn't matter if you come from money. You're super-hot and, if you wind up making lots of money one day, no one will care where you came from."

A loud clatter drew his attention. Nicole tore off her oven mitts and tossed them onto the counter. "What is the matter with you people?" She snatched a baggie out of a box in a drawer, stuffed some scones in it, and shoved it at him. "You are so much better than this, you know." She stomped out of the room.

Wait, she was mad at *him*?

The Magnusson School of Business stood on north campus. The artsy types hung out on the south side, which meant he and Nicole wouldn't cross paths during the day. So it came as a surprise, as he headed out of his statistics class into the bright sunshine of a September day, to see Nicole in her floaty yellow and tangerine shirt wandering off the walkway and ducking into the woods.

He had an hour until his next class, and while he usually used this time to check in with his mom, he couldn't resist seeing where she was headed. Plus, he wanted to know what he'd done to piss her off that morning.

Following that blast of color through the green foliage, he was surprised when the thick brush gave way to a structured garden. A meandering stone walkway curved around patches of mowed green grass. Sprinkled throughout the park stood large, steel sculptures. She ducked off the path, disappearing. That's when he began to notice hidden enclaves tucked into the woods—small, enclosed spaces, each with a curving cement bench.

Nicole sat down on one of them, completely unseen from the path. She dropped her backpack, drew her legs up and crossed them, plunking a brown paper bag in her lap. Out came a sandwich in a plastic baggie. She tilted her head back, closing her eyes against the sun, and took a bite.

He watched her for a moment. She was so fucking beautiful. "Hey."

She jerked. "Oh, my God. You scared me. What're you doing here?"

"I followed you. What is this place?"

"The Sculpture Gardens."

"Makes sense." He sat beside her. The cement was cool under his ass. "How's your lab going?" She'd mentioned having a hard time in it, which seemed odd, since she loved cooking so much.

Her shoulders slumped. "Oh." She let out a breath. "I blew it."

"What'd you do?"

"I made some crack about the syllabus. Everyone was talking, so I didn't think he could hear me from the back row. Only, he wasn't in the back row. He was right next to me."

"What'd you say?"

"Well, you know how a lab is supposed to be a hands-on experience about whatever you're learning in class?"

He nodded, aware of how much he enjoyed just sitting with her.

"So, I assumed it'd be about food science. I get the lab's about cooking, and that's why we have Chef Henri, but it's about *sustainability*, so I figured we'd have to put together a whole meal using twenty dollars or using only locally grown products. But on the syllabus all I could see were sections on meat, fish, poultry, venison. I mean, what's that? It did say something about sensory evaluations of food products, and that's food science, for sure. But, God, everything else was just..." She actually shuddered. "Animal flesh."

Dylan smiled, eyeing her sandwich. Thick slabs of whole grain bread, tomatoes, cucumber, avocado, and alfalfa sprouts. It sure looked good. "So, what'd you say?"

Without even thinking, she gave him half. "I said, Wonderful, a carnivore's holding me captive. I was *joking*."

"What'd he say?" Dylan waved away the sandwich, but she thrust it at him.

"Try it. It's good."

"It's your lunch."

"I get half your bed, you get half my sandwich."

His body heated at the mention of sharing his bed. It made him think of her body pressed up to his, the brush of her silky hair on his arms, and the painful morning wood he woke up with every single day.

But she'd get her furniture soon and move into her own room, and that would be that. So, he'd take what he could while he had her.

In the only way he *could* have her.

"Thanks." He reached for the sandwich. One bite and his mouth went giddy with excitement. "What do you put in here?"

"It's the dressing. It's got lemon and sage in it."

He tipped the sandwich towards her. "So, what'd he say that makes you think he doesn't like you?"

"He said, 'Mademoiselle, no one is in this lab against her will.' And then he pointed to the door."

"You're overreacting. Damn, this is good." The bread had a crunch to it. Sunflower seeds, maybe?

"Dylan." She tipped her head back, staring up at the sky.

"He doesn't hate you for saying that. He knows it was a joke."

"He's looking for any reason to cut us. And there are plenty of other labs to choose from. The only students in his want to be accepted into the Culinary minor."

"You're usually such an optimist."

"I'm not giving up." She frowned. "It's just…I'm good at baking, just…not so interested in most of the other things he's got on there. But I really want to be in this program. How can I make sure everyone has access to healthy food if I don't know how to make and provide it? Plus, I'll be a better baker if I understand the chemistry of food."

"So, you'll do what it takes."

"I will. Oh, and guess what? I made some calls and the nearest bakery's all the way across the lake. Our business is good to go."

To be honest, he couldn't imagine making bank off selling a few cupcakes. But he had nothing to lose. He'd roll with it for a while, see if it turned into anything.

"*And*…I want to call it Sweet Treats. Before you make fun of me, I know it's not the most unique name, but I really like it."

He honestly couldn't care less about the name of the business. "Not gonna make fun of you. You want to take some pictures of your cupcakes and I can start building a website?"

She blasted him a smile that cut through to the heart of him. "You're really in."

He shrugged. "Sure." A tomato slice hung from the bottom of his sandwich, and he pushed it back in. "Why were you pissed this morning?"

"I wasn't pissed."

"You stormed out of the kitchen." He watched her carefully. He liked to read her expression. It revealed everything.

"I just hate that you think you're so different from the rest of us."

He scowled. "I am."

"No, you're not. Maybe you think you're different because of your mom's scene on the front lawn, but what exactly do you think goes on behind closed doors in everyone else's homes? Do you think because Caroline is from a wealthy family that her parents are like Disney characters? She didn't become a raging bitch because she was just so doggone pretty and rich and popular. Maybe Caroline's parents have no time for her. Maybe they cheat on each other, and Caroline's grown up seeing it. Maybe she was raised by a revolving door of nannies."

"I don't care what her issue is. She was right to kick me out of the house."

She reeled back. "No, she wasn't."

"My mom stole Garrett's credit card."

"That's right. Your *mom* did. God, Dylan. You're not your mom."

"But I'm associated with her. And if you think that's not true, you didn't see how they looked at me. In their eyes, I was my mom." And no one could pretend otherwise because even in his small town where the McCaffreys were respected, everyone had painted him with the same brush as Lorraine.

"But you're not. So stop defining yourself that way."

"Define myself what way? As my mother's son? As the kid who grew up in trailer parks? That's who I am. That's not a judgment. It's a fact."

Taking in a sharp breath, she looked appalled. "But you're not." She leaned forward, getting all worked up. "You're not poor, you're not working class, you're not middle class, you're not anything. Your parents might be, but you're just a college kid. Just like the rest of us."

"Right. Harry's white trash like me."

"Stop it. You're not white trash. And Harry's not rich. He didn't buy that ugly watch with money *he* earned. His dad gave it to him. His dad gave him that ridiculous car he drives. His *dad* is rich. *Harry's* just like you. Every single one of us is in the exact same place—the starting point. And you get to build from here. You get to decide what and who you become. This is the one time in your life when you can finally break free of all the labels. Dylan, you can be whatever you want. Starting now."

He'd had enough of her naïve bullshit, so he shoved what was left of the sandwich back at her and stood up. "Do you think this is somehow new to me? That so far I've lived and gone to school only inside the trailer park? Jesus, Nicole. My whole fucking life I've been defined by where I live and my mother's latest bullshit. So don't tell me it doesn't matter because it does. It means I can't play football because I have to work after school. It means the nice, clean kids can't play with me, and the good girls won't go out with me. It's how my world works, and I'm okay with it. In fact, I don't give a shit. I do my thing, and I don't get involved because I understand that no one wants to get near the ugliness of my world."

She'd watched him the whole time, unfazed. Which pissed him off because he liked when he could scare people away.

But she just set her lunch bag aside and got up, facing him. "I don't know what your life was back home, any more than you know what *my* life has been like. But I do know you get a fresh start here. So why are you slashing *White Trash* all over it in red Sharpee? You can be anything you want to be."

"Really? That's great to know. Because I want to be the guy who makes enough money so my mom never has to worry again about a roof over her head. That's it." Like she could begin to understand. It just pissed him off that she thought everyone had the same opportunities as her. "You don't know shit about my life, Nicole. Don't pretend you do."

# CHAPTER FIVE

**Lying on her back, the sky glittering with stars, Nicole** couldn't stop worrying about Dylan. Of course he was right—she really didn't know anything about his life. She should keep her mouth shut. It was just...God, she hated the way he labeled himself. The lack of options he saw. But, he was right, it *was* none of her business.

"I don't see anything." James patted the blanket, found her hand, and then squeezed. "Why are we here again?"

"It's what people who don't party do for fun."

"Right. I knew that. And this *is* fun, right?"

Nicole laughed and, God, it felt good. "Yes, it's fun. Just wait till the shower gets going."

A collective gasp snapped her attention to the black sky. Even though everyone watched the same spectacle, she couldn't help pointing to the streaking meteor. "Oh, my God, see? That was the money shot."

"That *one*?" James said. "You said shower, so I imagined, you know, a Star Wars kind of event, thousands of meteors blazing across the sky, slamming into each other. Explosions. You know."

"You're such a guy. This isn't the cataclysm. It's a meteor

shower. But if it were the end of the world, I wouldn't exactly mind."

James grabbed her hand and gave it a squeeze. "You'll be all right."

"Chef hates me."

"He doesn't hate you. He just doesn't appreciate your squeamishness."

"James, I don't want to work with meat. I'm not a butcher. I work with flour and sugar."

"It's one lab. You'll live. And you know what? It'll make you a stronger person. What if you have to go into the rain forest and learn how to fry some special bug that's super high in protein…or whatever. I'm just saying."

"You're right. I know you're right." But that didn't change the fact that Chef hated her. And that meant he wouldn't choose her for the minor. And then what would she do? She needed to conquer her food issues. More than anything, she wanted to put the past behind her. On an emotional level, she needed the sense of mastery that she would always, always, always be able to feed herself. She believed with all her heart that studying with Chef Desmarais would heal her.

"Nicole," a voice called from far away. "Nic?"

Deep male laughter followed, along with other shout-outs issued from drunken tongues.

"Is that who I think it is?" James asked.

"I don't know." She did know. She'd known him a matter of days and already she'd recognize his voice anywhere. Her heart gave a tug because he'd come looking for her.

"What is going on with you two?"

"Absolutely nothing."

"Don't give me that. He sleeps with you every night."

"Not like *that.* It's just until my furniture comes." Sydney's mom had ordered furniture fit for a master bedroom. They'd had to return everything and reorder for her small, office-like space.

"Nicole?" The voice came closer. She knew it was Dylan, but she'd never heard him drunk before. She didn't like drunk Dylan. "Nicole."

"You should just tell him where you are so people don't take out his knees with a tire iron," James said.

"I don't want to see him when he's like this." No matter how many years had passed since she'd lived with her mom, the barrier of time thinned when she was around drunks. But to know it was Dylan, someone she had feelings for…yeah. It just made it worse.

*Oh, hey, now. I thought we're* not *having feelings for him?*

"Where is she?" some guy said. "Is she even here? Nicole?"

"Wait, what the hell?" Yet another voice. How many people did he bring with him? "Is this like the Jamestown massacre? Why're they all lying there?"

The first guy said, "Are they dead?"

"It's a meteor shower," someone sober called. "Shut the fuck up."

"Oh, sorry," one of the drunken idiots said. "Shhh. We're scaring away the stars."

"Nicole?" Dylan barked.

"Jesus, whoever Nicole is, can you please tell your boyfriend to shut up?"

She whipped up. "He's not my boyfriend."

"There you are." Dylan's voice was filled with relief and a happiness she'd never heard from him. In long strides, he came to her quilt, forced his way between her and James and sighed. "I found you."

"You're drunk."

"You wanted me to take off the White Trash tag, so I put on a Sigma Phi one instead. Do you like it better?"

"It doesn't matter what I like. Do you like it?"

"I'll get pussy."

James choked on his laughter.

"You'll get pussy without being in a frat. Isn't that why you work out every single day of your life?"

"You think that's why I work out?"

Someone said, "Ow," as the other guys stumbled through the crowd. They sat on random blankets, amidst a chorus of pissed-off stargazers.

"You're still mad at me," he said.

"When you sober up you'll recall you were the one who was angry with me."

"Just saying, this is way more entertaining than the whole meteor thing," James said.

"You're not mad?" Dylan's hand clamped down on her bare leg.

And, God, did that possessive grip feel good. "Well, I am a little now. I don't like hanging around drunks."

"I'm not a *drunk*."

His hand rode higher up her thigh, sending a shot of heat straight to her core. "Why don't you go back to the frat and get some pussy?"

James snickered.

Dylan rolled onto his side and nuzzled her ear, reeking of beer. "I don't like when you're mad at me."

"Dylan."

"I hate when you use that voice. You sound like Mrs.

Ellis. The prin—priss—principal of my high school. She expected so much better from me."

"Well, she was an idiot. You're incredible."

"You don't know anything about me, so you can't say that." And then right into her ear, he whispered. "You should stay away from me."

She rolled—big mistake—so that they were nearly nose to nose. Close enough to feel his warm beer breath on her face. "I do know you. I might not know all your stories, but I know how you are here and now. Well, not literally here and now, because you're drunk and that's gross, but outside of this exact moment, you're a really good guy. I don't understand why no one ever told you that."

"Because I did bad things."

She turned more fully, leaning in close so no one else could hear them. "Did you?"

Color tinged his cheeks, and her heart went soft for the guilt he carried.

She touched his cheek. "Did *you* do bad things? Or did your mom?"

And she could see from his pained expression he didn't think there was a difference, and that just made her crazy. She wished so badly she could get through to him.

"Dylan…" She drew in a breath. "You did the best you could with what you had. That's what we all do. Are you doing bad things now? Because I've seen you do only good things."

His grip on her thigh tightened. "You've got some weird ideas."

"What's weird is blaming yourself for what your mom does. That's beyond your control. You're away from your parents now, so you don't have to define yourself by them or by their choices."

"You should stop talking about my parents. I don't have a dad. Never did."

"That's not your fault either."

"You gonna be my champion?"

"If it means I get to wear a cape, then yeah."

He nuzzled her neck, sniffing. "You smell good." He licked her earlobe. She shivered, which was stupid, because he was drunk. He wasn't really hitting on her. She knew that. Still, the connection between them throbbed like a live wire.

His lips brushed over her cheek, and she sighed.

"Wait, do you like me? *Like* me like me?"

She pushed him away, but it was like pushing a boulder. His body pressed up against hers, and as much as she wanted to be repulsed by him, she couldn't stop her body's response. "Can you please go away? I don't like you right now."

"I don't want to go away from you. I never want to go away from you." He caressed her skin, slowly drifting toward her inner thigh.

Desire burned under his touch. But he was drunk, so she pushed it off. "Okay, that's enough." She started to get up, but his hand on her stomach pressed her back down.

"Stay." He held up his hand, as if to say, See, not touching you. But the way he looked at her, the intensity and desire in his eyes, made the blood roar in her ears.

And when her gaze lowered to his sensuous mouth, when she took in a shuddery breath, he nuzzled her neck. Chill bumps exploded on her skin.

He ran his fingers over them on the sensitive skin of her inner arm, his knuckles brushing against the side of her breast. "Fuck. You *do* like me like me."

Her whole body flamed with desire. She jumped up.

"Oh, my God, enough. What's the matter with you?"

James shot up, too. "Maybe you should go, Dylan. You okay, Nic?"

She took off down the hill, angry at him for messing with her, angry at herself for feeling anything for him. He was drunk. He didn't actually want her.

God, she was such an idiot.

"Nicole," Dylan shouted, and she could hear him running after her. "Fuck." He stumbled, but she didn't bother turning around to help him.

"Nicole, wait," James said.

She quickened her pace, blinking back tears. She hated that he'd treat her like some stupid hookup.

"Leave her alone, Dylan," she heard James shout. "Go back to your frat friends and leave her alone."

It didn't take James long to catch up with her. He grabbed her arm and yanked her back. "Wait. God, just hold up."

She looked behind them, making sure Dylan wasn't following. She didn't see him anywhere.

"What'd he say to you?" James looked so worried.

"He was getting all…worked up."

"Oh, well…"

"Oh, well, what?"

"You sleep in his bed every night. What did you think would happen?"

"It's not sexual."

"He's a guy. You're a girl. You sleep in a twin bed every night. Come on, Nicole."

"It's not like that. He shows zero interest in me."

He ran a hand through his dark hair. "You can't be this naïve."

"What?"

"You can't not understand what's happening here, right?"

"What are you talking about? He's looking for a drunken hookup."

"He's not that drunk, Nicole."

She knew that. She did. Then why had he touched her like that?

"He's drunk enough to finally loosen up a little, but he's not drunk enough to not know what he's doing. Believe me, tomorrow he'll remember everything."

"Then what does he want? Not me, obviously."

His brow curved up. "But you want him?"

"Well, obviously, I'm attracted to him, but I..." She wasn't going to lie. "Yeah, I do. I mean, I can't help how I feel." God, why had he gone and messed with her like that? "But I'm not going to be some hookup."

"And you shouldn't." He started walking. "Let's go back to the house."

As they found their way to the path, she rubbed her arms, the cool air finally getting to her.

"Listen," James said. "If there's anything I know about, it's wanting what you can't have."

"Please don't tell me I can't have him. I *know* that."

"He wants you. Of course he does. He just doesn't think he can have you."

"Oh, please." Hope popped like a prairie dog out of its hole.

"I see how he looks at you, and it's probably the same way I looked at Jason Rountree for about three years. The poor guy had to know how bad I wanted him. But he was straight." He shook his head. "I just couldn't stop the way I felt."

"And how did you feel?"

"I'm not attracted to the flamboyant guys. I like 'em manly. You know? The jocks. The alphas. And Jason was our school's hottest jock. That dude was fucking hot. But he wasn't gay. And I knew that, but I couldn't stop wanting him."

"Uh, Dylan can have me, obviously."

"Not in his head he can't. I don't know his demons, but I do know his mom is on him constantly."

"Yeah, either he's super popular or she calls and texts him a *lot*."

He nodded. "I'm pretty sure he supports her."

"*Supports* her? Seriously?" Oh, God, how awful. Dylan was right—she didn't know anything about his situation. She felt terrible. God, she'd lived with an alcoholic, but she'd never been responsible for her. "That's awful."

He blew out a breath. "Look, I don't know what all's going on, but we saw what his mom did that night. And I'm guessing from the way he handled it, it wasn't anything new to him. So…a guy grows up with embarrassing things like that…I'm guessing he doesn't feel too good about himself. And you? You're, like, this sweet, fresh-faced girl. You're, like, purity and shit."

"Pretty sure I'm not pure."

"And there's that naughty smile that makes men want to open your book and turn the pages. You sexy little surprise, you."

They came out onto the main road, and she felt a little better. "I guess I kind of overreacted."

"Maybe a little."

"I'll apologize."

"Might be best to leave it alone. He's gonna be pretty

embarrassed tomorrow." He paused. "I'm just saying, if you're going drama-free this year, then your best bet is to stay away from a hot mess like Dylan McCaffrey."

He was right. She knew he was totally right.

If only her heart listened to logic.

******

With his drink order ready to go, Dylan turned away from the bar and started toward his table in the dimly lit, upscale restaurant in town where he'd scored a job as waiter. A hand rubbed over his ass and squeezed. He jerked hard, nearly toppling his tray.

Brittany, one of the waitresses, shot him a sexy smile. "Overreact much?"

Ignoring her, he brought the drinks to the small, corner booth and found the couple engrossed in their menus. "Would you like a few more minutes?"

The woman looked up. "We would like five minutes. Five minutes, and we'll be ready to order."

"You got it." *Professor OCD.* His gaze flicked over to Brittany. She looked up from taking an order to give him a seductive look. O-kay. He'd take his five minutes in the alley.

Pushing out the door, he breathed in the air—thick with moisture and a hint of mildew this close to the lake. He crouched, cradling his head in his hands.

His mom hadn't shown up for work, and she'd lost her job. Now what?

He had to get her back on track, but he wouldn't be home until Thanksgiving—two months away. Hard to look out for her when he wasn't physically there.

The door opened, light pooling beside him. Fingernails scraped across his scalp. "Hey."

Brittany stood over him, lighting up a cigarette. She took a drag, squinting against the smoke, and held it out to him.

He waved it away.

"Todd's having a party tonight. Want to go?"

And just like that the weight bearing down on him lifted. "Yeah, maybe." This was exactly what he needed—to make a life for himself away from the house. Away from Nicole.

Last night at the meteor shower…fuck, the way he'd touched her. *No more.* He was losing control and had to stay away from her. And Brittany had just given him an opportunity to make new friends.

What Nicole didn't get was that even if Caroline had been raised by nannies, her parents didn't *steal cars.* They didn't get in hair-pulling fights on the sidewalk in the middle of town or get hauled off by cops for running drug deals in the high school parking lot. Sure, everyone had problems, but he doubted the kids at Wilmington had his kind.

And he had a feeling Brittany was more like him. If he was going to have any kind of social life for the next four years, it'd be with her and her friends. He just had to be careful about the partying.

His grades had always been a handgrip in his clusterfuck of a life. Something he could latch onto so he wouldn't go down the wrong path with his friends. The way he'd partied with the Sigma Phis the night before? He hadn't done that since freshman year of high school.

And why had he done it? Because of Nicole. Because as pissed as he got when she talked about shit she didn't know anything about, he still liked what she said. A clean slate? Hell, yeah. The idea they were all starting out at the same point—the bottom—and they could build from there. He *wanted* to build. More than anything.

But how could he build when his mom kept screwing up? She'd lost her job. Did that mean he had to go back to Gun Powder? Go to CU and commute the hour and twenty minutes? He didn't want to do that. He wasn't ready to give up this opportunity yet.

His family had pulled the plug on her once again. His uncle had said flat-out they were done. So that meant it was up to Dylan to keep her safe.

So, what the hell did he do?

Brittany hip-chucked him, knocking him down on his ass, and then sat down beside him. She reached between his legs and rubbed him.

*Oh, fuck.* Sensation shot up his spine and down his legs. He'd been fighting a hard-on from the first night sleeping with Nicole in his bed, and he sure as shit didn't need to get worked up when he had an order to take in one minute and thirty seconds.

He looked at his new friend. She was hot, with her long blonde hair, big tits bursting out of a button-down top, and glossy lips. She could probably make him forget a lot of things.

"I think we're gonna get along real good." She took a drag, blew it out the side of her mouth, and smiled.

"Gotta take an order." He got up, reached for the door.

"Party after work?"

Holding the door open, he turned to look at her. "Definitely."

He couldn't think of a better way to put distance between him and Nicole.

# CHAPTER SIX

**With his clothes reeking of roasting meat and beer,** Dylan headed home for a shower instead of meeting up with Brittany and her friends. Just as he reached for the doorknob he heard someone call his name.

He turned to see Brittany jogging up the walkway to him. He was pretty sure she wanted him to see her tits bounce. He did—and he didn't. He did because he wanted to stop thinking about filling his hands with Nicole's sexy curves, but he didn't because next to Nicole, this girl just didn't compare.

"Thought you were gonna party with us?" Smiling, she nudged his chest.

A group of guys came up behind her. "Nice house," one of them said. "We can party here."

"No." His tone had them all going still. "Let me shower and I'll meet up with you guys."

Just then the door opened. "Hey." Some of his housemates and their friends slipped past him, while Brittany's group pushed in.

*Dammit.* He'd make this quick.

He was about to lead them up the stairs when he noticed

a bunch of people standing around the granite island in the kitchen. In the center of it all was Nicole, her hands gesticulating, features flushed, as she told a story.

A rush of energy flashed through him, and he bypassed the stairs. "What's going on?" he asked James, who was dumping a tray of cupcakes onto the cooling rack.

"She had a bad day."

Why the hell were they laughing if she'd had a bad day? And suddenly he understood the flush. She'd been crying. He pushed through and reached her side, touching her shoulder to get her to turn to him.

"What happened?"

She held his gaze for a moment, and he could tell she hadn't forgiven him for the night at the observatory. It took a moment for her to make a decision, but when she did, he was relieved. He had her back. "I got sick in lab."

"What? Why?"

Tears pooled in her warm hazel eyes. "He made me touch monkfish liver."

He had no idea what that was, but it couldn't have been that big a deal. "Okay?"

"He said we were going to make something rich and creamy, velvety to the palate. He was looking at me the whole time he was talking, so I thought maybe he knew about our business, you know? And he asked *me* to come up and help him, so I thought that meant we'd be working with dough or custard—something he knew I'd be good at."

A tear spilled down her cheek, and he couldn't help but brush it away with his thumb. Christ, he loved that smooth, soft cheek.

"Like he even knows about my baking." She rolled her eyes. "Like anyone does. We're not even getting any jobs."

"We just put the article in the parent newsletter yesterday. It'll happen. Now, back to the monkfish."

"So, I get up there, and he hands me a bag and asks me to take the monkfish liver out of it. And I'm thinking *liver*? But everyone's staring at me, waiting, and I couldn't freak out so I reached in, and my hand closed around this slimy disgusting…" Her features pulled in, and tears brimmed. He pulled her against his chest, and she clung to him. She smelled like sunshine and honeysuckle, and he knew right then why he'd come home instead of going out with Brittany and her friends. Nicole was the only person in the world he'd ever truly wanted to be with.

He had to stop doing this. Holding her at arm's length, he bent his knees to look her in the eye. "Do you want to be in this program?"

"Of course I do. I want it more than anything."

"Then you have to suck it up. You can't get grossed out by this stuff."

"I know that. You think I don't know that? I made a fool of myself."

"It was one day. The next lab you won't freak out no matter what he throws at you."

Tears spilled down her ruddy cheeks, and she swiped them away. "He's such an asshole. After he saw my reaction, he goes, *That comes from this*. And he pulls this monkfish out from under the table."

"Nicole."

"Do you know what a monkfish looks like?"

"No."

"It's black and disgusting and it has sharp teeth."

"You sound like you're twelve."

She sucked in a breath. "Thanks, Dylan. Really." She

turned away from him.

With his hands on her hips, he pulled her to him, and she resisted at first, but not with enough effort. So, he turned her to face him, and they had this disturbing moment when something sizzled between them. A sharp, crackling connection.

He wanted her so fucking badly. He didn't want Kelsi or Brittany or anybody. He just wanted Nicole. And he was a selfish prick because, while she was the best thing that had ever happened to him, he'd be her worst nightmare.

He let her go. "I might not be telling you what you want to hear, but I'm telling you to suck it up if you're going to make it in this minor."

"I know. And you're right. I *am* being immature. I've always gotten sick around raw meat or fish. I just…you don't understand. It's…stuff from my childhood. It makes me sick. But I've really tried. I haven't let him see how working with meat affects me until today. When he tricked me."

"You haven't let him see anything? Sunshine, you can't hide *anything*. Everything you feel is written all over your face." Like how she felt for him. He could see it, and it made him feel like the king of the world and sick to his stomach at the same time.

Because he knew the damage his mom could inflict if he let Nicole get close to him. And he wasn't hurting Nicole. Not for anything. "All right, so I'm going to go." The look in her eyes when she gazed up at him…Jesus, everything in him gave an answering cry to claim her right there and then. But he couldn't go there.

"Hey, babe, you comin' or what?" Brittany said. "Thought you were gonna shower?"

Nicole's eyes flared, but then all emotion shut down and

she waved him off. "Go. I'm fine."

He kept his gaze on Nicole. "You're okay?"

She gave him a half-hearted smile. And that was what got him—this girl was *all* heart. So seeing her upset made him want to beat back everyone who stood in her way.

Worse, he knew she'd do the same for him. If he let her, she'd give him her whole heart.

Need roared through him—fuck, he wanted that more than he'd ever wanted anything.

He stepped back from her so quickly he landed on someone's foot. *Shit.* He had to get out of there. Keep his damn distance.

Because it was just torture, wanting what he couldn't have.

"Let's go." He broke through the group clustered around the counter and led them out of the kitchen.

******

Nights like this, Nicole could understand why people got wasted. Just to shut down all the noise in their heads.

She flopped onto her back. *Stop thinking about it.* Dylan had never shown any romantic interest in her—drunken gropes didn't count. So whatever he did with other girls shouldn't affect her.

A rap at her bedroom door had her sitting up. "Yes?"

"It's Dylan."

*Dylan?* She had bedroom furniture now, so she didn't need to sleep with him anymore. "Come in."

Yellow light spilled across her comforter, as he came in. "Hey." He stood at the end of her bed.

What was he doing back so soon? An hour ago he couldn't wait to get away from her. Not that she blamed him.

She'd made a fool out of herself, freaking out over liver. Throwing up in class? *God.* The prickly heat of mortification flushed through her.

Seriously, everything he'd said had been right. If she couldn't work with meat, she had no business being chosen for the minor. But she wanted to overcome her issues—*had* to.

She wished she hadn't told him about it. "You're back early."

"Yeah."

He looked like he was struggling—like he didn't know whether he wanted to be in her room or not. Well, it wasn't like she'd invited him in. "What's up?"

He sat on the edge of her bed, but she didn't make room for him. And not just because she was embarrassed, but because she was pissed at him. For choosing to spend time with Brittany over her.

She shouldn't care what he did with other girls. Except…she did. She felt…owned by him. Did that even make sense? Of course it didn't. It was all in her head.

He pushed a lock of hair off her face, his fingers brushing over her cheek, leaving a tiny trail of sparks. "Come with me?" His phone buzzed, but he ignored it.

Like a total idiot, she threw off her blanket. "Where?" Really? Just like that, she'd forgotten how quickly he'd run away from her in the kitchen? To hang out with *Brittany*?

"Downstairs." He got up.

Jamming her feet into her shearling slippers, she glanced at the clock. Twelve-oh-two in the morning. She had class at nine, but honestly? She'd follow him anywhere.

At the top of the stairs she could see a single lamp illuminating the massive entryway and living room. At the bottom, he turned, grabbed her hips and held her in front of him.

Confusion had her wanting to spin around to face him.

"Trust me." He held her until she relaxed, and then he covered her eyes with fabric. She breathed in the scent of laundry detergent, felt the softness of the cotton, and knew he'd blindfolded her with a kitchen towel. "Okay?"

She just stood there. What was he doing?

Hands still on her hips, he guided her forward. His phone continued to buzz, and he continued to ignore it.

"Do you have to get that?"

"No." He steered her slowly, and with every step they took, their bodies collided.

She wanted to push back against that rock hard chest, feel those big arms belt around her. She wanted to get swallowed up in him. God, she could just sink into his warm, powerful body, and stay there forever.

"Right here," he said, his mouth at her ear. No one was around, so she didn't know why he whispered, but she liked it. Especially because she was shrouded in darkness, only the faintest sliver of light peeking under the edges of the towel.

He took her hand. "Trust me." When he just held it, not moving, she understood he wanted her acquiescence, so she said, "Okay."

And then he dipped her hand into something wet, cold, and slimy.

"Oh." She jerked back, but he held her firmly.

"You said you trusted me."

"Is this cow guts?" She couldn't believe he'd prank her like this. "Are you making *fun* of me?" Yeah, she had issues, but he didn't know what they were. She wasn't just prissy. She had *reasons.*

"Of course not." His calm dismissal made her relax a little. He didn't sound like he was playing with her. He caught up her hand again and put it in something else—round, slimy. Like eyeballs.

"Oh, my God, Dylan." She probably sounded as scared as she felt. He shifted behind her, his arms bracketing her waist in a show of protection. He was letting her know he wouldn't hurt her.

"Just feel it. Okay? Just let yourself feel it." His hands moved around the slippery balls with hers, his chin came down onto her shoulder. "It's not so bad, is it?"

Well, not when his chest pressed into her back, not when she could smell his fresh scent—soap, wide open spaces, and that hint of cinnamon.

"Come on," he whispered, threading his fingers through her. "Feel it."

Oh, God, she was feeling it. Not what he wanted her to feel, but she was definitely awash in sensation. She wanted to sway her hips in rhythm with the pulse of her blood, feel his arousal—the sure sign he wanted her as badly, as desperately, as she wanted him. She wanted to turn in his arms, so she could finally taste that beautiful, sexy mouth.

But she knew he wouldn't let her. Let *himself.*

"Let's try the cow guts again." He lifted their joined hands, plunged them into the other bowl. This time he purposely moved her hands around the soft, slimy substance. "You ready to see what it is?"

She let out a shaky breath. "I'm ready."

He pulled off the blindfold. On the counter, he'd placed two silver mixing bowls. One held peeled grapes. The other had cooked fettuccini noodles, broken into pieces. Both slathered with oil. She smiled at him over her shoulder. He stood so close she could see the five o'clock shadow on his chin. "Halloween's not for five weeks."

"This isn't about Halloween. It's about getting over your fears." He gestured to the bowls. "Go on. Stick both hands in there."

She hesitantly touched the grapes.

His smile, inches from her own, set off little electrical impulses along her nerves. "Next time you have to touch raw meat, imagine it's this. Slimy grapes and slimy noodles. Okay?"

"Okay," she breathed, her every cell open and calling out to him. She wanted him to wrap his arms around her waist. She wanted to be free to touch him. "You didn't go to the party."

"No, I went to the store."

"For me?" Their mouths were so close.

*Please kiss me. Please.*

"Yeah, Nicole. For you." When the air thickened, when her heart pounded so loudly she was sure he could hear it, he smirked. "Can't have a roommate with no glow."

"You going to make sure I find mine?"

His phone vibrated again.

"You can take that."

Briefly, he closed his eyes.

"Is it Brittany? Do you have to go?"

He bristled with irritation. "No."

"How come you hang out with those guys but not with us?"

His head lowered, and he looked almost defeated.

"I just don't get why you can be with her and not me."

Grabbing a kitchen towel, he wiped off his hands. Then, he cupped her waist and hoisted her onto the counter, stepping between her legs. For several moments he just looked at her. Her heart beat so hard it actually hurt. Was he going to kiss her now? Oh, please, just do it. *Do* it.

"I'm not interested in dating anyone, okay?" He smoothed the hair away from her eyes.

"Just hooking up?"

"Do you really want to talk about my hookups?"

"No." When she pushed him aside so she could jump down, he stilled her with his hands.

"Nicole. What Brittany wants…that's all I'm interested in. I'm not here for relationships. I'm here to get my degree, and that's it. I don't have time for—nor do I want—a girlfriend."

"Whatever."

"What does that mean?"

"It's just a stupid thing to say."

"What? That I don't want a girlfriend? I don't. It's true."

"It doesn't work like that. Relationships happen no matter if we want them or not. You meet that special person you spark with and that's it. You're in. It's not like you can help it."

The way he looked at her—like he was trying to read her—figure out if she was telling the truth—made her uncomfortable. Because of what she hadn't said. She may not want a boyfriend. She certainly didn't want boy drama. But she did want *him.*

"Things *don't* just happen. We let them happen. We can control what happens to us. I choose to not get involved. That's who I am." He stepped away, brought the bowls to the sink. "So, are we good?"

"Super." Whatever. Why did she even bother with him? He was so closed off to anything real, he wouldn't let it happen. She screwed the cap back on the oil and wiped it with a towel.

He pulled the towel out of her hand. "Go. You have an appointment with Professor Davison before freshman seminar." Putting the bottle back in the cabinet underneath the stove, he turned and dumped the contents of a bowl into the garbage bin. He hit the faucet, turned it as hot it could go. Steam rose out of the sink.

He knew her schedule so well he could automatically tell her she had an appointment in the morning? Uh, mixed signals much? "I don't—"

His phone buzzed, and he tipped his head back. "Jesus fucking Christ." He slammed the faucet. The phone had been going off all night. Why was he blowing up now? "Nicole. Go. I have to take this call."

Blustery and agitated, he stood there waiting for her to leave before he answered his phone. Instead of washing her hands, she grabbed the towel and wiped them on her way out.

Halfway up the stairs, when she was no longer in his line of vision, she heard him say, "What's going on, Mom?" And he said it in the kindest, most patient voice.

She wanted to hate him, but he just wouldn't let her.

Just as she was drifting off to sleep, when she'd exhausted the endless spool of Dylan-thoughts, her door opened again. Dylan came in, wearing nothing but a T-shirt and pajama bottoms, and climbed into her bed. He didn't say a word as he drew the comforter up to their chins, belted his arm around her, and tucked it in around them.

*God.*

"Jesus, why does the whole house smell like you?" Dylan burst into the kitchen with his new entourage.

Nicole ignored him, focusing on the syrup, which was just the right consistency. She pulled it off the stove. His friends started grabbing up the cupcakes she'd baked earlier.

"She's making a honeysuckle pound cake," Sydney said. "It smells so yummy."

Dylan swiped a finger through the batter, brought it to his mouth and sucked. His eyelids drifted shut and his expression turned orgasmic. "Holy shit."

"What is it?" Brittany leaned in so close her boob pressed into his arm.

The familiarity grabbed Nicole's heart and squeezed. She wanted the freedom to touch him like that. It wasn't just attraction she felt. It was…she craved him.

Dylan turned sideways, forcing Brittany to step back. "What's in this?"

"Honeysuckle." She shouldn't sound so snippy. He wanted who he wanted. Not his fault.

"Yeah, but how do you get it in the batter?"

"I use a little honeysuckle extract and coconut milk, add some sugar and make it into a syrup. You like it?"

He just smiled.

"You got any we can eat?" one of his friends asked.

"This batch is almost ready." James peered into the oven window. "But they're for a professor's birthday party."

"We got a job?" Dylan asked.

"No, James and I got a job." Well, that came out bitchy.

"Uh oh," one of the guys said. The others snickered.

"You know, he's got other shit to do," Brittany said.

Nicole ignored her, pouring the syrup into a bowl to cool.

"Did I miss something?" Dylan asked.

"What do you think?" Nicole knew she sounded like a fishwife. Well, she was hurt. He'd *peeled grapes* to help her overcome her fears, and yet he hooked up with *Brittany*? Had he memorized *her* schedule, too?

"If I'm supposed to do something," Dylan said. "You need to tell me."

"This is supposed to be a partnership. Me telling you what to do sounds an awful lot like you'd rather be an employee."

His gaze flicked to James.

"We're not getting many jobs," James said. "We could use some help."

"He's got a *job*." Brittany said it like she thought Nicole was some rich princess who didn't understand the concept of work.

Nicole bit the inside of her mouth to keep from going off on this girl. She needed to focus on her cake, not get into a battle over a guy who didn't want her.

Arms open wide, Dylan herded his friends out of the room, but Brittany pulled away.

"You know, maybe people don't want *lavender* cupcakes. Maybe they just want chocolate. Did you think of that?"

"Yeah, Brittany, I have. If you've looked at the website, you'll see the first flavors we mention are chocolate and vanilla." She tried hard to keep her cool. "Underneath that is our list of specialty flavors. And I'm always experimenting with other flavors, hence tonight's honeysuckle pound cake."

Dylan grabbed Brittany's arm and led her and the others to the basement door. When he went downstairs with them, Nicole whirled around to face James.

She pointed a finger at him. "Not a word." She dragged the back of her hand across her forehead. "I'm pathetic. I know it."

"Just a 'lil bit."

"I don't want drama this year. I really, really don't."

"Then don't make any." James shoved his hands into the oven mitts and pulled open the door.

"But he's not working with us at all. We should cut him loose."

"Cut him loose from what? We've gotten two jobs." He withdrew the cupcake trays and set them down on trivets.

"Okay, but he shouldn't get any of the profits."

"There are no profits. But he did set up the website, which was huge. And the two jobs we got came from the article he put in the parent newsletter."

"Whatever." She turned on the mixer to cream the butter.

"You won't believe what I heard." Dylan's voice shot through the noise of the motor, startling her.

He motioned for her to shut it off.

"What?" James pulled off the mitts.

At the same moment, Harry swept into the kitchen, his huge diamond watch glittering in the light. He dangled his BMW keychain off a finger, as he eyed the cupcakes. "*Yes.*" He tipped the tray over, catching one of them before it toppled onto the granite countertop.

"What is your problem, Mr. World is My Oyster?" James said, but Harry just stuffed the whole thing in his mouth. James turned the other cupcakes right-side-up on a cooling rack. "Didn't your nanny teach you manners?"

"Damn, that's good," the son of a billionaire said, his mouth full of white cupcake. "Hey, you should make this shit for my family for Thanksgiving. We have it in Costa Rica. We got a place there. You want to?"

"We're not really set up for shipping," Nicole said.

"No, I meant I'd fly you out and you could have Thanksgiving with us. It's a—"

"Compound?" Dylan said.

James fought back a smile.

"Yeah, it is, but I was gonna say, it's a free-for-all, our family holidays. Everyone brings people. It's a blast. You want to come?"

"I'm going home," Dylan said.

"Fuck that shit. Ever been to Costa Rica?"

Dylan shook his head. "Ticket's already bought."

"So? I'll buy your ticket to Costa Rica. Who cares? I'll buy all of 'em. You in?" He looked to each of them.

Nicole was about to speak, but Dylan said, "*I* care. I paid for it with money I earned. And I'm not leaving my mother alone for Thanksgiving."

Harry looked at him completely confounded. Not offended, not angry, not anything other than at a loss as for why Dylan was making such a big deal about a thousand dollar plane ticket. "She can come, too."

Dylan froze, and she knew he had to be remembering his mom's visit. Like he'd ever bring her around his college friends again. "I don't think so."

"Thank you, Harry," Nicole said. She saw Dylan shoot her a look, saw his features flush, and she wondered what she'd done to embarrass him. "But I'm looking forward to spending it with my family. My brothers come home, so it's the only time we're all together."

"Yeah, thanks, man," James said. "I've got to see my family, too." He rolled his eyes. "Gotta get drug tested."

"Maybe Christmas then. Plan on it. Gotta bolt." Harry snagged another cupcake and headed out.

"I haven't even frosted them," James called out to him. The door slammed. "Savage."

Dipping her pinkie in the syrup, she found it had cooled, so she poured a little into her frosting, then turned the mixer on again.

"So, what did you hear that we won't believe?" James said over the noise.

But Dylan kept watching her, inching closer. "Was I rude?"

She shut off the mixer, shrugged. "He wasn't being mean. He just got excited about the idea of bringing us all to Costa Rica. He's probably got a—"

"Compound," Dylan and James said at the same time. They high-fived each other across the island.

She ignored them. "Place on the beach. He wanted us to surf and Zip Line and stuff with him. He meant it in a nice way."

"It's not that simple."

"For him it is. He wants something, and he's got all the money in the world to make it happen. I don't think there's a mean bone in his body. It's just…that kind of wealth, the ability to do whatever he wants when he wants, is all he knows."

"Yeah, well, not me."

"Yes, we know that, Dylan. You make that very clear. And, so, yes, you were rude to him. You could've just said no, thank you."

He looked uncomfortable. She didn't want to get pissy with him. James didn't get upset with him because James didn't have feelings for him.

"What did you hear?" James asked gently.

Emotion cleared from his face, Dylan said, "A guy in my language lab had a birthday a few days ago. Last week, I told him about the website, told him to show it to his parents. Never heard back from him. So, I brought it up today. Apparently, his mom said, At that price, they probably use Crisco."

"I don't use Crisco." She shot a look to James. "Should we put the ingredients on the website?"

"No, we don't give away the goods, sweetie."

"But we should at least say something like, Only the finest—no, *freshest* ingredients."

"Go on," James said, gesturing to Dylan. "What else did she say?"

"They look boring."

Her gaze landed on the unfrosted cupcakes cooling on the wire rack. Usually, she just used a knife to slather on a nice, thick layer of frosting. No designs, no special swirls or patterns—and certainly no sprinkles or toppings. That would be heinous. "I guess I'm more interested in flavor than appearance."

"As you should," James said. "They're the best-tasting cupcakes I've ever had in my life."

She smiled. "Thank you, but I'm not hurt. I'm actually glad for the input. How else can I get better at what I do?"

"You guys don't think it's hilarious that we need to charge more to get people to buy our shit?" Dylan asked.

Her eyes narrowed. "Oh, it's *ours* now?"

"No, I get it," James said quickly. "My dad's the sickest consumer on the planet. He only wants the most expensive car, house, clothes. No lie. When we need a new refrigerator, he calls the appliance store and literally tells them to deliver the most expensive one they've got."

"Why?" Dylan asked.

"Because he assumes it's the best. And it makes him feel good."

"So, he grew up poor," Dylan said.

"Poorer than you."

Nicole sucked in a breath, her whole body on alert. Why would James be so cruel?

But after a tense moment, Dylan burst out laughing. "Not sure that's possible, but okay. I get it."

"So we need to raise our prices and decorate better." She should've known that. Who wanted to give out plain cupcakes for a celebration? "I like *baking*. I don't really care about the decorating part."

"You know what I need?" James asked. "Those fun bags. Let me spend some time with 'em. Can I play with yours?"

Dylan looked horrified, his gaze going right to her chest. "What's the matter with you? Don't talk to Nicole like that."

"Oh, my God." James laughed so hard he cried.

"I think he means decorating bags. You put the frosting in and add a tip to the bag to make different shapes."

Dylan's cheeks colored, and he looked from James to Nicole. Slowly, he broke out into a shy smile. God, she loved when he smiled. And then he slid between her and the counter, his back to a howling James. "You pissed at me for not helping more?"

"Yes."

"What do you want me to do?"

"I don't know. If you don't want to add this business to your schedule, I understand. I was just being bitchy because of—"

"Brittany." He lowered his mouth—so close to hers—but then shifted at the last minute and whispered in her ear.

"She doesn't smell half as good as you."

James swung around the counter, slapped Dylan on the back. "Well, I think you've saved our business. You take care of the prices on the website, and I'll work on the frosting."

"We should probably work on marketing, too." Nicole took a step back. She didn't even know what he meant by that comment—she smelled better than the girl he was screwing? Wow. *Cool.* "The newsletter isn't enough. How many parents actually read it? My dad probably just deletes it."

She felt Dylan's gaze on her. When he looked at her like this, like he was digging down through the layers, trying to get to the heart of her, it just electrified her.

"We should get the word out to the athletic department, let the teams know," he said. "The clubs, too. As soon as you figure out what you want to do with decorating, take some pictures and I'll send a new advertisement out to the different department heads."

"Sounds good." James brought dirty bowls and scrapers to the sink.

Even though she and Dylan didn't touch—anywhere—she could feel him—this band of heat and energy, this pulsing, pounding connection. No, she didn't want drama, but times like this she *knew* he felt it, too. Not that it mattered. That, plus the fact he smelled nice, amounted to one big ball of frustration.

He was waiting for a response, so she had to focus on the conversation. "Sounds good."

"Better get back downstairs."

And as she watched him leave, she realized she'd done it again.

She'd given a piece of her heart to another guy surrounded by orange hazard cones.

# CHAPTER SEVEN

**Dylan's friends sprawled all over the game room.**

He wasn't clueless. He knew he shouldn't keep bringing them to the house. But he never got to see Nicole, so whenever they asked what he wanted to do, he always suggested going to his house. But he could see that it hurt her. Seeing him with Brittany hurt her. He really needed to keep his friends in town.

"Be right back," he said to no one in particular, as he climbed the stairs. He wondered if Nicole was still in the kitchen.

"Where you going?" Brittany followed him.

"Gotta make a phone call." He turned to see Todd flicking a lighter on the black leather couch, having just finished a couple games of foosball. They were getting restless.

"I'll come with." She gave him a seductive smile.

Did she think *make a phone call* was code for *hook up*?

"Let's go back to my place," Joe said, getting up. "I can't light up in here."

"You got any shit in your room?" Kevin asked.

"Nope." Why did he have to keep telling them he didn't

do drugs? "You go on ahead, and I'll catch up with you."

But they didn't go. They followed him up the stairs. Just as he reached his room, the bathroom door opened. Steam billowed out, along with the familiar scent of honeysuckle body wash.

Oh, hell. The image of Nicole naked, lathering up her gorgeous breasts in the shower made him hard.

"Dude, you got any shit?" Todd asked him.

"He already told you he doesn't." Brittany pushed her way through the guys to reach him. "But we can go to my place. My mom's not home tonight." She reached up to whisper in his ear. "I get so fucking wild when I'm high."

The bathroom light shut off, and Dylan herded his friends into his bedroom. He didn't know why. Well, sure he did. He wanted to avoid another scene between Brit and Nicole. Not that Nicole ever initiated anything. It was always Brit, looking to claim territory she didn't—and would never—own.

Dammit all to hell. He had to stop spending so much time in this house.

Towel wrapped around her, she came out of the bathroom and nearly plowed right into him. Looking up with alarm, her hand pressed the top of the towel over her chest. Her gaze flitted to his room, where his friends laughed about something.

"'Night." She quickly looked away. Hurt.

He blocked her way but didn't budge. Wet hair hung around her face, trickles of water sliding down her shoulders and disappearing into the towel. She looked so pretty, so fucking sweet.

Caught in that magnetic force that always bound them together, neither one made a move. His dick hummed, his hands fisted. He wanted…what did it matter what he wanted?

And then she smiled, breaking the tension. She reached around him for her doorknob.

His heart pounded, his nerves vibrated. He wanted to say something to keep her, but he *couldn't* keep her. He couldn't have her at all.

Her door opened, and she stepped inside. She'd shut him out in one second, and he'd be stuck with Brittany, Todd, Joe, and Kevin for the night. For all the nights of his college life. And then he'd go home to his Colorado friends and sink back into the sameness, the ugliness of *that* life.

And this girl? She was like a portal to a whole different world. Fresh, clean, pure.

*Fuck.* He could feel her warm body curving along his under the covers, smell her subtle, sweet scent, see the look in her eyes in the darkness just before they fell asleep—the soundest sleep he'd ever had in his life—and he fucking wanted that. Wanted it so badly his body throbbed with it.

Her features softened. She had no idea what she did to him. "Hey, you know what I was thinking in the shower?"

The image of her naked in the shower…Jesus fuck, desire slammed him so hard his fingers curled into fists at his sides.

She gazed up at him like he hung the moon. "In the Apocalypse? You're the one everyone's going to look to. You're going to be the world leader because you're strong, smart, and you can do stuff. Harry's cowering in a hollowed-out tree, peeing in his pants."

"That's what you think about in the shower?"

"Well, it didn't start there. It started with Harry, because you let him get you so riled up. And then I was thinking that you just don't seem to understand that you have the potential to make billions of your *own* dollars, because you're so smart. Harry's a decent guy and all, but he doesn't have your potential. Which led me to the Apocalypse, and how you'd be a world leader." She smiled. "A really hot one. I pictured you in a loin cloth. Shirtless." She gestured to his chest. "All those muscles rippling every time you move."

Blood roared in his ears, and need crashed over him. He cupped her chin. Those warm eyes gazed up at him, those beautiful lips parted. When her tongue flicked out to dampen them, he couldn't take it anymore. He touched his mouth to hers. So sweet. So incredibly sweet.

He tried to hold back. Tried to get a handle on this thoughts—remind himself why this was wrong—but she opened her mouth—just a little—just enough for him to feel the rush of her breath on his lips. And then she leaned into him—so gently, so easily. Christ, like they belonged together.

Holy hell. This was bad. This was so fucking bad. He should stop, walk away while he still had possession of his balls. But he needed this taste. This one little taste to make the want go away.

He pressed his mouth to hers—lightly—just to keep a hint of her to savor for later—but she opened to him, tilting her head to let him in. She got up on her toes, a gentle hand wrapping around his neck—and God help him—but he leaned into her, gave into her. He fell into that delicious mouth, stroking inside with his tongue. And it was so fucking hot, it just cut him wide open, letting all that need come gushing out.

He reached for her ass, covered in the damp terrycloth towel, and he stroked the curves, familiarized himself with her shape.

Oh, fuck, she felt good. Firm, round, with enough flesh to get a good grip. He couldn't help himself, he took handfuls of her luscious ass and squeezed. She moaned, her hips pushing hard into his, and he slipped his tongue inside her mouth, taking advantage of her vulnerability, selfish bastard that he was.

Their tongues tangled and danced, while his heart threatened to beat right out of his chest. He wanted her, needed her beyond his ability to control.

It was too much, too overwhelming, so he broke the kiss but not the contact—God, he could not let go of her ass, couldn't remove himself from the scent that invaded his dreams, his every waking moment.

He felt her breasts against his chest, felt the sting in his scalp when she gripped the hair at the back of his head, as his lips moved across her soft skin, gliding down to the graceful curve of her neck. He sucked on her, letting his tongue flick over the pulse point, relishing this warm, sweetly-scented place to hide from the world.

"Dylan," she said on a breathy, exhale. "God." She pressed up harder to him.

They fit together so perfectly it was like coming home, finally falling into the place he belonged. This moment, this overwhelming moment with her, felt like they'd created their own time and space outside the cold, impossible world. It was intoxicating—this closeness, this profound connection. Fuck, she felt so good. His mouth sought hers, his tongue seeking, exploring, begging for connection.

And when he got it, when he got her total surrender, his hands slid deeper between her legs and he lifted her, backing her against the wall. He pressed his aching cock between their bodies and ground against her hard enough to tear a cry from her throat.

Her hips bucked, and her kiss turned desperate. Jesus, the rush of blood in his veins made him dizzy. She kissed him like she felt the same kind of urgent, frantic need.

"What the hell?" Brittany's voice landed like a punch to his stomach.

Tearing Nicole away from him was like ripping his heart out of his chest. But he did. Breathing hard, he set her carefully to her feet. She wobbled, bracing her hands on his chest.

"Are you *fucking* her?" Brittany asked.

Dylan turned away from Nicole, wanting to shield her. His heart raced, his palms tingled, and he felt like he'd been slammed into a wall. "Don't talk about her like that." He glanced to his bedroom door, but the others hadn't come out.

Brittany nailed him to the spot with her hostile glare. "Answer me."

He needed to take care of Nicole first, but when he turned back to her, she was gone. Her door closed.

He hadn't even heard it shut. "It's none of your business what I do."

"What is your deal? I don't get you at all. I've been trying to get with you for weeks, and here I find you nailing some chick in the hallway."

Todd leaned out of his doorway. "What's going on?"

And then Joe came out. "Let's roll."

Dylan had had enough. He looked over her head to Joe. "Can you guys get her out of here?" And then to her. "Don't come back here if you're going to talk to my friends that way. I've never misled you. We're friends. We hang out. If you can't handle that, it's not my issue."

"Fuck you." She spun around, racing down the hallway

and trampling down the stairs. "Stupid fucker." Her voice rang in the cavernous entryway, and Dylan just closed his eyes against the familiarity of the moment. His mom, Kelsi…all the women in his world.

"Dude, what just happened?" Joe said.

But Todd grabbed his arm. "Come on."

He watched his friends leave. Standing alone in the hallway, he flicked off the light, wanting darkness, wanting to hide.

"See you," he heard James call from downstairs, and then the front door banged shut.

Great, how many others had heard the scene? He hoped to hell no one knew what he'd done to Nicole.

*Nicole.*

He turned to face her room, just for one fleeting, stupid moment, falling back into their kiss. Kiss? Right. He'd practically banged her against the wall.

Blowing out a breath, he tipped his head back, rubbing the spot on his neck she'd touched. If Brittany hadn't interrupted them—shit. He started to get hard again.

Oh, hell, no. No, he couldn't go there. Couldn't think about her like that. He didn't need to imagine how good they'd be together. He did not need those images winding through his brain.

He had to talk to her. Apologize. He rapped lightly but, as expected, she didn't respond. Probably for the best. He didn't think he could apologize at the moment—not when he had a semi.

But he couldn't just leave things like this. If she wouldn't answer, he'd have to—

His phone buzzed. *Kelsi?* What the hell? They'd agreed to cut off their relationship cold turkey and she'd—

surprisingly—held to their agreement. So hearing from her only meant one thing.

He opened the text.

*Remember Jeff Blakely? Saw ur mom with him 2nite at Pit Stop. Just thot u shud no.*

Fuck, fuck, fuck. *No.* Jesus, she couldn't be going down this path again. Not so soon.

He had to talk to his mom. He started for the stairs. Too many voices downstairs, so he couldn't go there. He needed to get a hold of her now. Locking himself in the bathroom, he hit her speed dial. He had to stop her from going down this path. It rang three times, four. *Answer the damn phone.* He felt like he was standing on the highway with an eighteen-wheeler bearing down on him.

Had he been neglecting her lately? He forced himself to think about it. Truthfully, yeah. Between classes, work…yeah, of course he had. Look at him—tonight he'd been completely out of control. *Fuck.*

This is what happened when he pulled his attention off his mom.

******

Nicole stumbled into the kitchen, glancing at the oven clock. Great, she didn't have time to eat breakfast before her nine AM class. She'd hardly slept last night. Every time she'd remember last night's kiss a bolt of electricity would shock her wide awake. It had been the hottest moment of her life.

And yet…the whole time Brittany had been waiting for him in his room. What was that about? One woman in the hall, another in his bed?

She'd heard him tell Brittany they were just friends. Could that be true? If she thought back, she could clearly remember Dylan pushing the girl away every time she'd laid her hands on him. He always seemed irritated with her. But, then, he didn't seem the type to like clingers.

God, his mouth. That kiss—so fierce, so wild. His hands on her ass…oh, God. He'd wanted her so badly. Just…maybe he wanted all girls the same way?

She came downstairs to find the pretty pink box of cupcakes all ready to be delivered to Professor Englander. *Thank you, James.*

"Hey, can I have one?" Harry met her at the door with a pack of his Sigma Phi friends.

"Sorry, these are for someone's birthday."

"Nice." One of the guys eyed them hungrily.

Nicole glanced down at them. *Oh.* James had made perfect purple swirls. *Guess he figured out how to use the fun bags.* "Yeah, thanks."

She headed out the door, her thoughts immediately returning to Dylan. What if he was ready to be with her? Last night, beyond a quick knock on her door, he hadn't tried all that hard to get in. And, really, after the way they'd gone at it, a guy who was ready to be with her would've shouldered that door open and claimed her.

A shudder rocked through her. She wanted—no, needed—him to claim her. *Please, Dylan.* But her gut told her he wasn't ready.

She needed to talk to James. Pulling her phone out of her back pocket, she shot off a text.

*You up yet?*

*Of course. What's up?*

The air had just started to turn chilly, as the end of September neared. *I need to talk to you.*

*Is this about Dylan and the ho who went all trailer park last night?*

*Yes. Meet me for lunch?*

*K. Where?*

Definitely not in the house. *I'll make us a picnic. We can eat at the lake.*

*OMG. Who are you? You're like some gift from God. I can't believe you fell into my life.*

She smiled. James was crazy. *What do you mean?*

*You're good for me. I need wholesome and healthy, and I sure got it in you. Did my dad hire you? He totally would, you know. Yes, I'll meet you at the lake. I'll bring my bible. We can read the part about how Jesus sent you down to smite temptation right the hell out of my life.*

*So there's nothing tempting about me at all?* Every time doubt crept in, she remembered Dylan's hands on her last night.

*Not my kind of temptation, peaches. See you.*

About to shut her phone off, she thought of the box of cupcakes. *Love what you did to the cupcakes. xoxo*

*I got even more ideas online last night. Need to order some shit. Don't worry, using Dad's credit card. Now shush. I'm in class. Daydreaming.*

*About Jason Rountree?*

*Bitch.*

And then, a few moments later, he wrote, *Yes.*

She smiled and shut off her phone.

"Miss O'Donnell?"

Oh, damn. She'd taken a spot in the back corner of the lab, hidden behind a guy with hair so wild and frizzy she'd thought for sure Chef wouldn't notice her.

"Yes, Chef?" She shifted slightly into view.

"And how are we this morning?"

"Fine, thank you."

"And your stomach?"

"Strong. Like a steel drum."

"Excellent. Shall we try again?" He motioned her to come forward.

Couldn't he just leave her alone? She headed towards the front of the room, her rubber soles squeaking on the polished linoleum.

As soon as she got there, he ignored her. "Let's get busy, shall we?" His usual line to start class. "Today we make marinade."

*Oh, thank God.* Marinade, she could do the hell out of.

As class got going, the kitchen filled with the scents of garlic and herbs. She pulled a large glass bowl off a shelf and dumped the minced garlic into it.

And then Chef said, "Please get the meat from the refrigerator."

Oh, dammit all to hell. He *was* messing with her. "Sure." She could do this, of course she could. She wasn't that little girl trying to figure out what to do with raw meat because there was nothing else to eat. She could totally do this.

She stood in front of the refrigerator. Fear crept along her spine, biting down at the base and triggering a spasm. What was she going to find in there? She opened the door, and a blast of cold air hit her in the face.

A tray of shoulder clods sat on a shelf. *You've got to be kidding me.*

"You found them?" Chef called. She couldn't speak. She just stared in horror.

And then she heard, "Do you need a hand, Miss O'Donnell?"

She swallowed hard. He was such an ass. "I'm good." She could do this. Dylan came to mind, his hands on her hips, guiding her into the kitchen, the blindfold making her hyper aware of his breath at her ear, of his scent, that hint of cinnamon.

She remembered the feel of oily peeled grapes. So these clods…they were clay. Yep, slabs of clay. No problem. She lifted the tray—and oh, God, it smelled so bad—but she breathed through her mouth and brought it out of the walk-in, kicking the door closed.

Several of her classmates looked up, eyes going wide, but she maintained a placid expression, ignoring the roiling of her stomach.

"Excellent. Thank you. Set it right here." Chef gestured to the space beside the big glass cutting board.

After depositing the tray without a single roll of nausea—*yay, me*!—she looked to him for further instruction. Now that she'd done his dirty deed, she hoped he'd let her go back to her seat because she was starting to see pieces of a hacked-up cow—no, no, clay. It was simply clay.

"Do you know how to cut stew beef out of chuck?"

"No, Chef." This was a beginner's class. He was teaching the fundamentals. He didn't expect her to know. Just to be willing to learn.

"That's fine." He handed her a slicing knife with a wide, shiny blade, and she could feel his eyes on her, watching. She took it, letting it hover over one of the shoulder clods.

"Follow my example." He used his own knife to quickly slice the meat into cubes.

She saw blood ooze onto the cutting board, coat his fingers, and bubble out of the raw flesh. Bile shot to the back of her throat, but she forced it back down. This wasn't cow. This was clay. The red was paint. She could do this. And she would. She'd get through this so he'd choose her for the program.

She couldn't wait to tell Dylan what he'd done for her.

Exhilarated, Nicole came home with a fresh perspective. Not only did she pass Chef's test, but she had clarity on her relationship with Dylan. He didn't want to want her, but he did. He'd let her sleep in his bed. He couldn't keep his hands off her when he'd had a little too much to drink—when his inhibitions had been down. He'd given up a party to buy pasta and grapes to help her get over her fear of working with raw meat. And last night? That kiss. Holy cheeseballs, *that kiss*.

No doubt about it. He wanted her as badly as she wanted him.

But for some stupid reason he thought he was too different from her—too tainted by his mom. But she'd make him understand he wasn't. He was a great guy doing the best he could in a terrible situation.

As soon as she got inside the house, ready to charge up the stairs and get to him, she spotted him. Right there in the living room. Surrounded by his usual friends, he stood a head above the others. A petite and buxom brunette, dressed in skin tight jeans and a halter top, bounced around him like a Chihuahua. She kept touching him, pressing up against him. He smiled at her.

Nicole stood there, watching, all the happiness draining away, leaving her gobsmacked. Not eighteen hours after they'd gotten so lost in each other they could've had sex up against the wall had they not been interrupted, he was already onto someone new.

So he hadn't been that into her. That was how he acted when hooking up. He was a hook up artist. A master of the hookup. A hookup prodigy. A—oh, screw him. He'd been as into it as she had. Which meant he'd pulled back again.

The coward.

Okay, but even if he regretted last night, he shouldn't flaunt a new girl in her face. If he was trying to hurt her, then she kind of hated him.

Her legs felt rubbery, and she shook with a volatile mix of hurt and anger. White trash? How about *asshole*?

And then the girl stood up on her toes, lifting both arms to his shoulders. A look of confusion crossed his features, and just as his hands went to her hips, Dylan jerked his gaze right over to Nicole.

Pain exploded in her chest.

She charged across the room, heading for the stairs.

******

Dylan stalked up the stairs, and Mindy—Melanie?—trailed after him. "I'll be down in a minute." He needed her gone. He needed to get to Nicole. Seeing the hurt on her face had gutted him.

"I'll come with."

The sound of Mandy's boot heels clacking on the wood made frustration whip into anxiety. He stopped on the stairs, and she plowed into him. Her features went seductive, and she practically vibrated with sexual energy.

"Wait downstairs."

Her plump lips pouted. "I wanted us to have a few minutes alone."

"No." *Fuck*. He was a mess. The image of Nicole looking destroyed clawed at his heart. She must've thought he'd set the whole scene up. To deliberately hurt her.

He charged down the hall, knocked on her door. She didn't answer.

Low voices from behind him had him spinning around, bursting into his room.

James held Nicole in his arms. Dylan was on her in a flash, but she wrested out of her friend's arms and chest-thumped Dylan. "Leave me alone."

"No."

When he reached for her, she swerved around him. "I mean it, Dylan. Leave me alone." She tore out of the room and slammed her door. He heard the click of her lock.

He tapped his forehead against the wall. "Fuck, fuck, fuck." He was going out of his mind.

A swish of fabric, and then James stood beside him. "So. New girlfriend. You move fast."

He closed his eyes. "She's not my girlfriend."

"Last night you had Nicole up against the wall, and tonight you bring someone else home? That's kind of a dick move, don't you think?"

"I'm not—"

"Oh, shut up. You hurt her. That's all there is to say."

Why the hell had Nicole walked in at that exact moment? His chest felt tight, making it hard to breathe. "Obviously I didn't mean to."

"Didn't you?"

For three days she'd avoided him. Turned out to be a good thing, because it enabled him to get his thoughts together. Now, he knew what he needed to say.

Dylan waited outside her lab. She'd had a party tonight with her classmates, and he could smell the roasting meat, the warm bread and, over it all, the hint of lavender. He closed his eyes, breathed it in, and it drove him straight into the heart of *them*.

Them under the covers, bodies pressed together stoking the heat and combustible energy they created together.

And then the door burst open, and clusters of students walked out. He leaned a shoulder against the wall, watching for her.

But she never came out. Shit. He peered into the room to find it empty, lights out. How had he missed her? He took off down the stairs, burst out the doors, to find the group of them fanning out in different directions. One lone figure headed off campus. Nicole?

He took off after her. The closer he got, the louder his pulse ticked in his ears. His mind tried to tell him that girl couldn't be Nicole. Nicole didn't wear figure-hugging dresses and sky high heels. Her hair didn't look sleek and perfectly straight.

But his heart knew. He knew those gorgeous curves, the slope of those shoulders, the taut roundness of that ass.

Dylan caught up with her as she crossed the quad. "Nicole?"

The campus glowed with the diffused light of streetlamps covered in fog. Music floated out dorm windows and couples, arms entwined, moved silently down the walking paths.

"What are you doing here?" She didn't look happy to see him.

"Looking for you."

"You found me. What's up?" She stepped onto the curb, faltering when her heel sank into the soft grass. He reached to steady her, but she pulled away. "Stop it. Just stop…touching me."

"I'm sorry."

"What are you sorry for?" She sounded exasperated.

"Look, I'm not fucking Brittany or Mindy—hell, I'd just met Mindy that night."

"Oh, yuck. I so don't want to talk about this."

"I just want to get it out there."

"Okay, Dylan, it's out there. You brought a new girl home the day after you made out with me. We good now? Is that out there enough for you?"

"No, I mean, I wasn't trying to hurt you."

"Well, you did. But it's cool because you already told me you don't do relationships, and then you *showed* me. Which, wow, way to reinforce the whole telling thing."

"No, I mean, I didn't plan it. Mindy doesn't mean anything."

"God, Dylan, yeah, I get that. I get that kissing doesn't mean anything to you, but at least have the decency to understand that it does for others. Including *me*."

"Ours was a mistake." *Dammit.* "I didn't mean it like that." The cool night breeze teased her hair, and he found it hard to think.

She strode off in those outrageously high heels. "Don't make it worse. Just own it, Dylan. Kissing me was a mistake."

"Yeah, it was. But I didn't mean to say it like that. I don't want to hurt you."

"Big fail. *Huge* fail."

"Stop, okay? Just stop. I'm sorry. Look, I'm obviously attracted to you, and I let myself get carried away that night."

"You're attracted to *me*—or you'll hook up with any girl who's standing in front of you practically naked?"

"What? No." He hated the look in her eyes—searching, questioning—the look he'd put there. He'd treated her carelessly. "I'm attracted to *you*." Like she couldn't tell he wanted her desperately? Like his mouth, his hands, his rock hard dick wasn't obvious enough?

"What're you doing here?" she asked Dylan. Seriously, what the hell did he want?

"I'll just get in the car now." James left them alone.

"I got back from the gym, James was on his way out the door and asked me to come help carry the heavy stuff…" He shrugged.

"I think between us we can manage a twenty pound bag of flour, but thanks."

"You don't need me? That's great, because I've got a paper to work on this morning."

"Dylan." James gave them an exasperated look from the side of the car. "Are you part of Sweet Treats or not?"

Dylan's gaze flicked over to Nicole, his features blank. "Obviously."

"Then get in and help us shop for the ingredients. We're a team, right? Act like it."

"Whatever." Nicole headed for the SUV, but Dylan grabbed her arm, drew her back to him. The moment his gaze hit hers, all that need and want bubbled up. *Not fair.* She'd been doing so well. But the vulnerability in his eyes, the way he swallowed so hard, it just rocked her to the bone.

"Can't we be friends?"

She hated the way he looked at her, so intense, so serious. Why did he even care? She pulled her arm out of his grip and got into the car, forcing James to climb over the seat to the back row. Dylan shoved in next to her, sandwiching her between him and Terri, another of their housemates.

"Nic can sit on your lap," the girl behind them said.

"No," Dylan said. The car went silent from the snap in his tone. She looked at him, wondering why he'd find the idea so repulsive. "She uses a seatbelt."

Dylan dug under Nicole's ass, pulling up the strap. Then,

he reached across her, his shoulder and arm rubbing against her breasts, and locked it into place.

There was no way he didn't know what he was touching. His nostrils flared, color infused his cheeks. But he didn't stop until she was securely buckled in.

The girl on the other side of Terri rolled her eyes. "Fine. I'll take the jumpseat." She crawled over into the back row. Dylan stared straight out the tinted window.

She honestly didn't know if she could be friends with him. No, wait, she did know.

Her feelings ran too deep, her attraction too strong. It would kill her to see him with other girls.

Turning to him, she gazed up into those guarded eyes. "No. We can't."

******

Well, *that* was a great idea—spending an entire morning at her side, watching her face light up with happiness as she tossed peanut butter, chocolate chips, and bags of confectioner's sugar into the cart. Not to mention her rapturous expression as she tasted the various samples around the warehouse, all while acting like they barely knew each other? Fun.

And now he had to sit jammed up next to her, looking down on her breasts as they jiggled with every pothole they drove over. Her scent rising up to him every time she whirled around to talk to someone in the back seat.

Why the hell had he come on this trip? Because he was part of Sweet Treats, and he *did* have to do his share. So far his contribution had been limited to deliveries and website updates. Other than that, he didn't interact with Nicole at all. She avoided him, and he couldn't stand it.

"If my family didn't summer on Nantucket," one of the girls said. "I'd totally work in Costco. Those samples? Did you *try* the cheesecake?"

"No, you'd get fat," another one said. "You'd never do it."

"Don't say that," the girl said, laughing. "Way to ruin my fantasy."

"Spending your summer hauling crates of tampons is no one's fantasy."

The tinted windows brought him back to his bedroom at night. And Nicole's body pressed up so close reminded him just how it felt to sleep with her tucked against him. How many times had she shifted in her sleep, jamming that tight ass right against his junk?

Fuck. He couldn't go hard. Not here.

"Where do you summer?" Terri said, turning around to face James.

"My dad and I take off for a month somewhere. Last year we surfed Bondi Beach. Uh, let me rephrase. The summer before this last one. This past summer, I was in lock-down. Spent it at the beach house on St. Simons Island. Can we say bor-ing?"

Dylan forced his thoughts elsewhere. He thought about all the hours he'd wasted coming on this shopping trip. He had a paper to write—no, forget school. Instead of fucking off, he could be earning money. The lunch crowd at the restaurant didn't tip much, so he should be grabbing any extra cash he could. The only way to keep his mom away from assholes like Jeff Blakely was to make sure he covered her costs.

And Sweet Treats would never bring enough money to make an impact. Even if they made a profit from selling cupcakes, they had to split it three ways.

Who was he kidding? The only reason he was involved in the business was to stay connected with her. Which was pointless, because nothing would change. He'd never have Nicole in his life. He looked down on her shiny hair.

It took everything he had not to touch her. He had to stop this. It was a dead-end. Worse, it distracted him from what mattered. Maintaining his scholarship and keeping his mom safe—those were the only things he should be thinking about.

"Where do you guys summer?" Terri asked Nicole and Dylan.

"We don't—" Nicole began.

"I summer in Gun Powder. At the Lazy Days Trailer Park."

A terrible silence strangled the car.

He'd meant it as a joke, but still. Why would they talk about "summering" in a group of people from different backgrounds? Not every student at Wilmington had gone to prep or boarding schools.

"Well, no more summering in the Hamptons for me." Terri broke the tension. "I'll be doing internships from now until I graduate." She leaned across Nicole to address him. "You should, too. There's not much value in a finance degree without work experience. You're getting an MBA, right?"

"No."

"According to my dad, if you're going to get a job on Wall Street, you really do have to get the MBA."

"I won't be working on Wall Street."

"Well, maybe not literally. But for a hedge or private equity fund."

"Not sure they have any of those in Gun Powder."

Once again, he'd shocked the car into silence. Only this time he hadn't been joking.

"You're going back to your hometown after you graduate *Wilmington*?" Terri asked.

He felt the press of Nicole's thigh against his—was she trying to tell him something?

"Yup."

"Why bother getting a degree from Wilmington just to go back to Gun Powder?" James asked.

"Oh, look, there's a service plaza in two miles," Nicole said. "Anyone hungry?"

Dylan shot her a look. She couldn't be hungry, not after all those samples. So, she was either taking the heat off him or she was embarrassed by his answers.

"Seriously, you have to get the MBA," the girl in the jumpseat said.

"That'd be nice." He'd be lucky to graduate with the way things were going with his mom. Add on another two years of school? Forget it.

"Well, in any event, if you change your mind, my dad works for Pearson Greene, and they have a great college internship program. I know you're super smart, so I wouldn't mind hooking you up there if you wanted."

Pearson Greene was one of the world's biggest hedge funds. Landing an internship there would be golden. "Thanks."

"That's awesome." James nudged Terri. "That'd be so great if you could do that for him."

Oh, Christ. He had to stop things before he wasted anyone's time. "I appreciate the offer, but I'll be going home for the summer."

"You have to do the internship, man," James said.

"Gotta make bank." Dylan bore down on his rising frustration.

"Wall Street internships pay," Terri said. "It's the smartest thing you can do."

"Opportunity of a lifetime."

"Guys," Nicole said, softly.

He didn't need her damn protection. Did she think he'd never faced this kind of shit before? "It's not like I have a choice, okay? I don't get to choose between summering in Nantucket, interning on Wall Street, or surfing in Australia. Not everyone has choices. Now, seriously, thank you for thinking of me for the internship, but I can't do it."

"You *can*," Nicole said. "Everyone has choices. You just choose to believe you don't."

Sydney pulled into a parking spot in the plaza.

"I choose to wash my cheesecake down with a Venti soy latte." James climbed over the seat, his big black boot nudging between Terri and Nicole. He fell onto the girls, making them laugh. As everyone got out of the car, Dylan found his anger billowing out of control.

Nicole started to slide across the bench seat to follow Terri out of the car, but Dylan grabbed her arm and pulled her back. She looked at him wide-eyed, *What?*

"You gotta stop talking out your ass," he said. "It's really pissing me off."

"What're you talking about?"

"Do you actually think I'd give up an opportunity like Pearson Greene if I had a choice? Do you think I don't know how important an MBA is? Stop minimizing my situation."

"Oh, come on. You're eighteen. *Of course* you have

choices." She glanced out the open door to watch the group heading into the plaza. He could practically feel the anger radiating off her. "If you never talk to anybody, you'll keep thinking there's only one way to deal with whatever's going on. But, God, Dylan, do you really think your situation is so unique? Talk to someone—talk to *me*—and get some perspective. You don't have to live like this."

Why did he even bother? She'd never understand.

She reached over and slammed the door shut, sealing them in the dark space created by the tinted windows. Then, she slid right up to him with an imploring expression. "Look, you haven't told me anything, but it's pretty obvious your mom has a problem. I don't know the whole story, but you seem to think you're responsible for her. The thing is, you're not. And I know that because I thought I was responsible for my mom, too. I didn't take it as far, obviously, because I made the choice to leave her and move back in with my dad."

"It's not the same thing. You had a dad, brothers. My mom has no one."

"My mom has no one either—and that was *her* choice. My dad had to make one, too. And it tore him apart. It tore the family apart. But he made the one he thought was best for him and for us. And having my dad and brothers had absolutely zero impact on making *my* decision because they weren't involved with my mom at that point. It was just me. And when I left her, I left her completely alone."

Pain in his chest had his hand covering his heart. He hated what she'd lived through, preferred to think of her living in some mansion in Greenwich, Connecticut with a kind old dad, a cute lab, and two rowdy brothers chucking her on the chin. But he tore himself away from those thoughts and forced himself back to the conversation. "I can't do that."

"I'm not telling you *what* decision to make. I'm trying to make you see that you have options. You're not stuck. Life just doesn't work like that. But nothing will ever change if you don't allow the *possibility* of change."

She started to go, but he grabbed her arm. Confusion flashed in her eyes. "Let me go."

He couldn't. He didn't want her to leave. If she left, she took hope with her. And how could he think when she was sitting almost on top of him, her chest rising and falling with her rapid breaths? When all he wanted was to feel her body pressed to his? "I'm sorry for what you went through with your mom."

She exhaled so roughly she nearly collapsed. Her features melted into the sweetest expression, and she pushed even closer to him. "My dad gave her the choice of rehab or divorce. She chose vodka. She chose *alcohol* over her family. I lived with her five years—every day, she had a choice. Me or the bottle. She chose the bottle. She chose booze over *me*."

"Jesus, Nicole. She's sick. No one in her right mind would choose anything over you. You're amazing. You're fucking amazing."

"So are you." Finally, she touched him. Those warm hands cupping his cheeks. "That's why I keep talking to you about this. You won't open up to anyone, so you only hear one voice—that you're stuck and you don't have options. Whether you like it or not, I'm going to be another voice in your head, pointing out that you *do*. Because you deserve so much better than this tiny box you've put yourself in." Her pretty hands stroked down to his shoulders, and she tipped her forehead to his. "Just because you're doing something one way doesn't mean it's the only way. And if you opened up and talked to people, you'd find that out. You think you're trapped, but you're not."

"I don't see it that way. She's my mom. I'm responsible for her."

She shook her head. "No, *she* was responsible for *you.* And it's sad that you don't get that. But you're in college now. It's a whole new ballgame. Neither of you needs to be responsible for the other. You're both adults. You have a chance for a different life, Dylan." She reached up to him, but he grabbed her wrist before she could touch his face. "Take it."

He hated the hope she gave him.

She gazed up at him, like he was someone special. It didn't make sense. Meeting her didn't make sense. He'd expected rich college girls, easy sorority girls. But Nicole? Where had she come from? "What the hell do you see in me?"

"A really, really good man," she whispered, and then he just couldn't take it anymore.

He caught her behind her neck, pulling her forward, their mouths colliding in a rush of heat and frantic desire. Her hands clasped his shoulders, like she needed to hang on. Something inside him gave way—he hadn't realized how badly he needed her touch—and he couldn't help himself. He devoured her, lost himself entirely in her hot, welcoming mouth. Her light honeysuckle scent made him dizzy and achingly hard. Because it was her. *Her.* And he wanted her so badly he could barely keep his shit together.

Need kicked in with a force that shook him. She kissed him back, her mouth hungry for him, her hands grabbing fistfuls of his hair.

Hands cupping her ass, he dragged her onto his lap because he had to feel more of her, all of her. She straddled him, rolled her hips down hard, making his dick surge. She felt so fucking good, with her breasts pressing against him, her thighs squeezing him, her hot core riding him so urgently a tingling started in the base of his spine.

He squeezed her perfect ass through the thin cotton dress, pulling her so tightly against him she gasped.

He tore his mouth off hers to take a breath, clear his head. "Fuck, Nicole." But he couldn't clear anything because he was drowning in her. His body on fire, his cock was ready to explode with the hot friction she created as she rode him roughly. He should stop, shove her off his lap. But his hands kept kneading the plump mounds of her ass, dragging her over his hard, aching cock. He tried to stop his hips from bucking, but for fuck's sake, he couldn't. He couldn't stop. He was desperate, out of control. Had to have more of her. His mouth found hers again, and he sucked her tongue in, making hard, fast love to it.

The sounds she made—little cries that grew more desperate—and the way she ground on him with such desperation made him wild with need. Jesus, when her hands fisted in his hair, holding his head in place so she could kiss him wholly and completely, he lost it, just fucking lost it.

His hands left that glorious ass and tried to get under her dress, reach some skin, but it was caught under her legs. She got up, grabbing at the material, and then he found skin—the softest skin he'd ever felt in his life. He swept up her ribcage, cupping her breasts. Ah, those fucking breasts he'd wanted to touch for so long. God, they felt so good. But it wasn't enough. He needed skin. So he shoved the bra up and over her breasts, filled his palms with their delicious weight.

His head fell back and he groaned because holy mother of God he'd never felt anything so perfect in his life. Those soft, plump mounds, those beaded nipples.

"Dylan," she cried, as though in pain, as her hands tipped his head down, and her mouth found his again.

He pushed her breasts together, loving the feel of them, rubbing his thumbs over the pebbled tips, as he fell back into the heat of her mouth. She moved frantically now, arching her back, ramming her pussy over his dick so hard it hurt.

God, he needed relief or he was going to lose his mind. He reached a hand under the elastic waistband of her sexy boy shorts, a finger sliding inside her slick heat. Her back arched, and she hissed in a tight breath.

"Oh, my God, oh, my God. *Dylan*." God, he loved hearing his name in that passion-drenched voice. She rode his fingers, her head tipping forward, her hair spilling onto his shoulders. He could smell her arousal, her sweet-scented shampoo, and he stroked her faster, making sure with each upstroke his finger swirled around her clit. Each time she about leapt off his lap.

She was crying out, writhing on his lap, when he checked out the window. He spotted James jumping off a ledge, the group heading toward them. Shit.

He rubbed her faster and then, to get her *there*, his mouth closed over her breast through the dress and he bit down on the nipple. He sucked it into his mouth, pulling hard.

She cried out, her fingers digging into his shoulders. Her body stiffened, and her knees squeezed his thighs. "Oh, God." He continued stroking her, as her movements slowed. And then she let out a satisfied sigh. Looking dazed and thoroughly satisfied, she collapsed against him.

"They're here," he said quietly into her ear, avoiding her eyes.

She slipped off him, quickly adjusting her panties and bra. The door opened. Light and noise infiltrated their private space, and he quickly tugged on her dress so it covered her legs.

Before they all piled in, he tucked her up to him, wrapped an arm around her.

"Nic?" James said. "Shit, what's the matter?" He climbed into the SUV and scrambled over to her. "What happened? I thought she was starving."

"Car sick," Dylan said.

James smoothed the hair off her forehead. "You're sweating. Are you sure it's just car sickness?"

Dylan kept his expression free of emotion. He shrugged.

"Nic? Are you okay?"

She nodded. "I just want to get home."

"Of course." James took control, getting everyone into their seats and the driver on the road. "I hope all this food doesn't make it worse." He leaned over the seat, stroked her hair. "Come sit back here with me. I'll take care of you."

Dylan's arm tightened around her. "No."

James's hand recoiled. Everyone stared at him, like he'd overreacted.

"She needs the window." And then, continuing the stupid ruse, he hit the button, letting in a current of cold air.

As they sped down the highway, conversation was more subdued. Dylan leaned his head against the window frame. He'd touched her. Made her come. *Fuck him.*

How did he go back after something like that?

Alone in the garage, Dylan hauled the last case of water from the trunk and set it on the stack by the door to the kitchen.

He closed his eyes and blew out a breath, but startled at the image that appeared: Nicole's beautiful face softened with passion, breasts bouncing, fingers gripping his jeans.

*Christ.* What had he done? Why couldn't he stay away from her?

Because he fucking craved her.

So, if he couldn't stay away, could he at least have some of her? Stupid question. She'd never be happy with what he could give. Nobody was. His friends back home called him No-Show McCaffrey. They thought it was hilarious, but he'd always hated it.

Like he'd wanted to bail on camping trips? Walk out in the middle of dinners or parties because his mom needed him for some crisis? He knew his relationship with his mom wasn't healthy—obviously. But he did the best he could.

No, it wouldn't work, and yet…his blood burned for her. What could he do?

The moment he entered the house, Tatiana rushed up to him with a note in her hand, looking completely freaked out.

"What's wrong?"

"Campus security came by." She shoved the note at him. "Your mom called. She needs to talk to you."

*Shit.*

Tatiana's concern drew others around him. "Is everything all right?"

He pushed past the group. He didn't need an audience. "I'm sure it is. I'll call her." He looked for Nicole, found her in the kitchen watching him. That concerned expression, the wondering…he couldn't deal with it right then.

Heading outside, he hit his mom's speed dial. She answered right away.

"Dylan," she said in an accusing tone. "Where have you been?"

"You called campus security?" He came down the porch steps and strode around to the side of the house. A little stone path between a tall wooden fence and the house led to the backyard.

"You're not returning my calls, and I don't know any of your friend's numbers out there, so yes, I had to call the school."

"This isn't high school, Mom. I'm in *college*. You can't call the school." The lawn furniture hadn't been brought into the garage yet, but at least the weather had turned chilly enough that no one was out sunbathing. No one needed to hear him talk his mom down off the ledge.

"Then answer my damn calls."

Each of the dozen times a day? Not possible. Sometimes he had to turn his phone off just so he could concentrate on something other than the vibrating in his pocket. "I was busy today."

"It isn't just about today."

"Mom, listen to me, I'm in classes. I'm taking sixteen credits—way more than other freshmen—so I can graduate early." *So I can get home to take care of you.* "I work two jobs." *So I can send you money to keep you from hooking up with yet another abusive asshole.* "I can't talk to you all the time."

"I know that, Dylan. But I needed you last night, and you weren't around."

"Needed me how?" He stopped, swiveled around, and faced the backyard.

"I had some trouble."

"What kind of trouble?" Anxiety buzzed along his nerves.

"Dornen picked me up."

"You were in *jail*?"

"Yeah, but it's fine. I'm out." He could hear her sucking on a cigarette. Which meant she was spending money on them.

"Mom, who got you out?"

"It doesn't matter. I'm fine now."

"I couldn't have paid your bail anyway, Mom. I have no money. I have to pay my rent, my food, textbooks. I *have no money.*"

"Yeah, I get that. But I need to hear from you. It's hard not having you here for me."

"I know that. But I'm *not* there. I'm here, doing the best I can. And I really need you to do the best you can, too. I need you to go to your meetings."

"I know that, Dyllie. I know. Hey, I got a job."

"You did?" *Oh, thank Christ.*

"Yeah. It sucks, but it's a job."

"Tell me about it."

"Nothing to tell. I stand behind a counter and ring shit up."

Reaching for the fence, he gripped the top of the wooden post. When she was evasive, it made him wary. "What kind of store?"

"Who cares what kind of store? You want me to have a job, I got one."

"Yeah, but doing what?"

She blew out a breath. "Working at the Medicine Man."

"You're selling *pot*?" He had to cool it. Yelling at her wouldn't do any good. But working around drugs? Terrible idea. "Do you think that's a good idea?"

"It's a job. And if you've got a problem with it, talk to your uncle. I wouldn't be in this situation if he'd just give me my damn inheritance."

"There's nothing we can do about that, Mom. We have no control over the situation."

"He doesn't get to keep *my* money from me. The money *my father* left me. And there *is* something you can do about it. You can tell him you need it. He'll do anything for you."

He hated this rant more than any of her others. "I'm not asking Uncle Zach for money."

"It's *mine*. They stole it from me. Look, you're all the way across the country. You're hardly sending me anything. They need to give me my money. They're my *family*. All you have to do is ask."

"I don't take money from anyone. That's why I'm here on a scholarship I earned and working two jobs."

"You wouldn't have to do any of that if you came back home. Just go to school in Boulder. Stop punishing me."

"Punishing…Mom, I'm not punishing you. I'm getting an education." He blew out a breath, tipping his head back to look at the cloudy, grey sky. No point explaining. She heard nothing.

What was it his uncle had said? He wasn't talking to his mom, he was talking to the drugs and alcohol. Getting into the loop with her solved nothing.

"Okay, Mom."

"Okay, you'll come back?" She actually sounded hopeful.

"No. Okay, I'll try to answer my phone more often."

She sucked on what he hoped was a cigarette. "It's you and me, Dyllie. Don't you ever forget it. You and me against the whole world. I'm your mom, and no one in this world will ever love you the way I do."

He had a sick feeling that was completely true.

# CHAPTER NINE

**"He kicked me out." In her anger, Nicole whipped her** hand out of the dough, flinging a piece at her cheek. Her hands were too sticky to wipe it away.

James set the frosting bag down and took the big ceramic bowl away from her.

"I swear I didn't make a big scene. I didn't even think it showed on my face."

He walked her to the sink, turned on the faucet, and held her hands under the warm water, gently washing the dough off her fingers. "What does haggis have to do with sustainability? I don't get what he's doing." Still holding her hands, he leaned across her for a towel and then dried them.

God, she'd made a fool of herself yet again. "He said organ meats are the most concentrated source of nutrients. And they're cheap. So you can feed more people using all parts of the animal. It was *disgusting.* I swear he did it to test me."

He took a paper towel and wiped the dough off her face. "Was this haggis section on the syllabus?"

She nodded.

"Then he wasn't testing you."

"No, not that part. Making me come up to the front of the room and help him. He only chooses me when it's something gross."

"What did he say exactly?" The timer went off, and James left her to pull the two cake pans out of the oven.

She thought back to class when Chef had asked her to hold up the heart, liver, and lungs in front of everyone. The vile smells had hit her right away, and she'd known eating them would be a huge challenge. But she was determined not to fail. Unfortunately, after just one bite of the finished product she'd gagged.

"Tell me what he said."

Her head hurt. Her brain felt stuffed with cotton. "He said, *Enough*, in this big, booming voice. And he kicked me out of the room. He kept yelling at me as I packed up my stuff. What was I doing wasting his and everybody's time, this is college, not some cooking class for pampered princesses." She imitated his deep voice. "What if he kicks me out of the class?"

"For what? Gagging? I don't think professors can do that."

"He's not a professor. God, I was doing so well. I hadn't gotten sick in weeks. And now this." She looked away. "I blew it. There's no way he'll choose me. Dammit, I thought I'd made progress."

James stood beside her patiently.

"He's not, right?" she asked. "Choosing me?"

Her friend didn't say anything, but his lips pursed and his brow pulled in tightly.

"I know. He's not. I'm not getting in." Tears welled, blurred her vision.

James pulled her into his arms, and she just let go. Just

wept. She'd wanted it so badly, but she'd failed.

"Maybe you should tell him."

"No. I can't. He'll think I'm trying to get his pity. I don't want his pity."

"Tell who what?" a male voice demanded.

Oh, dammit. She'd thought she was alone. Tuesday night, the house had been so quiet. When had *he* come home?

Dylan stood a few steps behind James, looking fierce. Flanking him were two party favors—Brittany and a new girl—and his usual guy friends. She lowered her face into James's neck, hoping the jerk would just leave.

She hadn't talked to him since Saturday. After his conversation with his mom, he'd headed into town. Since then, he'd acted like nothing had happened in that car. What an ass.

"What's going on?" Dylan demanded.

James twisted around, and she couldn't stop herself from watching the silent exchange between both guys. James tightened his hold on her, using his body to block Dylan's view.

Dylan turned to his friends. "Listen." He walked forward, forcing the whole group back. "I'm gonna call it a night."

"Are you serious?" Brittany said.

He didn't even answer, just herded them out of the kitchen. "I'll catch up with you later."

Nicole watched over James's shoulder as Dylan closed the door behind them, and then stormed back to her. He reached out, but James blocked him. "I've got her. Just go."

Dylan stood firm. She didn't know what they were doing with each other, but she did know there was something between them. Something special. For whatever reason, he didn't want her as his girlfriend, but she suspected she got the one thing he didn't give any of his hookups—a piece of his heart. The moment she let go of James, Dylan tugged her into his arms.

She burrowed into his chest, letting those strong, powerful arms band around her.

"Nic?" She heard the frustration in James's tone. *Are you sure you want to go there?*

But before she could answer, Dylan turned to him with a look that said, *Let me.* And she couldn't miss the edge of *I need to take care of her.*

With a soft smile, she let James know she was okay. The moment he left, Dylan took her hand and led her to the bench seat by the window. Sitting down, he put her on his lap, tucked her under his arms and held her. "Talk to me."

"I blew it."

"Culinary?"

She nodded. His big hands stroked her hair.

"Tell me."

"He made me touch sheep organs in front of the class."

He waited.

"I got sick."

She tensed, waiting for his response. Her dad would tell her to lighten up, it couldn't have been that bad, and to go back to class ready to handle whatever came her way. Her brothers would make endless jokes. Well, Brandon might. Ryan wouldn't even be around to hear about it.

Dylan kept stroking her hair. "I'm guessing he didn't like that."

"He kicked me out."

He didn't even flinch. Just kept gently stroking her hair,

twining a lock around a finger every now and then. "Of that class? Or class in general?"

"I don't know."

"What is it that James thinks you should tell him?"

Outside her family, only three people knew her story. Her best friend, her ex, and James. No one else needed to know. Including Chef Desmarais. "He thinks I should tell him why I react the way I do."

"There's a reason?"

She shrugged, sitting up, conscious of her weight pressing on him. When she started to move, his hands clamped down on her thighs to keep her in place. "I'm too heavy." She slid back a bit, until her butt hit the cushion and her legs draped across his thighs. "He's not going to choose me for the culinary minor."

"It doesn't seem likely. Which is why James wants you to tell him what exactly to convince him to choose you?"

She knew she could trust him. But he'd hurt her so badly, flashing hot and cold, that part of her wanted to shut him out. "It doesn't matter. I'm not going to."

He was quiet for a moment, but he didn't stop sifting his fingers through her hair. Huh. He wasn't going to push for more information? "So what do you want to do?"

She shrugged. "I don't know. If I ignore it, he'll keep thinking I'm some kind of spoiled brat. But I'm not. Yeah, raw meat and haggis make me sick, but I fight through it. I do my assignments. It's not like I run out of the room crying."

"You could tell him that."

"That I think he's being unfair to me?"

"No, that'll just piss him off. Tell him how much you want to be in his program, and that you know you've had some bad reactions, but that you're working through it."

She shook her head. "No, he told us from the start he didn't want to hear from us. He doesn't want to hear our sad stories."

"Does your sad story have to do with your mom?"

The way he looked at her made everything in her soften, leaving her with nothing but the warmth and trust she felt for him. "Yeah." She'd already told him she'd been neglected. Why not give the details? She knew he'd be able to relate. "So, I told you that when my parents divorced, I went with my mom. My brothers were a little older, so they chose to stay with my dad."

"Why would your dad let you move in with an alcoholic?"

She shrugged. "She didn't fight for the marriage or her sons, but she fought for me. From what I'm told, she was getting help at that point. Or she told my dad she was anyway, and I guess he believed her. I don't know. I was seven. All I know was what she was like around me. She'd go on benders all the time. I didn't know what to do. My clothes were dirty, there was no food to eat. I mean, I was starving."

"Jesus, Nicole."

She hated the look on his face. "Hey, don't feel bad for me. I've more than made up for all the meals I missed out on." She patted her belly.

Grabbing her wrist, he pressed a kiss into her palm. "You can't expect me not to feel bad for the little girl who lived through that."

The darkness outside the window, the warmth of his body where they touched, brought back all their moments of intimacy. How could he feel this connection and then forget it ever happened? How could he hook up with someone else? She couldn't even think about other guys when all she wanted was him.

"So your food issues came from that?"

She nodded. "I remember this one day I was so hungry I passed out. Of course, I didn't know what happened at the time. Only that the world shifted, I felt nauseous, and I woke up on the floor."

His body tightened. "Fuck."

"Yeah. My mom rarely shopped, but even when she did, she didn't cook anything. She'd just leave the bags right in the entryway and then go straight for the freezer. Stuff as many bottles of vodka as she could fit in there. And then I wouldn't see her for days."

His hand came down to her thigh and squeezed.

"I, um, I'd eat whatever I could find. Sometimes…" A knot formed in her throat. Heat washed through her. This was the one little bit she hadn't shared with anybody. Because it made her sick to think about it. Because it was too…God, it was just so awful. "There'd be packs of raw chicken legs or meat in the refrigerator, you know? And I didn't know what to do with them." She paused. "I just…I was so hungry." Her voice sounded thick.

His closed his eyes.

She should probably stop. He didn't need to hear this. But something compelled her to go on. "One time, I tore off the plastic from the chicken, and it didn't smell right. But I was so hungry my mouth watered. I was just sitting in front of the open refrigerator in my nightgown and bare feet, holding this rancid chicken. I didn't know what to do. I'd looked through all the cupboards, and the fridge was empty except for a few packs of raw meat. So, I ate it."

"Jesus fucking Christ."

"Yeah, it was awful. I got really sick, and that was it. After that, my dad took me away from her."

"Good. I don't know why he let you live with her to begin with."

"He didn't know she wasn't going to meetings. And after she stopped getting help, she scared me into not telling anybody what our lives were like. Before he'd come pick me up for visits, she made me promise not to tell him about whatever had happened that week."

"I understand that."

She was sure he did. "I did my best to hide it, but at some point it was really confusing because as much as I didn't want to live with her anymore, I couldn't stand leaving her all alone. But after I ate that bad chicken…well, the next time he came to pick me up, I told him how sick I'd gotten that day."

"Wait, who took care of you? When you got sick?"

She couldn't believe how quickly she could be thrown back into those memories of helplessness and abject fear. That day, with her stomach cramping, she hadn't known what to do. She'd curled up on the kitchen floor, sweating and balled up in pain. So completely alone in the world.

When she didn't answer, Dylan said, "Your mom didn't help you?"

She shook her head. "But as soon as I told my dad, he packed up my stuff and took me home. And that was it. The nightmare was over." She remembered so vividly waking up that first morning in her old bedroom in a warm, fully-stocked house. The utter relief she'd felt.

"You left her."

She didn't appreciate his judgment. "She didn't feed me, Dylan. She—"

"No, no. I'm just saying. You left her. That must've been hard."

"It was…but it mostly wasn't."

"No regrets?"

"None. Best decision I could've made."

"And how is she now?"

"Still an alcoholic. She married another alcoholic. He's more functioning than her. He's an insurance agent, with his own practice. They lead a very sad life."

"Do you see her?"

"No. I send her a birthday and Mother's Day card. But she really isn't capable of any kind of relationship. I used to go over there on holidays—with Jonathan, my ex. My brothers wouldn't go. They have no relationship with her at all. But I could tell how uncomfortable it made her when I visited. She tried to be sober for me, but she didn't want to be. She wanted me gone so she could get back to drinking."

"Does she…"

"Does she what?" She gentled her voice.

"Does she hate you? For leaving her?"

"At first she did. She was so ugly and mean."

"Did you feel guilty? Did you want to go back to her?"

"No, never. And I don't feel guilty. I can't help her. For years I tried to fix her. I'd hide her booze, pry bottles from her hands. I'd crawl into bed with her and shake her, begging her to stop drinking. I mean, she'd fought for me to live with her, right? But I figured out much later that she only wanted me to live with her because she couldn't bear being alone. The best thing I could do was leave her—for myself, obviously—but for her, too. She can't change. She won't change. And having this kid around just caused her more grief, more guilt, more burden. Now, she's free to drink herself to death."

"Are you really that detached?"

She held his gaze, feeling his censure down to her bones. "Yeah, Dylan, I am. My mom's not reachable. She's never going to change. I let go."

"But she's your mom."

"I can't help her, Dylan. There's nothing I can do. She chooses the life she's leading. I chose a different one."

"Don't you miss her?"

"I'm sorry if I sound like a cold-hearted bitch to you, and that's why I don't talk about her, but no, Dylan, I don't miss her. What's to miss? Her yelling at me when she's blasted? Slurring all the time? Vomiting during my playdates?"

He swallowed, his eyes so filled with pain, she could barely stand to look at him. He cupped her chin, kissed her. "You amaze me."

Maybe she misunderstood? Maybe he didn't think badly of her. The way he looked at her, with such admiration and...well, like he *liked* her, made her want to run her fingers through his silky hair, press her lips to his cheek. She shifted on his lap, her knee bumping into his erection. Desire tore through her, and for a few moments, she didn't pull away. Because, God, she wanted him so badly.

But then she remembered she wasn't doing drama. She wasn't going to pine for a guy she couldn't have. And Dylan had made it clear she couldn't have him. His life was not his own, he'd said, and he wasn't open to seeing things any differently.

How many years had she hoped for Jonathan to change? People don't change. Her mom hadn't, Jonathan hadn't. And if she wanted to be sane, she had to make the choices that were right for her.

She couldn't help Dylan any more than she could help

her mom or Jonathan. Her leg shifted away, but he clamped a hand down, holding her in place, right up against his erection. His breathing changed, and his gaze drifted to her mouth.

"Nicole." His hand went around the back of her neck and brought her down to meet him in a hard kiss. It grew urgent immediately, his tongue brushing hers, sending sparks along her nerves. "Fuck," he breathed against her lips, both hands going around her back and pressing her tightly against him.

No one had ever kissed her like this—with so much urgency and need. Like he *had* to have her.

But then she remembered the two girls he'd brought home tonight.

She pulled away from him and got off his lap. "I'm not one of your party favors."

He looked confused, eyes still glazed, mouth still wet. "My what?"

She motioned to the archway, where his girls had flanked him. "The girls you bring home with you. If you want to be my friend, I guess that's fine." They lived and worked together, so it was unavoidable. "But anything else…" She shook her head. "Keep your hands off me."

His mouth shut, jaw muscle working. He stood, crowding her in the small space, forcing her to step back. "What the hell do you think I've been trying to do?"

******

Five days since he'd seen her.

He didn't get attached to many people. His close friends, Kelsi, but that was it. And in spite of what Nicole thought about him having random hookups, he didn't find himself attracted to all that many girls.

But with Nicole—he was out of control. He couldn't stop thinking about her, *missing* her, dammit. His body craved her.

Dylan stumbled on a crack in the sidewalk—the same block of concrete he passed every day, several times a day. Only tonight he wasn't paying attention. He caught himself before he hit the pavement, but it woke him up. Jarred him out of the fog he'd been living in.

His knuckles hurt like a bitch, and every time he moved his mouth, his split lip cracked and started burning again.

Instead of going in the front door, he ducked along the hedges at the side, heading around back to look into the kitchen windows. He imagined Nicole at the stove, stirring the honeysuckle syrup, that dreamy expression coming over her. That pink tongue licking the spoon, her expression so sensual. He went hard imagining that tongue licking his cock, that same look on her face as she took him in her mouth.

And, really, why her? Why the fuck her? Any of the girls he'd met so far would gladly fuck him, so why didn't he want them? Why did he want the one girl he couldn't have?

Through the window he could see the yellow glow from the lights under the cabinets. The kitchen looked clean, boxes stacked neatly for his delivery the next day.

He entered through the back door, tread quietly through the kitchen, and climbed the staircase. Immediately, he noticed her door was open, while his was closed. Murmuring grew louder the closer he got to his bedroom. Great, the two of them in bed again.

He headed into the bathroom first and cleaned himself up as best he could. He hadn't gotten too involved in the brawl. He'd just thrown enough punches to get himself cleared of the ruckus and out the door. Still, he'd wear his bruises for the next few days.

The moment he opened the door, conversation ceased. Dropping onto the edge of the mattress, he untied his boots and kicked them off.

A desk lamp flicked on. "What happened to you?" James asked.

But Dylan didn't look at James. He looked at his girl. Er, Nicole. She was so fucking beautiful. She didn't look at him accusingly or hurt or anything like he expected. She just looked…accepting.

"Nothing."

Without a word, she got out of bed in her little rubber ducky pajama shorts and yellow tank top and left the room.

"So now you're getting into fights?" James pushed up against a mound of pillows. "What is the *matter* with you?"

"What do you care what I do?"

James rolled his eyes. "Of course I care what you do. You're my friend. I just don't understand your choices."

When Nicole came back, she sat down beside him. Brushing the hair off his forehead, she dabbed a wet cotton ball at the scrape over his forehead. She smelled like honeysuckle and a hint of rose, and he went hard—full on raging erection—his skin screaming for her touch, his cock aching to bury itself deep inside her.

Setting a bag of frozen broccoli on the back of his hand, she wrapped it up in a kitchen towel. Finally, she spoke. "You worked so hard to get here. And what do you do? Recreate Gun Powder all over again. Why bother? If this is the life you want, just go back home." She got up and walked out of the room.

He sat there for several moments, feeling gutted and cold. Really cold. So cold, he tossed the ice pack to the floor, got under the covers, and turned his back on James.

Quiet chuckling got his attention, and he rolled back. "What?"

"She's so right."

"I'm here for the education. Nothing more."

"Pretty sure Colorado offers higher education."

"Trying to get rid of me?"

"Don't be a bitch. It's just…you've built this whole life for yourself away from campus. I'm not saying Sigma Phi was right for you. But other than one night at a frat party, what've you tried on campus? What friends have you made? You're not even giving it a chance. She's right. You just recreated your old life. Why not just go home—because it seems like that's what you want deep down."

"Deep down? You think you know what I want deep down?"

"I only know what you do. The world you've created for yourself since you got here. Obviously, you could have anything you want. You've got the grades, the looks, the brains. Everything. You could've joined Sigma Phi—they'd have let you in for free. You could fuck any girl on this campus—but you don't. You could have friendship—but I guess we're just not your kind of people. That's okay. I'm not everyone's cup of tea. Neither is Nicole. She knows that."

"She thinks I don't like her?"

"Not enough."

"Enough for what?"

"To be with her, asshole."

"I *can't* be with her."

James reached for the light, shut it off. "You're such a dipshit."

He couldn't sleep. How could he with this hard-on? Every time he closed his eyes he saw her. He saw her in his bed, those long eyelashes fanning in perfect arcs on her creamy skin. Or on his lap, straddling him, her face taut with sexual tension. Or, worse, he imagined her on her back, hair spread all over the pillow, breasts bouncing as he slammed into her. Jesus, he ached just thinking about it.

He had to stop this. He had better control over his emotions than this—how else would he have survived this long?

What was happening to him? That first night, when he'd brought her into his bed—he'd felt it then. This connection, this bond. He hadn't even known her—but he'd felt her. Inside, he'd felt her. When had she become essential to him?

*Oh, shit.* That was bad. Very bad. No one could ever be essential to him.

What she'd said tonight—about recreating Gun Powder. He *had* done that.

He'd hated his life back home. The town itself was beautiful, but it was filled with his big, extended family—family that wanted nothing to do with him. They'd given him a choice—him or his mom. Of course, he'd chosen his mom. But that had narrowed his social life to the guys who weren't going anywhere.

Or maybe he'd chosen those guys because he thought they'd understand his life a little better.

And, yeah, he guessed he had done the same thing here.

But he couldn't stop thinking about what James had said about what he wanted deep down. He'd never been allowed to think about what he wanted. For him, it was about survival. Nothing else.

And yet, he *had* worked his ass off to get into a top school. Why? Like James said, if he planned on going back to Gun Powder, why bother with the expense and hassle of Wilmington?

Hope rose in him, a force so strong he couldn't ignore it. He came here because he wanted more. *Nicole.*

He did have something deep down. And that something was a *someone.*

Holy shit. Adrenaline crashed his system.

*Nicole* was his deep down. She was his home, his heart.

His mom had never felt like home. How had he not seen that before? He loved his mom, of course he did. But he felt…wary around her. Never trusting her, always waiting for the next patch of trouble. He could never let down his guard around her.

But Nicole? She was his someone. She was *his.*

Throwing back the covers, he stalked out of his bedroom and right to her door.

*Fuck.* She was his heart. His deep down.

His hand closed around the doorknob, but there was no give at all. She'd locked it. Locked him out. Because his inability to man up had hurt her.

No more.

He tapped his knuckles against her door. "Nicole? Let me in."

The lock popped, and her sleepy head peeked out. "Dylan?"

He stepped inside and closed the door. Using his body to push her back, he watched the backs of her legs hit the mattress and she sat with a bounce.

"What do you want?"

"You."

She gave a sharp intake of breath. Her hands went to his stomach, and his dick got even harder. "Are you sure?"

He hoped the absolute certainty showed on his face because he had no words. She looked so beautiful, so incredibly sexy in her little tank top and short pajama bottoms.

She crawled back on her bed, and he followed her, laying his body on top of hers. He cupped her face with one hand, taking her mouth, and finally, finally giving into his heart. Why not? She owned it anyway.

Her arms wrapped around his neck, and her body shifted restlessly beneath him.

Lifting off her, he shoved the blankets away, got rid of his boxers, and climbed into bed. Completely awash in her heat, her sweet scent, and warmth, he kissed her again. Licking into her mouth, stroking her soft skin with his thumb.

"Dylan…?" She tried to speak, but her mouth kept coming back to his, taking more of him.

"I have to have you. I can't fucking take it anymore."

He gazed into her troubled eyes. "I can't just sleep with you tonight and then have you go back to your girls tomorrow."

"I have no girls. I want you. I've never wanted anyone the way I want you." He lowered his mouth to her ear. "I need you."

"But Brittany—"

"No. I haven't been with anyone since I've been here, and I got tested right before I left. *Please.*" His mouth burrowed into her neck, licked the sensitive skin. She stirred beneath him, her hands roaming his back.

He kissed her tenderly, the corner of her mouth, her jaw, and then his tongue swiped across her lips, and she lifted her hips, grinding against him. He skimmed the precious ducky shorts and panties off her hips, pulled the tank top over her head, and then filled his palms with her breasts. She gasped, and he licked a hot path down her neck to suck one sweet nipple into his mouth, circling it with his tongue.

"Oh, Christ." His mind practically shorted out with intense pleasure. "Fuck, Nicole. I want you. I have to have you."

"Yes." Hands in his hair, she arched into him, hips rocking, and his cock nudged at her opening—so slick and hot he nearly lost himself.

"Ah, Jesus, Nicole." His mouth skimmed down her body, his hands caressing her breasts. And then he pushed her legs apart, his tongue licking inside her. When he found her nub, he flicked his tongue over it, hard, fast, because he had to have her. Jesus, *now*.

She clutched his hair, her hips rocking, twisting, slamming her against his mouth. Christ, the sounds she made had him going out of his mind. He gripped her ass and lifted her to him.

"Oh, God, Dylan." She cried out his name over and over and then her body shuddered, her legs stretching straight out, her back arching off the mattress. "*God.*"

After her body settled down, she reached for his shoulders, dragging him up to her. He kissed her, couldn't get enough of her mouth, her tongue.

"Birth control?" he asked.

"Yes."

*Thank God.* He grabbed his cock, slid it through her juicy

folds and then thrust inside her. Her ass came off the bed, as she cried out. "Dylan."

He powered into her. He'd never felt anything like it in his life. Her heat, her scent, her hands clutching him, drawing him deeper. He rammed her so hard, she nearly hit the headboard. Jesus Christ, he couldn't stop. Needed her. More. All of her. Holy fuck. Sliding his hands underneath her, he cupped her shoulders and dragged her down the bed, hips locked tightly against hers. And then he was pumping, out of control, slamming into her so hard his teeth clacked together.

Her cries, the way she clutched him, let him know she was in it with him.

Everything tightened, narrowed to one sensation. Raw, carnal desire. For *her*.

"Nicole." Sensation grew so acute he could hardly take it. Her back arched off the mattress, fingers digging into his ass, as she slammed up into him. But he grabbed her hips, held her to the bed, and came so hard sparks filled his vision.

He collapsed on top of her, their bodies slick with perspiration. Her hands roamed his back, his shoulders, her breath hot on his neck.

Easing himself off her, he cupped her chin, turning her to claim that pretty mouth. His chest pressed to her back, his hand skimmed down her throat, cupped her breast, then palmed her stomach. She pushed back into him, like she had to be skin-to-skin, too.

"Dylan." His name coasted out on a sigh.

Fully awake, he listened to her breathing even out, felt his skin cool down, until he lay there chilled.

He was out of control. He'd lost it completely with this girl.

The red alert of danger clanged in his mind, making sleep impossible.

The worst thing he could do was lose control. Shit. How had this happened? What was it about her that made him so crazy? Sure, attraction was normal. But what he felt for her? It was insane.

And dangerous.

Fuck. He had to get out of there.

He couldn't bail on her, obviously. He wouldn't do that.

He just needed to think, to get a hold of himself.

Yeah, that was all he needed. Some time to get his shit together. He could have her, just…in a more controlled way.

He pulled away from her, but she stirred, gripping his hand.

Too soon to go. He'd wait until she'd fallen more deeply asleep.

Then he'd leave.

# CHAPTER TEN

**A beam of sunlight hit her eyelids, waking her. She** should really use a clothespin or a paper clip to hold those curtains together. It would be nice to be able to sleep in on a day when she had no early class.

An ache between her legs made her wonder—and then she lit up like a fuse.

*Dylan.* He'd come to her.

She smiled. He'd spent the night. And, oh, what a night. Burying her face in the pillow, she smiled at the way they'd loved each other. So intense. So wildly delicious.

She already knew he was gone. Sometime in the night, she'd felt him untangle his body from hers. Vaguely, she recalled trying to hold onto him, but she'd been too exhausted to fight.

How would he act around her today? Because last time they'd gotten intimate, he'd ignored her for days and then he'd brought party favors home. She'd told him not to treat her that way—to stay away from her if he couldn't be with her. He'd understood, so, no, he wouldn't do it again.

If he'd gone back to his own bed, though, she'd be pretty disappointed. He loved sleeping with her, so leaving her for his own bed would definitely be a sign.

Rolling out of bed, she winced at the soreness of her muscles. Shower, definitely.

Tying her robe, she opened her door at the same moment James came out of the bathroom, hair wet, towel wrapped around his waist.

"You little whore," he whispered, looking all excited and happy.

She shushed him, pointing toward the bedroom, in case Dylan was in there.

He cocked his head, confused. "He's not with you?"

She shook her head, trying hard to keep her spirits from plummeting. On Fridays, he had a lab at ten and then he worked the lunch shift in town. No way would he need to get up before eight.

"Oh, shit." James grabbed her arm and led her into his room, pushing her onto his bed. "Every detail."

She and Dylan…no. It didn't feel right to share what they did or said together. "When was the last time you saw him?"

"Last night. I haven't seen him at all this morning. But, damn, girl, I heard you two going at it. Who knew you could get so dirty?"

"Maybe he went to the gym." Yes, that made sense. *That* made her feel better.

James sat on the bed, reaching for the lotion he kept on his desk. He poured a good amount in his hand and slathered his shoulders and arms. "Text him."

"No." She'd give him space. Especially if he was lifting.

"You think he's freaking out?"

"Maybe. But he's probably at the gym."

James glanced at the alarm clock on his desk. "Fuck me." He got up, dropped the towel and pulled on his boxers and jeans. When his head popped out of a thermal Henley, he said, "I'm so late." He jammed his feet into his boots, didn't even bother tying them before he got up and smashed some papers into his messenger bag. "I'm sorry for bailing on you." He started to leave the room. "You going to be okay?"

She nodded.

"You going to text him?"

"I'm going to give him some space."

"He's crazy about you. You know that, right?" He came back and kissed her cheek. "Just give him time. He'll get there."

By the time she got back from class at two-thirty, she still saw no sign of Dylan. If he'd gone to the gym, he'd have come home to shower and change. Unless he'd brought his clothes and toiletries with him to avoid coming back to the house. But, no, his toiletries were in the bathroom, his bed the same mess it'd been that morning.

James found her sitting on Dylan's bed with his pillow on her lap.

He tossed his messenger bag on the floor near his desk. "Oh, shit. You haven't heard from him?"

She shook her head.

"Fucker pulled a runner." He pulled his phone out of his back pocket. "I'm texting him."

A few seconds later, they heard a vibration. Dylan's phone danced on the desk right next to his bed.

James's eyes went wide. Not taking his phone was huge. It meant his mom couldn't get a hold of him. The last time she hadn't been able to get through to him, she'd called the school.

Nicole set the pillow back down. "I'm going into town."

"Yeah, good idea. Let's get a coffee."

They walked in silence, James kind enough to leave her alone with her thoughts. Without a word, they both slowed in front of the restaurant where Dylan worked. James held the door open for her.

It took a moment for her eyes to adjust, but she walked right up to the hostess station.

The young woman grabbed some menus, the smile fading when she saw Nicole's expression. "Can I help you?"

"I'm looking for Dylan McCaffrey. Is he working today?"

"No, sorry. He's not in today."

"But he was supposed to work, right?"

The girl looked uncomfortable. "I don't know his schedule. I just know he's not here now."

"Okay, thank you."

James belted his arm around her as they headed back outside into the cold air.

"So, what do we do?" she asked him.

"I don't know."

"We should find his friends. You know, Joe and those guys."

Brittany came racing out of the restaurant. "Hey, wait up. Are you looking for Dylan?"

"Yes," Nicole said, fearful and hopeful at once.

"He didn't show up for work, and he's not answering his phone," she said.

"Do you have any idea where he might be?" James asked.

"I mean, the only thing I can think of is Joe's place. Maybe he crashed there?"

"Where does Joe live?" James asked.

"I'd take you there, but I can't get off work." She looked

down the street, unseeing. "God, he's never missed a shift. He didn't even call in sick." And then she turned to Nicole. "What happened last night? Was he with you?"

"Nothing happened. I know he slept at home."

"But he was gone before we woke up," James said.

Brittany took a step closer. "You've got to back off. He's got enough shit in his life. I mean, he's just…he doesn't need one more person to take care of, you know?"

"You know about his family?" Nicole instantly regretted asking.

"Of course. He tells me everything."

Nicole's heart squeezed so hard it hurt. Why would he open up to this girl and not to her? Why didn't he trust her?

"Except where he is." James pulled out his phone. "Listen, if you hear from him or find out anything, will you text me?"

"Yeah, sure." They exchanged phones and punched in their numbers. "I've got to get back. But I'm serious. He needs to hang around people who're fun and don't add to his load. Why do you think he spends his time with us?" She hurried back into the restaurant.

*Ouch.* Nicole stood there, letting her words sink in. She wasn't fun to him. He didn't like to watch meteor showers or bake cupcakes or dance to Drake in her tiny bedroom. He liked to party and hookup with his friends from town. She turned to James.

"No." He gave her a hard look. "Don't let her get to you. You don't seriously think he tells her his shit, do you? That dude's sealed up like a vault. And you're not trouble for him. He's into you. He wouldn't have howled at the moon like that last night if he weren't."

"He bolted."

"We don't know anything yet. *If* he ran—and we don't know that yet—"

"He ran."

His shoulders slumped. "Yeah, he probably ran. But it's not because you add to his load. If anything, it's because he thought his whole life had to be about taking care of his mom. He didn't think he could have something for himself. He'll come back to you, I swear. It might not be easy, but he'll work it out. I'm sure of it."

Nice words, but she knew better. Dylan might not work it out. He was incredibly strong. He'd had to be, to live through his childhood. And if he didn't think he could fit her into his life, he'd push her out.

His priority was his mom. She'd always come first for him. And, of course, she had to.

******

On his way back from the mountain, Dylan knew he'd made the right choice. It sucked that he hadn't told anyone where he'd gone. Bailed on classes, work, and on her. He hated thinking what he'd put Nicole through the last two days.

But he'd needed the time and the distance to get his head on right. He was relieved he'd come up with a solution that would allow him to be with her but not become *consumed* with her.

Because no matter what, he couldn't put her at risk. His mom ruined every relationship he'd ever had. Showing up drunk at his school, making scenes in public. He'd never forget Carol Mylon's expression, back in ninth grade, when the cops had busted into the apartment to arrest his mom and her drug-dealing boyfriend. Carol hadn't been too keen on dating him after that. Actually, she'd never talked to him again.

Thing was, his mom was already spiraling out of control.

Somehow, he'd thought if he'd stayed vigilant with her, she could make it to the frequent school breaks when he could go back and be with her.

But it wasn't working. She'd lost her first job. She'd spent time with Jeff Blakely, her dealer. And now she worked in a pot shop.

So what was he doing spending every free moment with Nicole? It wouldn't work. History told him that. He needed to keep his focus on his mom. And the only way to do that *and* keep Nicole was to move out.

Shrugging his backpack higher onto his shoulder, he turned down the brick walkway of the house. But, as he stood on the porch, all his confidence, the absolute certainty, drained right out of him when he thought of Nicole in this house. In the kitchen, brow furrowed in concentration as she folded syrup into the frosting, her scent lingering in the bathroom, the feel of her soft, warm body under the covers. Because it wasn't some girl he lived with, some body he'd slept with. It was *Nicole*. His deep down.

He would miss living with her.

But it would be fine. He had a plan.

He turned, looking back at the road, the campus across the street. Until he found a place in town, he'd have to crash with Joe. Because he was already feeling it—the dread of leaving her. And the longer he lived with her, the harder it would be to leave. Limiting his time with her was the only solution to the problem.

He blew out a hard breath. Yeah, he needed to move out right away. Since it was unlikely anyone else was up yet, he'd talk to her now, let her know his plans.

Opening the door, he stepped into a living room filled with people.

"Oh, my God." Tatiana jumped out of a chair.

"He's here," Harry said.

"Dylan." Sydney flew at him, wrapping her arms around him and hugging him hard. "Where have you been? Are you all right?" She released him, scanning his body, head to toe.

He looked around the room, everyone gathered as though in a meeting. And then his gaze landed on Nicole. Peering at him over the back of the couch, pillow cuddled in her arms.

He heard their voices.

*We were going to call the police this morning.*

*The only reason we didn't is because Nicole said you'd taken your sleeping bag.*

*Where'd you go?*

His entire being narrowed on her. He dropped his backpack, crossed the marble foyer, and made his way around the couch. His heart hurt just looking at her. She didn't seem angry. She didn't seem hysterical. She just watched him. With interest. Wondering.

He crouched in front of her, aware the room had gone quiet. Holy Christ, he melted just looking at her. His hands slid under her ass and he scooped her up. Her legs wrapped around his waist, her arms around his shoulders. She burrowed her face into his neck, as he carried her up the stairs.

"Holy shit," Sydney said.

"Fuck me." Terri's voice.

"You wish." Their laughter faded as he hiked up those stairs.

He couldn't get to her room fast enough. Kicking the bedroom door closed behind him, he set her down on the bed. It took all of five seconds to yank his long-sleeved T-shirt over his head, kick off his boots, and rip open his jeans.

Blood roared in his ears, and desire flashed hot across his skin. His body trembled with restraint.

She watched him, and he crawled on top of her, so fucking relieved to feel her, smell her. Jesus, he needed her hands on him. He kissed her, and thank God, she opened her mouth to him, let him inside.

Finally, her arms came around him, stroked down his back until she cupped his ass and drew him more firmly against her. Fuck, he wanted her. Had to have her. But he'd been in the mountains for two days. "I should shower."

She tucked her nose into his neck and inhaled. "You smell like pine and fresh air and you."

"Me, only ripe."

"Oh, Dylan," she breathed. "Don't you get it? I love everything about you. Just the way you are."

Holy mother of God, she made him wild for her. That soft voice, those hungry hands…and her words. Was she fucking kidding with what she said to him? Either she was crazy or he was in a dream he never wanted to end.

He captured her mouth, his tongue lacing with hers, as his hand slipped under her T-shirt and cupped her breast. But he couldn't stand the lace barrier, so he shoved the bra up. Holy fuck, the feel of her soft, round breast in his hand. He had to be inside her now.

"Get up." He helped her up so he could take off her shirt, unhook her bra, and pull down her sweats and panties. All that warm, soft skin. "Fuck."

He licked her nipple, then took a deep pull.

"Oh," she sighed, rising off the mattress. "*Oh.*"

"I can't wait." He could barely speak, his words fractured, more air than sound. Just as his fingers reached between her legs, she drew them closed.

He froze, looking up at her.

"Have you been with anyone?"

"What?"

"You were gone two days. I don't know where you've been. I looked for you in town, but Brittany said no one had seen you."

He closed his eyes, hating the pain he caused her. "There's no one else, sunshine. You know there's no one else for me." He surged into her, his face burrowing into her neck. "It's you. Only you."

"Dylan." Her hands tangled in his hair, hips rising to meet his.

He slid inside her—oh, mother fucking hell she felt so good—and he tried so hard to take his time, show her how much she meant to him, but he couldn't. He was out of control. He hammered into her, mindless, consumed with her—her hands, her sweet fragrance, her slick heat.

It wasn't enough—he couldn't get deep enough, close enough. He lifted her legs, bent them back until her knees nearly hit her shoulders, and he pushed in even deeper. She cried out, her hands fisting the sheets.

"Oh, Jesus, Nicole, oh, fuck, I can't…I can't…oh, fuck." His climax hit him with explosive force, blasting through every molecule in his body. He bore down on her, holding her in place, as he came in a scalding, blinding gush of heat.

His hips slowed, as he glided in and out of her, enjoying every last rush of sensation. When he slumped to her side, he pressed his nose to her cheek. "I'm sorry." His hand stroked down her stomach to her slick heat, his finger finding her nub. He swirled around it, watching her features ride the wave of ecstasy that crashed over her. Tremors wracked her body, and she cried out his name as she lifted off the bed.

"You're the most beautiful girl in the world."

"And you're the most beautiful boy." When she settled down, she turned to him, stroking the damp hair off his face. "Where did you go?"

"Up the mountain."

"I didn't know what to do. The only reason we didn't call the police was because we saw you took your stuff. Was it me? I mean us? Being together."

He nodded. Not playing games.

"Why is this so hard? You obviously want to be with me, so I don't see the problem. You're *here*, Dylan. Two thousand miles from Colorado. Your friends, your mom, they're a world away. So why can't we be together?"

"Because I'm not good for you. Especially after you told me about your mom, what your childhood was like. I don't want to expose you to my…" *Mother.* But he didn't say that. "Life."

"Am I good for you? Do I make you happy? Do you want me? Because that's all that matters."

"Yes, yes, and fuck yes." He kissed her hard on the mouth. He was a weak man, but it was too late. His heart made the decision for him. "I have to go shower." He got up, but she grabbed his arm.

Leaning up on an elbow, beaming him with her sincerity, she said, "You are good for me, Dylan. No one has *ever* looked out for me the way you do."

He shook his head because she didn't understand what happened when he took his focus off his mom. Nicole's mom had been capable of living on her own. Not Dylan's. His mom had no life skills. She'd go off the rails without him.

He didn't want to hurt Nicole. But…fuck. He wanted her.

And she wanted him. With what little she did know about his life, she still wanted him.

Fuck moving out. He'd have her while he could.

# CHAPTER ELEVEN

**As Nicole poured batter into the cake pans, Sydney** pulled the cupcakes out of the oven. "These smell so good."

"Look at your fine, fancy self, helping us in the kitchen and shit," James said.

Nicole's gaze shot to him, but Sydney laughed. "I know, right? If my mom could see me now." She set the pans down on trivets. "I love this. It's so much more fun than going to another frat party." She gave them a wistful look. "You know what's so sad? I wouldn't let anyone live here but Thetas and Sigma Phis."

"You let us in." James didn't look up from frosting the birthday cake.

She pulled off the oven mitts. "I only let you in because we went to the same high school. And well…*Dylan*."

"You wanted him, huh?" James said.

"Well, duh. Who doesn't?" Sydney smiled.

When Nicole scowled, Sydney's grin disappeared. "No. God. I don't look at him like that *now*. Not since you guys got together."

"Well, I'm just so grateful everything worked out the way it did." Nicole set the dirty bowl in the sink. "I love living here. If we lived in the Scholar House, we'd never have come up with Sweet Treats." She smiled at Sydney. "You've been so great, letting us use the kitchen like this."

"It's good to see it getting used. If it weren't for you guys, this house would totally be party central. With you guys working all the time, it forces everyone to go somewhere else to party. My dad's eternally grateful."

"We'll have to send him a cake," James said.

"Oh, God. You don't send my parents *anything* with sugar. Or butter. Or flour."

"Hm, what do you think?" James said to her. "A new line of lavender cakes that have no sugar, butter, or flour?"

Nicole made a face. "So, basically, we sprinkle lavender water on cardboard? Sounds awesome."

The front door opened. Dylan strode in. Good God, the man took up the whole foyer with his powerful body and bristling energy. His gaze found hers immediately and went from seeking to positively feral. A bolt of electricity shot through her. She took off running for him. A hint of a smile cracked that beautiful mouth, and she could see how hard he tried to remain cool and aloof. But the moment she went airborne, his eyes closed, and she caught a look of total bliss on those handsome features. His arms belted around her, as she slammed into his chest.

"You're so cold," she said, as she licked his chilled earlobe.

"Not for long." His hands slid down, cupping her ass and hoisting her higher. She wrapped her legs around him.

Bringing them to the couch, he perched on the arm. "Hey, sunshine."

She filled her lungs with his scent. "You smell like fresh air—"

"I smell like a man who wants his woman." He burrowed into her neck, kissing the sensitive skin.

She pulled back, covered his cold, rosy cheeks with her warm hands and kissed him. "Welcome home."

He tipped them onto the couch, then dragged them up until he could stretch out his long legs. Their bodies pressed together, legs entwined, as he held her chin and pressed his mouth over hers.

"How was work?" She scraped her fingers through his hair. "Did you get good tips?"

"I got great tips. The closer we get to the holidays the more people drink and the freer they are with their wallets." He kissed her some more, rolling just slightly on top of her so she could feel his erection against her thigh. "How's it going in the kitchen? Much more to do?"

As his thumb stroked her cheek, his gaze turned gentler, more loving, and she lost the ability to speak. She just shook her head. He smiled and brought his mouth back to hers, this time letting himself go, kissing her deeply. His tongue stroked into her mouth, licking, coaxing her tongue into play. God, he was such a sensuous kisser. She drove her hands into his hair and shifted to get as close to his body as she could.

He cupped her ass, pressing her tight against him, as his tongue continued its slow, voluptuous dance with hers. Oh, God, he felt so good. Her blood simmered, as desire flared, sparked, and ignited. Her leg climbed over his hip, tucking in between his ass and the couch cushion, and she locked him hard against her.

"Nicole?"

Vaguely, she heard her name being called, but the blood roared in her ears and his kisses grew more heated, more urgent, and she couldn't think, couldn't get her mind to rise to the surface.

"Nicole, honey? Peaches?"

She tore her mouth off his and looked up to find James standing behind the couch, hands on hips, a kitchen towel hanging out of his back pocket. "While I'd give my left nut to be you right now, your syrup's boiling and we need to finish up in the kitchen."

"Oh, sorry." She untangled herself from Dylan and got up. "Sorry about that."

James swatted her with a kitchen towel. "You are so not sorry."

She glanced back at Dylan, sitting up and watching her with a mischief in his eyes. "Yeah, no. Not sorry at all."

*Where r u?*

Nicole smiled when she saw his text. Between his job at the restaurant, classes, and Sweet Treats, they didn't get much time alone. So every time he sent a text like this one, she got a jolt of pure joy.

She quickly replied. *Magnusson Library. Basement.*

*Don't like u studying down there alone.*

*Best place to concentrate. No one's ever here.* Immediately after, she sent another. *Where r u?*

But he never responded. She pictured him slunk low in a chair in his study group. The brain power everyone relied on.

Nicole turned back to the article she was reading for her Global Studies class. She had a paper due on Friday, and she had to get through dozens of articles in preparation for it.

Footsteps trampling down the metal stairs set her heart

racing. Dylan always worried some pervert would find her alone down here, but, seriously, she'd never seen another soul on this bottom level of the library.

Clothes rustling, boots pounding let her know someone had landed on her floor. And then the hottest man she'd ever seen rounded the corner, a black knit cap on his head, his shoulder-length hair hanging down, those intense hazel eyes trained on her. Dylan dropped his backpack and swooped in for a kiss.

Not just a kiss, though. His mouth opened, his tongue slipped in, and his big hands cupped the back of her head. He did this to her *every time.* Swept her away, made her lose all sense of time and place until she was thoroughly immersed in his scent, his heat, his intense energy.

Tonight he smelled of coffee, and his cheeks were icy cold.

He pulled away, grabbed a chair from the carrel behind her and sat down so close their knees touched. "I want to talk to you."

Uh oh. That didn't sound good. But…gah. *Look at him—so gorgeous.* He just took her breath away.

"Did you eat dinner?" he asked.

She couldn't think beyond these feelings he evoked. He was such a big guy; he took up all the space in the small carrel. Plus, the way he looked at her, like he was holding himself back from consuming her—she couldn't take it. She needed more, so she leaned forward, smoothing her hands up his hard, powerful thighs.

He held her gaze, not saying a word. He did that a lot, like he was too full of emotion to speak. Like he couldn't believe they were together. She understood. She felt the same way.

Her heart pounded, and she squeezed those muscular thighs.

Shifting onto his lap, she kissed him. Pressed against his solid chest, she tasted the need and want on his tongue. She tugged his cap off, letting her hands slide into all that silky hair, and when he deepened the kiss, when he growled deep in his throat, she fisted handfuls, holding him as close to her as she could get.

Those big hands came down on her hips. "Up." He lifted her, spread her legs so that she straddled him, and then slid down in the chair, lifting his hips so his thick erection pressed hard where she ached for him.

Oh, God, she went up in flames. She felt so hot she needed to shed a few layers of clothing. As soon as she tossed off her sweater, Dylan's hands swept under her shirt, gliding up to cup her breasts and pull down the cups of her bra.

His mouth moved urgently over hers, as he palmed her breasts, thumbs rubbing her nipples. God, the man never just made out with her. He *possessed* her. And she loved it.

"Off." He pulled the long-sleeve T-shirt over her head, tossing it on her desk. His hot, hungry mouth came down on her breasts, both of them, tongue sliding from one nipple to the other. He sucked first one, then the other, and then, Oh, God, he took a deep, hard pull, making sensation explode inside her. Her fingernails scraped along his scalp, and she pressed him to her.

"*Goddammit,* Nicole." His hand pushed into her jeans, but there was no give. "Get these off."

As soon as she got up, her legs wobbled, but he caught her around the waist, jerking at the top button, tugging down the zipper, and then yanking down the tight jeans and panties.

With shaky hands, she undid her bra and tossed it. Once she was naked, he lifted her onto the desk, spread her legs, and dropped down in her chair.

The moment his tongue licked inside her, heat spread in a slow burn. She leaned over him, her hair curtaining them, closing her off in this intimate, wild moment with him. Her ankles crossed behind his neck, her hands cradled his head, and she let herself go into the brilliant sensations flooding her body.

He licked and swirled, gripping her ass, pulling her tight to his mouth. How could it be like this? This intense, this powerful? She couldn't even breathe for the pleasure taking hold of her, twisting her into a tight knot of energy, a powder keg ready to—

"Oh, God." Heat exploded within her core, radiating out in sparkling bits of light. Her head tipped back, as waves of sensation tore through her.

He looked up at her, this big, gorgeous man, who seemed to have a soft spot only for her.

Gently lowering her legs, he lifted her, carrying her to the wall between the metal bookshelves and the staircase. Pinning her there, he undid his jeans, shoved them down to his knees, then bent and thrust up into her.

She cried out, and he covered her mouth with his, but it was too intense. He was ravenous, his tongue twirling with hers, as his hips pumped madly, jolting her bones. She'd never been penetrated so deeply. She dropped her face into the crook of his neck and bit down on the wedge of muscle.

"Fuck, fuck, oh, fuck." Dylan rocked into her, one hand covering her tail bone to protect her from the hard wall. The other hand, the one gripping her ass, was right there between her legs, caressing where their bodies joined, as he powered into her. And it just felt so sexy and so erotic that heat flashed along her limbs.

The constant friction against her clit had her so aroused, the pleasure turned almost unbearable. The tension rose, tightened, until it ejected her out of her body and into a place of pure, floating, spiraling pleasure. She clung to him tightly, as the wild sensations took her for a ride. Just then his head reared back and he slammed her against the wall, over and over, and it was so intense that she felt another orgasm taking form.

"Jesus." He clamped his hands on her ass, pinning her to the wall, as he thrust hard and tight three, four, five times.

And then his rhythm slowed, became languid, and God, did *that* feel good, sending shivers up her spine. "Oh, fuck me." Still gliding in and out, he found her mouth, kissed her deeply, passionately. Her heart swelled with so much emotion she nearly burst into tears.

But he would freak out if she did that. If she expressed that depth of emotion. She'd have to let her body say what her words couldn't. He wasn't ready for all she felt for him.

Her legs couldn't take it anymore, so she uncrossed her ankles, and he slowly let her down. She needed to get her clothes back on, in case someone wandered down there.

But he held her in place, brushing the hair off her face. "You okay?"

"Better than okay." Wrapping a hand around his damp neck, she brought him down for a kiss. "You dazzle me." She headed back to her carrel and grabbed her panties off the floor.

He smiled, fixated on her bouncing breasts, as she hitched up her jeans. "Can you hand me my bra?"

"No."

be with your family, but do you want to hang out with me for a few extra days? I could fly out on Tuesday instead."

She flung herself into his arms. "Of course I want to stay here with you. Of *course*."

He tugged on her hair, tilting her head back to give her one of his all-consuming kisses.

"God, yes. But isn't it expensive? To change a ticket?"

"No price on three days alone with you."

# CHAPTER TWELVE

**Slick heat gripped his cock, the friction in her tight** channel sending erotic shockwaves through his limbs. With Nicole on her knees in front of him, he could see his glistening cock pistoning in and out of her, and it spun him into a frenzy of desire.

Hands braced on the white headboard, she pushed back on him so he could slam inside her all the way to the root. One hand squeezed the firm flesh of her ass, while the other plumped her breast, a thumb rubbing the hard nipple, and the ferocious need he felt for his girl drew his balls in tight as his dick exploded, releasing all the unbearable tension.

His pace didn't let up, as he kept coming in hot, shattering blasts, his finger rubbing her clit furiously until she threw her head back, cried out, and locked her ass to his pelvis.

"Fuck." Nothing had ever felt so good.

They both collapsed, sweaty and spent, onto her bed.

"You're going to kill me." She flopped onto her back. But, as he climbed up to rest his head on her pillow, she turned to her side, draping her body alongside his.

He squeezed her bottom, and she laughed. "What is your thing about my ass?"

"I love your ass."

She went quiet, and he had no idea what she was thinking. He figured it wasn't good—since girls had weird thoughts about their bodies. So, he said, "I love your breasts. I love your mouth. I love your hair. Love it all."

Still, she was quiet.

"You don't like how I touch your ass?" Some girls didn't like when a guy touched a part of their body they didn't like. Made them self-conscious. He didn't want her distracted when they were together—he certainly wasn't. He wanted her to lose herself completely—which he thought she had been doing.

"I love how you touch me. Everywhere. I *love* it."

"So what's the problem?"

"Nothing. I just…the way you touch me…no one's ever wanted me this much."

"Not even Jonathan?"

She looked up at him. Yeah, he never asked intrusive questions. But for some reason, tonight, he wanted to know. She'd be seeing her ex over the break.

"Are you serious? After a seeing-to like that you want to compare past lovers?"

He laughed—and, honestly, no one made him laugh the way she did. Sure, he laughed with his friends back home. But that was raunchy humor. Or drunken humor. His girl was snarky, and he never knew what would come out of her mouth. "You don't have to tell me." He was in no position to force anyone to talk about their private lives.

"Ugh." She got up, grabbing their water glasses from her desk. "I'm getting us some water. Be right back." He heard the faucet run in the bathroom, and he wished he hadn't said anything. Just because he'd never had this kind of sex with anybody before didn't mean she hadn't.

Handing him a glass, she drank hers down, then turned on the desk lamp. She pulled on his T-shirt and a fresh pair of panties from her dresser. "Jonathan's a drunk."

"Jesus, Nicole." He sat up, stacking pillows behind him. "Your boyfriend of three and half years was an alcoholic?"

"Not in the beginning. When we met he was just like me. That's how we became friends. Both a little nerdy."

"You're not nerdy."

"Whatever. We were both independents in a school full of stereotypes. I wasn't a jock like my brothers. I wasn't a brain or a thespian."

"Well, you weren't a nerd."

"Fine. The point is that neither of us was in a group. Which meant we didn't have a huge social life. We were friendly with everyone, but we didn't go to football games and stuff like that. So we found our own little group of misfits."

"What about Gina?" He'd heard her Facetiming with her closest friend a lot.

"She didn't go to my school. She went to a private one, like my brothers. But, anyway, after Jonathan and I lost our virginity together, then we did a lot of, you know, exploring."

*Wonderful.* He never should've asked.

"And then sophomore year things started to change. His parents were always on him about grades, but in tenth grade they really started pressuring him. He wasn't going to get into an Ivy League school if he didn't do research in the summer, win contests, publish articles. He didn't want to do any of that. He wanted to play with me. But they wouldn't let him. So, he started partying. And I, of course, didn't, so we fought a lot. Basically, after that first year together, the sex turned into him trying to get with me. Drunken hook-ups."

She watched his face, and he tried to keep it clear of emotion, even though he felt sick. He'd touched every inch of her; his tongue had traced her every curve. His hands knew her so well he could make her out in a stadium full of women in total darkness.

She was *his*.

Shit. He couldn't *actually* have her, but she still felt like his. And he hated the idea that some guy had treated her so badly. Some guy she'd stood by, given herself to.

When she slid off the chair, crawled across the bed to fall into his arms, kissing his forehead, his cheeks, his eyelids, his chin, he knew he hadn't hid his emotions.

"It was never like this." Pulling off the t-shirt, she brought his hand to her breast, and he cupped her tightly. "Nothing's like this."

He palmed her ass, dragging her leg across his lap so she straddled him. "Nothing." He doubted anything ever would be. How could it? He was hard again—which made no sense given the number of times they'd had each other the last three days. But he was leaving for the airport at the crack of dawn and wouldn't see her for five days. He needed to get his fill.

"How did he handle the break-up?"

She rocked on him, playing with his hair. "Not well. I'm pretty sure he's still waiting for me to get over it and make up with him."

Damn, but he loved the way she felt against him, loved the way her breasts bounced when she rocked. He pushed his dick between her pussy lips, sucking in a breath at the feel of her slick heat sliding along the length of him. "I'll *bet* he wants you back."

She gasped, her head tilting, hair spilling behind her. "I will never get back with him. He was drunk, so he wouldn't remember things the way I do. We fought all the time. I begged him to give up drinking, you know the drill. Huge drama, shouting, crying. Why wouldn't he quit drinking for me? Finally, right after New Year's, I ended it. Done. No more drama."

"Did he cheat on you?"

"Who knows what he did when he was wasted, right? I don't want to think about it ever again." She lowered her mouth to his, kissing, stroking, rocking, until she'd worked him into a frenzy all over again.

Hand on her ass, he lifted her, positioned his dick, and thrust inside.

"God, Dylan." She arched her back, hands gripping his thighs behind her, all that pretty hair falling like a silky veil down her back. Those gorgeous breasts bounced with her every move, and he had to sit up and taste them, lick them, suck them into his mouth.

She gasped, rolling forward to clutch him to her chest. Locked together like that, his dick enveloped in her tight, hot channel, her arms belted around him, he felt a kind of happiness, a completeness, he'd never felt before. Never even believed possible. He wanted her, all of her. Every single drop of her.

As his hips powered into her, as his dick swelled inside her, all he could feel was the need to protect her, be with her forever. He wanted to be there for every moment of her life—to fight for her and with her.

*Fuck.* He should *not* be thinking like that. About things he couldn't have.

He'd always accepted his lot in life. But now—for the first time—he wanted something else. So fiercely it made his heart seize up.

He'd always been so careful not to want the things he couldn't have—experience had taught him that lesson. But he had no control when it came to Nicole.

Maybe coming to Wilmington was one big colossal mistake.

They'd showered and packed, ready to leave for the airport at five. She'd said it was on her way to Connecticut, but he'd checked Google maps. It was completely out of her way. Which would make her even later to see her family.

"So, what's Thanksgiving like in the O'Donnell house?" he asked, as they clung to each other under the covers in the last few hours before the alarm went off.

"Oh, it's a big scene, my brothers and their entourages, all my dad's clients and friends."

"Does your dad have a girlfriend?"

"Not that I know of. He never brings women home."

"Why?" Wouldn't that have been nice, if his mom hadn't brought anyone home?

"From the moment he got me back, he's been very careful with me." She pushed up, looking at him. "Do you know where I got my love for baking?"

He shook his head, loving these moments with her. She looked so pretty in the soft light of the desk lamp. Her hair all shiny. Everything about her was so feminine and strong and real.

She was so fucking real.

"My dad."

"Really?" For some reason, he'd assumed it came from a

good memory of her mom. He had a clear image of her as a dark-haired little girl, standing on a chair and watching her mom drop a spoon full of batter on a baking sheet.

"You can imagine, when I came back to live with him, I was really weird about food. I kind of hoarded."

Shit, he hated to hear how traumatized she'd been. His TV-land images of her had long ago been blown out of the water.

She sank down again, cuddling up against him, a finger tracing figure-eights on his chest. "He'd find food stored everywhere. Under couch cushions, in my drawers. There were certain things I really liked, and with my brothers and their friends over all the time, they literally ate everything in sight. So I'd hide the things I wanted. Sometimes I'd find them months later, all moldy and nasty. So it wasn't like I was starving and needed them."

Stroking the hair off her face, he said, "What did you really like?"

Her features turned pink. "Oh. I really liked cinnamon bread." The flush deepened. "I'd hide bags of it in my ballet bag at the back of my closet."

He smiled, but inside he ached for the little girl sneaking a loaf of bread into her room.

"Anyhow, my dad made a big thing about food. He took me shopping, stuffed the pantry and cupboards. But he didn't know how to cook. He could grill, so he'd make steaks and chicken and stuff for my brothers, but he didn't know how to make vegetarian dishes for me. So he started making pancakes and waffles for dinner. And that turned into biscuits and scones. Then pumpkin and banana breads. Really, cooking for him was baking. And while my brothers and their friends were always coming and going, on their way to a game or practice, the only real time I had alone with my dad was in the kitchen."

"He sounds like a great dad. I'm glad he was there for you."

Her arm belted around him, and she shifted so her breast pressed into his ribcage. He fucking loved that. "What about you? Since I can't be there with you, give me a picture of what it'll be like. Who're you going to see, where're you going to spend Thanksgiving?"

He wouldn't tell her the truth about his *holiday*, but he'd give her something. "Okay, well. I guess I'm like your brothers, always hanging out in a pack." It was how he'd kept himself safe from his mom's friends. "Mostly, I try and stay home as much as I can." Because nothing was more embarrassing than having his mom show up drunk, looking for him.

"Your friends don't party?"

"We can do that at my place."

Her finger stilled for a moment, and he figured it would take her a moment to work that one out. His mom, the supplier. But then she went back to touching him. "Do you have a traditional meal?"

Jesus, she had no idea. "Sometimes." Not since his grandpa had died, and the rest of his family had turned their backs on them.

He didn't want her to become uncomfortable, so he figured he should change the subject. "But when we do get out of the house, we head to the mountains. We hike, camp out."

"So, like, who picks you up from the airport? Who'll be waiting for you when you walk in the door?"

"Sawyer'll pick me up. He's my closest friend. We'll hit

the diner on the way into town. Everyone'll be there, Brian, Craig, Paul. My girlfriend'll already be at my mom's—" *Oh, shit.* He knew it the moment the word came out of his mouth. He tried to pull Nicole back, but she jerked away from him. "Ex. My *ex*-girlfriend." *Fuck.*

Grabbing a pillow, she covered her body with it. "Your girlfriend?"

Jesus, she looked horrified. "My ex-girlfriend. I promise you, Kelsi's in my past."

Swear to God, she looked like he'd clubbed her, all stunned and dazed. "When did you break up?"

He didn't know how to answer that without sounding like a jerk. "August."

"*August?* You mean right before you came out here?"

He nodded.

"So you didn't break up. You went to college."

"It was over." He didn't want to explain his relationship with Kelsi.

"Did you love her?"

He shrugged. Any form of the truth would make her hate him. "I guess so."

"You *guess* so? How long were you with her?"

"Two years."

She flew off the bed, taking the pillow with her. In the pale lamp light, he could see fresh tears glistening on her cheeks as she bent to pick up her sweats.

"It's not what you think at all. We didn't have that kind of relationship. It wasn't about love."

"You were with her for *two years*. And you didn't break up with her. You just left for college."

"It's not…she doesn't…" How was he supposed to explain this shit to a good person?

"Have you been talking to her this whole time?" She stopped what she was doing, features contorted in pain.

"No."

Standing there in sweats and no top, her features froze in a mask of horror. "Are you going to be with her this week? *Tonight?* Is that—" Her hands covered her mouth, her nose, leaving only eyes full of horror.

He lunged for her, grabbing her wrist and tugging her onto the bed. She fought him, wrenching out of his grip. "Of course I'm not going to be with her. I told you, it's not like that. It was never like that." *I want you.*

"What was it like for two years with a girl you only stopped seeing because you weren't physically in the same state?"

"She gets me."

"She gets you? She *gets* you?"

"No, I mean my life. She gets my life."

"Is that because you *talk* to her? Let her in? Well, I'm sorry if I don't *get* you, Dylan, but you never tell me a damn thing." She swung away from him, scooping her bra off the floor and jamming her arm through one of the straps. "I can't believe this. You have a girlfriend. A real one."

What did she mean, a *real* one? "Kelsi's not…" *You.* "It was never like that." He scrambled out of the sheets, reaching for her.

"You never once, in all our time together, thought to mention you had a girlfriend?"

He thought about it. Again, it made him look like a total dick, but, no, he hadn't. "No." He looked away. "I don't think about her."

"You were with her for *two years*. You didn't have some fight or some big falling out. She didn't cheat on you. The only reason you're not sleeping with her tonight, right now, is because you left for college."

He blew out a breath, scrubbed the back of his neck. "Sunshine—"

"Do not *Sunshine* me. I am not your sunshine. I'm just another one of the bimbos in your line-up."

Anger roared through him. He'd had enough. "You are *not* a girl I fuck. Now, stop this. You're freaking out on me, I'm afraid I'm going to lose you, and I just need a goddamn minute to think." He let her go. "Can you give me that?"

She let out a shuddery breath. "Yes." She threw on a sweatshirt, then sat down on her desk chair.

Shit. How had he fucked up so badly? He took a few moments to pull his shit together. His heart felt like it might explode.

"Actually, no." She got up again, reaching for her shirt. "I'm going to take a shower and then we should go."

"You already showered. We should get some sleep."

"I'm not going to sleep, Dylan." She stopped what she was doing to pin him with a determined look. "There's nothing you can say right now to take away what I've just learned." She pulled off the sweats, took off her bra, and strode out of the room.

Dylan watched her go, listened as the shower turned on, and felt the cold hands of fear curl around his throat. Had he lost her?

*Fuck, no.* He couldn't lose her. Jesus. Not over this. What had just happened? Why had he called Kelsi his girlfriend?

He should go in there, force her to hear him out.

Right. Because what he had to say would win her over. Make him sound like the great guy he was.

"What is it about Kelsi that makes you let *her* in?"

He practically jumped out of his skin. She stood in the threshold, naked, water streaming down her body. She swiped hair off her face.

She looked so heartbroken, standing there, completely vulnerable to him. She'd given her whole self to him and he'd…taken.

Approaching her, he swallowed, fisting his hands at his sides so he wouldn't reach for her. He needed to hold her, love the hurt right out of her. But he knew he couldn't do that.

He looked down at his bare feet. "She didn't run. She got a front-row seat to my fuckfest of a life, and she didn't run. She didn't think anything of it because her family's just as messed up." But a truth struck him, so he could look her in the eye. "I didn't let her in. Yeah, she knows about my shit, but she's not…she and I…"

"What? Just say it. Why can't you just say it? It's not like you can hurt me any worse than you already have." She turned, and he didn't know if she'd given up on him. But then he heard the shower cut off and she returned with a towel around her. "You lied to me."

"I've never lied to you."

"Bullshit. Reverse the situation. Imagine you're just finding out about Jonathan right now. How would you feel, after spending these last three days together, holding me in your arms and hearing me say, *My boyfriend'll be waiting for me at my dad's house?* Can you even imagine what that would feel like?"

He sure as hell could. The rage—the betrayal—shook him to his core, and it hadn't even happened to him. "I wouldn't be standing here right now." She was so much stronger than he.

"I feel like every moment I thought was so special was just you getting off. Maybe I'm just more convenient, being right across the hall. You have to walk into town to hook up with Brittany or any of the others in your harem."

"Jesus, Nicole, you know that's not true. I don't care about those girls." Okay, he had to just get it out because nothing would make him look more like an ass than what she already thought of him. "I don't know what to say. I…you're nothing like Kelsi. *We* are nothing like…you have to know how I feel about you."

Her features collapsed in total disappointment. She brushed past him, giving him a whiff of that fragrance that narrowed his world to them, together, under the covers, naked bodies entwined.

Normally, she took her time slathering on her scented body lotion. This time she rubbed it quickly into her skin, threw on her clothes, and focused on packing up her toiletries.

The first three hours of the ride to the airport, he'd driven so Nicole could sleep. The next two and a half hours she'd driven. As the car slowed in the clot of traffic narrowing to the departure terminals, she edged nearer to the curb.

He motioned ahead. "Go all the way to the end."

"But your airline—"

"Go."

Not a chance would he leave without setting her straight. He'd had time to get his thoughts in order.

He never freaked out—he couldn't afford to. No matter the situation, he had a clear head so he could handle crises. But the fear of losing Nicole? It had loosened a screw. He'd lost his balance. But he was back on solid ground now.

She pulled over at the very end of the terminal, well ahead of the cars dropping off passengers. They sat quietly for a moment. She looked straight ahead, tapping her fingers on the wheel.

Okay, enough of this shit. He shifted his seat back as far as it could go, then lifted her onto his lap.

"No." She struggled, pushing him away. "Stop it."

He situated her in his lap and threw an arm over her thighs to keep her in place. "I didn't mention Kelsi because when I left her in August I was done. Completely done. Not because she'd done anything wrong, but because I wanted to get out of there and start a new life. As far as my feelings for her? I felt… grateful."

Her expression turned angry, like she didn't believe him. Well, he was sorry if it made him sound like a piece of shit, but it was true.

"I've lost a lot of relationships because of my mom—I don't speak to anyone in my family, and whatever friendships I might've started in school ended the moment my mom pulled one of her stunts. And believe me, in my small town, everyone knows what my mom does." Her name could be counted on to show up in the Police Report section of the local paper several times a year. "But Kels didn't care about any of it. She was always there for me."

He tipped her chin, wishing he could take the pain he'd caused away. "What *we* have? You and me? It's on a whole different level. I know you think I've slept with a dozen girls since I got here, and I guess I can see where you'd get that idea, but I haven't. I've only been with you."

"You wouldn't have stayed with a girl for two years if you only felt grateful to her."

*This* was what he loved about her. She was real. "You're

right. In the beginning I did have feelings for her. But, still, not the way you think. It was never what *we* have. Look, Nicole, I fucking hated my life. I worked my ass off so I could get out of there. And Kelsi? She's everything I hated about my life. Her ties to my mom, her attitude, her lifestyle—she represents everything I couldn't wait to get away from. Did I care about her? Sure I did. I was grateful to her for helping me manage my mom."

"Then don't try to pretend you had no feelings for her so you can get back in my good graces."

"Well, I don't know how to get back in your good graces. There's no fucking way I can explain to a girl like you what my fucking life is like. You won't understand that Kelsi and I weren't exclusive." He hated to say it. Hated her expression. "We partied, Nicole. We got wasted. She wound up with other guys, and I wound up with other girls. But we had each other. I was overworked and overstressed, and she was there and more than willing, and that's the relationship we fell into with each other. So, when I left, I was ready to go. And, no, I don't think about her. I don't *want* to think about her."

"But you're going to see her."

"Yes, I am. She's part of my group of friends. Just like Jonathan is for you."

"And you're going to get wasted, and she's going to be there."

"Yes, that's right. But I'm not going to touch her. I don't *want* her."

"You say that now, but people do things when they're wasted." She gave him a look that said, *Believe me, I know.* "It's only been three months, Dylan. You're going right back into that world."

She said *world* like it was a used syringe she'd found on the street. Her disgust lit the fuse inside, and a flash fire of shame burned through him. "I *told* you that you weren't going to like me. I told you not to get involved with me." He lifted her and dumped her back in her seat. "I knew this wouldn't work." He was such an asshole. He'd known from the beginning not to get involved with Wilmington girls. He'd been right to focus on the girls from town.

Fuck him for letting this one in. He shouldered open the door and slammed it shut. Opening the trunk, he pulled out his duffle. He'd already filled her gas tank, so at least he didn't have to burden her with that expense.

He threw the bag over his shoulder and strode into the terminal, never looking back to see her leave.

# CHAPTER THIRTEEN

***Landed. Let me know you got home.***

Nicole looked up from reading Dylan's text to find her dad and Gina watching her.

"Mr. Hot Sexy Pants?" Gina's chair scraped back on the hardwood floor. She gathered the lunch plates from the table and carried them into the kitchen.

"And that's my cue to head back to my office for a few hours." Her big, burly dad got up and ducked out of the room.

"It's not like she's flipping out or anything," Gina called after him. "Jeez, you'd think you were a drama queen the way the O'Donnell men scatter when you have a problem."

"Is that normal? I mean, if I'd had a mom or sisters, it might not be so bad, but they don't talk to me about anything."

"When I become the Man Guru, I'll get back to you on that." Gina set the dishes on the counter next to the sink, just as Inna instructed. Their housekeeper hated when people stacked plates and cups inside—said it made her job harder and broke things. "In the meantime…" She nodded toward the cell phone in Nicole's hand. "You gonna answer him?"

She supposed she would. *I'm home.*

"What'd you tell him?" her friend asked.

"Just that I'm home."

"So…you're not going to ask him if he broke up with you?"

"Not ready to hear it."

"Yank the Band-Aid, pull the trigger. Just get 'er done. You know it's killing you not to know." Gina leaned back against the counter, arms folded across her stomach.

Honestly, Nicole was devastated. To go from the kind of intense intimacy they'd shared to losing him—just like that—it left her reeling. She couldn't get over the way he'd dumped her into the driver's seat and walked away from her. "I don't know what to do."

"Of course you do. You talk to him."

"No, I know that. But I mean I don't know what I want."

"Meaning?"

"Meaning, even if he didn't break up with me, I'm not sure I want to be with him. I can't give my whole heart to someone who can't give me more than a tiny slice of his."

Her phone buzzed. His name filled the screen.

"Him again?" Gina asked.

*Sorry.* "He says he's sorry."

"That's it?"

"He's a man of few words."

She shook her head. "You're being ridiculous. You've known him five minutes. Trust takes time to build. Give him a break."

"I think he gave himself one."

"Nicole, sweetie. We are women of *action.* What do you want?"

She wanted to get back into bed with him, feel the heat

of his hard, muscled body, feel those strong arms tighten around her. He made her feel loved, cherished, wanted. "I don't know. Everything was so perfect and then…"

Gina pushed off the counter. Reaching into the waistband of her black leggings, she pulled out her phone. "Perfect, huh? Memory is such a fluid thing, isn't it? Let's find us some perfect." She scrolled down. "Okay." Her friend read from the screen. "He brought home three hos tonight. WTF?"

Nicole remembered the night she'd written that one. He'd visited her in the Sculpture Gardens that afternoon. She'd thought it had meant something, that he'd take time out of his day to be with her. He'd even shared a cookie he'd picked up at the Trough. But then he'd come home that night with three townie girls, flaunting them in her face. Well, flaunting. He didn't actually flaunt. It had just felt like it.

Gina continued reading. "Having great talk, then his phone rings, and he just leaves me. Who the hell is he talking to all the time?"

"Okay, I get it. Not perfect." But the last three days sure had been.

Her friend's gaze was still fixed to the screen. "I literally know nothing about him other than what I see with my own eyes."

"Stop. I get it."

Gina started out of the kitchen. "Come on, I have to do my nails before we go out tonight." She led the way to Nicole's bedroom, shut the door, peeled off her oversize sweater, and flopped onto the bed. "I want something dark and ugly. What do you have?"

"Get it yourself. I'm having a crisis here."

"It's not a *crisis*. Crisis is what you lived through with your mom and fuckface. This one's your own doing because you won't talk to him."

The last two and a half years with Jonathan had been traumatic. She'd tried to save him, tried to get him to choose her over booze. She'd been with him for three and a half years—a lot longer than Dylan and Kelsi—but she'd *never* mistakenly refer to him as her boyfriend.

Gina got up, pulled off her long sleeve T-shirt and rolled the manicure table closer to the bed. Her friend grabbed a hideous shade of puke green. "This one's disgusting." She held it between two fingers like it was a dead mouse.

"Thank you. You bought it for the prom I never went to."

She smiled, her eyebrow piercing catching the overhead light. "I did." Struggling to open it, she scowled. "Hey, it's never been opened."

The door flew open. "Yo." Brandon leaned into her room, and then froze when his gaze landed on Gina. His jaw hung open. "Fuckin' put some clothes on, Gina. Jesus."

"Bite me." She didn't even look at him as she carefully applied polish to her pinkie toe. "We're in triage over here, if you care even a little bit about your sister. Besides, the door was closed, dickhead."

Nicole watched her brother's expression carefully—he wavered between pissed off and lustful. "You should knock first." And then she turned to Gina. "And I don't know why you need to be half-naked to do your nails."

"I can't do it when I'm all constricted. It's *art*."

Brandon tore his eyes reluctantly off the bountiful curves nearly bursting out of her friend's skintight cami. "Dad wants you to go to the store. We need snacks."

In a flurry of motion, Gina screwed the cap of the bottle back on before lobbing it at him.

Luckily, Yale's starting quarterback caught it. "What the hell's your problem?"

She got off the bed, big boobs bouncing, hips strutting. "Bill didn't ask you to come in here and tell Nicole to go to the store. He asked *you* to go, but you're too self-involved to do it."

Her brother smiled. "She likes shopping for food."

Nicole's phone rang. Her heart flew up into her throat. Of course, it could be James. It could be anyone. But she wanted it to be Dylan. She unearthed it from the bedding.

When she saw his name light up her screen, anxiety stabbed into her nerves. "Hello?"

"Hey. We're still sitting on the plane."

That was it? That was all he had to say? "Okay. Got plans with Kelsi tonight?"

He sighed. "Yes."

"Cool. Have a great week." Her thumb stabbed the off button, and she tossed her phone aside. She felt too hot, her clothes too tight. Her stomach hurt, and she had a hard time taking in a full breath. Oh, God, was she having a panic attack? She had to breathe. Nothing was wrong. This wasn't trauma. Just because the man she'd given her body and soul to was spending Thanksgiving in the arms of his ex-girlfriend didn't mean her world was falling apart.

When she looked up, she found Gina and her brother watching her. "I'm fine. I overreacted." And then she closed her eyes and tilted her head back. "God, I'm such an idiot." He'd warned her against getting involved with him. Why hadn't she listened?

"What happened, sweetie?" Gina sat on the edge of the bed, rubbing her arm.

"Nothing. He's waiting to get off the plane." Her friend turned blurry, viewed as she was through the wall of tears Nicole refused to shed. Because Gina was right. It had *never* been perfect. Yes, they did great when they shut out the world and clutched each other in the deep of night. But they lived in the real world. And that world involved his mom, his ex, and all the baggage Nicole herself dragged with her. "And his girlfriend's waiting for him to get home."

She looked up through the screen of tears to find Brandon looking at Gina…enraptured. What the hell? She had to blink away the tears to be sure, but he seemed to be looking at Gina with want. And that made no sense. None at all. Her brother was the clean-cut frat boy, the All-State quarterback for three years in high school. And Gina was a pierced, tatted, foul-mouthed…pin-up girl.

"No, that's *not* what he said." Brandon stepped into the room. "You asked *him*. You said, Got plans with Kelsi tonight? In your bitchy voice."

"She's not bitchy, she's hurt." Gina shot up, so they stood face to face.

For one moment, her brother seemed to lose his train of thought, as he took in Gina's body in a slow sweep. But when his gaze returned to her face and met with a brow arched in challenge, he shook it off.

"Then she should say that. We're guys. We don't know what you're thinking unless you say what you mean."

Her phone buzzed, and she leaned across the bed to reach it.

*Surrounded by people on the plane. Can't talk now.*

She quickly shot off a response. *Can you ever talk? I mean, with someone other than Kelsi?*

"My point is," Brandon said, turning from Gina. "If you attack us, we're going to run. Plain and simple."

"Then you're weak, and we don't want you," Gina said.

"What's weak about not wanting to be around people who bitch at you? That's just all kinds of fucked up and immature. There's no *strength* in sniping. What do you accomplish with your cutting comments when we have no idea what we've done wrong?"

Nicole looked from one to the other. What was going on between these two?

"It's not possible to hurt someone who doesn't care."

He tipped his head back to look at the ceiling. "It's not that we don't care. But if we don't understand, then we obviously *can't* care. If we hurt you, then just say, *You hurt me.* You'll get a better response if we know what we've done."

He was right, and she instantly regretted her text. She stared at her phone, wishing she could take it back. As upset as she was, she couldn't quite get past the fact that she *did* know Dylan. She knew a lot about his character based on his actions in the short time she'd known him. And no one could pretend to want her the way he did.

She shivered at the thought of how he consumed her. Her phone buzzed with a text. Dylan.

*I'll call you later when I'm alone.*

But she already knew he wouldn't be alone. He'd be surrounded by his mom, his friends, and his *girlfriend.*

"You're a pig," she heard Gina say.

"Because I'm not telling you what you want to hear?"

"No, because you're not there for your sister."

Nicole's head snapped up. No one talked to her brothers like that. They were revered in their social circles—in the whole community. Girls would lick the soles of their boots if they thought it'd get a minute of their time.

Brandon's face…God, he looked gutted. She wasn't sure how she felt about Gina's attack. Her brothers cared about her—she didn't doubt that. But, no, they hadn't really been in her life.

"Fine. I'll go to the store myself." He turned and walked out of the room. "If you want anything, text me."

The silence in his aftermath throbbed with electricity.

"Your brothers are so fucking arrogant." Gina flounced back onto the bed and resumed painting her nails. "So, are we done brooding? Should we get our Wild Woman on and go to Bar None?"

The last thing Nicole wanted was to go to her brother's crowded, loud, underage club in the city. She didn't want to dress up, and she didn't want to get groped by drunken guys.

Gina threw a wicked glance over her shoulder. "Or you could stay home and feel sorry for yourself while his ex goes down on him."

******

Dusk bathed his mountains in a deep orange glow. The scattering of snow on the ground reminded him of Nicole's confectioner's sugar, and he smiled as they passed his cousin's bakery, Hot Cakes. Nicole would love it in there. His cousin had studied and apprenticed in France, so she created incredible desserts. So good, brides from Denver to Aspen had turned her little bakery into a specialty wedding cake shop.

"And Turner knocked up Amy Kessler." Kelsi bounced around in the driver's seat. The girl never stayed still, not for a moment. "Can you believe that shit? She's going to have the kid, too. I swear she's just trying to bag and tag him. But even if she does get him down the aisle, who cares? It's not like he'll ever be faithful to her."

As Kelsi continued to fill him in on everyone, he felt a sharp pang in his chest.

Had he ruined everything with Nicole? It was probably for the best. But he was a selfish prick, and he…he just…*fuck*…he wasn't ready for it to end. Not even close. It felt too good, too right. And, especially, to end it over Kelsi. He glanced at her. She'd surprised him by picking him up at the airport instead of Sawyer. And, worse, he could tell she was expecting something from him. As soon as she'd gotten in the truck, she'd peeled off her coat, twisting towards him to pull her arms out of the sleeves—a move designed to show off her impressive rack.

It did nothing for him.

She'd blown her dyed blonde hair straight and put on a ton of make-up. But maybe it was for the party tonight and not him. Nicole had put ideas in his head. He and Kelsi weren't like that. Never had been. She'd never even asked to be exclusive.

He jerked his gaze away when he realized he'd replaced her face with Nicole's, imagining his girl driving, turning to him with that soft smile she had for him. A shot of lust grabbed hold of him, and he had to look out the window.

"What about Loughlin?" He caught a glimpse of his Uncle Zach striding out of the Outfitter store. Dylan turned to see where he was going in such a rush and found his cousin Amy struggling with a screaming baby in a carrier strapped around her chest and three-year-old Elle prancing around her. His family kept growing. He'd missed a lot.

"He finished basic and now he's in Infantry School in Fort Benning. He's having the time of his life at the base, if you know what I mean." She shot him a knowing smile. "I'll bet you are, too."

He quickly looked away. No, he shouldn't do that. He should face the issue head-on. In case she did have expectations, he needed to make things clear right off the bat. "I met someone."

"Yeah?" She smiled. "Hopefully, lots of someones."

"No. Just one."

"Come on, tiger. You're at college. You're supposed to join a frat, fuck around. Get shit out of your system."

"I like her." The relief rumbling through him took him by surprise. He actually wanted to talk about Nicole. A girl's perspective would help.

"You've been there three months, and you've already got your fuck buddy? Come on, shake things up. You're not in Gun Powder anymore. You've got the rest of your life when you get back here to be with one girl. Live it up."

He ran a finger over his lips as he watched the streets of Gun Powder roll by. Did that mean she considered herself his fuck buddy? Or the one he'd be with the rest of his life when he got back? He got a sick feeling, hoping to hell it wasn't the latter. Should he address it now? Or leave it be—let time and distance do its thing?

"You seeing anybody?" he asked.

Another sly smile. "Me and Perkins. But it's just for fun, obviously. Doesn't mean anything."

"You always had a thing for him."

"Yeah, now that his girlfriend's in Fort Collins, suddenly I'm all right to hang out with." She shook her head, like she didn't care. But he knew better.

"He and Tammy broke up?"

"Don't know. Don't ask." She squeezed his knee, then ran her hand firmly up his thigh.

His hand shot out, cutting her off before she reached his

package. All the humor drained from her expression, and she looked surprised and hurt.

"I'm seeing someone." He held her gaze, his tone dead serious.

"Yeah, in school. Two thousand miles away." But she kept her hands to herself.

The truck pitched, as she turned into the rutted driveway of the sad apartment complex. At least his mom hadn't gotten evicted yet. "Have you seen her with Jeff?" He assumed Kelsi would tell him if she had, but he needed to be sure.

The sky had darkened, making it harder to see the nuances of her expression. She bit her lip, as she jerked the gearshift to park. "I have, yeah." The parking lot lights cast a yellow glow to her features.

He closed his eyes. "Why didn't you tell me?"

"Because you can't do anything about it. It has to play itself out, you know that."

"Is that how's she paying for this apartment then?"

She worried her bottom lip, one finger stroking the console between them. "Babe, I don't know. You know I can't ask. Neither can you."

Because his mom would just lie. The back of his head hit the headrest. "Fuck." What could he do about it? He could pick up a few days of work with his old boss over the break, but it wouldn't amount to much.

"But she's off the wagon right?" Obviously, if she was seeing Jeff again. Still, he needed confirmation. "I'm guessing she's not going to her AA meetings?"

"Dylan, really?" She looked incredulous. "I'm not her keeper, but I'm pretty sure AA meetings aren't on her to-do list."

"Yeah, I know. I just need to be sure. I can't believe she'd get back with Jeff."

"I'm not sure if they're together or anything."

"What have you seen?"

"We should go in." She motioned to his phone, which his mom had been blowing up since he'd landed. He'd texted to let her know he was on his way home but hadn't fed her obsession since.

"Just tell me what you've seen. I need to know."

"You don't get it, do you? You still think you can control her."

"Kels."

"Okay." Her fingers made a slow, sensual slide around the steering wheel. "Bri and I were driving by the Pit Stop and saw her coming out with him."

"Were they together, as in dating? Or was she buying something?"

"She could barely stand up. He was practically dragging her out."

"Was he hurting her? Did he look pissed?"

"Um…" She looked thoughtful, like she was remembering. "They were laughing. He was wasted, too."

"And? Any other times?"

Her features pulled in, like she'd bit down on a bug.

"Tell me."

"Well, okay, but I didn't see this. Perkins said she came to pick up her truck. I guess her credit card didn't go through, and he wouldn't let her leave without paying."

His stomach pulled into a tight knot.

"And…she made a call." She shot him a worried look. "Jeff came by to pay for her."

"Why didn't you tell me?"

"It's all been in the last week or so."

Of course it had. While he'd been with Nicole, his mom had strayed. *Of course.*

He closed his eyes, the image of Jeff grabbing his mom's arm and shaking her filled the screen of his mind. "Let's get in there." As he got out of the truck, the biting late November air slapped him hard in the face.

"Dyl." Kelsi met him in front of the truck. "She's having a really hard adjustment. She's never been without you. I don't know why you thought you could pay her rent for two months, set her up with a job, and think she'd just start this new life." She stepped in front of him. "You had to know she couldn't handle that job."

"No, I didn't know. We're talking about survival. She *has* to do it this time."

"She knows you, Dyl. Deep down she knows. You'll never leave her."

His skin went clammy, and he felt sick to his stomach.

"We all know that." She gazed up at him like a bride on her wedding day.

Holy fuck. He'd thought he'd set it all up—got his mom situated in a new life, let Kelsi go in the cleanest way possible, but no one had believed him. They'd humored him, thinking they knew him better than he knew himself.

How could he stay at Wilmington knowing his mom was getting involved with a drug dealer? Kelsi could be with whoever she wanted, he didn't care. But he couldn't have her thinking he'd come back to her. That they had a future together.

"Dyllie." A yellow rectangle of light on the second floor drew his attention to his mom, standing there in worn jeans and an off-the-shoulder sweatshirt. She waved to him. "My boy." She shrieked, jumping up and down. "Get up here."

One woman at a time. First his mom.

He'd deal with Kelsi later.

Surrounded by loud music and a crush of bodies, Dylan leaned against the wall and watched his mom. High as a kite, she partied with his friends. But then she pulled her phone out of her back pocket, read the screen, and quickly headed for the door.

He'd bet his scholarship she was meeting Jeff Blakely.

Fucking drug dealer. She'd hooked up with him years ago. He'd roughed her up—put her in the hospital—and then he'd left town for a while. And now his mom was messing with him again.

Too many years of this shit had taught him not to intervene when she was high. Kels was right. He couldn't control his mom's choices or her behavior. All he could do was manage her world to keep her safe. He'd slipped up a little, allowed that fucker to step in during his absence. But he'd talk to her when she was somewhat sober and get her back on track. She didn't need a damn drug dealer to keep a roof over her head. He'd get another job—

Kelsi slammed into him, eyes glazed, beer can in one hand, cigarette in the other.

He pushed her away.

She pouted. "You've been ignoring me all night."

The front door opened, and his mom stumbled back in with Jeff wrapped around her, hugging her from behind. Both wasted.

Dropping her cigarette into the can, Kelsi set it on the floor, clasped her arms around his neck and pressed her pelvis tight against his. "Mm. I've missed you. Let's go to your room."

Anger pounded in his veins. A dangerous, wild sense of aggression—like he could hurl a couch off the upstairs balcony—caused him to tear her arms off him and step away from the wall so roughly she lost her balance.

"Get off me, Kels."

"What the fuck's your problem? I'm not the one banging a drug dealer."

Before he could ram his fist through the wall, he tore out of the room.

Locking himself in the bathroom, he ran the cold water and splashed his face. Too drunk to call Nicole, he dropped his head in his wet hands. The problem was he *only* wanted Nicole.

Had he fucked up giving Wilmington a shot? Obviously he could still earn decent bank graduating from Boulder. It's just…he'd wanted more.

And look what he'd found. *Nicole.*

Fuck it. He was too drunk to have self-control. He dialed his girl. A hip perched on the edge of the sink, he tilted his head back, listening to the shrieks of laughter, the thump of bass, and rumble of conversation. After four rings, she didn't answer. He wouldn't leave a voicemail.

But then he heard her voice.

"Hello? Dylan?" She shouted over the loud music in the background.

Energy flooded him. "Where are you?"

"Wait. I can't hear you." She paused. "Hang on a second."

Was she in a club with Jonathan? The drunk from Greenwich, Connecticut? Clean up that little drinking problem, and the guy would be perfect for her.

"Dylan?" It sounded quieter now.

Drunk as he was, he knew he had to calm down. "Where are you?" He was glad she hadn't heard him the first time.

"You're drunk." She didn't sound disappointed. Just…cold.

"Yeah."

"What do you want?" Crisp, professional. Like he was a telemarketer who'd interrupted dinner.

"I miss you."

"Dylan, we're not going to talk when you're drunk. Besides, didn't you dump me this morning? Which is great timing, actually, since you're with your girlfriend right now."

He was too drunk to properly respond. He didn't trust himself to not blow up.

"You are with her, right?"

"Kelsi's not my girlfriend. I told you that." He had his girl on the line, and he couldn't bear to let her go. "I didn't say it right the first time. Will you let me try now?"

"Not when you're drunk."

"Don't be so cold with me." He needed to tone it down. "It's me, sunshine."

"I know."

"So, give me a chance here. When you get all hard with me, I can't think straight."

"You can't think straight because you're drunk."

"Nicole! Jesus. I'm trying here." Yeah, he understood her history with drunks, but come on. He wasn't her mom or her ex.

"Okay, okay. I'm sorry."

"I'm not that drunk. Can you please just give me a chance to tell you how I feel? It's not easy for me."

"I know that." Her soft voice spread through him, soothing like nothing else.

"Kelsi's a friend. That's all she is to me anymore. She's been there for me. We never had the…fuck, what do we have, sunshine? Fire? Because even just thinking about you gets me all stirred up. It's like there's this little flame burning right in the center of me, and the minute you come close, it turns into this raging fire. I want you, Nicole." Emotion choked him. "*You.*"

"You're drunk. Everyone looks really good to you right now."

"No. I want you. Only you."

"You broke up with me."

"I didn't break up with you. I just don't know how to do this. My mom's—" *Shit.*

"Uh oh. Were you about to share something with me?"

"It works, you know. When you shoot me with that nail gun mouth of yours? It works. I'm trying to talk to you, and you're fucking nailing me."

"I'm sorry. A, you told me you had a girlfriend, B, you broke up with me, and C, you're drunk dialing me. Three strikes, I'm out."

The line went dead.

He'd told her how he felt about her, and she'd shot him down.

Fuck. He hurled his phone against the wall, then turned and left the bathroom, diving right back into the party.

# CHAPTER FOURTEEN

**Her hand fisted his cock, her tits pressed against his** back. Sensation burned through him, rousing him from the deepest sleep. "Nicole, oh, Jesus, Nicole." God, he wanted her. And not just her hand. He wanted her mouth. He wanted inside her. God, he needed her so badly.

But something didn't feel right. The way she jerked him off. It was—too rough, too…his eyes shot open. What the fuck? Where was he?

He felt her pressed up against him—but no. It didn't smell like her. And those weren't her tits.

*What the fuck?*

He shot up, only then realizing he was on the edge of the mattress. No, couch. Falling onto the floor, he landed on something hard, cold. A beer bottle.

"Hey, baby." Kelsi lifted on an elbow. "Oh, my God, what happened? Are you okay? Get back up here. Let me finish you off."

He tucked himself back into his jeans, stood up. The world swayed, and his stomach flipped over. "What the hell're doing?"

"You were hard as a baseball bat. I was helping you out."

He got to his feet, his vision adjusting enough to see beer, vodka, and wine bottles littering the living area. Bowls and bongs everywhere. Someone was passed out under the kitchen table. A few other bodies curled together on the floor, against the wall. The whole place stank of body odor, pot, and beer.

Two days ago, his life had been so…sweet. Clean. Perfect. And now…Jesus, imagine if Nicole had come home with him? Had seen *this*.

Kelsi sat up, pulling her shirt off, revealing the huge globes of her breasts. "Come here, baby, it's all right." She held her arms out to him.

"I have a *girlfriend*, Kelsi." He leaned low, spoke quietly but deadly. "Stay away from me." He started for the bathroom, but she flew off the couch, following him.

"Would you shut up about the girlfriend already? You're fucking some girl at school, big deal. That has nothing to do with us." She grabbed the back of his shirt and yanked. He turned to face her, so damn sick of this life. "It's us, baby." Her eyes went hooded, as she pressed those naked tits up against him. "I can make you feel good. And I've missed you so much. No one treats me like you do."

He had to get out of there. He thought of Nicole—and fear skittered down his spine. He remembered calling her in the bathroom. Drunk. She'd hung up on him. Jesus Christ, he'd called her when he was *drunk*. She would hate that.

And even right then he was still drunk. He'd gotten completely trashed. He didn't want Nicole to know about this life—

*Then why am I living it?*

He strode back to the couch, snatched up Kelsi's T-shirt and tossed it at her. "Put it on so I can talk to you."

She held it up against her chest, standing there all defiant with her tangled, over-processed hair and smeared mascara.

"I should've talked to you before I left, but I didn't. At the time, I guess I thought we were on the same page. I thought you understood, but now I can see that was just chicken shit. Kels, we're over. Even if I didn't have Nicole, you and I are still over."

"Are you sure about that, Dyl? You got anyone else to keep an eye on your mom?" She lowered her arms, revealing those tits again.

A familiar uneasiness slid through him. He *didn't* have anyone else. Everyone but Kelsi had bailed on them long ago. He sat on the edge of the coffee table, knowing he was still too drunk to have this conversation. "You're right. I don't have anyone else. But I'm not going to pretend to want you to get that help. You've been a good friend to me, Kels. I'd like us to still be friends. But I'm serious about this girl." Even though he'd blown it so badly he didn't know if she'd take him back.

But, God, he hoped she'd take him back.

Kelsi made a sound of disgust. "That's so sweet, Dylan. I'm super happy for you. But don't forget who you're talking to. I know the truth. So, while I genuinely hope you have fun two thousand miles away in Disneyland, let's keep it real when we're together. I hope your little Disney Princess gives good head and all, but in four years, your scooter's going to turn into a pumpkin. You're going to come home and guess what? Your real life's going to be right here, just as you left it."

She flounced back on the couch, bunching her T-shirt in her hands. "Now go take a piss or whatever it was you were going to do and let's go to sleep. You don't want me touching the goods Princess Wilmington has recently sucked?" She shrugged. "We'll see how long that lasts. But I know you better than anyone. You won't be able to keep up the charade. How long can you fake the whole Prince Charming routine? I know you, Dylan. And you're going to want what we have together. The fact you're even worried about cheating on her—are you fucking serious? You're eighteen years old. You *should* be screwing around, getting it out of your system. I give you exactly what you need. Now let's get to sleep. We've got Mason Dean's turkey fry at noon."

She lay back on the couch, patting the space she'd made for him.

He turned and left the room.

When Dylan lifted the toilet seat, he caught a gleam of silver out of the corner of his eye. His phone lay on the floor by the waste basket. He grabbed it. Maybe Nicole had called back?

He opened it to find a text from her. Hope hammered in his chest.

*I'm sorry for the nail gun thing, but you have to know how I feel about you drunk dialing me.*

Yeah, he did. *Fuck*. He grabbed a quick shower and then headed outside. Kels had already fallen back asleep on the couch.

Hitting Nicole's speed dial, he headed down the stairs. Damn, it was cold this morning. But the fresh, brittle air cleared his head. He felt better, stronger.

"Hey." She didn't sound good. "I'm glad you called."

Relief flooded him. Just her willingness to talk. "I'm sorry for last night. I shouldn't have tried to talk to you when I was wasted." He found himself wandering the parking lot, looking for his truck. The truck he'd sold to pay bills before he'd left. *Shit.* It felt weird not having any wheels. Normally, he'd take off into the mountains.

"Dylan, I know what we have."

His heart kicked in his chest. She was back. His girl was back. She wasn't angry anymore. He waited for her to go on.

"So, I don't think you're hooking up with Kelsi."

He tensed. His mind told him to be happy with what she was saying, but his gut sensed something was wrong. "No, I'm not."

"But I don't *really* know because I don't know you. Maybe you *are* that guy."

Oh, shit. Where was she going with this? That soft, sweet voice had an edge in it. "You know me."

"I know the five percent you're willing to show me. But everything else is hidden, and unless you're willing to share it with me, then I don't see that we even have a relationship to end."

"Nicole."

"No, I know you're hung-over, and this isn't a good time to talk about this, but you called me, you want to talk, so I'm going to just say this. This is really hard for me because I'm crazy about you. No, it's more than that. I feel this connection with you, and I've never had it with anybody before, so believe me when I say, this is hard for me to do. But I want more—I need more from you. I'm sorry, but I know myself, and I can't settle for the five percent you're willing to give. Do you understand?"

"Yes." Of course he did.

"You warned me from the beginning, so I'm not blaming you. But after learning about a girlfriend you've had for two years, after finding out she knows all of you and I only know a tiny bit, I guess…I guess I just now understand what you were trying to tell me."

"Don't do this, Nicole." No, no, what was he saying? She was right. She *shouldn't* be with him. He should let it go. He needed to let it go. Focus on his mom, work, school, not a fucking *relationship*. The ninety-five percent she didn't know about? Was disgusting. "The five percent you have is the best part." Why was he pushing it? *Let it the fuck go.*

"Yeah, well, I don't want just the good parts. I want all of them. All of *you*." She paused. "Will you give them to me?"

This was it. The turning point. He could have his deep down, or he could let her go.

He thought of his mom, beaten unconscious in the parking lot of the Pit Stop two years ago. He thought of Kelsi, completely wasted, face in his lap, sucking him off before they both passed out. Nicole wanted to know *that* part of his life. Was he willing to let her see it?

"No."

And that was it. The end.

It sucked, but at least he'd done the right thing.

******

Gina came in the back door. "It's like walking into my own personal restaurant every time I come here. What is that yummy smell?"

"That's the sweet potato casserole." Nicole watched her dad roll out the dough for the crust for the pumpkin pie.

Gina leaned in and gave a loud, "Mwah," as she bussed cheeks, and then pulled off her red cashmere wrap. "Why does your kitchen smell so much better than mine?"

"Because your mom orders Thanksgiving dinner from

Dunbars." Brandon tromped up the basement stairs with three cases of beer.

"What can I do to help?" Gina hovered over Nicole's shoulder.

"Uh, take some of these for me?" Brandon said.

"You're the superstar athlete," Gina said. "Why go all candy-ass and ask for help?"

"You're standing right there. Doing nothing." He set the cases down next to the refrigerator.

"What is going on between you two?" Nicole couldn't make any sense of the underlying anger between the two of them.

Brandon's features turned crimson. He turned his back on them and squatted, tearing open the box and shoving bottles on the bottom shelf.

"Not a damn thing." Gina's fingers moved across the keypad of her cell phone.

Nicole figured she'd better change the subject. She'd talk to Gina privately. "How long can you hang here?"

"We're not eating till five-thirty, so I've got all day."

"Do you want to set the table?" Nicole knew her friend preferred design to cooking.

"Oooh, yeah. You guys are so weird. You're all about the food. You don't give a fig how anything *looks*." Casting a mischievous glance over her shoulder, she headed out into the dining room.

Nicole double-took when she noticed Brandon staring at her friend's ass in nothing but a pair of black leggings. She was about to say something, when her phone buzzed.

Dylan. *Can you talk?*

She shot off a reply. *Is there anything left to say?*
*What do you want to know?*

She froze. Did that mean what she thought it meant? Was he saying he would open up to her? She had to find out.

*Let me get the stuffing in the oven. One sec.*

She brought the casserole dish to the oven. "Guys, I'll be right back."

"Where you going?" Brandon asked, accusation in his voice as he tore open another box and shoved more beer bottles into the refrigerator.

"To make a quick phone call." She took in the kitchen. Turkey was in the oven. She had time before she needed to peel the potatoes or wash the green beans. Her dad had the pies covered—apple and two pumpkins. He wouldn't make the whipped cream until they were ready to eat the pie.

"You've been on that phone a lot this morning," her dad said.

Brandon cut her a look. She waited, almost hopeful they'd ask her something—anything—to take an interest in her life.

But nothing came. "Yeah. Friend from school. I'll be quick." She took her phone and went up to her room.

Dylan answered right away, his voice gravelly and tired. "Hey."

"You sound terrible." Her bare feet padded across the thick white carpet.

"I feel like shit."

Completely disgusted and one second away from killing the call, Nicole said, "That's a hang-over for you. Listen, I'm in the middle of cooking." She had zero patience for people who partied so hard they became sick the next day.

"I'm not talking about physically. I hate that I called you when I was drunk."

*Oh.* "No big deal." Forehead pressed to the window, she

took in the backyard—the pool and terrace, the gazebo, the broad expanse of green lawn.

"It is to you. I'm sorry."

"You seem to be sorry for a lot of things. You asked me to call you, so what's up?"

"Enough, Nicole."

Her head snapped up. She didn't say a word. His shift from apologetic to commanding unsettled her.

"I know I hurt you, but we're not going to get anywhere if you keep sniping at me. I'm sorry for the way I told you about Kelsi, I'm sorry for the way I left you at the airport, and I'm sorry for calling you when I was drunk. I can't take back any of that, but I'd like to go forward. Think you can give me a chance here?"

"I gave you a chance yesterday, and you didn't take it." She said quietly because Brandon had basically delivered the same message about sniping yesterday. It had made sense to her then, yet she couldn't seem to control herself. "You hurt me."

"Then show me hurt and not the fucking cold shoulder."

She closed her eyes, wishing she could be with him. It was so much simpler when they were wrapped up in each other under the covers. "Okay."

He blew out a tired breath. "Look, Nicole, I'm all fucked up over this. I can't…I don't know what to do. My mind tells me to let you go, but the rest of me—my fucking heart—just can't do it."

His heart? She couldn't believe Dylan McCaffrey was talking to her about his heart.

"But here's what I figured out last night. Whichever way I chose, I lose you. If I let you into my fucked up life or if I shut you out of it, either way you're gone. At least if I let you in, I have *some* chance of being with you. The other option leaves me no chance. So, I'm going to take my shot. If you still want me."

"Oh, I want you." She wanted him all in, not one foot out the door, but she'd take him. He was *trying.*

"Yeah?" He sounded as relieved as she felt. "And one other thing, no more drunk-dialing, I promise."

She felt a squeeze at the base of her spine. "Hey, careful, I do want to hear from you now and then."

"You'll hear from me all the time. I'm done partying."

Irritation flashed through her, and she turned from the window. "Okay, this…I'm not going to do this with you. I can't go there, with the promises and apologies. Seriously, Dylan, that will kill me."

"Exactly."

"No, Dylan, listen to me. This is the one thing I really can't handle. All the promises, the disappointments, the begging, the drama." She'd had a lifetime of it. "I can't go there with you. You can party as much as you want. Just don't do it around me."

"But I want to be around you. So I'm not partying."

"Dylan, no. I would never ask you to stop drinking for me. What kind of relationship is that if I'm telling you not to party?"

"The kind where I care about you more than I care about booze."

Her chest seized. Those were the words she'd wanted to hear from her mom, from Jonathan. She nearly reeled backward from the impact of them. "You don't have to do that. Let's not even talk about it." She couldn't bear the disappointment if she were to believe him and then he failed her. Like her mom and Jonathan had done a hundred thousand times.

"Nothing good comes from booze."

Tension gripped her spine—something in his tone made her think he'd done something bad the night before. God, what had he done? "You asked me what I wanted to know."

"I did."

Did she really want to know if he'd done something bad? Maybe he hadn't hooked up with someone. Maybe he'd done drugs. She *didn't know*. "Did something happen last night?"

"I partied too hard."

She wasn't stupid. She heard how guarded he sounded. "Dylan…just tell me. You had a lot of booze. Did something bad come from it?"

"No. Except I feel like shit today. And I hurt you."

Okay, she'd have to get more specific. God, she *hated* this game. "Did Kelsi spend the night?" Whoa, that came out aggressively. She hadn't even known how deeply that question was lodged into her gut until it popped out. But she had a right to know the truth.

"Yes."

"In your bed?" The pause told her everything. "Fuck you." And she hung up. *Oh, God, oh, God, oh, God.* He'd slept with his ex-girlfriend. He called her right back, but she ignored it. Deal-breaker. Total and absolute deal-breaker.

Too agitated to go back downstairs, she paced around her room. He called again. And then she got a voicemail message. Then, a text. She hated that he'd done that to her. Hated it. All those times he'd warned her off him.

Why hadn't she listened? This was her fault for ignoring what he told her. She knew that—you always had to listen to what a guy said. He was telling the truth. More texts came in. He was frantic.

Fine. She'd read them, but only so she could let him know to stop. She opened the text.

*Need you to hear me out. Talk to me.*

And another that said, *Ur killing me here.*

And a third. *I did not sleep with Kelsi. I don't want her.*

So, fine, she called him back.

"Nic. Jesus Christ, *stop that.* You're going to give me a fucking heart attack."

"Dyllie?" she heard a woman call. "What're you doing out here?"

"I'm on the phone," he said firmly. "I'll be in soon."

"Who're you talking to?" Was that his mom? She didn't sound young enough to be Kelsi.

"Is it Sawyer?" his mom asked. "Tell him to come over."

"Mom." His voice snapped like a branch.

"What? God, fine."

"Sorry about that." He came back on the line.

"Your mom?"

"Yeah. And, no, I didn't tell her about us. Believe me, you don't want her to know." He let out a shaky laugh.

"Did you sleep in the same bed with Kelsi?"

"We slept on the couch together."

She sucked in a breath. "Did you touch her?"

He paused. "No."

"Don't lie to me on a technicality."

"I don't lie. I don't have to. I own what I do. I didn't touch her because I don't want to. I'm not attracted to her. I want you, Nicole. Only you. How do I get through to you?"

"I believe you didn't sleep with her. I do. But I have to know what happened last night."

"Fuck. Do I really have to do this?"

"If we're going to have any kind of trust, then yes, you do."

He blew out a breath. "I woke up…she woke me up…" He paused. "I didn't even know I was on the couch with her. I was drunk, in a deep sleep. She was jacking me off."

"Did it feel good?"

"What do you think, Nicole? Yes, it felt good. Because I thought it was you."

"What did she say when you went, *Oh, Jesus, Nicole*?"

It took him a moment to figure it out, but when he did she was pretty sure he smiled. His tone changed, sounded lighter. "To be honest, I don't think she noticed. Either she didn't notice or she didn't care."

"Did you…finish?"

"No." He sounded outraged. "About one second after I said, *oh, Jesus, Nicole*, I realized it didn't feel right. It didn't feel like you. So I woke up and got off the couch and told her to knock it off."

"What did she say?"

"Come on, Nic. I didn't do anything. I told her it was over, and that I was serious about you. It won't happen again."

"You don't know that. What control do you have when you party?"

"I'm not drinking anymore, remember?"

"You can't make promises like that."

"I'm not an alcoholic, sunshine. I'm a social drinker. My friends party. I've never partied the way they do—didn't have the time or interest."

She didn't see him party much at school, so she believed him.

"You know," he said, quietly. "As a kid I learned to never

leave myself vulnerable. And to never get drunk unless I was surrounded by my friends. They had my back around all the sketchy people my mom brought over. But last night…" He sounded so disappointed.

"Your friend let you down."

"Big time. I'd told her about you. I'd told her it was serious."

It was serious? By the rush of blood to her ears, she realized how badly she'd needed to hear that he was as into it as she was. "She didn't care."

He was quiet.

"What did she say? I have to know what she's telling you, so I can tell you my side of things."

"She said Wilmington's like Disneyland. She says you're my Disney Princess."

"Meaning I'm not real? I'm some fantasy for you? College is some kind of escape from reality—as opposed to a bridge between the life our parents made for us and the life we build for ourselves? That's really sad that she sees college that way."

"But not that she sees you that way?"

"Sweet cheeks, I'll be whatever Disney princess you want me to be. I'll even buy the costume."

"Which one wears a really short skirt?"

She smiled, folding an arm across her stomach and touching her forehead to the window.

"Tell you the truth," he said, "I never really got hard for Disney characters."

"But those big eyes, and those perfect figures. And they're so docile. They never fight back."

"I'm pretty sure there aren't too many guys who want to give it to Snow White."

"But Ariel is so pretty."

"See, this is the thing girls don't get. It's not the pretty face that gets us. It's what we see in your eyes. The attitude, the spark. We want intelligence, because it means we're in for a fun challenge. We want spice."

"Mulan had spunk."

"Five minutes in a room with Cinderella, and I'd be looking up the skirts of her handmaidens."

"Ooh, then I want to work in Prince Charming's court. What else did Kelsi say?"

"She said in four years my scooter will turn into a pumpkin."

"At which point, you'll have to go back to Gun Powder and give your happily ever after to her?"

"That's what it sounded like." He actually sounded relieved.

"Okay, first of all, I'm not a damn princess."

He laughed.

"Secondly, God, Dylan why do these people want to hold you back? I don't understand. I don't know the whole story with your mom, but I do know she's a grown woman who's supposed to take care of *you*. Not the other way around. And what kind of life is it for either of you if you give up yours to take care of her? What a colossal waste of potential."

When he didn't say anything, she figured she'd overstepped her bounds. No one wanted to be told how to live his life. "I'm sorry about my inspirational speaker rant. I truly don't know your situation. You probably think I'm a terrible person for bailing on my mom."

"I think you're amazing. And I want you so badly right now I don't think I can stand to stay here one more minute.

I want to get on a plane and fly out there and get back in bed with you and kiss you all night long. My life here? It's dark, and it's ugly. And that includes my friends. You're my sunshine. You make me happy."

For the first time in days, peace spread through her. They'd fought for each other, and they'd won. She couldn't wait to get back to school and just be with him. Really be with him.

"It may be too good to be true, but I'll take it while I can have it," he said.

Oh, damn him. She closed her eyes against the rush of disappointment that bordered on pain.

He had to go and ruin it. Remind her she didn't have him. Not all the way. And if he didn't believe he could ever have her, then what did she do?

She'd hang in there. This connection they had? What else could she do?

Later that night, while everyone crowded in the kitchen to clean the dishes, her phone buzzed in her pocket. She finished scraping the leftover green beans into the glass storage container, put the lid on, and shoved it in the refrigerator so she could open Dylan's text.

*I changed my ticket. Coming back Saturday.*

She couldn't type her response quickly enough. *Expensive for one day.*

*Worth it. Want u.*

The smile spread across her face, heating her body, filling her with so much joy. *Want u 2.* And then she wrote again. *Give me your flight information, and I'll pick u up. Want to come to my house?*

*Already booked the shuttle. Don't think anyone will be back at the house yet, so rather be alone with u there. Good?*

"I'm guessing you worked it out with that guy?" Brandon looked over her shoulder.

She quickly typed, *So good*, and stowed her phone.

"What guy?" her dad said. "You're seeing someone?"

She nodded.

"I thought you said no drama?" Her dad looked surprised. "You didn't want to date?" Maybe he listened more than she thought.

"Why would she say that? She's in college." Her older brother Ryan leaned in the doorway. Emma, his model girlfriend, peeked around his muscled arm. "You gotta live it up while you can, squirrel."

She shot him a look. Why did he still use that nickname? She hadn't hid food in years.

Brandon winged an apple at him. "She's your sister, asshole. You don't want her to fuck around."

Ryan looked thoughtful. "True." He pushed off the wall. "Hey, we're out of here."

"You're not going to help with clean up?" Nicole asked.

"Gotta check in with her family." Emma stepped out from behind him and came into the kitchen.

She reached for Nicole, giving her a hug. "Thanks so much for dinner. Delicious as always."

"Thanks. Great to see you." Nicole watched them leave together.

"Asshole," Brendon called.

But Nicole didn't care. She was totally wrapped up in Dylan. He'd changed his ticket. That's how much he wanted to be with her.

It would work out with them. She knew it.

# CHAPTER FIFTEEN

**She'd showered, put on the yellow sundress, and aired** out her room. After all, they'd practically lived in it for three days.

*Where r u?* she texted him.

*On 134. Just passing the Freeze.*

Five minutes away. *I'll meet you in the parking lot. Outside Admissions? Or the gym?*

*No. Stay put. No screw-ups.* And then a second later. *Stay in the house.*

The jolt she got from his intensity set her pacing. Sydney had hired a cleaning crew over the holidays, so the place looked like a showcase home. She breathed in the scent of baking bread. She hadn't made a meal exactly, but she'd warmed a baguette, put together a platter of fruit, cheese, crackers, and nuts.

They'd take it to bed. Her blood heated at the thought.

*Turning into Wilmington. Don't move.*

She smiled. *I might take a little nap.*

*That's fine, sunshine. Just make sure ur not wearing panties.*

*Oh, didn't I tell u? Bought us purity rings yesterday! Yay! Now we can prove our true love for each other.*

*WTF???*

*Need to know you want me for me. Not just my ass.*

*Not just your ass, sweetheart. Love ur tits, too.*

*Think how much sweeter it'll be when u finally get to touch them again after we're married!*

When he didn't respond, she worried she'd freaked him out. Probably not a good idea to joke about marriage to a guy who only recently decided to give a relationship with someone outside his world a go. No matter how ridiculous the whole Disneyland idea, she knew it had to have rattled him. Because, on some level, he believed it. Kelsi had given voice to his fear.

She should diffuse the tension, say something else. Way to ruin their reunion, getting him all wound up over nothing.

Just as she composed her text, she heard his voice outside. "Nicole!"

She ran to the door, flung it open.

He strode up the walkway, leapt onto the porch, and tossed his bag into the house. Leaning down, he whisked her off her feet, his mouth finding hers. He kissed her like a man possessed.

Setting her down, he kicked the door shut and locked it, then cupped her face. "Missed you."

She couldn't speak through the hard knot in her throat. His big hands swept down her back, gripping her ass, and he lifted her. Her legs automatically wrapped around him, as he carried her to the couch.

With a grunt, he fell back onto the cushion, holding her tightly against him. His mouth fused with hers as he gave her a searing kiss. After crazy, long moments of feeling nothing but the warm, wet heat of his mouth, she pulled back. Foreheads touching, breaths mingling, she sighed. "Missed you, too."

His hands yanked up her dress, coming to rest on her bare bottom. "Oh, fuck, yes." He cupped her cheeks. "So sweet." His body shuddered, as he squeezed her flesh, his hot breath at her neck. "You feel so good." Sliding lower on the couch, his hips rocked up. He tipped his head back to look at her. "*This*." She'd never seen him look so happy, so completely at peace.

She leaned into him, fingers sliding into his hair and whispered, "Us."

His hands gripped her hips, pressing her down on him, and then they slowly glided up her body, fingers tracing her ribs, until he reached her breasts.

Chill bumps burst in a shower of sparks along her arms, and she shuddered at his gentle, reverent touch. Lightly, he cupped her breasts, stroking the undersides, fingertips brushing her nipples. He held her gaze, never wavering, as his palms rounded the curves and gently squeezed.

Her eyelids fluttered closed, her hips rocked, and she thought she might die from the sweetly erotic sensation of his touch.

And then he pinched her nipples, and a shock of lust struck her core. She jerked against him, eyes opening. His smile looked painful. "Take this off."

She pulled the dress over her head, tossed it aside.

"Look at you."

Look at her indeed, naked on his lap, his big hands covering her breasts, her nipples peeking between his fingers.

"I need you." He thrust up, pressing his erection to her. Desire flashed through her body.

She reached between them and unbuttoned his jeans. His ass lifted off the cushion, and he shoved down his pants and boxers. She grasped him, guiding him to her entrance.

Before he slid inside, he clamped a hand at the back of her neck and brought their mouths together. Just when she relaxed against him, lost herself in the hot, wet heat of his mouth, he rammed his hips up into her as he brought her down hard on his erection, fusing their bodies. She gasped, tearing her mouth off his, and clung to the back of the couch as he filled her up completely. And then she started moving on him, every slide lighting up her nerves, the friction creating sparks that set her on fire. It felt so good she could barely breathe.

His hand came between them, a finger finding her clit and swirling. He brought his mouth to her ear. "I'm not gonna last, sunshine."

Clutching the back of the couch, her knees digging into the cushions at either side of his hips, she rocked hard and fast on him, electricity flashing across her skin.

"Holy fuck." His fingers curled into the flesh of her hips, little beads of perspiration popping out on his forehead.

And when the first swell of her orgasm rose, that hint of coalescence, she ground down on him. His legs went rigid as he braced his feet on the floor and his hands clamped down on her hips as he held her in place and thrust up into her. Her head tipped back, as a cry tore out of her throat.

He shouted, thrusting in hard, powerful jabs. "Jesus, fuck." When he finished, he bound her in his arms, tight to his chest, and breathed heavily in her ear. "Let's go upstairs, sunshine. I'm greedy for you."

Holding her to him tightly, he lifted off the couch, carrying her up the stairs. His mouth turned at her ear. "Thank you for giving me more."

A sharp sting hit her right in the center of her chest. She

wanted to think he meant coming back to Wilmington a day early, but she suspected he meant in his life. Because he was so convinced they'd never last.

Damn him.

She'd prove him wrong.

******

Dylan woke up feeling cold. He opened his eyes to an expanse of white sheets nearly glowing in the shaft of moonlight from the crack in the curtains. He listened for sounds but heard nothing. They'd slept together every night since Thanksgiving. He wasn't used to waking up without her. Where had she gone?

He got up, put on his gym shorts, and checked the bathroom. Not a sign of her. He headed down the stairs, found the white light from the kitchen spilling onto the foyer tiles.

His girl stood at the granite island, brow taut with concentration as she swirled the spatula around the silver bowl. Sliding his hands around her waist, he breathed in her warm, sweet scent and kissed her cheek. "What's got you up?"

"I was thinking about lemon cupcakes."

He smiled. That was what she thought about at two in the morning.

"You know what's missing?"

"What, sunshine?" He slid his hands under her T-shirt so he could feel the warmth of her skin.

"You know chocolate lava cake? That yummy molten chocolate in the center?"

He nodded, kissing her neck, loving the softness of her skin.

"Imagine cutting into a springy, moist lemon cake and having warm lemon custard ooze out. A sprinkling of confectioner's sugar, and then a drizzle of raspberry sauce on the plate under it. Does that sound good?"

His hands pushed under the elastic of her panties and cupped her between the legs. The slick moisture on his fingers made his cock go hard and lodge into the crack of her ass.

"Oh," she said, all breathy.

"That sounds really good, sunshine. Are you making it now?"

"Not right now."

"That's good. So I don't need to turn off the stove or the oven?"

She shook her head, pressing back into him.

"Why are you thinking about lemon custard right now?" His hands pulled out of her panties, stroking up her stomach to cup her bare breasts. Holy fuck, the shot of lust that struck him just from the feel of her soft round curves, heavy in his hands. His dick surged between her legs, as he caressed those firm globes.

"I, um…it's hard to think when you're touching me like that."

He stepped away from her, smoothing her T-shirt down her stomach. Leading her to the bench seat, he sat down and pulled her onto his lap. "Talk to me?"

She sighed, wrapping her arms around his neck, dropping her forehead against his temple. Her silky hair brushed over his eyelashes, tickled his nose. He tucked it behind her ear.

"We're doing fish in lab today."

"Got any memories of slimy fish?"

"No." She smiled softly.

"Stinky fish?"

She turned to him, pressing a kiss to his mouth. "But I don't know what he's going to do to me."

"In front of the class?"

She nodded.

"What would freak you out the most?"

"The most? Well, the most would be if he makes me take a fish out of a tank and kill it."

"Seems unlikely. What's the second worst thing he could do?"

She smiled, running her finger along his bottom lip, making his skin tingle. "Make me fillet it. You know, chop off the head, cut off the scales."

"That seems less unlikely. Can you do it?"

"I mean, I don't know if I can do it without getting sick to my stomach, but I *will* do it if he asks me. It's just that I think he's more interested in getting me to throw up. He seems to get a perverse pleasure out of my discomfort."

"What're you worried about?"

She kissed his cheek, rubbing her nose softly over his skin. "I honestly don't think anyone gets me better than you do. It's the weirdest thing. But, um, I guess I'm worried that he already knows he's not choosing me for the program, and he's just getting his kicks out of watching me squirm."

Dylan thought about it and figured she could be right.

"If I knew for sure he'd made his decision, I wouldn't let him treat me this way. But I *don't* know, so I have to go along with it. And that sucks."

"He's an ass if he's already decided. It's only December, and you're working hard to overcome your anxieties. He sees that. Is it easier to handle meat now?"

"Yes."

"See? You're acclimating."

"Gina agrees with James, that I should tell him about my childhood."

"You said he didn't want to hear your personal stories."

"Yeah, but he's deliberately playing with me, so they think if he understood why I get upset, he'd back off."

"What do you think?"

"I think a guy who would try to get a girl to throw up in class isn't capable of compassion, so it would only give him more reason to toy with me." She shifting, leaning back against the wall, stretching her legs across his lap. His hand slid between her thighs, and she turned just a little, tilting towards him. "Tell me what you think."

"I don't think he sees a spoiled princess because that's not who you are. I think he sees determination. Because that's what anyone looking at you would see. He might not understand your reaction in class, but he's fascinated by your response to it. You're not throwing tantrums, and you're not refusing to touch raw meat. You clearly have an aversion, but you're fighting through it."

She looked anguished.

"Hey." He drew her closer, scanning her features to figure out what she was feeling. "What did I say?"

"You said everything right. I just…" She kissed him, cupping his jaw and stroking her thumbs over his cheeks. "I don't know what to do with all these feelings. For you. You won't let me in all the way, so I have to hold myself back, you know? But then you say things like that, and you…" She looked down to where his hand gripped her inner thigh. "You touch me the way you do, and God, Dylan, what am I supposed to do?"

"I'm here. I'm *in*."

"Yes, but you tell me all the time that you can't really be with me, that it's just temporary. It's like you're on loan here until your real life calls you back."

"Well, there's truth in that. But I'm with you here and now." He tipped her chin, forcing her to look at him, to see he was giving her all he could. "Right now, I'm with you all the way."

"I know." She looked away, and he couldn't help the rush of frustration that tore through him. In a perfect world would he give her more? Fuck, yeah. But in his world? This was all he had to give.

But he wanted to finish their conversation, not worry about things he couldn't change. "So, when are his office hours?"

"Um…" She looked pensive. "Monday, Wednesday, and Friday. He's in from eleven to noon."

He did a quick scan of their schedules in his mind. "We're both free tomorrow at eleven, so let's go then."

"You're going with me?"

He brushed the hair off her face, cupping her chin to look in her eyes. "I won't go in with you, but I'll walk with you and wait outside."

Tears glistened but didn't spill.

"What, sunshine? You're killing me here."

"No one's ever…" Her breath hitched and she blinked back the tears. "You said, *We*, like we're in it together. I've never had that before. I just…sometimes I feel so close to you. And it feels so good, like I'm not alone."

"You're not alone." She had a great family, great friends. "You've always had close friends."

"Gina's the best, but she's got her own life, her own issues."

"So do I." Like he had to remind her.

"Yeah, but from the moment I met you, when you didn't even know me, you claimed me. Like we became a *we* right then. I've never been a *we*."

"You were with Jonathan for almost four years." He didn't know why he kept pressing when he felt it, too. But he *did* want to press. He wanted to know, because he couldn't explain it either.

"He never looked out for me like you do. I took care of him. Helping him fight his demons."

"I battle demons."

"Yes, but you do it while holding my hand."

Fuck, oh, fuck, her words struck deep. He'd never had anyone's hand to hold. Not ever. Jesus, she was right. From the moment he'd met her in the hallway outside their rooms at the Scholar House he'd felt something—a startling awareness. But when she'd stood up for him on the lawn? From that moment on, they'd been connected—they'd been holding hands.

"I love the way we're in this together," she said. "It's like we're both strong people, handling all the crazy stuff in our lives on our own, and then we find each other and it's such a relief to have someone to just…be with you while you go through it."

Emotion surged so hard and fast it made his heart hurt. He kissed her, his hand sliding up higher between her thighs, feeling the heat and dampness. He couldn't stop himself from pushing a finger under the elastic of her panties, slipping into her slick core. She squirmed restlessly on his lap, rubbing against his erection. His hips jerked up, grinding into her warm skin. Fuck, he wanted her so badly. All the damn time.

She shuddered in his arms when he found her clit and stroked it. "Take off your shirt," he said, though it came out more of a growl.

Sitting back, she tore it off, arching her back. He greedily pulled her nipple in with his tongue. God, she was so responsive, the way she moaned and writhed on his lap.

He let his thumb swirl around her clit, slid his fingers deep inside so he could feel her slick heat. When her body rolled and she let out a breathy moan, he knew she was getting close. And when she sucked in a breath, when her legs straightened, her toes curled into the cushion, when her nipple tightened into a hard bead, he knew she was coming apart. He pulled his mouth off her so he could watch her features tighten into sheer ecstasy, as her body shuddered.

And then she collapsed against him, draping herself over him, and he felt her heartbeat against his own.

"Upstairs, now." Wild with need, he practically lifted her off his lap.

She got up, grabbing her T-shirt. When she didn't put it on, he snatched it, shoved it over her head. "Cover up." And then he grabbed her hand and led her up the stairs. Shutting the bedroom door behind him, he flicked on the desk lamp because he wanted to see her—them—joined in every way possible. She tossed off her shirt, shucked off her panties, and started crawling onto the bed. He grabbed her hips, pulled her back, and slid inside her.

He thought of what Kelsi had said, how he held himself back around Nicole. And maybe he did. He figured his white trash upbringing informed everything he did, including how he fucked.

But Nicole wasn't his Disney Princess. And she hadn't balked at anything they'd done together. She'd been in it all the way—just as wild, just as frenzied. And so he tilted her ass higher, held her in place, and thrust into her. When her back arched, when her fingers curled into the duvet, he knew. It wasn't white trash to love her the way he did. It was just them. She made him crazy. She made him let go completely.

And it was such a relief to just be himself, act purely out of need and want, that he started pounding into her, shutting down his mind, immersing himself in the intense heat and tight, wet glove of her pussy, the sight of that gorgeous ass, the cheeks shaking with abandon at his every thrust. He squeezed her flesh, loved the firm feel of it, so he did it again and again. And, Jesus Christ, he'd never felt anything so good, so insanely erotic in his life.

He leaned over her, his chest on her back, and his palm splayed out on her pelvis, holding her tightly against him, his middle finger sliding into her folds and immediately finding her clit.

She moaned, her ass hitching higher, thrusting back harder, pushing tight against him so he could slam into her in tight, short thrusts, until he fucking exploded inside her.

Nothing had ever felt so good. Nothing. His cock pulsed, a never-ending orgasm. *Jesus fucking Christ.*

She pushed forward, flattening on the mattress, panting. "Holy cow."

He had no words. Collapsing beside her, he dragged her up against him, and closed his eyes.

Just as he drifted off, fear shimmered through him like heat radiating off asphalt. The heavy weight of sleep lifted with the realization of how attached he was getting to her. *Not good.*

What would happen when he had to let her go? *I don't*

*have to think about that now.*

Not yet anyway.

A buzzing sound awakened him. His phone, set on vibrate, rattled around on her desk. He reached across her to grab it, started to roll out of bed, when she tugged on him.

"Kelsi?" He quickly read Nicole's expression, but it wasn't jealousy he saw. She wanted him to stay and deal with his call. She didn't want him hiding from her.

"Dyl, listen, things are totally fucked up here." Kelsi sounded freaked out.

He sat up, body alert and primed for action. "What's going on?"

"Your mom. She texted me. Asked me to come get her. She was in a field. You know where the Sunoco used to be?"

"Is she hurt?"

Nicole sat up, clutching the sheet to her chest.

"No, but she's been kicked out of the apartment. She's got nowhere to go."

"So she wanted money?"

"No, she wants to crash at my parent's place. She's pretty fucked up."

"Drugs?"

"Yeah."

"What kind?"

"I don't know. She's passed out in my car right now. I can't get her into the house by myself."

"What do you want me to do?" He could call Brian. But it was four in the morning back home, and Brian had probably just gone to sleep. He worked as a bouncer at the Pit Stop.

"Well, I want you to be here, for God's sake. I can't do this myself."

"I can't be there, Kels."

"She's *your* mom."

"I know that. Let me call Brian. He'll come and get her."

"Brian lives at home, Dylan. His parents hate your mom. They're not going to let her into their house. Besides, his grandma moved in last month. There's no room."

"Well, I don't know what to tell you. Can you let her sleep it off in the car?"

"Oh, come *on*. It's twenty degrees out here. I'm not sitting in my car with the heat on while your mom sleeps it off."

"I'm sorry, Kels. Can you take her to a motel and let her stay there a few nights? I'll pay for it."

"This isn't working, Dylan." Her voice grew shrill. "I know you want to dance around the ballroom with your Disney princess, but you've got shit going on here that you have to take care of. I mean, I'm here for you. I am. And I'm happy to help. But I need you here, too." She paused. "You can't just throw money at us."

*Us*. Fuck. He didn't want Kelsi to be part of his family, his problem. But what else could he do? He had no one else to help him. He glanced at Nicole. With a calm expression, she had a hand on his back, letting him know she was there for him.

But she *wasn't* there for him. No one was. No one could help him with his goddamn problem because it wasn't anyone else's responsibility.

And in this moment he perfectly understood the division between Wilmington and Gun Powder. Kelsi might have a personal agenda, but she was right. Five minutes ago, wrapped in Nicole's arms, he'd felt whole and perfectly happy. Safe and clean. And if he had a choice, he would choose her. Of course he would choose this future over his real one.

But Nicole would never fit in Gun Powder. She'd never be part of his family. Picking up his mom in a field littered with broken glass and hubcaps, sitting in a car with her while she slept it off? No fucking way. Even if she told him she wouldn't mind, he wouldn't do that to her. She deserved so much better than that. He would *never* expose her to the ugliness of his world.

His world was divided cleanly in half. He'd already made the decision not to feel guilty for this half, the one he shared with Nicole, but the only way to handle the other half meant dropping out of school. Enrolling at Boulder next fall.

Nicole leaned against him, wrapping her arms around him and resting her head on his shoulder.

*No.* He wasn't going to give her up. And he wasn't dropping out of school. He would find a way to make this work. "Take her to a motel. The one by the park. I'll text you my debit card number."

"You can't afford this, Dylan."

"I'll get another job."

"How many jobs are you going to get before you figure out that throwing money at her isn't the answer? You need to be here to take care of her."

"And give up my education? So that, what? I can work in a gas station and make minimum wage the rest of my life?"

"You don't need to be the president of a corporation, Dylan. You can go to community college for two years, transfer to CU, get a job here in town."

"I don't want to do that."

"Okay, great, you don't *want* to do that. So explain to me

how it's going to work? After you've paid for this motel? Then what? What about the next time she's passed out in a field at four in the morning? Am I supposed to come get her? I mean, I will. You know I'm here for you, Dyl. But, come on."

"I know, I know. Look, I'll be home for Christmas break in a couple weeks, and it's a long one. Over a month. I'll deal with it then."

"Fine. But you know as well as I do, play time's coming to an end."

# CHAPTER SIXTEEN

**With her pretty mouth wrapped around his cock, Dylan** couldn't think about how many minutes he had left to catch the shuttle. Steam filled the bathroom, hot water hammered his back, and his knees shook. Jesus, mother of God, Nicole sucked him deep, her tongue swirling just under the head.

The feel of her fingers digging into his ass, her mouth sucking him deeper into her mouth, sent him shooting into the stratosphere. He shouted so loud his voice echoed off the walls. He watched his glistening cock slide out of her mouth, loved the sexy look in her eyes, and couldn't bear the fact he was leaving her for five and a half weeks.

Helping Nicole to her feet, he kissed her voraciously. The idea of not seeing her—of possibly never seeing her again—brought out the beast in him. Made him want to kick through the shower door and tear the vanity out of the wall.

"I'm going to miss you." She snuggled against him.

She'd never know how much he appreciated her lack of drama. Sure, she didn't like not being able to see him for the entire winter break, but she didn't throw a fit. She made no demands on his time. She understood—to the extent she ever would—his situation.

"I wish I could drive you." Getting out of the tub shower, she gazed up at him, offering a weak smile.

But she couldn't. She had two more finals and a paper due. He'd taken one of his tests early so he could get home sooner.

Without talking, they dressed. He took her hand, as they headed down the stairs. At the front door, he dropped his duffle, cupped her face, and kissed her senseless. When he pulled away, she drew her lips into her mouth. He could see the strain as she swallowed back emotion. And then he left.

No promises, no tears.

And no goodbyes.

The cold air stiffened his fingers in the unheated warehouse.

"You're going to work yourself to death."

Dylan ignored his uncle, hauling the box he'd just labeled to the loading dock. Setting it on top of the stack beside the door, he quickly strode back to find his uncle still standing there.

"You don't have to work this hard over your winter break," his uncle said. "You know I'd give you money. Your aunt and I would give you anything you need for college."

The qualifier—*for college*—wasn't lost on him. His family wouldn't give money if his mom could somehow get her hands on it. But that was what Dylan needed. Cash to keep a roof over her head and food in her refrigerator.

Dylan focused on taping the next box shut, then got to work on the address label.

His uncle blew out a frustrated breath. "How is she?"

If he'd cared, he wouldn't have bailed on her the first time she'd relapsed. *Second,* he reminded himself, remembering her stumble over the summer. But maybe if

Uncle Zach hadn't bailed, if he'd given her a little support, he could've helped her find her way back to sobriety.

*Could* she find her way back to sobriety? In all his life she never had.

Not that it mattered. The *only* thing that mattered was helping her. And he just couldn't understand how his family could leave her care on his shoulders, but whatever. It was what it was.

A hand clamped on his shoulder but gave no resistance when Dylan pulled away. Dylan looked up to see his uncle's hardened expression.

"Put the tape dispenser down."

Since the man paid him a generous wage, Dylan did as requested, then straightened to his full height.

"When we cut her off, it's not because we don't care. It tears your aunt apart to see your mom living the way she does. But giving her money doesn't help her. You know that."

"I'm not here to talk about my mom."

"No, you're here to earn money for her."

*Oh, fuck this shit.* Dylan was tired of the elephant in the room. Time to just throw down. "You know, maybe if you and my aunt hadn't taken my mom's inheritance, I wouldn't *need* to earn money for her."

Shock gripped the man's features. "What the hell are you talking about?"

"If you'd given her her share when she'd asked, she'd have a house to live in, and I wouldn't have to work my entire vacation to make enough money for her rent."

"She *got* her share of the estate. Everyone did, as stipulated in the will. Are you talking about the ranch? Your mom wanted us to sell it so she could have the money. Her sister and brothers wanted to keep it in the family. So we bought her out of her fifth, even when none of us could afford it. She got everything that was coming to her. Didn't you know all this?" He shook his head, looking off somewhere, clearly unhappy. "Dammit, boy. All these years, you've been buying her sh—"

His uncle cursed under his breath. "Excuse me while I try to find my *nice* words, as your aunt likes to call them. But I don't have a whole lot of them where your mom's concerned."

Honestly, Dylan didn't know what to think. The idea that his mom blew through the inheritance, all while telling him she couldn't afford the instrument rental fee he needed to play in the school band or the uniforms he needed to participate in school sports…that they couldn't *eat* that week…Jesus, he wasn't sure he could handle knowing that about her.

But he guessed he needed to know. "You gave her the money?"

"*I* didn't do it. Your aunt and I have no power. The estate was divided five ways. Your mom got her share."

Dylan stood there, letting it all sink in. He looked down at his boots, letting the truth slowly form in his mind. His mom had run through all that cash to pay for her drugs and alcohol. The ground became a little shaky, and he reached for the wall of boxes. "Maybe it's in a savings account."

"Bullshit." His uncle's voice boomed in the huge warehouse. Other workers stopped what they were doing to look over. "Goddammit. That was not a nice word. Nor was it my inside voice."

Dylan just looked at him like he was crazy.

His uncle shook his head. "Too many years with a damn

preschool teacher." Then the familiar look of pity took hold of his rugged features. "I'm sure glad you had the balls to bring it up with me or you never would've known the truth."

"I don't know whether I'm glad I asked or not."

"I can understand that. I just hope that now that you *do* know, you'll consider coming back to us. We miss you, son. The ranch…it's your home, too. You've still got your own room there, and it's yours to use any time you like."

"If I come without my mom."

"Yes. Without your mom. And I do not feel bad about that decision. None of us does. And I'm pretty sure you're starting to see why. The only thing we feel bad about is that you're stuck taking care of her."

*Stuck?* This was his *mom.* "What choice do I have?" And, dammit, he really needed an answer.

"Well, now, son, that's the thing. You do have a choice. All this money you're earning for your mom? I think you know where it goes. You get that, right? That your money enables her to buy the booze and drugs? It's not making her stronger—you don't see her relieved and thankful to have a place to live, do you? It's not giving her the foundation to go out and make a better life for herself. It only fuels her addiction."

"You think this is new to me? It's not. But if I stop taking care of her…" His throat tightened so hard it hurt.

His uncle stood there a moment, and then he clapped a hand on Dylan's shoulder. "I know it scares you to picture her living on the streets, shacking up with that drug dealer she's been hanging around again, but son, even if you bought her a mansion and had it fully staffed, you couldn't stop her from making the same choices she's making now."

He'd heard it all before, but the same stab of fear gutted

him every time. "I get that, but I'm not like you. I can't live with myself knowing she's on the street."

"I live with myself just fine. Because when we let her in our lives, she destroys us. Takes us right down with her." His eyes narrowed. "And that is not acceptable." Then, his features softened. "Come on, boy, of course it cuts me up to see how she's living. But it's her *choice*. I live with myself because I know we tried everything. How many interventions did we have for her? Hell, son, you were there. Crying your eyes out when you were not even ten years old and she was screaming like a lunatic when we tried to get her help. No boy should have to go through that. We pooled our money and got her in rehab, only to have her walk out after three days. I paid for the next one myself—and I did it for *you*. She didn't last a week. Dylan, come on, you're nearing nineteen. Honestly, you're scaring the hell out of us."

He stilled, cocking his head, hyper aware of the tension on his uncle's features, the harsh breaths he took, the tight set of his shoulders. Yeah, he'd heard this lecture before, but he'd never seen his uncle so worried.

"When you went off to college, we were so damn proud of you. For the first time in I don't know how long, we could breathe. We could sleep straight through the night."

"Then why did you bail on her? If you'd been there, you could've helped her get back to her meetings."

"Come on, boy. Did you hear anything I just said? We've tried. Over and over. It doesn't work. It doesn't stick." His uncle tipped his head back, he scrubbed his face. "We love you. We'd do anything to help you, but you just won't see it. You won't let go of your mom."

"She's my *mother*. I'm all—"

"Stop right there. You hear how twisted that sounds? She's your mother, all right. So shouldn't *she* be bending over backwards to take care of *you*? And if she is all alone it's because no one will let her steal from them anymore. Why are you so willing to let her destroy you? Why is her life more important than yours?"

"This isn't the point. The point is that she has no one else. I can't abandon her. I have to do something." What, though? *What can I do?*

"Dammit, Dylan. Listen to yourself. Don't you see the way she manipulates you? That you believe *you* have to do something? No, son, *she* has to do something. *She* has to take responsibility."

"Well, she isn't, okay?" *Therefore, I have to.* Everyone liked to talk at him, but no one offered solutions.

"I don't know how to get you to see it." His uncle scratched the back of his head, staring down at his boots. "I can't just stand here and let you waste your life." His jaw hardened. "You know how I know you're something special?"

He didn't give a shit. It didn't solve his problem. Dylan reached for the tape dispenser, but his uncle's hand blocked him.

"Because after you stole your aunt's car, you never got into trouble again. Your whole ugly history with vandalism, theft, getting into fights, it ended. Just like that."

Dylan looked away. Facing his uncle that day had sickened him. Knowing he'd betrayed his family had made him hate himself. He vowed that day he'd never cross those lines again. And he hadn't. He'd just worked his ass off to make enough money to support her.

Money she used to buy drugs.

"You were fourteen years old, and you could have easily followed in your mom's footsteps. Why wouldn't you? The life—the sick bastards—she exposed you to? Yeah, you could've gone down that road. Ended up just like her. But you didn't. Instead, you got some steel in your spine and forged your own path."

His uncle's gaze turned hard, intense. Like he wanted to drill the message into his brain.

"Unlike your mom, you've got a moral compass. After you stole that car, you set up boundaries for yourself. That showed us all what you were made of. Dylan, you've got to know, we're rooting for you. You impress the hell out of us."

He appreciated hearing that. He did. But it didn't offer a *solution.*

His uncle sighed, scrubbed his face. "And now you've got a great chance to make something of yourself. We don't want to see you blow it. Son, every time you do something for her, you cheat her of having the ability to do it for herself. Every time you give her money, you're keeping her an addict. You want her to change? Then give her a reason to. *You* change. If she wants you in her life, then she's gonna have to do things differently. Make different choices. Give her the chance to decide which is more important to her. The drugs or her boy."

He turned sharply to look at his uncle. His uncle had nailed it. That was it, right there. That's what it all boiled down to.

But dammit all to hell—was he ready to find out the answer?

Dylan checked his phone. Nothing from his mom. He hadn't heard from her in three hours. Excusing himself from the kitchen table, he made his way through the rowdy crowd to get some quiet in the hallway outside the bathrooms.

Living with Kelsi and her parents wasn't working for his mom. It put a strain on her because she had to be on her best behavior or risk getting kicked out, and she didn't handle stress well. Obviously.

And Nicole certainly didn't appreciate *him* staying with Kelsi's family. But, as Kelsi constantly reminded him, he couldn't think about Nicole just then. He had a huge problem to handle and no real options. He wasn't wasting the money he'd earned the past two weeks on a motel. He'd found some trailer homes to rent in a safe-looking park outside Carbondale but doubted his mom would live by herself so far from her friends.

But he did know his mom couldn't keep staying with Kelsi's parents.

Did this mean he had to quit school and get a full-time job to pay for rent and bills and food? His gut screamed no because, come on, where the hell would that lead?

A couple of the guys he'd grown up with got up when they heard a Limp Bizkit song, all of them completely wasted. They grabbed the nearest girls, grinding on them, and Kelsi stumbled her way through the crowd to get in on it.

It struck Dylan right then, as he watched his friends party the same way they had throughout high school, how familiar it all felt. He'd only had a few months away, but he just didn't want to be part of this scene anymore.

Pulling up his phone, he texted Sawyer.

*Let's get out of here. Meet you outside.*

As he headed for the door, he tried to get Kelsi's attention to let her know he was leaving, but she had her head tilted back as she ground her pelvis into some guy he didn't recognize.

And then he saw Sawyer with his usual swagger and cockiness making his way across the living room. The moment he saw Dylan, he raised a hand.

Once they reached each other, Sawyer dangled his keys. "Let's ride."

They headed outside into the fresh but icy cold air, and Dylan was relieved to have this time alone with his closest friend. As they trampled down the metal stairs in their boots, Dylan said, "Hey, you never told me how school went." His breath came out a pure white fog.

"Good." Sawyer shrugged. "You know."

"No, I don't. You haven't said shit about it." They hadn't talked much while his friend had been in motorcycle repair school.

"What's to tell?"

"It was your dream, man. You finally did it. So, how come you're back working for your dad?"

"It's *winter.* There're no motorcycles to repair in Colorado."

"You could've stayed in Florida. What's keeping you here?"

He shrugged again. "Family."

"We always said we'd get out of here. See the world. Do shit."

"I did shit. I went to school in Florida for three months." Finally, he cracked a smile. At his truck, he hit the keypad and the locks popped up. "We gonna talk, or we gonna ride?"

"Ride." Dylan jerked the door open. "Cold as shit out here." He got into the truck, with the crumpled fast food bags and engine parts littered everywhere, and it hit him again, the sameness of it all. He was back in the world he'd grown up in, but for some reason it no longer fit.

Some reason? How about Nicole? Because it didn't matter that he'd only known her a few months, she'd gotten deep inside him. She'd become a flickering light, a constant reminder of what he could have. If he could only figure how to manage his mom.

As they headed down the street, the glove box popped open and boxes of chew tumbled out. "Still a slob."

"Give me a break, man. You've been gone three months." At the stop sign, Sawyer looked in both directions. Left would take them to the mountains—a long drive they'd fill with music, conversation, and a lot of laughter. Right would take them back into town—with a stop at the diner, where they'd find others to hang out with.

Sawyer turned right. "Roads are closed up around the Pass. Shit ton of snow up there. So, how's school?"

"It's good. I like it."

"Yeah? What're the girls like?"

Dylan ran a finger over his top lip, not sure what to say.

"What's that expression?"

"What expression?"

Sawyer stepped on the brake, jerking them to a stop in the middle of Pueblo Boulevard.

"What're you doing?" Dylan snapped.

"You got a girl."

He looked away, only because he couldn't stop the smile. "Yeah."

"What the fuck, man? That expression—you're serious."

"Yeah, I'm serious."

"Then what are you doing back in Gun Powder living

with Kelsi fucking Reynolds?"

"My mom."

Sawyer's expression—man, it gutted him, knowing his closest friend didn't get it, either. Only Kelsi seemed to understand Dylan's responsibility.

Someone honked behind them. Sawyer opened his window and motioned for the driver to go around them. The engine roared as the truck passed, guys hanging out the window swearing and giving them the finger.

Sawyer laughed. "Perkins and Daughtry."

"You know I can't bail on my mom."

"What I know is that she's never gonna let you do shit in life, and that's fucked up." The moment Dylan opened his mouth to argue, Sawyer held up his palm. "Stop. Forget it. Look, you're my brother, man, and I'm with you no matter what. Let's just drop it and go have a fuckin' burger."

A Florida Georgia Line song came on, and they didn't talk again until they reached the diner. As soon as Sawyer angled into a spot in front, Dylan got out of the truck. Motion across the street caught his eye. Bodies entangled, an elbow cocked back, a punch to the gut.

Sawyer followed his gaze. "What the fuck? Dude's hitting a woman."

They raced across the street, dodging traffic. A couple other guys mobilized, too, so when they got to the scene, the victim threw her head back and screamed.

It was his mom.

Dylan started for the bastard—realized right away it was Jeff Blakely. But Sawyer gave him a shove in his mom's direction. "You take care of her. We got him."

Sawyer and the others took off after Jeff, leaving Dylan alone with her. He held onto her shoulders. She turned away from him, tears shining on her face. She reeked of booze. "That cocksucker. I'm gonna kill him."

"Careful, Mom. You're bleeding."

"It's nothing. Let's get of here." When she started to walk off, she winced, a hand covering her rib.

"He hurt you. Dammit." Taking her arm, he led her away from the seedy bar to a streetlamp and examined her there. She'd have some bruises, but otherwise her face looked okay. But the way she kept wincing—she could have some broken ribs. He pulled out his phone.

"Who're you calling?"

The guys came walking around the corner of the building. Dylan lowered his phone. "Did you get him?"

"Nah, fucker's long gone." A couple of them headed back to their trucks, a few went into the bar.

"I'll get the truck." Sawyer loped across the street.

Dylan's mom had collapsed on the sidewalk, her back against the lamppost. He crouched beside her, a hand on her leg, and called Kelsi.

"Hey, baby, where'd you go?" She was completely wasted.

"Listen, I'm heading to the hospital. Just wanted to let you know I'm not coming back to the party."

"No. No hospital." His mom started to get up but cried out in pain.

"Stay put." He heard the rumble of Sawyer's truck, as headlights whipped around.

"I'll be there in a second." Kelsi hung up, and he immediately called her back.

"What, baby?" she answered.

"You don't know where I am, and you're not driving drunk. Sawyer's taking us."

"No. I'm fine. Just give me…ow, fuck. What's your problem, bitch?" He could hear two drunk girls shouting and couldn't deal with it, so he hung up.

Sawyer's truck eased to the curb, country music blaring. The music shut off, and Sawyer leaned toward the passenger side window. "Let's go."

Dylan reached under his mom's arms to lift her. She whined and moaned until Dylan shot Sawyer a look. "A hand?"

Sawyer got out of the truck and swung around to the sidewalk. Together, they lifted his mom and got her into the front seat.

"Oh, shit, oh, God, Jesus, Dylan, it hurts. It hurts so bad."

"Yeah, I know. We're gonna get you to the hospital."

"No. No hospital."

"You have to go, Mom. Jesus, he beat you up."

"Take me home. I just need to rest. I'm not going to a hospital."

Sawyer leaned forward. "Dude, she's strung out. She's not gonna cooperate. You don't want to take her to the hospital like this."

*Fuck*. He slammed his palm into the dashboard.

"Where to?" Sawyer asked.

"Police station."

"No fucking way. I'm not going to the cops." His mom lunged across him, trying to open the door.

He had to physically restrain her. "What's your problem? The guy beat the shit out of you. Of course we're going to the police."

"He'll kill me. The bastard will kill me. Is that what you want? You want me dead?"

"No. I don't want you dead." *I want you normal.*

"It'd be for the best. Then you could stay at your fancy college with all those rich pieces of shit and never have to worry about me again. Because I'm such a burden. I'm such a pain in the ass. Do it, Dylan. Take me to the cops. I'll be dead by tomorrow."

Dylan sat there, his mom muttering, his oldest friend watching him. He had no options. No matter which path he chose—dropping out of school, staying in school, setting her up in another apartment, arranging for her to live with Kelsi's family until school ended in May—his mom would still hang out with drug dealers, spend the money he sent her on drugs and booze, and make the shittiest choices possible.

A sense of calm came over him. Because it was so perfectly clear.

Finally.

"Mom."

She didn't stop her ramblings.

He gave her a shake, and she looked up at him with watery eyes, jaw slack, skin grey and harsh-looking in the streetlight. "You've got two choices."

Her jaw snapped shut. She seemed a little more alert. He rarely used that tone with her.

"We go to the police and report the assault or you go to rehab. That's it."

She let out a bark of mean laughter. "Go to hell. Not doing either one."

"Well, then, here's a third choice. You can go back to the guy who beat you up. He'll continue to take care of you. But I won't."

She looked away, not even blinking. "Fuck you."

# CHAPTER SEVENTEEN

**Nicole collapsed on her bed. Her hair smelled like** cinnamon, and her shirt had tomato sauce stains, but she'd had a great day. The O'Donnell's post-Christmas holiday bash was always a huge deal—an open house with people hanging out from noon till midnight—and this year didn't disappoint.

She hadn't heard from Dylan in two days, so she'd stopped checking her phone, what with the party and everything. But now, missing him pretty hard, she reached for it. Swiping the screen, she noticed several missed calls, texts and voicemails. So many from Dylan. *What's going on?* She hit his speed dial.

He answered right away. "Hey, sunshine."

Hearing his voice made her ridiculously happy. She pushed back against some pillows. "Hey."

"What's doin'?" It sounded like he was in a car. She could hear voices in the background, laughter, tunes on the radio.

"I caught you at a bad time."

"Nope."

"You're in a car?"

"Sawyer's truck."

"Sounds like you're having fun."

"Yep."

"So that's why I haven't heard from you in two days." It hadn't even occurred to her that he'd been drinking. He'd been on a bender.

"No, I—"

"Dylan," she said, "I'm not angry. I want you to have a good time."

"I wasn't going to say that. Look, we're here. Let me call you back in a few."

Whatever. He was the one who'd left a million messages. She'd been so worried when she hadn't heard from him—had imagined the worst things happening with his mom. Turns out he was having a great time.

He just didn't have time to talk to her. *Super.* She rolled off the bed. She wasn't going to sit around feeling sorry for herself. She hadn't planned on tackling clean up until morning, but maybe she'd get a head start now. Pocketing her phone, she headed downstairs.

"Hey, pumpkin," her dad called from the couch. Ryan and Brandon stretched their long legs out beside him, three pairs of big, sock-covered feet lined up on the coffee table.

Gathering up her hair, she pulled the elastic from around her wrist and drew it into a ponytail. She grabbed some beer bottles on her way to the kitchen.

"You're cleaning up *now*?" Ryan didn't sound happy about that.

"Wait till tomorrow and we'll help," Brandon said. "Not doin' shit right now."

"Eh. I'm a little restless." She reached down to pick up a crostini someone had dropped on the rug. "I'll get started now."

"Still haven't heard from Mr. Hot Sexy Pants?" Brandon asked. Ryan elbowed him, leaning forward to grab a water bottle.

She smiled because it seemed Brandon had really gotten Gina's message. Since she'd reamed him for ignoring her, he'd been hanging around more often, asking her questions. She'd wound up telling him all about Dylan.

"No, I just talked to him."

His brow furrowed. "I saw you five minutes ago."

"We could only talk for a second. He's going out with his friends. He'll call me back."

Her dad muted the TV. "What happened, sweet pea?"

She rolled her eyes. "Gina got to you, too?"

He motioned for her to come closer. She set the bottles on the table and faced him. "Gina was right, pumpkin." He patted the broad arm of the leather couch, and she perched on it. "I'll tell you what, we love you something fierce."

Her gaze shifted to her brothers, both watching her carefully.

"But when you came back to us, sugar buns, we didn't know what to do for you."

Ryan looked away uncomfortably. He'd ignored her more than the other two.

"You came back all fucked up," Brandon said.

"Thank you." She scooped up a handful of peanuts and tossed them at him. She wasn't insulted. She *had* been weird. Detached, watchful, and—

"You fucking hoarded food." Brandon scooped up some peanuts, cracked them open, and tossed them in his mouth.

*That.* "Yeah, well, I went days without it, jerkface."

Her brothers cringed.

"Anyhow," her dad said. "My point is that we didn't

know how to act around you. And I think it really just built on itself. I'm not making excuses—we should've made a bigger effort." He looked at the boys, and they seemed chastised. "But we didn't know what to do."

"All I've ever wanted was for you guys to feel comfortable around me. I mean, I know we don't have much in common, but I just wanted to hang out with you, talk to you. You guys were all about sports and hanging out with your friends. It just felt like you didn't have time for me."

To his credit, Brandon's features colored.

"Well, now I feel like shit," Ryan said. "You make it sound so easy."

"I know I must've scared you guys. I get that you didn't know what to do with me."

"I still don't," Ryan said. When he got sharp looks from Brandon and his dad, he said, "What? I thought we're being honest here."

"We are." Nicole laughed at his total confusion. "And I appreciate it."

"So, you want to come to a party with me?" Ryan flashed his trademark smile.

"She doesn't party, asshole," Brandon said. "And she doesn't want to be around all your shallow friends."

"Oh, now they're shallow? This from the same guy who begs to come to my parties?"

"I didn't say *I* didn't want to be around them. I said *she* doesn't. See, you don't know her at all. *I* do." Brandon punched his shoulder. "And you better fuckin' invite me."

"Not sure you can handle it."

"Handle what? Of course I can *handle* it."

"Don't want you embarrassing me." Ryan brought the water bottle to his mouth to cover his grin.

"You think I can't handle myself around your friends?"

"I see the way you look at Emma's friends."

"They're fuckin' models. Who wouldn't look at them the way I do?"

"Gettin' boners around them's embarrassing."

"I don't get *boners*. Jesus."

"So, basically, this is what I've been missing out on by not hanging out with you guys?" Nicole smiled at her dad.

"Exactly," he said.

"She missed out on years of sage advice from the oldest," Ryan said.

"I should take advice from a guy who dates a model?" She made a face, and he tossed a pillow at her.

"I go out with the women in my dating pool." Ryan grinned.

"How do I get into that pool?" Brandon asked.

"Stop hanging out in underage clubs," Ryan said.

"I'm twenty, asshole."

"Ever hear of fake IDs?"

They all looked at their dad. "No."

And then all of them burst out laughing.

Just then her phone chimed. She checked the screen and energy rushed through her.

"Mr. Hot Sexy Pants." Brandon said it like it was the most obvious thing in the world.

"Dylan?" She waved to her family and headed up the stairs.

"Hey, sorry about that." No more noise in the background.

"It's fine. If you're out with your friends, we can talk tomorrow."

"We *are* going to talk tomorrow."

"Okay."

"In person."

"What?"

"I'll be at the airport at seven AM."

Adrenaline punched through her system. "You're coming here?"

"Is that all right?"

"Of course it's all right. Oh, my God. You're coming here—for the rest of the break?"

"Yes."

"Oh, my God. I'm so happy. But…I don't understand…what's going on with your mom?"

"It's a long story."

"Where are you right now?"

"Sawyer's."

"Can you talk?"

"Yeah, I'm in his bedroom." He paused. "My mom had an incident the other night."

Ah, *that's* why she hadn't heard from him.

"And I gave her an ultimatum. She could either go to the police or go to rehab."

"And she chose rehab?"

"She chose neither, actually. So I talked to my uncle. And, damn, if he didn't come through for me."

*Oh, thank God.* "What'd he do?"

"First, he called my uncle Brad, a lawyer in Aspen, who'd done some work for a rehab facility out there. They know the story, and they're going to give us a break on the price."

"I thought they're done helping her."

"My uncle said…" She waited, his voice sounding a little thick. "He said…" He cleared his throat. Her hand went over her heart, wishing so badly she could be there with him.

God, this was killing her. He was so strong and had such a fierce heart. No matter what anyone could say about his choices, his loyalty to his mom told her everything she needed to know about his character.

"They said no matter what they don't want me quitting school. And with the deal my uncle Brad made with the facility, my family agreed to give it a shot."

"That's wonderful. That's just…I'm so happy for you."

He was quiet, and she had no idea what he was thinking. Was he overwhelmed that his mom was finally getting the help she needed?

"They're helping me." He sounded like he couldn't believe it. "They've given up on her, but not on me. They're doing this so I can stay at Wilmington."

"That's so great."

"Yeah, it's just…she can't contact me. If we have any hope of it working, of her staying in, I can't be there for her. So, I'm going to change my number. Make sure she knows I'm not around to save her. Because the only alternative to me is her drug dealer. Who beats her up."

Okay, wow. That was more than he'd ever revealed before. "I'm so glad they're giving you this chance. But…how are you? Can you do that, have no contact with her?"

"I feel good about it. I don't think I could leave if she wasn't in a detox program. Also, my uncle arranged it so that he'll be the intermediary. If she needs me, she has to go through him. If he thinks it's a valid, healthy reason, he'll let me know and I can call her."

She wished she felt hopeful for his mom, but she knew rehab never worked unless the addict wanted the help. But at least Dylan finally had help dealing with her. "Well, she's in for the seventy-two hour detox period, so we'll see how she feels when she's got a clearer mind."

"Sometimes I forget that you know all this stuff. I wish you didn't."

"Yeah, well, I do, and that means I can understand what you're going through."

"See you tomorrow?"

*Oh, my God.* She couldn't wait.

Watching the top of the escalator, Nicole nearly jumped out of her skin when he appeared. Tall, gorgeous, and devastatingly masculine, he stepped onto it, looking like a warrior come home from battle. With his gaze trained on her, her body flooded with anticipation.

He looked focused, intense, and hungry.

The moment he stepped off, she flew into his arms. He dropped his duffle, lifted her, and then kicked his bag toward the nearest wall. Without a word, he walked her over and pressed her against it.

He didn't kiss her. He cupped her ass, and his hips pressed between the legs she'd locked behind his back. He turned his face into her hair. "I almost lost this."

"Lost what?" She could feel the slight tremble in his limbs, the long inhalation as he breathed her in.

"You."

She pulled back to look at him, the fear, the want in his eyes. "I'm so glad you didn't."

He pressed his lips to hers, the gentle contact igniting the need burning inside her. She couldn't help sinking into him, opening her mouth to taste more of him. And once his tongue touched the tip of hers, sparks went off in her core.

His fingers tightened on her ass, as he deepened the kiss,

leaning into her, pressing his erection *right there.* He hitched her higher, tearing his mouth off hers.

"Car. Now." He set her down, grabbing his duffle and reaching for her hand.

They walked quickly out into the freezing cold New York City wind. At the stoplight to the parking garage, she said, "I can't believe you're here."

He squeezed her hand, and she noticed the way his jaw worked. He was worried about his mom. Maybe he felt guilty about leaving her behind. "How far's the car?"

She smiled. No, he just wanted to get his hands on her. "At the far end of the highest level in the most remote spot."

The tension broke slightly, as he cracked a grin. "I knew there was a reason I liked you."

They broke into a run, darting in front of a brigade of taxis barreling toward them. Once inside the parking garage, she punched the button for the elevator, turned and found herself in his arms again, his mouth on hers as he backed her into the empty car. She pressed the button for the fifth floor, so glad they were alone.

Until a businessman called, "Hold up," as he slipped through the closing doors.

Dylan leaned back against the wall, wrapping a muscled arm around her waist, pulling her against him. He rested his chin on top of her head.

The man got off on three, and Nicole turned into Dylan's chest, her hand shoving beneath the waistband of his jeans. She grasped his erection, watching his eyes squeeze shut as he pushed into her fist.

The doors opened, and they race-walked across the nearly empty lot. "Good choice." He headed to her yellow Jetta in the far corner. Not another car in sight.

She hit a button on the keypad, and the trunk pop opened. Dylan tossed his duffle inside and then opened the back door, gesturing her inside.

"Start the car." He leaned over, his big body sliding into the backseat. "Don't want you cold."

He *always* looked out for her. Leaning in, she turned the key in the ignition and blasted the heat. Then, she joined him in the back seat. Her fingers trembled with her eagerness to be with him. Unbuttoning her jeans, she skimmed them off her hips, and straddled his lap.

Heat enveloped her as he wrapped her in his arms, kissed her with a passion that set her on fire. He squeezed her ass hard, as he drew her tighter up against him.

"Jeans," he said.

She got up on her knees, fingers fumbling with his top button. He shucked his jeans and boxers down to his ankles, then set her back on his lap. He sighed with such relief that she had to smile.

Immediately she gripped him, her thumb stroking over his crown, as she guided him right where she ached for him. He sucked in a breath, rocking against her. "I missed you." He lifted her, grasped himself, and set her down on top of him.

As he filled her, every nerve-ending lit up, flooding her body with heat. "Dylan."

Right away, he started moving, those big hands clutching her ass, lifting her up and slamming her down to meet his thrusts. And, God, he hit so deep, it made every cell in her body burst open and sing. She grabbed the seat behind him, fingers curling into the cushion, as she rode him hard and fast. "I missed you. So much."

"You have no fucking idea." He slid lower, looking at her

with such tenderness it made her eyes sting. "Lean back. I have to see you."

She loved the feel of his silky hair on her skin, the smell of him, so starkly masculine, but she pulled back, bracing her hands on his thighs. Color flooded his cheeks, his nostrils flared, and a look of pure ecstasy took hold of him.

"You are so fucking beautiful." His hands found her bare skin under the sweater, glided up her body with reverence, and then cupped her breasts, giving them a lusty squeeze. When he pulled down the cups of her bra and pinched her nipples, a bolt of electricity flashed to her clit and she nearly convulsed with raw, intense pleasure.

"I don't want to lose you," he murmured. "Oh, fuck, I want you so bad." And then he sat up, pulling his hands out from under her sweater. Holding onto her ass, he tipped her onto the seat. One leg on the floor, the other knee braced against the cushion, he cupped the top of her head and started stroking into her. Deep, long, powerful thrusts that had her breasts shaking, her senses awash in desire.

"Fuck, Nicole, oh, fuck. Ah. Jesus Christ." Sweat beaded over his lip, his jaw hardened, and she tilted her hips to draw him in even deeper.

Holding onto his thickly muscled arms, she slammed her hips to meet his. She knew when he was going to come, could tell from the sounds he made, the tightening of his grip on her. He powered into her with urgency before shouting his release. Her whole body tightened, squeezed hard, and then burst into an ecstatic frenzy of sensation.

Collapsing on top of her, he said, "I'm not getting up."

"Now, we both know that's a damn lie."

He turned his sweaty face towards her, smiling.

She wiggled her hips beneath him. "You'll get up in no time."

He laughed, kissing her mouth.

******

Dylan couldn't believe the winter wonderland outside the window. This stretch of Connecticut highway looked like something right out of some kid's Christmas book. A canopy of snow-covered trees made it feel like they were gliding through a tunnel.

When she got off the exit in Greenwich, his jaw dropped. He'd never seen a world like this one. Trees, expensive cars, wrought iron gates. Flashes of cupolas, glimpses of rolling lawns behind stone walls let him know he was in rich man's country.

They drove down narrow, windy roads, heading deeper into the countryside. More trees, houses—houses? Right. *Mansions*—further apart. And then she turned onto a stone driveway. A quarter of a mile later, behind a wall of trees, rose a white clapboard house—uh, *mansion*—with deep blue shutters.

In the center of the circular driveway sprawled a huge garden. He'd think it was overgrown, but on closer inspection it was intentionally wild. Spots of pink caught his attention, and he noticed plastic flamingoes scattered randomly throughout it.

"Nice flamingos."

She smiled. "Ryan sent them for my brother's birthday."

She parked outside the six—count them, *six*—car garage.

"Nice place."

Reaching to the sun visor, she hit a button. One of the garage doors opened and she eased in. She killed the ignition, leaned over, and kissed him. "We're home."

She smelled so damn good, he couldn't keep his hands from cupping her face, keeping her close to him so he could kiss her more deeply and run his fingers through her soft, silky hair.

She pulled away. "Everyone should be here in an hour, if you want to shower."

"Shower sounds good, but what about your hair?"

She smiled against his mouth. "I would like nothing more than to shower with you, but you'll be enjoying one of the guest bedrooms while you're under Big Bill's roof."

"Uptight Easterners." He kissed her one more time, a slow, sensuous glide of tongues. "Let's do this."

They entered through what Nicole called a mudroom. She sat down on a bench that had a woven straw seat and tall wooden frame and pulled her slippers out from under it. He leaned against the wall and toed off his boots.

Reaching for his hand, she motioned to the stairs. "I can either take you to your room, or you can meet the guys."

"Nicole," a male voice bellowed. Seriously, the most booming voice he'd ever heard. "You home?"

"Yeah, Dad." She shrugged. "Just leave your bag here."

Passing through a massive—he'd go so far as to say it was industrial-sized—kitchen, sparkling white and stainless steel, with copper pots hanging over the stove and endless white, glass-fronted cabinets, she led him through a dark-paneled dining room with a table that could seat an NFL football team, through to a huge family room. The place was jammed with furniture—big and comfortable. Leather couch, leather love seat, leather recliners, and then these fancy high-backed chairs with blue velvet cushions. The house smelled strongly of pine and cinnamon. A fire blazed in a huge hearth.

"There you are." A big, beefy man heaved himself off the couch. Not fat—just brawny. With a big smile, he reached out his gigantic hand, as he headed toward him. "Bill O'Donnell."

"Dylan McCaffrey." That paw engulfed his hand and shook firmly. "Nice to meet you, sir. Thank you for letting me stay here."

"A pleasure." He turned his head aside still holding Dylan's gaze, as he barked, "Boys."

Jesus, that voice rattled his bones.

"Hey." Nicole touched his arm. "Let me show you to your room so you can shower and get ready."

"Nah, let him meet the boys first. Your friends are gonna be here soon, so you go on up and get ready. I got this." Her dad dismissed Nicole firmly—but not meanly—and focused on Dylan. "What can I get ya to drink? We got beer, water, soda?"

Nicole gave him a private look, asking if it was all right for her to go. What was he supposed to say? No, stay here and protect me from your big, bad father whose energy screamed *Hurt my daughter, and I'll tear your head off*? He gave her a short nod, and she took off toward a wide, curving staircase. A glittering crystal chandelier hung down over it—like something found in a palace. Funny thing, the house was huge and all, but it felt homey and warm. Comfortable.

"Water would be great."

"Water?" Her dad seemed surprised.

Nicole glanced at him from the middle of the stairs. He couldn't read her expression at all. Was she waiting to see what he'd do? Like if he'd drink around her dad?

"Yep. Just water." It would take her awhile to trust him, he got that. But, come on, like he gave a shit about partying compared to being with her?

"Okay, then. Come on with me into the kitchen." On his way, he stood at the top of a staircase that led to a lower level. "Boys? Come up and meet your sister's boyfriend."

Dylan followed him into the kitchen. As the big man pulled a glass down from a cupboard and filled it with ice from a drawer next to the sink, he said, "So, you're dating my little girl."

Why did that question sound so loaded? It made him stop and think what her dad was really asking. He'd never thought about it before, what he and Nicole had, but dating didn't begin to define it. "It's not really dating."

The older man's brow furrowed. He folded those big beefy arms over his stomach, glaring now. "Come again?"

"It's more than that. I mean, we're together."

Water sloshed out of the glass, dripping down the man's hand. The intensity of his gaze made Dylan wonder what he'd said wrong. He wouldn't be here if he'd just been *dating* Nicole.

She was…well, hell. "She's…" How did he explain it? "She's fucking amazing." Oh, shit. Nice language. To her *dad.*

He grinned, thrusting the glass out to him. Dylan took it, but he didn't want to drink. He wanted this man to understand what she meant to him. "It's so much more than *dating.* She…" *Lights up my whole world.*

The man's smile faded. "Well, you're freshmen in college. You just met…"

Dylan shook his head. "It's not like either of us wanted it. But it happened, I found her, and…I'm in." Well, he was trying his damnedest anyhow. And even if he wouldn't get to keep her, he knew in his heart, in his gut, she was the one for him.

By the time Dylan had showered off his day of travel, changed his clothes—not that he knew what to wear to an underage club in New York City—and made it downstairs, Nicole's friends had probably been waiting a good twenty minutes.

Hearing the laughter and conversation, he stopped midway down the stairs, as the group came into sight. Jesus, when Nicole dressed up she looked like a movie star. At the airport, she'd worn tight jeans, fancy snow boots, and her yellow parka. He was used to seeing her in regular clothes. But tonight? With make-up, deep red lipstick, and glittering diamonds in her ears and around her throat, she looked sophisticated. A true beauty. But it was her dress that blew him away. A rich, deep blue, it tied around her neck, perfectly cupping her breasts and highlighting the feminine slope of her shoulders. The skirt flared below the waist.

She was stunning and, at that moment, completely preoccupied with her friends. He couldn't take his eyes off her as he continued down the stairs. Just then the door opened and a tall, lean guy walked in. He stumbled a bit, but they were too busy talking and laughing to notice. *Jonathan?*

He was decent-looking, with his shaggy dark hair and soul patch. His tight-fitting black pants and clunky-soled shoes gave him a hipster look.

The guy got a bead on Nicole, whose back was to the door, and he moved in fast. He put his hands on her hips and then leaned in. His chest pressed up to Nicole's back, and Nicole just stood there, smiling, giving him her cheek.

of wrapping paper. Nothing expensive, just cute things. A book—the retelling of Star Wars through Shakespeare's voice, a bag of nuts and raisins, a couple protein bars, and a plastic keychain with a picture of their Sweet Treats logo.

"Who's down?" Jonathan held a flask in each hand. He shook one. "Vodka." And then the other. "Jack."

"I've got Coke, so I'll take the Jack," one of the girls said.

"I'll take vodka," someone else said.

Jonathan poured a good amount in each glass. Then, he got to Dylan. "What'll it be?"

He shook his head. "I'm good, thanks."

"Oh, come on. It's a party. I know you want some." His gaze slid to Nicole. The fucker.

"Actually, I don't. But thanks." He pulled Nicole tighter to him.

"You're seriously going to let her pussy whip you like this?" Jonathan might have talked to him, but he watched Nicole the whole time.

"I thought you wanted to get her back, you ass." Gina stepped into the circle they made and shoved him.

Jonathan stumbled back, knocking into the person behind him. He kept that stupid laugh going until he straightened, then took another swig from each flask. "Taste testing." And then he leaned toward Dylan, tipping the flask over his glass.

"Cut it out, Jonathan," Nicole said quietly. "He said he didn't want any."

"Look at him. He's a big, bad ass. No one tells him what to do." He sneered at Dylan. "You gonna let her lead you around by your dick?"

"I don't *make* him do anything," Nicole said.

"Why's it so important to you?" Dylan shrugged.

"You're being such an asshole," Gina said to Jonathan.

"And please stop thinking about my dick," Dylan said. "It makes me uncomfortable." Everyone stopped and stared at him, and then they burst out laughing.

"Come on, let's dance." Gina made a grab for Nicole.

She turned to him, lifting up on her toes so their faces were close. It was such an intimate gesture, it made him go all caveman, wanting to throw her over his shoulder and drag her back to his lair. "Dance with me?" she asked.

Cupping her chin and holding her gaze, he said, "No."

"Please—"

"Don't dance. Nonnegotiable. Now go have fun."

She pressed her mouth to his, and then pulled away. But she didn't go. She sighed, her gaze dropping to his lips. He smiled, and then Gina tugged her and she disappeared into the crowd.

An hour later, Dylan watched a very drunk Jonathan come up behind his girl and start grinding on her. *That's it.* He pushed off the barstool and drove into the crowded dance floor.

Yanking the asshole off, he gave him a hard shove. Nicole watched in horror as her ex stumbled back, circled his arms, and then fell down, clearing a space on the dance floor.

She didn't go to him. Gina didn't, either. Two of the others did, crouching beside him.

"Is he hurt?" Nicole slid her arm through Dylan's.

"No."

"Good, then let's get out of here."

"You want something to drink?" Spending nine bucks for a glass of water pissed him off, but she'd danced pretty hard for a solid hour. She needed to hydrate.

She shook her head, leading him off the dance floor. They wound through tables until she stopped against a painted concrete wall. He wrapped his arms around her, then turned so his back was to the rough surface. Didn't want to hurt her bare skin or tear the filmy skirt of the dress.

"Fun night, huh?" he asked.

Tears pooled in her eyes. "I hate when he's like this." She sounded apologetic. "He's been egging you on all night."

"He's drunk. He doesn't know what he's doing."

"I'm so sorry we went out tonight. It's your first night in town. I wish we'd stayed home and just been alone."

"Why didn't we?"

"We'd planned it before I knew you were coming, and my friends have been so good to me this whole break."

"Because of me?"

She nodded.

"I'm sorry."

"It's not your fault. I just...I didn't know what was going on."

"We talked every day." It wasn't like he'd dumped her.

"Not for the last two days."

"Those were the best two days of my life—minus the not talking to you. But getting my mom taken care of? Huge."

That got a smile out of her. "Huge. But when I stopped hearing from you, I didn't know—I thought maybe you were partying."

"I told you I stopped."

She rolled her eyes. "I know, but..."

He cupped her chin, forcing her to look at him. "No buts. When I say something I mean it."

She held his gaze, and it took a moment for her to finally

smile and relax against him. "Okay." Her hands scraped through his hair, and she got up on her toes to reach his ear. "Let's go home."

He squeezed her hips. "Yes."

"Um, one thing. You should probably know we can't do anything with my dad and brothers around."

"Don't worry about it."

"Oh." She sounded disappointed. "You're not going to try anything?"

He smirked. Like he could keep his hands off her. "Oh, I'll try."

"With my dad around?" She looked worried.

"You act like I don't find you irresistible or something."

She gave him a dazzling smile.

"Sunshine, nothing will keep me from you. Nothing."

"Okay, then." She pulled away from him, reaching for his hand. "Let's get out of here."

"What about your friends?"

"They'll want to stay." She glanced briefly to the dance floor.

"Okay, you go tell them what we're up to. I'll find Jonathan."

"Jonathan? Why?"

"He's pretty messed up."

"So? It's his fault. He does this all the time."

"Sunshine, where I come from, we don't leave anyone behind. If I don't think he's capable of getting home on his own—"

"He'll go home with Gina."

"Come on, you know as well as I do the trouble he can get into in his condition. How many times has he not gone home with his friends?"

"A lot." She worried her bottom lip with two fingers. "Yeah, okay. I don't want him with us, but you're right." She wrapped her arms around him and hugged him tight. "You're pretty amazing."

# CHAPTER EIGHTEEN

**No one was around when they got back from taking** Jonathan home. Ryan had probably gone to Emma's, and Brandon would definitely be out partying with his friends. She suspected her dad, though, was waiting up for her.

Dylan surprised her when he took her wrap and hung it on the hook in the closet. "Thank you."

"Yeah, well, now the dickhead's got nothin' on me."

Ah, so he'd noticed when Jonathan had gotten it for her. "He never did." She wrapped her arms around his neck. "I'm sorry this night was so terrible."

"I'll bet we can make it better. Where can we go to just hang out alone? Do you have a finished basement or something?"

She felt the restraint in the arms he'd wrapped around her waist, hovering just over her ass. It made her smile because she knew where he wanted his hands. "Why don't you go up to your room for right now? I need to talk to my dad, okay?"

He seemed wary.

"Give me a few minutes with him." She didn't bother explaining herself, in case she couldn't convince her dad.

Heading up the stairs, she heard canned laughter and found her dad on his bed, reading glasses on, newspaper spread out before him, and a late-night TV talk show on the flat screen.

She sat beside him. “Hey, Dad.”

“You’re home early. Have a good time? Where’s your fella?”

“I had a terrible time. Dylan’s downstairs.”

He lowered the paper, hit the mute button. She loved Gina to pieces right then. Not just because her dad had tuned everything out, but because he no longer looked uncomfortable talking to her. “Things go bad with you two?”

“Jonathan got drunk. We just dropped him off at home.”

“Ah. Well, you got to give that boy a break. Hard for him to see you wrapped around a guy like Dylan.”

“What does that mean?” She hadn’t told him anything about Dylan, other than that he was from Gun Powder, Colorado and had a full-ride to Wilmington.

“He’s damn good-looking. Quite a build. He could probably be a line-backer for Yale. Or anything he damn well wanted to be.”

She smiled. “That’s true. But, lucky me, he’s just a student at Wilmington.”

Her dad’s humor faded. “He said some things tonight.”

*Oh, no.* “Oh, God, Dad, what did you say to him?”

“All I said was, So, you’re dating my little girl.”

“Okay…? And what did he say?”

“He said you weren’t dating—”

Her spirits toppled. Weren’t dating? What did that mean?

“He said it was more than that. When I pointed out you were just freshmen in college—I mean, come on, kid, you’re eighteen, who meets Mr. Wonderful at eighteen?—he said you two hadn't meant to fall for each other but now that he had you, he was 'in.'"

If she hadn't been swooning at that very moment, she might've found her dad's confused expression comical. "He said that?"

Her dad shrugged. "You're not gonna run off and elope are ya?"

"Of course not. But he's right. Neither of us had any intention of getting involved with anyone this year. But he's got some…issues at home, and he's not sure he can stay at Wilmington." She took a breath. "He's not sure we can stay together…because of his mom."

"Doesn't sound good."

She shook her head, holding his gaze, and they shared an understanding of what she'd gone through with her own mom. "I think he wanted to give you a good answer."

"He did."

"Yeah. So, that's kind of what I want to talk to you about. We *are* more, Dad. I don't know how to explain it, but from the moment I met him, I felt this connection."

"Well, sure, anyone can see that between you two."

"You can?"

"You bet."

"So, I guess that's as good a segue as any because I'm going to ask you something. Dylan and I, we don't get much alone time. Between school, work, and his mom—"

"His mom lives in Wilmington?"

She might as well. "No, but she's…a lot of trouble for him."

"Uh huh. Go on."

"I don't want to disrespect you or your rules, but it would mean a lot to me if you'd let Dylan stay in my room."

His lips pressed together in disapproval.

"We just…need to be together."

His brow shot up.

"I don't mean like that. I'm not Brandon." She wasn't doing a good job of presenting her case. "I love him, Dad. And it's not small. It's not…some kind of freshman fun-times crush."

He smiled. "No freshman fun-times crush, huh?"

"We'll be respectful—he's a really great guy. Jonathan was awful to him tonight, goading him, and when I was ready to leave the club, Dylan insisted we bring Jonathan home so he wouldn't get into any trouble."

"Good guy."

"Really good guy. So, would you mind? Can he stay with me? I know it's not fair to Brandon, but it would mean everything to me."

He looked away, thoughtful. "You know, if he hadn't answered me the way he had tonight, I'd probably say no. But he sees you…well, let's just say he's pretty taken by you."

Happiness expanded inside her chest. "Thank you, Dad. We won't gross you out, I promise." She gave him a kiss on the cheek and ran out of the room.

"I'm gonna hold you to that." His voice boomed down the hallway.

Nicole entered the guest bedroom to find Dylan on the floor doing crunches.

She knew he exercised every day, but she'd figured he'd allow himself a day off every now and then. He'd been traveling all day. "Good news. We have a gym in the basement."

He smiled and got up. "Well, now, that is good news. I wondered what I'd do with all my time out here." The guy wasn't even out of breath, as he settled on the bed, back to the headboard.

She kicked off her heels and crawled toward him. "I've got lots of ideas to keep you from getting bored. And they're aerobic, too." Quickly unbuttoning his shirt, she pushed the material aside, baring his hard, chiseled chest, and pressed kisses along his collarbone, down the valley between his nipples, and down to his belly button. "Guess what?"

His hips pushed up, stomach muscles tightening. Watching him, she unbuttoned his jeans and reached in to grip his erection. She smiled as she stroked him, and his eyes rolled back in his head.

"What?" he said on a gusty exhalation.

"I talked to my dad. Explained our situation. Guess where you're staying?"

"In a hotel? In another state?"

"No." Pulling him out of his boxers, she licked him from the base to the tip.

His hips shot off the mattress, and he groaned.

Letting go of his glorious erection, she straddled his thighs. "I asked him if you could stay in my room."

"And then he put a hit out on me?"

She smiled. "Do you want to talk or can I get busy?"

He stroked the hair off her shoulder. "Sunshine, we're going to get busy no matter which room I stay in. But I don't want to cause any problems or make anyone uncomfortable."

His erection thickened, and she couldn't resist giving it a firm squeeze. He jackknifed up.

"I want you in my room. What do you want?"

He captured her ass in his hands. "I'll tell you exactly what I want. From the moment I came downstairs tonight, all I could think about was that little bow behind your neck."

She lifted her hair. "This 'ole thing?"

He reached around the back of her neck. "I was imagining what would happen if I did this." He tugged, the knot slipped free, and he lowered the top of her dress slowly. He sucked in a breath. "Look at you." Peeling the top down to her waist, his chest expanded, his eyes widened, as he took her in. Her nipples beaded under his rapt attention. "I don't think I've ever seen anything so pretty."

Her skin pebbled, and she trembled deep within.

With reverence, he gently cupped her breasts, drew them together, and then licked one nipple. "So sweet."

Oh, God, he made her feel so freaking good. She sighed, reaching for his erection. She gripped him, and he surged into her hand. So hard, so thick, and so hot. His warm, wet mouth closed over her breast, his tongue slowly licking the nipple. She pulled him closer, never wanting this delicious pleasure to end.

His phone buzzed and bounced on the nightstand. He pressed his forehead to her collarbone in defeat. "I have to take this."

"Is it your uncle?" She couldn't think of any other call he'd take just then.

He shook his head, scowling when he saw the caller ID. He punched the button to answer. "What?"

Nicole waited, figuring he'd tell the person he'd get back to them. Unless it had to do with his mom. She hoped nothing was wrong.

No, it was a girl's voice, and she talked a mile a minute.

"Goddammit, Kels, that was the whole point. That she

wouldn't have someone to call."

Nicole scampered off his lap. His ex. Great. She tied her dress back up.

Whatever. She tossed his duffle bag on the bed, then started throwing his clothes in. He'd showered earlier, so she headed into the bathroom and grabbed his toiletries, stuffing them back into the plastic freezer bag he kept them in. She should've gotten him a nice leather toiletry bag for Christmas, but they'd agreed not to give each other presents, and she hadn't wanted to make him uncomfortable. Maybe for his birthday.

"She *has* to stay in, Kels."

Quickly, she threw the bag into his duffle. Then she motioned to the door and mouthed, My bedroom.

He nodded, barely focusing on her.

Hot water pummeled her skin, steam swirled around her, and Nicole couldn't stop wondering what Kelsi had done. Knowing the lengths his ex would go to keep him—giving him a hand job while he was sleeping, *ew*—she couldn't help but wonder if the girl would do something to undermine his mom's care just to force him to come back.

That would be awful.

And completely messed up. No one knew better than Nicole that you couldn't make someone love you. She'd learned the hard way, and she'd never fight someone's demons again. Nope, they had to do it themselves.

Stepping out of the stall, she patted herself dry with a fluffy towel and then smoothed her honeysuckle-scented lotion all over her body—wishing it were Dylan's hands on her instead of her own.

Murmurings from the bedroom let her know he'd found

her room. She wrapped the bath sheet around her before heading out to find some nightclothes. However nice it was of her dad to let them sleep in the same room, she wasn't going to be naked. What if he knocked? What if her brothers barged in? She crossed to the door and locked it.

"Of *course* it's hard for her." He used his handler voice.

Inside her closet, she dropped the towel, found an old pair of navy sweatpants and a plain white tank top.

"No. That's the worst thing I could do. She has to believe I'm not there for her. She has to know there's nowhere for her to go." He paused. "Of course she's out of her mind. She's getting the shit out of her system."

After hanging the towel on the rod, she switched off the bathroom light and crawled into bed.

"Stop. Just…stop. Look, she can make all the threats she wants, I don't believe she'd go back to Jeff after he cracked her ribs." He cut a glance her way, and she saw him stiffen.

She shut off her lamp and turned away from him, giving him some privacy. She appreciated that he talked in front of her but understood how much he hated sharing such ugly bits about his life.

"No." He listened. "Because it won't help."

The duvet whisked off her shoulder, as Dylan got out of bed. "Dammit, Kels, no. It's not your call. We're giving this a try."

She closed her eyes, anxiety buzzing through her. She wished she could help him.

"She has nothing to do with this. It's about making the best decision for my mom. What we've been doing hasn't worked, so we're going to try this. Now, I'm getting off the phone. But I'm telling you, Kels, next time she calls, don't answer."

Nicole took shallow breaths, waiting for him to get off the phone.

"I'm getting off the phone now." He paused. "Yes, with *her*." The phone slammed onto the nightstand. Dylan strode into the bathroom. He stormed right back out, digging into his duffle bag and taking the plastic toiletry bag back in with him.

Fear got a grip on her.

Kelsi was playing a dangerous game—and the cost to everyone involved could be enormous.

******

A Greenwich, Connecticut diner had nothing on the ones in Colorado. First, the prices. Twenty-two bucks for some *eggs*? And who wanted salmon roe in an omelet?

But secondly, everybody dressed like they were headed to church. Dylan hadn't given much thought to clothing when he'd packed. He'd practically run to the airport to get to his girl, but even if he had, he still wouldn't have thought to bring a blazer and khakis just to grab breakfast at a diner.

Dylan shoveled eggs into his mouth, tuning back into the conversation between Nicole and Gina.

"Did it hurt?" Nicole gestured to the barbell in her friend's eyebrow.

Gina just shrugged. "A little."

"You going to keep doing this?"

Gina's eyes narrowed. "Doing what?"

"Tattoos, piercings. You have to admit it's a huge change for you."

"Hey, I live in Greenwich Village. This is normal."

Nicole reached for her orange juice. "But not normal for you."

"But it's sexy as fuck, right?" The tip of Gina's pointy stiletto jabbed him in the shin.

He kept his focus on his eggs.

"I just…I want to know what's going on with you. We haven't really talked this whole break."

"We talked." But Dylan couldn't help noticing the way Gina's gaze slid away.

Nicole set her hand on his thigh, gripping him, and he had the feeling she was restraining herself from asking more questions. He doubted Gina would open up around him anyway.

"You know what I mean. And what's going on with you and Brandon?"

Gina's facial muscles flinched, and then her whole body went still. "Your brother's a dick. How is this news?"

"You've never been so mean to him."

"I'm done with entitled assholes." She licked her lips, then gave a seductive smile.

"Did something happen between you guys? Now that you live in the city, do you see him?"

Gina dragged a fork through a pool of syrup on her plate. "I see him sometimes when I go clubbing." Her tongue flicked out to lick the syrup off the tines of her fork. "You should look out for him. He's partying pretty hard."

The waitress came by with a coffee pot. "Missing you two girls now that you've left me for college. You doing all right?"

He didn't know if it was intentional, but Nicole eased slightly closer to him, her light, sweet fragrance filling his sense. "I'm doing great."

"Super, Marta. How's things with you?" Gina's fingers whispered across her collarbone.

"Same old, same old. Just how I like it." She tipped the coffee pot toward Dylan's mug. "Top you up?"

The diner door opened, and Marta glanced over. Her gaze narrowed, her features freezing. A sober Jonathan entered. Nicole stiffened, taking her hand off his leg. "Crap."

Dylan reached for her hand and put it right back, holding it firmly. She owed this guy nothing.

"Looks like you got company," Marta said, before taking off.

As Jonathan neared the table, Gina glared at him. "Who invited you?"

Jittery, intense, he stared at Nicole. "Can I talk to you?"

Nicole gave him a bored expression. "You can say hello to my best friend and my boyfriend."

His jaw clenched, but he gave a cursory nod to both of them. Returning his focus to Nicole, he said, "Please?"

She put her hand on Dylan's shoulder and said quietly, "Excuse me."

But Dylan didn't budge. They'd had a shitty night. He wouldn't let the jerk-off ruin their day.

She softened. "It's okay. I'll be right back."

"You don't have to talk to him."

"And you didn't have to talk to Kelsi, but you did. You always do."

"Not fair."

"It won't take long, I can promise you that." She leaned close. "Unlike you, I don't care what he has to say."

Pissed, he slid out of the booth and let her out. He dropped back down, watching for them out the window. As soon as they stepped outside, the asshole grabbed her upper arm to get her attention. Dylan tensed.

The guy spoke rapid-fire, leaning forward and gesticulating. Nicole stood there calmly, listening. She had to be freezing. Maybe he should bring her coat.

"Is he high?" he asked Gina.

"I don't think so. Jonathan never did drugs. Believe it or not, when he's not drinking, he's a really good guy."

"Team Jonathan?"

"Oh, hell, no. He drove Nikki batshit crazy. I'll never be team Jonathan."

"But you're not Team Dylan."

"Not a chance. You're fucking with my girl."

"*Fucking* with her? Are you out of your mind? Do you know what I'm risking to be with her?"

"You don't know what she's gone through."

"Yeah, I do."

"How could you?" She eyed him meaningfully, the first time he'd ever seen her without her mask of seduction. "I've been friends with her since she moved back in with her dad. Right now, with all you've got going on, you're the worst thing for her."

Like he didn't already know that. "That's her choice."

"You gonna choose her?"

"I'm sure Nicole has told you—"

"Nicole has told me very little. She says you value your privacy."

He shot a look outside, emotion gripping him. It meant a lot to him that she hadn't shared the details of his life to her best friend. He didn't think he'd ever had anyone he could trust—other than Sawyer.

Jonathan lurched forward, gripping Nicole's arms. She jerked out of his hold, but he made a rough gesture, a sweep of his arm.

His pulse quickened. Why didn't she walk away? "What am I missing here?"

Gina didn't even bother looking. "She's the girl, when he's forty, married with kids, he's going to imagine when he's fucking his wife. She's the one he built a shrine for in his heart."

*Shit. Fuck.* "What about her? Does she…?"

"Not at all. Believe me, she gave it her all." Her gaze narrowed. "Nicole doesn't trust many people. Other than me and Jonathan, she hasn't really let anyone else in. But when she does? She goes all in."

He got her message, loud and clear. And as much as he needed that—fucking craved it—he knew he didn't deserve it. Because he couldn't go all in with her. Probably ever. One thing he was finally coming to understand, his mom would never get better. She'd never become the healthy, functioning woman he'd always wanted.

"Jonathan's not the threat."

He got Gina's meaning, but at that moment, his girl had had enough. She stepped back from Jonathan, features turning pink. Her hair shook, her breath came out in white puffs. And then, in the middle of ranting, she looked away. And her gaze caught Dylan's.

She stilled. Her arms dropped to her sides. Her shoulders relaxed, and then the sweetest smile spread across her face. A slow hum began in Dylan's chest, spreading out along his limbs until his body vibrated.

Walking towards him, she pressed her fingertips to the glass. He reached up, mimicking her gesture. Happiness danced on his heart.

And then she mouthed, *I love you*, and the breath left his lungs. The burn raced across his chest, up his neck, and curled around his ears. The soles of his feet tingled.

Her grin broadened, and then she was gone. Breezing past Jonathan, she swung into the diner, raced to the table and threw herself on top of him. He caught her in the tight space of the booth, her hair spilling all over him. He pushed it aside so he could find that hot, sweet mouth, and then he pulled her tighter to him, his hands sliding under her sweater to find the skin of her back.

"Gross," Gina said. "I'm going to the bathroom. When I'm done, you'd better be finished with this obscene display of public affection." She slid out of the booth.

Once she was gone, Dylan pulled back, nuzzled her neck—heart thundering, body trembling. "Say it again."

Her smile splashed light and heat all over him. "I love you."

He couldn't look into her eyes and hear those words. It was like looking into the sun. So, he burrowed into her neck, hips rolling into hers, pressing, and then holding her in place.

Her arms wrapped around him, and she turned his head to press her mouth to his ear. "I love you so much."

An hour later, Gina brushed past him, wearing nothing but a bra and thong. "Kelsi again?"

He stood outside the boutique's dressing room, setting his phone on silent. If Gina had noticed, then he'd obviously gotten sucked into the Kelsi tornado. Just like with his mom, when Kelsi got going, she wouldn't stop. She was on a tear about him coming back home.

He'd already said no and explained himself—two dozen times. So, enough. If Gina hadn't snapped him out of it, he might've gone back and forth with Kelsi all day.

Because he wasn't only trying to convince Kelsi he was

doing the right thing. He needed to convince himself.

"Excuse me?" Gina called, her centerfold figure on display for anyone in the lingerie store. The saleswoman looked up from the counter. "Do you have this in a triple D?"

The woman smiled, held up a finger.

*Why is she broadcasting her cup size?*

"You're gonna rip her heart into pieces, aren't you?" Gina stood there, hands on hips, bounteous breasts quivering in the filmy bra. He couldn't understand why she'd show herself off to her best friend's boyfriend like this.

"I don't want to hurt her."

"It's not looking good." She flicked the curtain open and stepped into her dressing room. When she saw him still standing there, she said, "Go help her choose a bra."

Dylan didn't like her bossy attitude. And he definitely didn't appreciate her interfering when she didn't know or understand the situation.

Kelsi was threatening to take his mom out of rehab. If she did…*fuck*. What the hell was he supposed to do? *She just won't listen.*

Gina arched a brow at him, waiting.

He leaned against the dressing room door.

"Dylan?" Nicole called in that sexy voice that made his blood heat.

"On my way." He smiled at Gina, letting her know exactly what motivated him.

He swept aside the curtain, stepping in to find dozens of bras jammed on the racks. The three-way mirror revealed his girl's backside in a yellow number that made his eyes hurt.

"Too bright?"

He nodded, couldn't speak because she looked so pretty

in her neon yellow boy shorts and bra. Her breasts jiggled and mounded out of the cups. He took a step closer, placing a soft kiss on her shoulder. "You might need a size larger."

She looked up at him. "Want to unhook me?"

"Every time."

He watched her in the mirror, as he caressed her shoulders, smoothing down her arms, and he loved the spray of chill bumps his touch elicited. Pushing her hair aside, he pressed kisses at the curve of her neck. "You smell good." Once he'd unhooked the bra, he flicked the strap off each shoulder, then peeled the bra off, exposing her gorgeous, round breasts.

"I love the way you touch me."

"I haven't touched you yet."

"Oh, yes, you have." Her hand came around the back of his neck, as her hips swayed gently. "Your eyes. The way you look at me."

Oh, Jesus, what she did to him. He went so hard he had to palm himself through his jeans. Her ass brushed over his hand, and he couldn't help but grab a cheek and caress it. She sucked in a breath, looking so fucking sexy.

He couldn't help himself. He crouched, kissing that ass through the boy shorts. He needed them off now. Lowering the waistband of her panties, he took a bite of her luscious rump.

She pushed back. "God, Dylan."

Yanking down the panties, he stood up, arms belting her waist, chin resting on her shoulder, just taking her in. Mouth on her neck, he palmed her breasts. Her ass shoved hard into him, and she moaned, eyes heavy with desire.

And then he couldn't take it anymore. He unbuttoned his jeans, shoved them down. Grasping her hips, he tilted her forward, then slowly sank into her slick heat.

"Fuck." Stroking one finger along her slick length, he watched her expression change when he circled her clit. She shuddered against him. "I want you, sunshine. I want you so much." A hand on the small of her back, he lowered her even more as he buried himself deep inside her.

She gasped, all that hair spilling forward, those luscious breasts rocking with his thrusts. His finger glided over her clit, his cock powered in and out of her, and everything in him quickened. Spots of light flickered in his vision, as heat rushed over him, and his legs went weak.

"I'm gonna come, sunshine," he whispered. "I'm gonna come so hard."

Her mouth popped open, as her body shuddered, eyelids fluttering closed. She slammed back against him, and he held her there, pinned to him, swiveling his hips hard and fast, biting his lip to keep from shouting as he came inside her.

He continued pumping, his hands skimming up her body, cupping and squeezing her breasts. Fuck, this woman was everything to him. *Everything.*

# CHAPTER NINETEEN

**"Dammit, Kels. I told you not to take her calls." Dylan** paced around the covered pool, the sharp air biting into his skin, making his ears hurt.

"Are you kidding me? She's all alone, Dylan. Everyone's abandoned her—including her own son. She's scared."

Somehow that didn't ring true, but he couldn't hold onto the thought when Kelsi jerked so hard on the guilt strings. "I know that. We've been over this a thousand times. Nothing about this process is going to be easy, but she has to go through it if she's going to get clean."

"It's too late. She's out. She's here."

"I can't *fucking* believe you took my mom out of rehab."

"I had no choice. Whatever. It's done. But I need you here. She's your problem, not mine."

"Yes, and I got her in a program. That was how I was dealing with *my* problem."

"Don't put this on me. She was walking out that door no matter what. If I didn't go pick her up, she'd have called Jeff, and you know it."

He cupped the back of his neck and looked up to the cloudy sky. "We'll never know now."

"Are you coming home?"

If he came home, he'd have to drop out of school. If he didn't come home, his mom would go back to Jeff. And he couldn't live with himself if she got caught up with the drug dealer again. He knew where that would end.

"I've *been* home. She was with Jeff when I was around. I don't know what I can do to help her, but dropping out of school isn't the answer."

The phone whisked out of his hand. He swung around to find Bill putting it to his ear.

"Pardon the interruption. This is William O'Donnell." He held up a finger to Dylan. "I'm going to guess by the circular nature of this conversation that we're not dealing with an emergency, so I'm going to hang up right now, let my boy clear his head a bit. He'll get back to you soon." He tipped his head back, squinting, and then turned the phone off.

Dylan had no words. What had this man just done?

"You play golf?"

He gave Nicole's dad the death glare. He had a crisis to deal with, and the man was talking about *golf*. As if he had the time or the money to play a rich man's sport.

Bill burst out laughing. "What do I know about your life, son? You could caddy at a country club for all I know." He slapped a hand on Dylan's back. "Come on. We're gonna go hit some balls."

Two hours later, in the warmth of an indoor driving range, Dylan took a swipe at the little white ball, watched it sail across the turf.

Bill followed the trajectory with an awed expression. "Hot damn, boy. You're a natural athlete. If you'd been an

O'Donnell, you'd be on the pro tour right now."

"Thanks. Can I get my phone back?" He needed to know what his mom was doing. Could Kelsi keep an eye on her? Stupid question. Her own son couldn't keep an eye on her.

He could not *believe* his mom had walked out of rehab.

"You work out?"

Again, Dylan just looked at him. This conversation was bullshit.

Panic clutched at his chest. Holy shit, *his mom was out of rehab.* He had to get the hell out of there and back to Colorado. What was she doing right then?

"Dylan?" He said it sharply, to get his attention. "You work out?"

What the fuck? Why…Dylan blew out a harsh breath. This guy'd had an alcoholic wife. He'd dealt with similar stuff. He should give him a chance. Maybe he could help. "Yes."

"How often?"

"A lot."

"How much is a lot?"

"Every day." Saying it out loud made it seem kind of…obsessive. "I used to just do it five days a week, but…"

"But you got a little anxious when a whole day would go by that you weren't tightening those muscles."

What could he say to that? True.

"I noticed you don't pig out with the rest of the crew. No pretzels, no chips. Even those desserts Nicole's always making. You don't eat 'em."

"I watch what I eat."

"Why?"

"Kind of defeats the purpose of working out if I'm just going to eat crap."

"No sugar?"

What was his point? "Not usually, no."

"What else you trying so hard to control, son?"

He pulled off the glove Bill had bought him. Play time was over. He didn't have these conversations with anyone, but then he thought about Nicole. Another seizure in his chest. He didn't want to lose her, but he had to focus on his mom right then. "I need my phone."

"Heard you got a full-ride to Wilmington."

"No disrespect, Mr. O'Donnell, but can you please get to your point?"

Bill led them away from the green, away from the other golfers. "I'm guessing you didn't have a whole lot of control growing up with your mom?" That was the softest voice the man had ever used.

"No. She's not…"

"She can't be controlled. Addicts can't. I know from my own experience. But it looks to me like you compensated in your own life." He motioned to Dylan's body. "You ever wonder why you work out so much?"

"It keeps me healthy. That's a good thing."

"Sure is. Four, five days a week'll keep you fit, too. You do seven. Why?"

If he was going to have this conversation, he might as well be real. "So no one can take advantage of me."

"You live in a dangerous town?"

"I live in a tourist town. Old Western shoot-outs and everything."

"So who're you protecting yourself from?"

He didn't answer. He'd never tell anyone about the creeps who'd threatened him throughout his childhood.

"The folks your mom brought around?"

He shot a look to Nicole's dad. No one had ever asked him that before. "Yes." Jesus Christ, he sounded like a pussy. Felt as vulnerable as he had when he was eleven. What was he going to do next, cry? It's just…damn, he needed to make sense of everything. It had all gone haywire.

Bill drew in a breath, his muscular chest expanding. "I think you know I was married to a drunk."

Dylan nodded, not liking the way that sounded. Too harsh for an ex-wife.

"I tried to control her environment. Became my full-time job."

"I know I have no control over what my mom does. Believe me, I learned that lesson. I'm trying to…"

"To what, son?"

"To help her."

"Help her what?"

"Keep her out of trouble."

"And have you done that so far?"

"Not as well as I should have."

Bill blew out a breath, kicking at the Astro turf. "So, it's your fault, huh?"

"I didn't say that. Look, she does what she does. I just have to at least pay her bills so she has a roof over her head."

"So, if you pay her bills, you'll keep her out of trouble?"

Dylan looked away, seeing nothing but his mom's expression when she was high over Thanksgiving. "You don't understand."

"What don't I understand?"

Yeah, he knew he sounded like a kid, but he didn't know what to say. Well, it was more than that. Bill was leading him to think about things he'd never considered, and it made him confused. "I'm her *son*."

He held up a hand. "I understand. I was Audrey's husband. Nicole was Audrey's daughter. We understand. And trust me, nothing you say or think about your mom or your situation is new. Every single enabler on the planet thinks the same way as you. Know how I figured that out?" He paused. "Al-Anon."

"You went to therapy?"

"Hell, yeah. I had kids. Nothing I did made things better. Nothing. Sound familiar?"

"I don't need therapy." He needed the help of his family. "She does."

"Therapy only works for people who want things to change. Do you want things to change?"

Dylan nodded.

"Does your mom?"

He didn't bother answering.

"Then, you might want to try therapy."

"It doesn't matter what I do, she's still going to…get into trouble."

He shifted, looking alert. "That's exactly right. No matter what you do, she's still going to do whatever the hell she wants. So, you can continue doing exactly what you're doing—and nothing will ever change. This will be your life." He paused, his gaze deep and probing. "Is this the life you want?"

*Of course not.* "I'm not going to abandon her."

"Interesting choice of words. Let's change 'em a little. Tell me what'll happen if you start to look out for yourself. And I'm talking bottom line. What happens after you decide to look out for you?"

His head snapped up. "She'll get into trouble."

"She's already in trouble. What could happen, Dylan?

What are you really afraid of?"

Dylan's stomach cramped. His breathing turned shallow.

"What happens if you take care of yourself? Let your mom take care of *her*self?"

He went a little light-headed, which only made him fight for clarity. Dammit, he needed to punch something.

"Dylan?" Bill nearly barked his name. "What happens to your mom if you take care of yourself?"

"She'll fucking die, what do you think?"

Compassion etched the man's features. And Dylan felt the snap of connection. Everything he'd done for his mom, the driving force in his life—he finally saw it. The responsibility for his mom's fucking *life* sat on his shoulders.

Bill clapped a big hand on his shoulder, holding his gaze. "Can you keep your mom alive?"

He'd never thought of it so literally before. "Yes."

"Son." Even though he didn't move, Bill seemed to come closer. "Can you keep your mom alive?"

Dylan looked away. His mom didn't listen to anything he said. She didn't have any boundaries, no discipline. If she wanted to drink, she drank. If she wanted to get wasted, she did. If she wanted to shack up with a drug dealer, she did. "I guess not."

"You guess not?"

"No. Okay? No, I can't keep her alive. But if I'm there, at least I can do everything in my power to keep her safe."

"And now we're going in circles again. Which means you're not ready to accept the bottom line. Okay, I get that. You need to get there on your own, but seeing how close you are to making a decision that will impact the rest of your damn life, I'm going to just say it. You can't keep your mom safe. Being there, paying her bills, whatever it is you do to keep her alive is like covering an arterial wound with a Band-Aid."

Dylan felt sick to his stomach. He turned into Bill, away from the green. "She walked out of rehab," he said quietly. "There's no one to take care of her."

Bill scrubbed his face with a beefy hand. "When you get tired of the hamster wheel, pull up a chair in an Al-Anon meeting. They'll help you get off."

******

Traffic jammed the highway into the city, but her friends didn't care. Wearing their New Year's Eve party hats, they drank champagne in the limo, everyone laughing and shouting over each other. Well, except for her and Dylan. They sat quietly, tucked in a corner.

Over the past few days, Dylan had been on the phone constantly. She'd tried to get information out of her dad, but all he'd said was that she needed to prepare herself. Dylan wasn't ready. Ready for what?

She pushed back in her seat, cuddling with him. The bright lights of Times Square splashed all over his flannel shirt and jeans, casting a reddish glow to his handsome face.

She was losing him. She knew that. But he was still with her—he could've bailed days ago when he'd gotten the call from Kelsi.

"Happy New Year," she whispered against his cheek.

He tightened his hold on her, still staring out the window.

He hadn't shared much of anything. She knew Kelsi had picked his mom up from rehab, but that was about it. She wished he'd talk to her dad again. Her dad knew so much about the issues he faced.

The limo pulled up to the club. Everyone spilled out, already half-wasted. As Dylan turned to her, finally, she held his face in her hands. "We don't have to go with them. We can go back home. You know I just want to be with you."

"It's fine." He nudged her, but she didn't budge.

"You're in no mood to party. Let's go talk somewhere."

"Don't want to talk."

"Fine. Then, let's go to a hotel." She tried for a sexy look, but she couldn't fake it.

"Forget it. Let's party with your friends."

Desperation clawed at her heart—she was losing him. God. What could she do? How could she hang onto him?

If there was anything she could do for him, she would. But he wouldn't let her in.

And that left her feeling completely and utterly helpless.

Which was, of course, the most familiar feeling in the world to her.

******

Standing at the end of a long hallway, the music muted in this remote part of the club, Dylan thought his head might explode if Kelsi didn't answer her damn phone.

"Dyl?"

Finally. *Jesus.* He'd been going out of his mind. "What's happening?"

"We need to talk."

"You think? I've been calling and texting you for *three days*. Where's my mom?"

Every second of her silence stabbed his nerves with an ice pick. "Fuck. *Fuck.* Just say it." His skin tightened, his lungs squeezed so tight he could barely get a breath. "Where is she?"

"She's with me."

His energy let down in a rush. "Is she all right?"

"She tried to kill herself."

The world spun. He couldn't get his bearings so he turned, slamming back against the wall. "You're in the hospital?"

"We're in New York."

"You're…what?" *Hang on. First things first.* "How is she?"

"She's alive."

"How did you get here?"

"I drove. I've been driving."

"For three days."

And in all that time, she hadn't thought to call him? Let him know? "What did she do to herself? Is it bad?"

"She tried to slit her wrists."

"Oh, Jesus." He clutched the back of his head. "You found her?"

"She called me at work. I got to her in time. Took her to the hospital."

He felt sick to his stomach. "How bad?"

"She's okay. No stitches, but she's all bandaged up. Mostly, she's devastated you chose some girl you just met over her."

"*She's* devastated or you are?"

"Fuck you, Dylan. *Fuck you.* Who do you think's been here for her? Who's been taking care of her while you're fucking off with the Trumps?"

"Where are you?"

"I don't know exactly. GPS says I'm about five miles from the club."

*Club?* "How do you know where I am?"

"Facebook. Your shiny new friends talked about their

plans for New Year's Eve. While I was playing nursemaid to your mom, you were making plans to party at an underage club in Manhattan. Well, party's over big guy. We're coming to get you."

"Just…stay put. I'll come to you."

"Are you fucking kidding me right now? You're still thinking about your Disney princess, when I've got your mom on suicide watch in my car?"

"You shouldn't have brought her here. You should've talked to me first."

"You want me to leave your suicidal mom alone in Gun Powder? What is the matter with you? What happened to you? You never used to be like this."

"Tell me where you are. I'll—"

"Too late. I'm almost there. Meet me outside the club in…twelve minutes."

This wasn't happening. He closed his eyes. Saw Nicole. Why did he always see Nicole? When had he stopped seeing his mom?

His gut twisted hard. He'd totally fucked up.

His mom was in Kelsi's car, wrists bandaged. She'd tried to kill herself. Because she thought he'd given up on her.

As much as he wanted to say he hadn't dumped her in rehab, one small part of him knew he had. Not that he doubted his decision. He knew she needed the treatment. But he couldn't deny the relief he'd felt when he'd boarded that plane—leaving her in someone else's care.

Had he dumped his mom for Nicole?

To some degree, yes, he had.

He thought of the O'Donnell's mansion, the stocked cupboards, the overflowing pantry, the refrigerator stuffed with food. He thought of the leisurely lifestyle, the comfort.

The lady who came each day to clean, even though Bill, essentially, lived alone.

Dylan had been living large, while his mom locked herself in a bathroom and tried to kill herself because her son had abandoned her.

What had he done?

He pushed off the wall. Thank God, she hadn't died.

He had another chance to make it right.

******

This whole night was just stupid. Dylan didn't dance, he hardly knew her friends. She hadn't even seen him in the last hour. She pulled her phone out of her bag and texted him.

*Let's go home.*

No response. She'd go look for him.

After roaming the perimeter of the club without success, she found her friends dancing. "Have you seen Dylan?" She had to shout over the music to be heard.

Gina shook her head, looking worried. She started off the dance floor, but Nicole stopped her. She didn't want to ruin their New Year's Eve. So, she smiled, waved it off.

She called him again. Maybe he'd gone outside? It was crazy loud in the club. God, she wished they'd just stayed home.

She headed for the door, figuring it wasn't too late to save their New Year's Eve. In fact, she'd call the car company now. She pushed through the throng waiting to get in and stepped out into the frigid air. Too late, she wished she'd thought to grab her wrap from the coat-check.

After calling for the car, she shot off a quick text to Gina.

*Going home. HNY! Talk tomorrow!*

Okay, so, he wasn't outside—

There he was. In the street. In front of someone's

double-parked car. He was talking to a girl. No, arguing. Nicole's heart stopped beating. The icy cold air stung the back of her throat so she snapped her jaw shut.

Her feet moved of their own accord, bringing her closer to Dylan and the girl.

And then her gaze drifted down. To the Colorado license plate.

*Oh, my God. Kelsi?*

Who else could it be?

But there was someone else—a woman, leaning against the car, arms folded tightly across her chest. Shoulders slumped, body agitated. Was that his *mom?*

What were they doing here? Dylan hadn't mentioned they were coming.

The moment she reached them, she put her hand on Dylan's arm. He flinched, turned to her, and dread washed over his face.

He didn't want to see her.

No one said anything. The girl had a challenge in her eye, as she watched Dylan.

Finally, the girl broke the tension. "So, this is her? Nicole?"

Dylan's mom, swallowed up in her oversize black parka, snapped to attention. She took one step forward, her expression turning livid. "*This* is her? This is why you dumped me in the fucking loony bin? For this cunt?"

Ice cold shock slashed through her, and her fingers curled into Dylan's arm.

He spun around to his mom. "Don't you ever talk to her like that. Jesus Christ. Get in the car and wait for me."

"Fuck you. *Fuck you!* You're not hiding me away again so you can spend more time with the rich bitch. What's so special about her? She's nothing. *Nothing.*"

"Mom." His bark reverberated down to Nicole's bones. He got right in his mom's face. "You talk about my girlfriend that way again, and things will not go down well here."

Long, awful seconds passed, where mother and son held each other's angry, searching gazes. The crazy seemed to ebb and flow in his mom's eyes, until it finally drained. Her shoulders relaxed, and she let out a rough breath.

Kelsi reached for Dylan. "Let's just go, okay?"

He yanked out of Kelsi's hold. "I need you both to wait in the car, so I can talk to Nicole privately."

"You're doing it again." His mom's voice turned low and scary. She pushed up the sleeves of her coat, revealing frayed white bandages wrapped around her wrists. "So help me God, you leave me for that uptight bitch, and I'll run into traffic right now. I will fucking finish the job."

"She's high?" Dylan grabbed Kelsi's arm roughly. "Did you give her something?"

"Fuck you." Kelsi yanked away. "You have no right. No right."

Oh, God. Nicole's heart ached for Dylan. His mom had tried to commit suicide. That was why they'd driven out here. But would she do it? Would she actually run into traffic?

The woman's lip curled into a sneer. "What are you staring at, you stupid bitch?"

Maybe if she hadn't had an alcoholic mom who'd yelled and snarled and screamed to be left alone, maybe then this woman could intimidate her. But she *had* had that mom, so Nicole's only thought was for Dylan. His agonized expression had her focusing solely on him. "How can I help?"

"*Help?*" His mom faked a laugh. "That's hysterical coming from you. You can help by getting the *fuck* out of my face and out of my son's life."

"Mom." She'd never heard him sound so scary. The veins in his neck popped and strained. The muscles in his arms bulged.

She touched him, trying to get him to focus on her. "Hey, talk to me. Where are you going? Do they have somewhere to stay?" She couldn't invite them to her home—not with his mom this angry—but she could at least set them up in a hotel. She pulled out her phone to look up Times Square hotels.

His big hands closed over hers, making her realize she was shaking. "Nic, stop. I have to go."

"I'll get you a hotel." She waited for the hotels to load. "You shouldn't drive anywhere tonight."

Dylan closed his eyes, looking like he wanted to die. "No. Nicole, you—"

"What do you mean *no*?" his mom said. "What're we gonna do, sleep in the car? Do you know what we've eaten the last three days? Jerky and granola bars. Let her set us up in a hotel." Her mom strutted up to her, hand out. "We need some cash, too."

"That's not a problem." Nicole tucked her phone back into her clutch. "Let me find an ATM."

But Dylan hooked an arm around her waist and towed her back. "No. I'm not taking your money."

"Dylan, I don't care. Let me help." She had to do something.

"Yeah," his mom said. "Let her help. She fucking owes us."

"I don't take money from anybody." His hardened tone

felt like a door slamming in her face.

Tears stung, and she sucked in a sharp breath. "I'm not *anybody*. It's me." She hated how her voice wobbled.

Kelsi slid a hand between them, letting her palm rest on Dylan's stomach. Looking disgusted, he jerked away from them and headed to his mom, grabbing her arm and leading her to the car.

Alone on the crowded street with Dylan's ex, Nicole had no idea what to do. She should probably let him go, but…it was hard. Because if he left right now…what would it mean? Was he *leaving* her?

And then Kelsi's bitchy voice broke through. "Just go, okay? Go back to your friends."

"No, I…" She looked helplessly to Dylan, restraining his mom—kicking and screaming, as though she wanted to make a break for the heavy traffic of Avenue of the Americas.

"You're just making this harder for him," Kelsi said.

"I want to help."

"Come on, Nicole. How can you help when *you're* the problem?"

# CHAPTER TWENTY

**Nicole blinked against the bright light slanting in** through the crack in her curtain. Why hadn't she fixed that already?

Oh, right. Because she'd liked that little slice of light when she'd had Dylan beside her. She loved to see moonlight glowing on his powerful body.

Her eyes squeezed shut at the pain barreling through her, making her whole body clench. It didn't fade. It didn't get easier.

She'd known he wouldn't choose her. Of course she had. He'd never misled her. And, of course, it was his *mother* they were talking about. Of course he had to choose her.

Rolling onto her side, her gaze fell on her textbooks, the slim laptop case she hadn't opened in…a while. What time was it? She reached for her phone. Twelve-oh-three.

A bolt of fear shot her out of bed. Twelve-oh-three meant she'd missed two classes. Wait, oh, God, what day was it? She checked the phone again. The eighth.

The eighth. What did that mean? What classes did she have today? Oh, okay. Just a lab at four. God, she was exhausted. She settled back down, got under the covers and drew them up to her chin, one piece of it covering her ear. Funny, she hadn't done that in ages. Not since she'd lived with her mom. Everything had scared her back then, including the fear of spiders crawling in her ears. Had she read that somewhere? That spiders crawled into ears?

A soft knock at her door jolted her out of her rambling reveries. It could only be either James or Sydney. "Come in."

Hallway light flooded her room, and she squeezed her eyes shut. Someone sat on the edge of the bed—someone big, considering the way the bed dipped so much she nearly rolled forward. A big hand clamped down on top of her head.

Only one person had a hand that big. She opened her eyes. "Dad?"

"Get dressed. We're going for a walk."

Weak and a little light-headed, Nicole could barely keep up with her dad. "Over here." She led him down the path toward her favorite spot in the garden.

"Nice." He took in the curving cement islands, the stretches of grass, the tall iron sculptures. "Spend a lot of time in here, do ya?"

She murmured a response, a sense of relief coming over her when she got to her bench and collapsed on it. Even though she was bundled up in parka, knit hat, gloves, and a scarf wrapped all the way up to her nose, the cold still burned her skin, making her bones ache.

Her dad sat beside her. "Cold as hell today."

"What're you doing here, Dad?" He'd already reassured her the boys were okay, Brandon safely back at school, Ryan gearing up for his final semester in college.

"I got a call from your friend."

She shot him a look. "James?" How did he have her dad's number? He'd probably gotten it off her phone.

He nodded, his nose red, his skin looking dry and chapped. "Yep."

*Oh, James.* She wished he hadn't involved her dad. "What did he say?"

"That you're not doing so well."

"Oh, no, Dad, I'm fine. I swear, I'm just fine." God, he'd come all the way out there.

"Nicole…" He gave her a disbelieving look. "You've lost your sparkle, sweet pea."

"It's been a week. I've haven't hit the limit on eating ice cream and wearing stained clothes yet."

Her dad settled back. "Aw, pumpkin, love sucks."

Laughter shot out of her. She hadn't expected to hear that. "That's what you drove five hours to tell me?"

"Naw, I'm sure you figured that out on your own. But maybe you haven't figured out that it's not the love itself that's the problem. It's the people. We're messed up. You know that, right? And it's pretty hard to love when you're all twisted up inside."

"I know, Dad. He has to take care of his mom. He told me from the start."

"I'm not talking about Dylan. I'm talking about you." He watched her, waiting.

"You think *I'm* messed up?" Her heart ached, and she really needed to lie down.

"Yeah, I do. We all are. Thing is, I know you're hurting, but what you're feeling right now is more than just a broken heart. You've got some old fears tangled up with it."

"This isn't about *fear.* I gave him my whole heart, Dad, and he didn't want it. It hurts, okay? *I hurt.* I just need a few days, and then I'll be fine." And she would. It wasn't like she'd never had a broken heart before.

He pressed his lips together, getting that stubborn look he had. "I don't want you to be *fine*. Fine isn't good enough. Not for my girl. And I wouldn't be here if I thought you were just getting over a broken heart. That, you can do on your own."

She reached into her pocket for a tissue and swiped at her nose. "Then what're you here for?"

He reached for her hand. "You know what's killing me right now?"

She held his gaze and saw true concern. And that just knocked the stuffing right out of her, leaving nothing but sadness. "What?"

"I'm looking into the eyes of that little girl I used to pick up from her mom's place on the weekend."

"That's…what…no. Why would you say that?" Her mind grappled for traction while it spun and whirled. "I'm not that girl anymore. I don't… God, I'm not…I don't hoard food."

"No, you don't. But this thing with Dylan's pushing all your buttons."

"Well, of course it does, Dad. My mom and Jonathan chose booze over me. Dylan chose his mother. I mean, how do you keep putting your heart out there when no one chooses you? It sucks. And it scares me to death."

He reached for her hand—his gloved in leather, hers in wool—but she still felt his firm grasp. "I know it does, angel. Anyone who's ever lived with an addict knows that same fear. We want them to change so badly, and when they don't, it messes with our heads. Makes us feel helpless. You just wanted your mom to love you more than the booze. When she didn't, that had to make you feel like there was something wrong with you. But there wasn't." He lifted their joined hands, tugged, so she'd look at him. "I want you to know that, sweetheart. You were one hell of a little girl."

*Oh.* A rush of heat flooded her. He'd never said anything like that to her before.

Her dad smiled broadly, pride and affection glowing in his eyes. "Your mom's neglect probably made you think you weren't loveable. And I'm guessing that's what's going on here with Dylan. You think he didn't choose you, which hits that same nerve." He brought his hands to his mouth, cheeks puffing out as he blew into them. "So, *that's* why I drove five hours to see you. To make sure you understand that your mom's choice, Jonathan's choice, *Dylan's* choice is not about you. You're exceptional. A gem. And Dylan knows that. He loves you, and he'd choose you every day if he could."

"But he didn't."

"You've got it wrong. He thinks his happiness—*you*—comes at the cost of his mom." He shifted to face her. "But those are his issues. I want *you* to understand that you were a kid when this happened with your mom. You felt helpless. If there was no food in the house, you didn't eat. If she didn't get you to school, you didn't go. How many times did you think she was dead?"

Nicole startled at the blunt question.

"How many times did you shake her, crying your eyes out, trying to get her to wake up?" He shook his head, and she thought she saw a gleam of moisture in his eyes.

"A lot." All those sickening feelings popped right back up to the surface. "I don't know what this has to do with Dylan." She didn't want to feel them. The horror at seeing her mom's lifeless body, the desperation in trying to get her to wake up. The utter helplessness she'd felt for years.

"When your mom chose booze, it meant you were hungry, alone, dirty, and lost. Remember the time that dog came into the yard?"

She held up a hand to stop him. That ferocious dog snarled, barked, drooled, and lurched toward her. She'd screamed, terror wracking her body, but no one came. When she'd finally gotten into the house, she'd run to the living room to find her mom passed out on the couch.

"I remember." She hadn't thought about that incident in years—yet she felt the fear as vividly just then as when she'd experienced it.

"You were helpless back then. This time…this time, sweet pea, you're a woman. You can take care of yourself. Now, I know he broke your heart, but you're not helpless."

Her chest tightened so hard it ached. His words connected right with her heart.

"What I'm saying is, you can handle this one. You'll hurt, but you can take care of yourself. And you should. You can't fight someone's demons. No one knows that better than us."

*Us*. Tears burned in her eyes. Why did hearing him say *us* touch her so deeply?

She sucked in a cold, shaky breath. Because she wasn't alone. He was here for her. He *understood* her.

Her dad's big hand clamped down on her knee. "But you also can't let those demons take *you* down. You love with all your heart, and that's a good thing. Don't stop doing that because it didn't work out with Dylan. Don't let someone else's failings shut down your beautiful heart. You carry on, and you try again."

She didn't think she'd ever loved her dad more than at this moment. She nodded but couldn't speak through the painful knot in her throat.

He exhaled a puff of fog. "You are *so* loveable, sweetheart. You're a one of a kind."

She lowered her head, unable to see her gloved hands through the blur of tears. "Dad."

"I mean that. You're special, Nicole. I know you think your brothers are. And, sure, they're damn good at what they do, but they've been preoccupied with their physical skills, while you've been developing your mind, your heart, your creativity. You keep that heart wide open, sweet pea, and I promise you'll get back what you give."

*Oh, my God.* She had no idea her dad thought this way about her. She leaned into him. Those big, strong arms cradled her to his chest, and his beefy paw cupped the back of her head. "Thank you, Dad."

"There's nothing I wouldn't do for you."

She pulled back, wiped the moisture off her face with her glove. "I'm going to think about what you said. And, you know, maybe shower a little more often from now on."

******

Shrieking women hurled profanities at each other.

"Don't put up with her shit," his mom shouted at the TV.

Dylan forced himself to stay focused on his computer screen. Just a few more questions, and he'd be done. *No, wait.* He still had the essays to write.

"Oh, that's it. That's it. Take that bitch down."

Apparently, one of the Miami housewives didn't like being accused of trying to hang onto her man with sexy lingerie and cosmetic surgery. And she was willing to brawl to defend her honor.

"Oh, my God! Did you see that? Oh, fuck me. She *did* have plastic surgery. Did you see that, Dyllie? I've got to check this out." His mom came up behind him, reaching for his laptop. "Can I use this for a sec?" She tried to turn it toward her.

"I'm working."

"It'll just take a minute. Can you Google Marianna Janson? One of those bitches pulled her hair, and you could totally see scars right here." She motioned to the hairline at her temple. "I want to look it up on the Internet."

Okay, that was it. Gently catching her wrist, he edged her away from the table. Shoving the chair back, he strode to the TV and flipped it off.

"Hey." His mom whirled around. "I was watching that."

"I can't think when it's on."

"Well, what am I supposed to do?"

Good question. His mom didn't read or have any hobbies. All her friends partied, so she couldn't hang out with them. She couldn't work at the moment—too unstable, since she'd only been sober five days. What *was* she supposed to do?

"Maybe I'll call Anne." She leaned over to grab her phone off the coffee table.

That wasn't going to happen. Anne was the one who'd introduced his mom to Jeff Blakely. "How about you make some cookies?"

Her features lit up like a child's. "That's a great idea. You love cookies."

Not exactly, but he wouldn't correct her. He was just glad to have her occupied.

Hooking the chair leg with his boot, he dragged it back

to the table. Okay, so where was he? The cursor blinked over the question. Why did he want to go to CU. Well, he didn't. He wanted to stay at Wilmington.

It took a moment to realize the kitchen was too quiet, so he glanced over to find his mom texting on her phone. When she caught him watching, color stained her features.

That familiar sense of dread poured through him, hot and prickly. Who was she talking to? He couldn't ask. Too much pressure drove her to act out. But if he kept her occupied and didn't make her feel too watched, she did all right.

Or did she? Because weren't they already back to their hide and seek games? How many times this week had he searched her drawers and under her mattress and couch cushions for bottles and drugs? How many fights had they had over his distrust?

Jesus, he needed to get out, get some air. It was so hard to breathe in this apartment. Maybe after he knocked out a few more questions, they'd go to the diner. Grab a shake or something.

Okay, so, why did he want to go to CU? He could talk about the business school program…maybe his preference for a small, mountain town—

An image flashed in his mind. Nicole on the street, the tip of her nose red from the cold. Her expression of shock and horror as his mom swore at her.

Jesus Christ, he would give anything to take that moment back.

Worst of all? It was his fault. He'd known not to pull Nicole into his world.

He'd *known*. But selfish bastard that he was, he'd had to have her.

And then his mom had gotten to her. He squeezed his eyes shut at the memory of his mom calling Nicole a cunt.

His mom's phone chimed, and he swung around. She gave him a bright smile.

"Hello? Oh, hey." Using that fake peppy voice, she hurried out of the kitchen and down the hall towards her bedroom. *Dammit.* He got up, walking quickly but quietly, straining to hear anything—to pick up any kind of clue—but by the time he got close enough to hear her conversation, she'd killed the call.

Coming out of her room, she smiled. "You done with your application?"

Christ, these games. "No, Mom. Who was that?"

"Who?"

He gave her an impatient look.

"On the phone? Just a friend from work. I might start back on Monday. That's why she called. To see if I was ready to come back."

"You're going back to the head shop?"

"I don't know. Maybe. We need the money." And then she got pissy. "What do you want me to do, run Apple?"

What could he come up with to distract her from going out? "How about after you finish the cookies, we go to the diner?" While she baked, he'd try to finish at least one question before tabling the application for the night.

"Yeah, sure. Sounds good." He recognized that vague tone. She was definitely up to something.

He settled back at his computer, but a moment later a drawer slammed shut.

"There's no more chocolate chips."

"Then make sugar cookies."

"I want chocolate." She came out of the kitchen, body

tensed and jittery. "I'm just going to head to the store."

Yeah, like that was going to happen. "Okay, let's see what we've got. We'll come up with something you like." Screw the application. He saved it and closed the screen.

Jesus, it'd been a tough week. She'd barely slept, and she'd snacked constantly. She was restless but didn't want to walk or hike in the cold. Really, unless it involved partying, she didn't want to leave the apartment. But all she did was switch from the stereo to the TV. Seemed like nothing held her attention.

And, since he'd cut Kelsi out of his life, he didn't have anyone to help him anymore. It'd just been him and his mom for the past five days since he'd been back.

Keeping her sober was a full-time job.

She'd settle down, though. Once she got the shit out of her system, she could get a job. She said she'd start back with AA next week. Maybe she'd even make some decent friends.

And then he could get back to school in the fall. Or…why not summer school? She'd do all right if she knew he'd come home at the end of the day.

*That's what I'm giving Wilmington up for?*

He hadn't pulled the plug yet, though. Why, he had no idea. But the idea of flushing away that scholarship sickened him. And of never seeing Nicole again? He broke out in a clammy sweat just thinking about it.

But, of course, he had to let it go. Put it—her—behind him. It wouldn't work, being across the country. His mom needed—

A sharp knock on the door had his mom bolting across the living room. The chair kicked back, and his longer legs ate up the short distance. He cut her off.

"God, Dylan. Let me get the damn door."

He gripped her shoulders. "Is that Anne? Are you going

out tonight?"

Her gaze cut away. "I'm going to go crazy if I don't get out of this dump." She struggled to get out of his hold.

"Stop it. Just stop. Talk to me."

She blew out a rough breath but didn't say anything.

"Is Anne at the door right now?"

"Well, why don't you let me answer it and we'll find out?"

"Mom. I don't want you going out with her. You know where it'll lead."

"We'll get a coffee. Some laughs. What's the big deal?"

"Bullshit, Mom." Drawing in a deep breath, he worked to keep his temper under control. "I'm here, Mom. You wanted me home, I'm home."

"Yeah, that doesn't mean I'm your prisoner. I can have a life, you know. I'm not going to go out and get shitfaced. Now, back off and let me out for a few hours."

Anger flickered and flared, but he pushed it down. "I'm transferring to CU to be with you, so think hard before you walk out that door to get wasted."

The doorbell rang again, at the same time her phone chimed. She rushed forward, and this time he let her go. "Don't do it, Mom."

"What? I'm answering the door. At least let me let her in. She can hang out here if you need to play jailor so badly."

And let Anne hand her a bag of coke?

"I'm not playing games with you. I know she's got shit on her, and I know she's going to find a way to give it to you."

"What do you want from me? You're sitting there in front of your computer, and I'm bored out of my mind. What's the big deal if I go out for a drink? One fucking drink, and then I'll come right back home. Big whoop."

"But it won't be one drink. We both know that."

"I need to take the edge off."

He couldn't let her go out. "You've been sober five days. Don't blow it tonight."

"I'm not blowing anything. I'm having a friend over." She looked at her phone, quickly texted. "Just…lay off."

"No, I'm not going to lay off. I'm giving up my full ride to Wilmington." *I've already given up Nicole.* "So, it's not okay that you can't last more than five fucking days. You have to try harder than this. Now, tell your friend to fuck off because unlike her *you're* trying to get your life on track. Or don't you want a decent life? Am I wasting my time here? Do you just want to get wasted and knocked around by drug dealers and wake up in dirty fields in the middle of winter?"

Pain flickered across her features. "No. Of course I don't want that."

"Then get in the kitchen and let's bake those damn cookies."

His mom looked thoughtful—had he gotten through? And then she typed something out on her cell phone. Finished, she tossed the cell on the couch. "Fine. Let me tell her I'm not going out."

He wanted to stop her—to physically block her—but he wouldn't risk pushing her too far, so instead he stood his ground and watched her open the door to speak quietly to her friend.

After the closed the door, she looked subdued.

"You ready to bake?"

"Yeah. Let me have a smoke first." She headed calmly back to her room, leaving the door open. He knew she'd pull a chair up to the window, lean forward with her arms against the sill, while she took deep drags and blew smoke out into the frigid night air.

He got started in the kitchen. Pulled butter from the fridge, the cookie sheets from the drawer under the oven. And then, when he opened the cupboard for the vanilla, he could've sworn he got hit with a whiff of lavender. He closed his eyes, and there she was. Nicole, with a mischievous gleam in her eyes as she turned from the stove to smile up at him. Jesus, he could feel the curve of her ass in his hands, her breath at his ear.

"Okay, ready." His mom breezed into the kitchen smelling faintly of pot.

A quick glance at her dilated pupils confirmed she'd actually scored a bag of weed from her friend in the thirty seconds it took to tell her she wasn't going out with her.

Something clicked into place inside him. He thought about his mom, her hands shaking, the constant texting, the hide and seek games, and he got it. He just completely got it.

For the first time he understood that he couldn't be the reason she stayed sober. She had to find her own reason. Otherwise, it was like trying to hold back a waterfall.

"Did you find any chocolate?" His mom came into the kitchen.

Giving up Wilmington wouldn't solve anything. Even if he quit school and got a job, he'd still be worrying about what she did during those hours.

Keeping her from using was a full time job. And even then it wouldn't stop her.

He'd give up a lot to keep her safe, but he wasn't giving up his scholarship.

She cocked her head. "Why're you looking at me like that?"

"Forget the chocolate. We're making cupcakes instead."

******

"Nicole?" Chef called, as everyone packed up their bags. Today, they'd find out who he'd chosen for the culinary minor. She'd only gotten to know a handful of the hundred and eighteen students, but she wondered which of them he'd choose. What about the twenty made them glow brighter than the others? She wished them well.

Lifting the strap of her messenger bag over her head, she adjusted it and headed to the front of the lab. "Yes, Chef?"

"You surprised me."

*Okay.*

"Not many people do that."

"Well, thank you. I…" She wouldn't lie and say she enjoyed his class. "I learned a lot. Thank you." She turned to go.

"I know I was hard on you."

She stopped. Turned to face him. Was he messing with her again?

"I thought you'd drop out." He shrugged. "You didn't belong here. But you *didn't* drop out, and it made me curious. So I pushed. I couldn't see how you'd fit into a culinary program with all your…sensitivities. But you didn't quit." He eyed her thoughtfully. "You never quit."

"This minor is important to me."

He nodded. "I got some decent final presentations."

Well, good for the select few he'd chosen. She wanted to leave, but she had the sense he wasn't finished with her.

"But no one gave me an action plan. Other than you. I like it, Nicole. I like it very much. I don't know if the residents of Wilmington will make use of the community garden you're planning, but we'll make sure all my future students do."

*Uh, was that the Queen's we or the Chef and Nicole we?* "That's great."

"I'd like you to oversee that project for the school, if that interests you."

"The project? You want me to oversee the building of the greenhouse? Using recycled plastic bottles?"

He hadn't smiled so broadly since the first student dropped his lab. "That's what I'm saying."

"I'd like that very much, but I don't know what my schedule will be like. I have to choose a different minor, and I'm developing my cupcake business."

He tipped his head, looking baffled. "You're in, Nicole."

"In?" Her heart pounded hard and fast.

"Didn't you see the list I posted on the door?"

She hadn't bothered to look.

"I chose you."

"You…" Emotion rushed her so fast she went dizzy. "Thank you." She was stunned. Honestly, just…stunned. "I…wow…I didn't expect that. Thank you." She turned once again to go.

"Hang on. Your final project…I want to know how you did it."

Seriously, he wanted to know about her vegetable, bean, and rice dish? Wait a minute. Was he back to playing games?

"I'm not a pastry chef," he said. "And I consume enough calories through my own creations that I rarely eat desserts, but I know a treasure when I find one."

*Okay, whoa.* Now she was completely confused. What did her final project have to do with dessert? She waited for him to continue.

Briefly, he looked confused. But then he just looked interested. "How do you do it? How do you infuse the scent of a flower in the batter of a cupcake? Usually adding syrup makes an overly sweet product. But yours…I thought I was biting into a lavender-scented cloud."

"I don't understand. You've had one of my cupcakes?"

His brow furrowed. "You turned in a cupcake, didn't you?"

"I turned in the rice dish."

"Yes, and then several hours later a lavender cupcake was delivered with a note that said it was yours."

"What? I don't understand any of this."

"You don't make lavender cupcakes?"

"No, I do. But I didn't turn one in for my final project."

"No, but a very large young man with shoulder-length hair did. Ring a bell?"

James reached across the scarred table to squeeze her hand. "Wait, you're serious? You made it?"

"Congratulations." Sydney leaned over and threw her arms around her neck. "We have to celebrate."

"Hey, this *is* a celebration," James said. "We got her out of the house."

Nicole gave him a smirk. Ever since her dad's visit, she'd gotten out more. But she'd heard Dylan had come back to school, so she hadn't ventured into town. But, hey, she'd pulled herself together enough to get through finals and get back to Sweet Treats. Her dad had helped her separate the pain of losing Dylan, the love of her life, and the debilitating fear of not being chosen. Irrational, but still. Her dad's insights helped her see that she could carry on, even with a broken heart.

She just had to stop giving her heart to people who *couldn't* choose her.

"So, um…" Wrapping her hands around the mug, she let

the heat travel up her arms. The hum of conversation in the coffee house relaxed her and, for the first time, the ache in her heart didn't pull her under. "I can't help wondering why he did it."

"He loves you." Sydney bumped her shoulder. "You know he does."

Dylan loved her enough to bake cupcakes and turn them in for her final project in culinary but not enough to be with her? If he'd come back to school, why hadn't he come to her?

Maybe he'd gotten back with Kelsi.

Nope. She didn't believe that for one second. She smiled at James. "So, do you think he just slopped the frosting on?"

Sydney and James shared a look, then Sydney smiled.

"What?" She nudged James gently under the table with her boot. "You did it? *You* frosted them?"

"Nutbag woke me up at six in the morning."

"He did?"

"He was going to turn it in with the frosting slapped on, because he figured it was all about taste, but then he got all worried you'd get marked down for presentation."

Sydney placed a hand on her heart and swooned. "He thought it should reflect you completely, and you'd never turn in something—"

"Half-ass." James finished her sentence.

"So, what do you think?" Sydney asked. "Are you glad to be in the program?"

"Nothing really pushes the needle, you know? My meter's pretty flat right now. But, yeah. I mean, there's nowhere else I'd rather be."

"Baby steps," James said.

A few other friends showed up, crowding around their

table. Nicole remained quiet. Talking about Dylan had stoked the pain to life. Times like this, the loss seemed unbearable. How did she move on after a guy who'd let her sleep in his bed because of a nasty roommate, who'd...well, who'd bake lavender cupcakes to make sure she got into the program that mattered so much to her?

Oh, dammit. Tears burned, and her throat started to close. She would not cry.

But, God, what a freaking *loss*. Fine, he was never hers to begin with—as he'd told her repeatedly—but how cruel to have had him in her life such a short time. She missed him.

She ached for him.

A rowdy crowd entered the coffee house. Her friends were so engaged in conversation they barely noticed.

Nicole did. She recognized Joe, Kevin, Dylan's whole crew. Why had she agreed to come into town? It was so small, her chances of seeing him—

He was there. The group shifted, revealing him in the center. Fierce pain slugged her gut. Out of everyone in the room, he stood out. Tall, powerful, and strikingly handsome. But he was wasted, she could see from the laziness of his eyes, the slouch of his shoulders. Someone said something that had them all cracking up, and then one of the girls wrapped her arms around him and rubbed his stomach.

Anger, disgust, *pain* fired her up and out of her chair. Turning sideways, she angled her way between the closely packed tables and blew out of the warmth of the coffee house into the bitter, freezing cold.

He *disgusted* her. He was a drunk just like Jonathan, just like her mom. Just like *his* mom. God, how could he watch his mom for eighteen years and then turn out just like her? She was so glad she hadn't turned out like her mom. Not wanting James or anyone to come after her, she shot off a quick text. *Tired. Going home. Alone, ok?*

*Sure you don't want me to come with?*

*Positive.*

*Here if u need me.*

Cold air stung her face, making her eyes water. Damn, she forgot her coat. God, what a pig. Right back to partying and hooking up. What a relief it must be for him to be free again. To be back in the world he knows best.

*Screw him.* God, it was cold. She race-walked down Main Street, only just then becoming aware of the sound of boots hitting pavement behind her. A hand clamped down on her shoulder.

She swung around to him, ready to ream him out, but when she saw the remorse, the pain in his eyes, she shut her mouth.

All the anger, the hate…just faded. Because she looked at this man she'd always thought of as strong and powerful and realized he was just a guy. Dealing with some heavy stuff he didn't know how to handle.

Like her dad said, it wasn't about *her* at all.

It took a moment before she noticed his offering. Her coat. He'd found it among the dozens on the hooks by the door, and he'd brought it to her.

"Thank you." She turned to go. Honestly, she couldn't bear to be around him.

"Wait."

And there it was all over again. That single word was the flint to spark her anger back to life. "For what? For you to be the man you could be? No, I don't do that. I keep moving forward. You of all people should know that." She'd learned her lesson. She'd never wait for another person again. Either they were marching forward, strong enough to face their own demons and create their own lives, or she'd quietly move on.

But he kept up with her, matching her pace. "We never got to talk."

"You never bothered trying."

"I did. I came to the house as soon as I got back to school, but your friends wouldn't let me in to see you." He didn't sound all that drunk.

"They were your friends, too." He'd just preferred the townies.

"They made a choice—they didn't want me to hurt you—and it was the right one. But I wanted to tell you I'm sorry."

"Shut up. Just shut up. I do not want to hear another word out of your stupid mouth."

"Fine. I just wanted—"

She stopped. "I don't care what you want. And guess why, Dylan?" She spat his name out like it was an olive pit. "Because your actions already told me what you want. Go back to your friends, your girls, the life that makes you comfortable. Stay away from me. You made your choice."

"My choice? Are you fucking serious? My mom tried to *kill* herself."

She exhaled, making sure he saw how bored she was with this conversation. "People don't *try* to commit suicide, Dylan. They *do* it."

His eyes went wide with horror. As if she were some kind of monster. But she didn't care. His mom had played him. Too bad he couldn't see it. But then he calmed down, took a few deep breaths. "Maybe you're right. But even so, it was different for you. You had your dad, your brothers. You had your mansion in Greenwich."

"My *mansion*? Really? Wow, when you go back you go *all*

*the way* back. Right back to the boy who flashed his White Trash badge to everyone he met. Well, screw you, Dylan. My choice was no easier to make than yours. I just made a different one. Stop making excuses—they only make you look more cowardly than you already are."

He reeled back. "I'm a *coward*? I'm a coward for taking care of my mom? Are you out of your fucking mind? I might have to give up my scholarship to keep her—"

"To keep things exactly the same. Because that's all you'll accomplish by giving up your future. As long as you allow her to manipulate you, as long as you do exactly what you've always been doing, *nothing* will change. Nothing you do or say will ever change who she is. Eighteen years of living with her has proven that to you. You *know* that, deep in your bones you know there's not a damn thing you can do to make her change."

"You're pissed because I didn't choose you. I wanted to. You don't think I wanted to?"

"No. You didn't want to. You wanted to keep things the way they were because that's how you feel safe." She had nothing more to say.

"You know I had to choose my mom."

She stormed up to him. "The choice was never between me or your mom. The choice has only ever been between your past and your future. And instead of choosing the life you could make for yourself—the life you can actually have if you had the balls to take it—you chose to stay in your past, the only world you've ever known. *That* makes you a coward." She narrowed her eyes. "Now, thank you for bringing me my coat, but I don't want you to do one more thing for me. Ever. Stay away from me. I choose *me*, my future, and you're not in it."

She walked back to the house, aware that he'd followed from a distance. As she pulled out her key, she glanced over to find him watching. Making sure she got in safely.

And the loss of that—someone caring about her, looking out for her—it just made her heart ache.

She entered the house and quickly closed the door on him.

# CHAPTER TWENTY-ONE

**He hadn't seen her in the Sculpture Gardens for weeks,** so he went to her spot. Dropping his pack on the ground, he pulled out his phone, and found the right number. Head still foggy from pulling another all-nighter—he still hadn't caught up from the week of school he'd missed—he tipped his head back and drank in the fresh, crisp air.

When he was a kid—couldn't remember the exact age—some guy his mom brought home needed the bathroom, but Dylan had been using it. In a rage, the guy had slammed the door on Dylan's arm. A couple of times. He'd heard the snap, felt the staggering pain. The music had been loud that night, so no one'd heard him scream. He'd crawled into bed, but the pain had kept him up all night.

He remembered lying there, wide-eyed from a pain so intense it made him sweat profusely, soaking the sheet. He remembered wondering when it would pass, thinking it *had* to pass.

Turned out he'd broken the arm in several places. But that pain? He lived with it now. Only instead of physical, it was his heart. And it wasn't getting better. Nor would it.

Because Nicole O'Donnell was his deep down. And he

couldn't do it anymore. He couldn't deny his deep down one more second.

He had to make the call.

Punching in the numbers, he wondered how the man would respond. Would he tear him a new asshole? Or see his name and just ignore the call? But Dylan realized right then it didn't matter how the man responded because it was time. And if this guy wouldn't help him, he'd go somewhere else.

Shit had to change, and it had to change now.

"Yello?"

"Mr. O'Donnell? Bill? This is Dylan McCaffrey. I was hoping I could talk to you."

The last time he'd been in this house it had smelled stale, like rotting gym socks. That was the day he'd come back to school, only to find his roommates blocking him from going upstairs. James had packed up his duffel and told him to hurry up and get his shit together because they missed him and wanted him back.

That was when he thought he could have school, but not Nicole. He couldn't mess with her again—not unless he was absolutely sure he could be with her.

Today, the scent of lavender filled the air. A few people sat in the living room, conversation halting as they noticed him. Last time they'd formed a vigilante group, ready to kick his ass out. Today, they watched.

Heading for the stairs, he noticed the boxes on the kitchen counter, waiting for delivery. He wondered who'd taken over his job but felt a little punch of excitement because he'd only worked peripherally for Sweet Treats before—but now? Now he was all-in.

He made it up the stairs without any confrontations.

Kicking the door open with his boot, he tossed the duffle bag onto his bed, dropped the backpack on the floor, and dumped the textbooks on his desk.

James, typing away on his laptop at his desk, twisted around. "Give me one more sec—oh." Surprise turned into disapproval, as he took in Dylan's belongings. "What's happening here?"

"I'm back."

"Oh, no, you're not." James got up, eyeing Dylan's belongings.

"Forget it. I'm not living in that hell hole in town anymore."

"You're also not living across the hall from the girl you destroyed."

"My room."

"Oh, that's just great. You've moved on, so you think you can just come back? God, how did I miss this prickish side of you?"

"Moved on? Are you fucking kidding me? I'll never move on from her. Never." He unzipped his bag and dug around for his sheets, tossing them on the mattress. "Get your shit off my bed."

"I'm not letting you back in here. You will seriously have to kill me first."

"I'm going to fix it. I'm fixing everything."

Dylan waited, watching emotion play across his roommate's features. Until James softened. "I'm not sure that's possible."

"Anything's possible if you hang in long enough."

"What changed?" He sat on the edge of his bed and crossed a leg over his knee. "Wait a minute, what have you done?"

"What I should have done a long damn time ago."

The sight of her on the concrete bench made his pulse quicken. She sat huddled in her puffy yellow parka, mittens, snow boots, and scarf, and he smiled. She wouldn't talk to him at home. She ignored him when they passed each other on campus, but he'd have her full attention here.

Gloved hands wrapped around a large paper coffee cup, she had her eyes closed as she breathed in the steam.

"Hey."

Her body jolted, the hot liquid lurching out the tiny opening. At first she looked angry to see him, but then she just looked annoyed. "What do you want?"

Same attitude she'd given him the past two weeks. "I have something to say to you. And before you leave, I know this is your special place, so I won't be long." He sat down beside her. "I talked to your dad last week."

"My *dad*? Why?"

"I needed his help."

"Okay." She looked away. "Well, I hope he helped you."

"He did. But it's because I was ready for it."

"Good for you." Clearly, she wanted him to leave.

"I want you to know that I'm not transferring."

She held up a hand. "I'm glad my dad could help you, and I hope your life works out, but it's not my business anymore. I don't want to hear about it."

"Your dad said something to me over the break. Remember when he overheard my conversation with Kelsi, and he took me golfing?"

She gave no acknowledgement. Her cheeks matched the pink tip of her nose and her dark hair flipped out of the blue beanie that had a big furry pom pom on top, and she was the most beautiful girl he'd ever seen. And he wouldn't quit. He just wouldn't quit till he won her back.

"On the way home that day, he said that when a kid grows up with parents like ours, we become anxious. For you, it was about food. Only you channeled a bad symptom of anxiety—hoarding—into something really good. You bake magical desserts. Well, that *and* you've made it your life's work to make sure people don't go hungry." He smiled, but she remained unmoved. "I didn't do that. I just held on tight to the idea that if I continued to control things, I could keep the worst thing from happening."

She let out the faintest exhalation.

"He told me that the only way to overcome my anxiety was to break away from the situation causing it. Unless I did that, I'd never have perspective. I'd just be in this endless loop of enabling. Nothing would get better, nothing would change. As you've pointed out so many times."

"Dylan…" She sounded tired, uninterested. Fortunately, he knew her better. Knew her enough to know the way she clutched the cup, the way her brow furrowed, meant she was very much interested in what he had to say.

"When I came back to school, after I ended things with you—"

"You didn't bother ending anything. You left me on Avenue of the Americas on New Year's Eve. I never heard from you again."

"I did that." He nodded. What could he say? "Not because my feelings for you changed, but because I felt guilt. At the time I actually believed that if I gave up my happiness, I could keep my mom alive. Weird, but true. When Kelsi told me my mom had tried to kill herself, I thought it was because I'd chosen you over her. The hit of anxiety made me…well, I couldn't think. I just acted. I went home, right back to the life I'd left. Because my worst fear had come true. I'd chosen my own happiness over hers and nearly cost my mom her life. But your dad was right. I needed to come back here, get away from everything, just be alone—"

"You've hardly been alone. Nor have you gotten away from anything—you've just recreated your life in Gun Powder."

"Yes, I know that, Nicole. It felt less like a betrayal—like I hadn't really left my mom and my friends behind—when I hung around people I thought were like me. My point is that in the time away, I thought about what you said, about the real choice I had to make. And I realized that letting guilt inform my decisions was going to fuck things up for everybody. So, I talked to your dad. I told him everything." He let out a breath, feeling lighter, more confident. "Your dad's a good guy."

"I know."

An icy wind cut through the garden, and he had to lower his head, turn his eyes away from the gust. "I cut her off, Nic. I changed my phone number." He let out a breath. "I told her I loved her and that, when she got better, to let Uncle Zach know so I could come see her."

She nodded, deep sadness in her eyes. "That's great. Really great. I'm happy for you." And then she got up, a rustle of bulky material, and she walked away from him.

He saw the moment she recognized him through the swarm of bodies leaving their classes and heading off in different directions. Nicole averted her gaze, as usual, but this time he blocked her.

"I need to talk to you."

Flanked by her friends, she easily sidestepped him. "I've got to get to Psych."

A hand on her shoulder, he pulled her back. "It's important."

She stopped, turned toward him, looked him straight in the eye, and said, "I asked you to leave me alone, and I meant it."

He forced himself to ignore the sharp stab of pain her brutal words delivered in such a soft voice. "I got a call from your dad."

"Why? Is there something wrong?" Digging into her bag for her phone, a look of concern gripped her features when she read the screen. "He called a half hour ago." She quietly told her friends she'd catch up with them later, as she hit her dad's number. "Did something happen?" she asked Dylan. He led her aside, out of the flow of passersby.

Her attention snapped to the phone. "Dad?" After a few moments of listening, shock hit her, sending her shoulders back, her eyes wide. "The *hospital*? What happened? Is he all right?"

He doubted Bill had gotten new information on Brandon's condition in the twenty minutes since they'd talked, but he tensed, waiting for her reaction.

"Oh, my God." Wincing, she placed a hand on her chest, like she'd taken a deep breath that hurt too much to expel. "Is he going to be all right?" For just one brief moment, her gaze locked with his—his heart lurched with hope that she'd turn to him—but then she looked away.

"Yes. Okay. Yes. I'm coming home now." Anger replaced worry, and she narrowed her eyes at Dylan. "No, Dad. I can drive myself." She started walking away. "I don't need him."

Oh, but she did. Not a chance in hell he'd let her drive five hours home in icy conditions when she was freaking out about her unconscious brother.

She grew even more agitated. "Forget it. Don't worry how I get there. Let me go so I can pack a bag. Okay, bye. Wait. Dad? If you find out anything—anything at all—let me know. Okay, thanks." She dumped the phone in her purse and took off across the quad.

With a hand on her shoulder, Dylan gently steered her toward the parking lot. "I've already packed you a bag."

"You what?" She shrugged away from his touch. "You went into my room? You can't do that."

"Well, I did. Now let's go."

Her eyes flashed. "No. I'll get James." She veered left, toward the Science buildings—he didn't know why, since James didn't take any science classes—and then stopped short, turning in a slow circle, as if disoriented.

"We don't have time to find James right now." His gut ached that she needed James and not him.

Her eyes filled with tears. "Okay." She started toward the parking lot. "Why did my dad call you?"

"You weren't answering your phone."

"I had it on silent."

"And he wanted me to drive you."

"You're not driving me. I can drive myself."

"Probably not a good idea in these conditions." Sheets of ice covered the roads.

"Then I'll get James."

"James is from Atlanta. He's not used to driving in this."

"Oh, my God, Dylan, I can't handle this right now. Just go." She scrounged around in her purse and wound up dropping her phone. They both lowered to get it, cracking heads. "Dammit, Dylan, just leave me alone." Clutching the phone to her chest, she inhaled. "Thank you for your help, but I don't need you anymore." She pulled keys out of her bag and then headed off. But she faltered, looking around. He could tell she'd forgotten where she'd parked.

He wrapped a hand around her waist, gently tugged. "Come on. Let's go see your brother."

"I feel sick. I think I'm going to be sick."

He suspected adrenaline was to blame, and he didn't really think she'd throw up, so he guided her to the parking lot where he'd found her Jetta.

At the car, he popped the trunk, tossed the bag he'd left on the ground into it. Then, he met her at the driver's side. "Get in, please."

"I don't want you."

"I know that. I brought your pillow. You can sleep. We don't have to talk."

"You don't get to take care of me."

He smiled because she made it sound like the privilege it was. "I know. Get in the car. Let's go see Brandon."

Saying his name out loud did the trick. She hurried around to the passenger side.

Dylan cranked the ignition and flipped on the defroster. Then, he grabbed the scraper from the backseat. After de-icing the windshield, he pulled her pillow out of the carry-on bag he'd packed and handed it to her.

Once on the road, she bunched the pillow in her lap. "What was he doing home? He should be at school."

"I don't know." He turned on the wipers to remove the melting ice. His skin burned as it made the transition from cold to warm.

"What if he doesn't wake up?" The anguish in her tone killed him. He reached out and cupped her knee. She tensed but didn't bat his hand away. "Who plays hockey in the middle of the night?"

"He'll wake up."

She set her phone in the cup holder. "They don't know anything." She tugged off her gloves, rubbing her hands together. "Oh, my God. What if there's a blood clot or something. People die that way."

"We don't know anything yet, so let's not make things up."

"You're right." She looked unseeingly out the window, features pulling in tight in concentration. "He'll be okay. He's strong. I just…I don't understand why he'd come home."

"You know his friend Troy?"

She nodded.

"It was his birthday. I guess a bunch of the guys came home for it."

She gave him the stink eye. "How do you know?"

"Your dad and I have been talking."

"Oh." She sniffed, reached into the glove box and pulled out a napkin. Blowing her nose, she tipped her head back and closed her eyes.

An hour later, she still hadn't said a word to him. With every mile that ticked by, he tried to come up with ways to get her talking to him. But nothing came.

Because words didn't matter. Actions did. He was the third person in her life she'd let in who hadn't chosen her. His only hope was to be there for her—prove it through his actions.

"Dylan." She reached for the stereo and lowered the volume. "Thank you for taking me home, but I don't want you to get the wrong idea."

"Okay."

"I'm not…we're not getting back together. I don't know if you even want that—"

"I want that more than anything."

"It's never going to happen. I'm glad you're not transferring, and I wish the very best for you, but we'll never be together again. You may think you see things differently now, but the truth is, you could go back to your mom at any time." She stiffened. "I didn't mean it like that. Oh, God, that sounded terrible. She's your mom. She's your priority—she *should* be."

"*I'm* my priority, sunshine. I should've been all along."

She looked a little stunned. "Okay…I…wow."

"This didn't happen overnight. When I was fourteen, my aunt and uncle had me in Alateen meetings. My penance for stealing their car. So I've heard all this stuff before. Borderline personality disorder, manipulation, accountability…it's nothing new. And it even made sense on some level back then, but my mom's influence was a lot stronger. I thought I was all she had. I thought without me…well, you know what I thought. But your dad asked me some hard questions, and it made me kind of sick to think my own mom would use me the way she has. She doesn't see me as her son. She sees me as a means of meeting her needs. That's pretty fucked up." He took in a breath, held it, and chanced reaching for her hand. When she didn't move hers away, he grasped it. She didn't turn hers over to clasp his back, but she didn't pull away either. "I'm moving on. And until she wants what's best for me, I don't have anything to say to her. I'm done with the life I hated so much."

She gave him a wary look. "I'm…happy for you."

Time to tell her everything. Put it all out there. "I'll tell you what did it—what pushed me over the line." He withdrew his hand, rubbing it over his chin. "If I didn't make a change…fuck, Nicole, I wouldn't have *you.* I mean, Jesus, it hit me hard. Missing you was this physical pain that wouldn't go away, and I couldn't really figure out *why* I had to give you up. How would it help my mom? Until I realized she just wants me for herself because there's no one else to pay her bills. If I let her, I'd give up everything I am to serve her."

She shot him a look, this one filled with compassion. He *was* getting through.

"And I *let* it happen. All the way up until she asked me to give up you. That was the game-changer. That made me see her for who she really is for the first time. And once I did, I realized that, yeah, I love my mom—she's my *mom*—but I'm only enabling her to continue to live this life she's created for herself. The only hope she has of changing is if *I* change."

"But you were so worried what might happen to her. How did you let go of that?"

"Well, that's the thing, isn't it? I could give up everything, and she could still wind up dead of an overdose."

"You think you can stick with it?"

"Absolutely."

"How do you know?"

"Because I see it now. You can't go back from that."

At the Help desk in Greenwich Hospital, Dylan asked for Brandon's room, while Nicole called her dad.

"No change." She looked up from her phone.

They headed for the elevator. He wanted to reach for her hand—more than anything, he missed touching her—but he couldn't risk upsetting her. Besides, even after all he'd said, she still hadn't warmed to him.

At the Intensive Care Unit, they had to press a buzzer to gain entrance. Fortunately, her dad waited for them behind the door, watching through the round window.

She threw herself into her dad's arms. He swallowed her up, one big hand covering the back of her head. "I'm so scared."

"Me, too, sweet pea." When he let her go, he led them down the corridor to Brandon's room. She went right to him, resting a hand gently on her brother's arm.

"He looks so peaceful."

Dylan came up behind her, standing close.

"How bad is it?" she asked her dad.

"Depends." Her dad jammed his hands deep into the pockets of his jeans. "He's in the ICU because of alcohol poisoning. Not sure about anything else yet."

"Alcohol poisoning. Oh, my God." She watched her brother. Dylan took in the tubes, the monitors, the steady beep of the machine. It was pretty damn scary.

"I didn't know he drank that much." Her dad seemed confused. "Sure, he drinks, but I've never seen him out of control."

Nicole shot him a look. "It's not your fault."

"We have alcoholism in the family. I watch for it with them." He nodded to the bed, to Brandon. "You, I don't have to worry about."

"What was he doing?" She looked to her dad.

Her dad shrugged. "Boyce and Parker came in for Troy's birthday. They went for some beers. I guess someone had the bright idea to skate on Pequot pond."

"Was he unhappy? Why would he drink that much?"

Her dad shook his head. "No idea, angel."

"He's got everything. *Everything.* And yet he's so miserable he drinks himself unconscious?"

And that was it. He'd given her enough space. He stepped around to her side, wrapped an arm around her. When he looked up, he caught her dad watching.

"Hey, now," a crisp voice said. They all turned to see a nurse enter the room. "Thought I told you to wait outside?"

"Now, Marnie," her dad began, his usual charm a little tattered.

"Hi, I'm Nicole." She stepped away from Dylan. "His sister."

"And your brother needs his room cleared out so we can get to him." She tipped her chin to Bill. "Which I thought I did a nice of job of explaining before. Now, scat, all of you. I will personally come to the waiting room when it's time for a visit—one at a time."

They headed out. She turned to her dad. "What about Ryan? Is he on his way?"

Her dad gave a terse nod.

"God, Dad, what if…"

"Nope. Not going there. My boy's going to be just fine."

******

"Hey, pumpkin. It's time to wake up."

That familiar voice tugged at her consciousness, and she fought to open her eyes. When she came awake, she saw an expanse of broad chest covered in a light blue button-down.

She jerked upright, her back and neck stiff and aching. Looking around, she found herself sprawled across Dylan in the waiting room of the ICU, her dad crouching before her. "Dad. Is he all right?"

"Still no change, sweetie. Listen, the doctor wants us to go home. If anything changes, he'll let us know."

"No, I'm…can't we just wait?"

"Pumpkin, I'm gonna camp out right here. I'd like you and Dylan to go home, get some sleep, and let me call you the minute I hear anything, all right?"

She glanced at Dylan, who watched her carefully. "Yeah, all right."

The moment they got inside the warm house, Nicole reached for her luggage.

But Dylan held onto the handle. "Hang on. I've got some stuff in there, too."

"Oh, of course." What was she supposed to do with all these emotions? She couldn't handle being with Dylan, when all her energy needed to be with her brother. She watched him set the bag down, unzip it, and rummage around for his plastic toiletry bag, a T-shirt, and a pair of gym shorts.

He zipped it back up. "I'll carry it upstairs for you."

"No, it's fine. I'll just see you in the morning." She wanted to thank him, ask him if he needed to get back to school, but the words didn't come.

She climbed the stairs, feeling him watching her, but she didn't look back.

She *never* looked back.

Teeth brushed, face washed, she grabbed her phone and walked out of the bathroom to find Dylan taking up the whole doorway. "Do you need something?"

"Sorry. I brought you this. Thought it might help you sleep better." He only came in a few steps, holding a mug of steaming tea. She could smell the lavender from where she stood.

"Thank you." She approached him, too aware of the thick muscles in his arms, his damp hair, and the strain of the shirt over his broad shoulders.

"You okay?"

She shrugged. "Not really."

"Do you want me to stay? Till you fall asleep?"

Her mind said, *No*, but she couldn't push the word out of her mouth. He stood there so strong and powerful, and she couldn't deny the need bearing down on her. Maybe she couldn't have him because, ultimately, his mom would always come first—as she should—but she could have the comfort he offered tonight.

She'd done such a good job of steeling herself against him. Talking herself out of the drama of wanting a guy who didn't want her enough to overcome his issues. If she let down her guard—even for one night—would she fall back into that morass of wanting what she couldn't have? She didn't think she could bear it.

He really did sound like he'd overcome his issues, though. And he'd said he'd done it for *her*.

"Just till you fall asleep." His voice, so calm, did more for her than the warm cup of tea. And, well, he'd made her a cup of tea.

She barely nodded, turning quickly to her bed and setting the mug on her nightstand. Pulling down the covers on her side, she got in. He got on top of the duvet.

"You're going to be cold."

"Your house is pretty warm."

"No, you're just a furnace."

"That, too."

She sat up, pulled the throw from the foot of the bed, and shook it out, tossing it over him.

He nodded to the mug. "Drink your tea. Someone I know says lavender relaxes you."

Okay, so she smiled. He was wonderful. That didn't mean anything, though, because in a month, a year, two years, his mom could do something drastic, call him back, and he'd leave her just like that. As easily as he'd done on New Year's Eve.

She lined up some pillows behind her, took the mug in her hands and brought it to her face, letting the steam rise up to her. "Do you want some?"

Resting on the pillow, he shook his head. Those soulful eyes watched her carefully.

And that's when it struck her. His eyes. For the first time, they didn't have that guarded look anymore.

Why did that make her so happy? "Maybe this isn't a good idea."

"It's a great idea."

"It's hard enough with you living across the hall again. I'm not sure I can handle you in my bed."

"I don't want to make things hard for you."

"What do you want?"

"Your forgiveness."

She set the mug down, shifting toward him. "You've got it. I don't blame you for choosing your mom. I understand it. It's not like I ever thought you were a bad person."

He swallowed, his Adam's apple jerking. "No, sunshine, you were right. It wasn't my mom I was choosing. It was my past. What I was most familiar with. But, Nicole, that lasted all of a week. One week before I called your dad and got help."

"I'm glad my dad helped you, but—"

"Not just your dad. I'm going to Al-Anon meetings, too."

"You are?"

He nodded. "But even if I weren't, I told you, I see things differently. I'm not going back to my past. I don't *want* to. I want to move forward. With you."

Swiping a bead of sweat from over his lip, he sat up, pulled off his shirt and lay back down, drawing the throw up to his collarbone.

But not before she saw the spot of yellow on his chest. "What was that?" She reached to pull it back down. He didn't stop her.

He had a quarter-size sun on his chest, not centered, but slightly to the left. "Is that a tattoo? Is it permanent?"

"Forever." Oh, God, the look in his eyes made her insides melt. Just freaking melt.

"You got a tattoo of a sun on your chest—"

"Over my heart, sunshine."

"Why would you do that?" She couldn't help touching it.

"Because I never stopped loving you. Even when I left you on the street in New York City, even when I went back to Gun Powder, even when I filled out the application for Boulder, I loved you. I love you, Nicole. You're my deep down. And I want you back. All the way back."

Her body felt stretched thin, her emotions strung tight as a bow. She had no words, so she drew her legs up and clasped her hands together over her heart.

"You're my sunshine, the very best thing in my life. And I'm not going to stop until I get you back. I swear to you, Nicole, you can keep pushing me away, you can wait as long as you want to see if I choose my mom over you again, but it's never going to happen. No matter what happens with my mom or to my mom, I'm going to be with you. Because I *have* to." He reached under her knees and straightened her legs, uncurled her fingers and placed her hands on his warm chest, right over the tattoo. Then, he dragged her up against his body. "I *have* to."

She couldn't think. Everything locked up inside her. Her body trembled, as her heart started to ache. The ache turned into pain, and the pain grew to the point she thought her heart would crack wide open.

His gaze bore into her, penetrating and deep. "I love you. I never stopped, and I never will. You make me happy. You make me *free*."

Pain had a grip so tight she couldn't breathe. She had to look away from him. Resting her head in the crook of his arm, she traced the tattoo. *He made me part of him. Permanently.*

"Your mom won't change," he said. "Jonathan's not going to change, but *I* did. I changed for you because I want you more than I want to stay stuck in my past. *I choose you.*"

That did it. Something burst inside her—only it wasn't her heart. It was the bindings around it. She felt the shift in her chest as vividly as if someone had lifted a weight off her. She looked up at him and saw the truth in his eyes. And she believed him.

Holding his gaze, time seemed to stand still. And then he licked his lips, the movement lowering her gaze to his mouth. That beautiful, sexy mouth that loved her so passionately, so ardently.

Her cell phone rang, and Nicole sat up in a rush. "Hello? Dad?" She pushed the hair out of her eyes.

"Your brother's awake," her dad said. "He's doing just fine."

"Oh, thank God. Thank *God*. Okay, we'll be there soon.

Does he need anything? Do you need anything? Should I bring your toothbrush?"

"Slow down, sweetheart. Don't bother with anything. He'll be discharged in the morning."

"Okay." She turned to Dylan, mouthed, *He's okay*. He brought her hand to his mouth and kissed her palm. "He's um…he's going to be all right?"

"Yup. Get some rest. We'll see you in the morning."

"Are you sure? I'd really like to see him."

"It's late, and the doctor's with him. Best thing for him is to get a good night's sleep."

"Okay. You're right. Goodnight, Dad."

She set the phone down, turned to Dylan. Her mind spun, a tangle of emotions. Too much to process.

"Come here." Dylan held his arm open for her, and she curled up against him.

His big arm reached across her to turn off the light, then settled around her, pulling her tight against him.

"'Night," she whispered in the darkness. Thank God her brother was all right. She didn't know what she'd have done if he hadn't been.

"I've missed this." He lifted a strand of hair, wound it around his finger. "I missed you."

Her body vibrated with both need and anxiety. She wanted his hands on her, his mouth on her, his body pressed to hers. She'd missed him with such fierceness she'd been unable to get out of bed for the first few days.

But she couldn't move. She wanted to let go and love him—*God*, she wanted to love him. But she shouldn't even be thinking about it right now. She was tired, and her brother was in the hospital. She'd sleep now, worry about her and Dylan tomorrow.

Only her mind wouldn't shut down. Not for a second. Not when she felt his heat, the tension in his body—from his muscled thighs pressing into hers to the arm that cinched her waist. Even his breathing sounded short, shallow. Anxious.

As a child, she'd go to sleep like this every night. All wired and scared. Just like this. But her dad was right—she'd been helpless back then. Now, no matter what happened with her and Dylan, she wasn't helpless. She could handle anything—it would hurt, but she'd live through it. She'd be fine.

Just like that, her muscles let go, and she relaxed in his arms. He must've felt it because he shifted, burrowing in closer.

His nose at her ear breathed in. "When we're like this, everything just feels right."

*Oh, yes.* She felt it, too. Desire streamed through her. This was Dylan. He was here, he was back. She smiled when she realized he'd *fought his demons for her.*

For *her.*

She turned in his arms, loving the feel of his heat and powerful body. It was all hers. *He* was hers. Reaching for his hair, she scraped it off his face. "Dylan."

She kissed him. And, oh, God, did it feel good. The slam of need had her heart hammering, her blood pounding. To feel him again, to have his mouth devouring her—she'd thought she'd lost him.

But then he abruptly pulled away. His hand settled on her hip and held her firmly. "Get some sleep."

Rearing back, she tried to see his expression in the darkness.

"You're tired. You're upset." He paused. "I want you to be sure. About me. Us."

Her blood turned to honey, thick and sweet. This was her man. And she loved him with everything in her. She cupped his cheek. "Do you choose me?"

"*Yes.*"

"Then show me."

He groaned and, just like that, he tossed the throw off him, whipped her blanket back and off the bed. His mouth claimed hers, his hands cupping her face. He shifted on top of her, his hands hot on her skin, gliding along her curves. "I love you. I love you so fucking much."

He shoved his gym shorts down, kicked them off before covering her with his hard, hot body. "My sunshine." His mouth moved to her neck, licking, pressing kisses to her collarbone. "Tell me you want me. Tell me you want this."

"I do. You know I do."

"Lift." He drew her top up over her arms and flung it aside, tugged her pajama bottoms and panties off her hips. Palming her breasts, he devoured first one nipple, then the other.

His hands were on her everywhere, under her back, stroking down her belly and cupping between her legs. "I need you. All of you." His mouth followed the path of his hands until his shoulders pushed her legs apart and he licked inside her.

At the first lick of his tongue, electricity pulsed through her, and her hips shot off the mattress. She gripped his hair.

Hands sliding under her ass, he lifted her to his mouth, taking his time to love her—so sensuously, so intimately. It built fast, her senses inundated with him, with desire, her heart so full she thought it might burst.

"Oh, *Dylan.*" Head thrashing on the pillow, hips rocking wildly, she came in a rush of heat and deliciously churning energy.

His big body rose over her, one hand lifting her leg over his hip, as he pushed inside. Her neck arched, as she rose to meet his thrusts.

"Oh, God, Dylan."

He stopped, pulled back to look her in the eye. "I *love you.* And I'm giving you all of me. Not holding anything back."

Everything in her softened, slowed down, until she felt his words stir her soul.

Hands under her back, cupping her shoulders, he pulled almost all the way out. As he thrust back in hard, he sucked a nipple into his mouth, and she cried out. She rocked up to him, pressing hard, harder, her cries growing more urgent.

"Ah, fuck, Nicole. Jesus." He pounded into her. Sweat formed on his brow, a single drop taking a slow slide down his cheek. His head reared back. "Ah, God."

Her body bloomed, stretched open, and she let him in—all the way. She had him back, her love, her heart, her man. And it was *everything.*

"I'm gonna come, sunshine. Oh, Christ, I'm gonna come." Big hands clamped down on her hips, pinning her to the mattress, as his strokes quickened. He gasped, short intakes of breath, and then he roared with his release, slamming into her so hard he rocked her up the bed until her head hit the bunch of stacked pillows. His features tensed, and he kept rocking, gasping with each new surge of his release.

He collapsed on top of her, their bodies damp. And then he nuzzled her neck, his hair on her cheek. As he rolled off her, his arm banded around her, pulling her until they were jammed against each other.

With a hand over his tattoo, she felt the rapid beat of his heart.

"It's you and me, sunshine," he said. "Whatever life throws our way, we deal with it together."

Something he'd said kept running through her mind, stirring up her blood. He'd called her his deep down. And she got it. She did.

Because that's exactly what he was to her.

Her deep down.

# CHAPTER TWENTY-TWO

**In the settling dusk, the edge of the horizon a brilliant** apricot-colored band of light, the greenhouse glowed. The solar lanterns they'd hung from the ceiling gave the place an ethereal look—almost like a spaceship.

Dylan dug his key out of his pocket, glad for the automatic lock he'd thought to purchase since Nicole spent so many hours in here at night.

The moment he opened the door the humidity hit him. His gaze instantly sought and found her. In her pretty white and yellow wrap dress, she scooped a handful of soil and dumped it into an earthenware pot. Her dark hair gleamed in the yellow lights.

Affection rushed him hard, and goosebumps popped along his arms.

*She's mine.*

Sometimes he couldn't believe it. Couldn't believe how his life had turned from dark and desperate to light and...well, happy. This unbelievable woman, who'd created a community garden a block off Main Street and on the edge of campus, who'd helped transform a fledgling sustainability culinary program into a model for top schools across the country, was his heart and soul.

He moved toward her, the door slamming shut behind him, and she glanced over her shoulder.

Her face lit up with warmth and happiness, and another emotion erupted inside him, this one making his blood hum. He loved her. He fucking loved her with every fiber of his being.

"Hey." Hands dirty, she swiped the hair off her face with her forearm. "Almost done here."

"Yeah? Everyone's on their way."

She did a slow sweep of his body. "You look like the pied piper of sorority girls."

In his khakis and button-down, he probably did look a little fratty. But he'd bought these clothes years ago for his summer internships at Pearson Greene. Plus, they'd graduated today and were heading out to celebrate in a few minutes. So, it wasn't like he had a choice. "You gonna join in?"

"Nah. I'm gonna keep you all to myself."

Coming up behind her, he belted his arms around her waist. "You and me. Just how I like it." He leaned down, pressing a soft kiss to her cheek, and breathed in her light honeysuckle scent. Her soft skin, her silky hair, the hitch of breath she always made when he touched her…it made him ache with desire for this woman who'd been by his side these last four years.

He kissed the curve of her neck, and she pushed back into him. *Oh, damn.* She always got him so stirred up. When her hips swayed against him with gentle pressure, desire pounded in his bloodstream.

They couldn't start anything. Not with everybody on their way into town.

But he didn't let her go. His mouth wandered up to her jaw, and he nudged aside her hair to lick the shell of her ear.

Her hand closed over his and squeezed. "Dylan." He loved that whispery tone, the urgent request.

Leaving a trail of kisses along her cheek, his fingers fisted in her dress, raising it just a little. And then she turned—just slightly—giving him access to her mouth.

She turned in his arms, wrapped her arms around his neck, and opened to him. Nothing felt as good as the silky heat of her mouth, the sensual slide of her tongue. And with her hips rocking into him, she made him burn.

She pulled away, resting her forehead on his chest. "I love you."

There it was again, that pounding rush of emotion. He tipped her chin, captured her mouth, and showed her with his kiss how fiercely he loved her, too.

Her fingers dug into his back. "Dylan."

It drove him crazy when she sounded like that, all urgent and desperate; when she got that sexy as fuck look of abandon in her eyes.

He needed her mouth. Needed the hot lick of her tongue, the fierce and sizzling connection. His tongue coaxed hers back into play, and—*fuck*—he burst into flames.

He drank in her love, inhaled it, completely reveled in it. Sometimes he felt starved for her. She filled him with her goodness and purity, her love and warmth, and he didn't think he'd ever get his fill.

Hands gripping her ass, he lifted her, and she wrapped her legs around his waist.

Angling his head, he deepened the kiss and breathed in her sweet, fresh scent. He couldn't get close enough. He wanted more. Always more. "I love you, Nicole. I fucking love you so much." Burning need swept through him fast and fiery—

"Dylan?" Sydney called in the distance. "Nicole?"

"Fuck." He relaxed his hold, started to put her down, but she tightened her arms and legs.

"Wait. Before everyone gets here, I just want to tell you how proud I am of you."

He could barely catch his breath, and his body shook with want, but he listened.

Because, yeah, it was pretty amazing. Four years ago he couldn't imagine graduating college—let alone with honors and Nicole by his side—but here he was.

"I remember once telling you that you were a coward but, God, Dylan, I was so wrong. You're a good man—*such* a good man. I didn't understand it then, but I do now. Because you fought for what you believed in. And you believed with all your heart that your mom was your responsibility—and *of course* you did. It's what she'd told you your entire life. But once you figured it all out, that you couldn't help her, that you needed to take care of yourself, you let her go. And you put all that strength, all that loyalty and energy, into your own life, into *us*. And I'm grateful—I mean, I'm so unbelievably grateful you chose me—and I'm so proud of you for the man you've become." She smiled, scraping her fingers through his hair. "My man."

Oh, hell. It wasn't about his accomplishments. It was about *him*. She had a way of making him feel like a fucking superhero. "How the hell did I ever find you?"

"We found each other." She pressed her sexy mouth to his, stirring up all that desire and need, and he backed her against the wall, grinding into her.

"Oh, look at the greenhouse." Sydney's voice came

closer. "It's so pretty."

Breathing hard, Dylan lowered his face into the curve of her neck. Nicole cupped the back of his head, shaking with laughter. "Later."

He didn't know if he could wait.

Sifting her fingers through his hair, she said, "We've got the rest of the night."

"The rest of our lives."

Their gazes locked, the meaning behind his words ricocheting between them, until he saw the moment it finally sank in. Her features softened.

"The rest of our lives," she whispered.

"How does she get it to light up like that?" Sydney neared the greenhouse.

"She leaves the solar lamps out all day and brings them in at night," James said. "But she also wrapped recycled aluminum around cardboard so the light reflects off it."

"This thing is *so* cool."

"Yeah. That's my Nic."

"I mean, it's like glowing." Sydney sounded like she was right outside the door.

Slowly, Dylan set her down. He cupped her chin, pressing soft kisses to her mouth.

"Dylan? Nic?" Sydney called again, this time right outside. The door rattled. "You in there?"

Nicole smiled up at him, radiant and sweet. The most beautiful woman in the world. He held her gaze, heart full. "Yeah."

"Might be cool if you unlocked the door," James said.

"One sec." Nicole smoothed the skirt of her dress.

He grabbed her hand, and they edged between the counter and the row of freshly planted snap peas.

"Guys, come on." James rattled the door. "The McCaffrey horde is advancing."

Dylan unlocked it. Stepping out into the peach dusk of a cool May evening, Dylan saw Uncle Zach waving, as he headed up the street toward their little community garden. The greenhouse took up a quarter of it, so the neighborhood and school could make use of it year-round.

"Diwin!" One of his little cousins squirmed out of her mom's arms and came toddling over to him. He scooped her up, her sticky hand cupping his face. "I wuv you, Diwin." She smelled of candy and baby shampoo.

And then they were all there. His aunts, uncles, cousins—the whole family had flown in for his graduation. They wanted to see the greenhouse before heading out for a celebratory dinner.

Just for a moment, he thought about his mom. She'd tried rehab once more, but it hadn't stuck. She was living with some guy in Carbondale. He talked to her from time to time, but she was so rarely sober they didn't connect much. He'd long given up believing she'd get better. Not that he'd extinguished all hope. He'd never do that.

"Dylan." Uncle Zach drew him in for a bear hug. "Proud of you."

"You skishing me." Little Emma squirmed between them.

"Nicole," a big voice bellowed.

"Hey, Dad." Nicole got swallowed up in her dad's arms. And then her feet were off the ground. "Oh."

Her brothers came up behind him, their women in tow. The men wore navy blazers and khaki pants, shiny leather shoes and well-groomed hair. The women wore curve-hugging dresses and expensive shoes.

His family couldn't have looked more different with their southwestern flair. The men wore pearl-button shirts and cowboy boots, while the women wore silver and tooled-leather purses. They looked just like what they were—hard-working mountain people.

As he took in their families surrounding him, peace settled over him. A happiness he'd never dared hope for reared up and just for a moment emotion swelled so hard he couldn't breathe.

*This is my life.*

Thanks to her. He reached for her hand, clasped it tightly. He'd done all right.

They'd take the summer off to travel, but in the fall he'd be at Columbia Business School, while Nicole started her job with Feeding America in New York City.

She squeezed his hand, and he knew she felt it, too.

As long as they had each other, everything was right in the world.

Thank you for reading this book! The next book in the Wild Love series, *Mine for the Week*, comes out soon. Please sign up for my newsletter to find out when it will be up for preorder. I would love to get to know you better, so come hang out with me on Facebook, Twitter, and Instagram.

**Newsletter:**
http://erikakellybooks.com/contact.html

**Twitter:**
@erikakellybooks

**FaceBook:**
https://www.facebook.com/erikakellybooks/

**Instagram:**
@erikakellyauthor

**Website:**
http://www.erikakellybooks.com/

**Mine for the Week**
**(book 2 in the Wild Love series), coming soon!**

# CHAPTER ONE

**"Like shootin' fish in a barrel."**

"I'm going for the hot blonde with the tight ass."

"That narrows it down."

Ryan O'Donnell's friends burst out laughing and then spread out to claim their fun for the night. A singles resort wasn't exactly what he'd had in mind when he'd called his buddies to take this trip, but what the hell. The dance floor teemed with grinding bodies—flashes of bare skin, red lipstick, and glittering jewels. He wasn't complaining.

He didn't dance, so when he spotted a hot brunette sitting alone at a table, he headed in her direction. She looked up as he approached, her features softening, eyelids lowering, and her tongue took a slow glide across her glossy upper lip. Then, she lifted a hand, curved her fingers into a claw, and meowed.

*Okay*. Maybe a drink first? Yeah, a drink. They'd arrived twenty minutes ago, and he'd been traveling all day. He could use to loosen up a little.

As he headed toward the bar, his phone vibrated in his pocket. He tensed. Pulling it out, he scanned a couple of the most recent texts.

*Everything okay?*
*When you coming back?*
*You okay dude?*

Damn, when he'd made up the story, he hadn't considered anyone's reaction. He hadn't thought about anything. He'd just run.

And then he saw a voicemail from his coach. His chest went tight.

Okay, so, he either returned the call now and listened to Coach tell him to come back to school, or he ignored it and took his break. What was it going to be? *You in or out?*

*Fuck it.* He had six days to forget about everything and have a good time—

"Hey, there."

Ryan's head snapped up at the sound of a sultry voice. The accompanying face and body didn't disappoint. He shoved the phone back in his pocket. "Hey. Ryan O'Donnell."

"Carrie Winters. I saw the three of you standing there." She blew out a slow breath. "The trifecta of holy hotness. It's like winning the lottery or something."

His smile broadened. As athletes, they tended to get attention like that. Jake, at six-six, with his dark hair and olive skin, had women falling all over him. Dixon might've been shorter than the two of them, but he was a powerhouse of pure muscle. His blonde hair, shaggy and overgrown like a surfer, got him the attention his height and looks didn't.

"Can I get you something to drink, Carrie?" Unlike most island resorts with tiki lamps and strings of lights, Isla de los Amantes had gleaming black lacquer tables, silver vases filled with exotic orchids, and crystal chandeliers. A safe haven for wealthy singles, it was known for its Vegas attitude. *What happens on Santa Grenada stays on Santa Grenada.*

He made a move to the bar, but she stepped in front of him, planting her hands on his chest.

"Let's just skip to the part where I'm in bed with all three of you at once."

*Yup.* He really needed that drink. "How about we start with a beer?"

"Oh, honey. Don't you know?" She got up on her toes, her breasts brushing against him, and whispered in his ear. "I'm a sure thing." Gliding a hand from his shoulder to his biceps, she gave it a squeeze. "You're seriously the hottest man I've ever seen. I can't wait to get you naked."

Step one in letting loose stood before him. This woman was ready to get down and dirty, no strings attached. He should go for it.

Instead, he stepped sideways and moved around her. "I'm gonna grab a beer. You want one?"

"Ah. A virgin."

"Excuse me?"

"Don't worry. I love virgins. I can't wait to break you in."

The last thing he should be feeling right then was irritation. With her long dark hair and curvy figure, Carrie was hot. Clearly, she had no inhibitions. He couldn't ask for a better way to launch spring break. "Virgins, huh?"

"Resort virgins. I can't wait to initiate you. Let's go to my room."

"I'm gonna grab that drink first." He pushed through to the bar and lifted a finger to get the bartender's attention.

Carrie's hand caressed his ass and gave it a squeeze. "I'm not used to resistance, but I admit the build-up's making me even hotter for you."

He grinned at her. "So, Carrie Winters, where you from?"

"Boston. You?"

"I go to school in Michigan, but I'm from Connecticut."

"You're still in school?"

"Senior, but yeah. What do you do?"

"I'm a realtor, and I'm about four years older than you. I've never been a cougar, but that's what I love about this place. I can be whatever I want."

"And what do you want to be?"

An ocean-scented breeze fanned her hair out. Her skin-tight dress revealed a toned body with generous mounds of flesh bursting out of the deep neckline. "When I'm here? Fucking wild. I work in my dad's firm, so I have to be perfect. All the time. And I love it. I'm not complaining. I make a ton of money, and the clients come to me. But sometimes I need to let loose, you know?"

"I do." Christ, did he know.

Her features turned sultry. "Obviously, or you wouldn't be here. I've been coming here for four years because there's no bullshit. You can just do your thing with anyone, anywhere, anytime. And there's no walk of shame. No worrying if the guy'll call you again. I love it."

He tugged at the collar of his shirt. Was it warm in here? He checked to see if he stood under a heat lamp.

"So, come on, Hollywood. What do you say we take that movie star smile up to my room? As sensational as it is, I'd love to replace it with something a whole lot filthier."

He appreciated her straight-forward approach—he did—but maybe what he needed was a work-out, a hot shower, and a good night's sleep. Tomorrow he'd start fresh.

Just then Jake bustled up to them. "Hey, how's it going?" But before either could respond, he clapped a hand on Ryan's shoulder. "Can I talk to you for a sec?" Then, he turned to Carrie. "Will you excuse us?"

"Sure. We'll catch up later." She smiled and headed toward the dance floor.

Jake led him to the side of the outdoor bar. "How's it going?"

"Great, why?"

"Looked like maybe you were gonna bail on that very nice young woman."

*And that's the problem with knowing someone all your life.* "I might work out. Been traveling all day."

"That's pretty much what you'd be doing if you were at school. But isn't that why you called me? To get a break from all that shit? Yeah, you could go to the gym like you always do. Or, I don't know…" He gave a chin lift to Carrie, who'd already turned her attention to another guy. "You could motorboat the bodacious tits of that woman who clearly wanted to climb you like a tree."

"I'll probably do both."

"Maybe she's not your type? Not a problem, since you've basically got a Babes-R-Us selection here. But, hell, man, look around. Every woman you see wants the same thing we do. That's the whole point of coming here—everyone gets what they want without the bullshit. So, come on. Who you bangin' first?" Jake gestured to the crowd like a game show hostess.

He took a step into Jake's space. "When I said I needed a break, I meant a break from the pressure. Six days to do what I want when I want. *That's* why I'm here."

Jamming his hands deep into his pockets, Jake looked thoughtful for a moment. "You wanna know why we'd let you blow off spring training?"

The reminder hit like a fastball to the gut. *Christ.* He'd never lied to a coach in his life.

And, come on, his *family emergency* happened to fall the week of spring break? Coach Harding deserved better than a cheap lie from the captain of his baseball team.

"'Cause you're gonna blow. That's why. You're on the edge, and it's better to pull your ass out of there than let your coach, your agent, the *scouts*, watch you fuck up." He squeezed Ryan's shoulder. "Number one shortstop in the country."

"I hear you. But I'm going to have to do things my way. I appreciate you guys coming out here with me, but…" Ryan blew out a breath. "You gotta give me room, all right?"

Looking thoughtful, Jake scrubbed his jaw. "Not tellin' you anything you don't already know or you wouldn't have called me." He stabbed his finger into Ryan's chest. "But you need to go hard this week. Trust me on this. You're too fuckin' controlled. Yeah, all that discipline and focus is great—you wouldn't be a first draft pick without it—but you gotta hit that release valve sometimes, man. You got one week here to blow it all off, and to do it you need some good, hard fucking to get you loosened up and relaxed."

Damn, that rang true. Just hearing the words relieved some of the pressure. His friend was right. He did need to go *hard.*

Jake spun around. When he spotted Dixon at the bar, he waved him over.

Dix gave a jerk of his chin in acknowledgment, then whispered in his date's ear before making his way to them. "What's up?" He glanced over his shoulder, as if to make sure the woman he was talking to hadn't moved on to someone else.

"Our man here needs a little help selecting tonight's entertainment." Jake shoved his hands in his pockets and turned to the dance floor. He elbowed Dixon. "Who's a good starter chick?"

"Cut the shit." Ryan had ended things with Emma over Christmas break. "I've been single for three months."

They ignored him, as Dixon checked out the dance floor. "You want someone like Emma? Blonde, skinny?"

"I've been with other women besides Emma. We've broken up a lot over the last six years."

"Not the point. You always had Emma in the back of your mind. This time, you're totally free." Jake turned to him. "You are totally free, right?"

"Completely."

"Let him find his own girl," Dixon said.

"Now that's what I'm talkin' about." Jake pointed to a curvy woman striding around the perimeter of the dance floor. "And see, the thing is, you can have fun with her tonight and not have to hang out with her tomorrow. *She* won't want to." His finger shifted to a woman who looked very much like Emma. Slender, long blonde hair, fragile. "Look at the way she's eyein' you, bro. Hungry little minx. I'll bet she's a tiger in the sack. What do you say? Feel like kickin' back and lettin' her do the work?"

Jake had no idea how appealing that sounded. Six years with the same woman. Ryan had had enough of the dead fish routine. He'd loved Emma, of course, but begging for sex? Never again.

"That one." Jake's feral gaze landed on a sexy blonde with an hourglass figure, half-lidded eyes, and shiny red lipstick. "Now that's my kind of woman."

Irritation whipped through him. He'd had enough. "Have at it, man." He stalked off.

With all this energy barreling through him, he needed to hit the gym, blow off some steam. The moment he headed out, he saw a dark-haired woman kneeling on a bar stool, surveying the area with a concerned expression. In her white shorts and pale pink tank top, she didn't look anything like the other women in the bar. The oversized white sweater she wore drooped off one shoulder and didn't cover the ample breasts straining against the top. Her round ass stretched the cotton of her shorts, and when she licked her pink lips, biting down on the bottom one, a jolt of energy blasted through him.

*Her.*

He knew the rules now, understood no one wanted conversation. That suited him just fine.

Bailing on spring training might've cost him the respect of his teammates and coach. Bailing on his ex might've cost him his lifelong relationship with her family—and her dad was practically a father to him. Even he could see that, for the first time in his life, he wasn't making the smartest decisions. But just then?

This woman with her rosy complexion, sexy as fuck mouth, and body so ripe he wanted to sink his teeth into her ass? He knew exactly what he wanted.

With every step he took toward her, his heart beat faster. When he reached her, electricity flashed across his skin. She was beautiful and undoubtedly the sexiest woman he'd ever seen.

It went against his nature to be so blunt, but what the hell. He'd play by the resort rules. He stroked a finger down her thigh.

She jerked, looking down at him. "What the hell?"

Holding her fiery gaze, his breath froze in his lungs. "I want you." And, oh, man, did he want her.

"Excuse me?"

Not exactly the reaction he'd expected. *A little outside my comfort zone here.* But he wouldn't give up. "You. I want *you.*"

"Are you high?" She let out a huff of breath, yanking the sweater back up her shoulder. "Wow. That was super classy." Confusion turned to humor. "Yeah, for sure. Let me just shuck off my clothes and we can do it right here. Or did you want to drag me by my hair to the nearest table?"

*Yes.* But the outrage in her eyes doused his lust, leaving him flustered and uncomfortable. "Take it easy. I didn't mean…" He lowered his head, shaking his head. "What a night."

She laughed. "Well, if that's been your approach, no wonder your night's not going so well. Little tip for ya? Start off with a simple hello. Then maybe offer to buy a girl a drink. Jeez."

Ryan dropped his head back, and he dragged a hand through his hair. What the hell was he doing here? He'd rather be sitting alone in his room working on code than trying to navigate the waters of a pervy singles resort.

"Fuck it. Never mind." He struck off, thinking he'd lift weights. Or maybe run along the beach. But he didn't get more than a few feet before he realized he'd been a jerk. He turned back to apologize and found her climbing off the stool, her round ass hoisted high, her leg reaching for the floor. He took her arm, helping her.

Once she had her footing, she looked up at him. "Thank you."

Her long, dark hair gleamed in the yellow lights, and her blue eyes were lit with intelligence and an irresistible spark. And suddenly he felt like a total ass for treating her the way he had. "Look, I'm sorry for touching you. I don't…I'm not like that." He let out a breath and scratched the scruff on his chin. "Can I buy you a drink?"

Her good humor seemed to fade. "Three things. I don't drink, I have zero interest in a one-night stand, and I really need to find my friend right now." Her phone clattered to the wood floor, and they both crouched at the same time to retrieve it. When she leaned forward, her breasts plumped in the top, and a surge of lust rushed him so hard his dick pressed uncomfortably against the buttons of his jeans.

He handed her the phone, his whole world narrowing to this woman who smelled like vanilla and flowers and looked so round and luscious he wanted to squeeze her.

She gave him a distracted, "Thank you," before touching the screen of her phone as she stood.

Heading out of the bar behind her, he couldn't help catching her conversation. "Hey. I don't see Laura anywhere, and she's not answering her phone." She paused. "I said I can't find Laura." She was nearly shouting now. "Yeah, well, she's got my wallet." Another pause. "I was taking pictures when we got off the boat, and I handed her my bag. Anyhow, I'll go to the front desk and see if they'll loan me some cash, but then I'll jump in a taxi and come get you. Are you going to be all right until I get there?"

They were both headed to the lobby, so he couldn't miss the way her shoulders hunched and her arm wrapped across her stomach. "God, Kat. I can't believe this. Can you talk to the bartender? Is there someone there you can trust? Yeah, yeah, okay, don't worry. Let me get some money, and then I'm on my way."

Ryan stepped up to her. "What do you need?"

She lowered the phone from her mouth. "I'm seriously not interested. I mean, at *all*." Striding down the stone walkway, she continued her conversation. "You sure you don't want to call the police?"

"I'm not trying to hit on you. You obviously need help." But she ignored him. Well, Christ. When did he become the creep a girl had to get away from?

All right, enough. Time to put an end to this day. He'd head up to his room and change into gym shorts.

"Kat, I *am* hurrying. But I need cash for a cab, and I think town's at least twenty minutes away."

They'd reached the door to the lobby, so he held it open. Blocking her way, he pulled out his wallet, yanked out some bills, and thrust them at her.

She stopped, gazing up at him as though trying to figure out his motives. "Hang on a second," she said into the phone. "Are you sure? I mean, why are you doing this?"

"I'm paying for sex. How much will this get me?"

When her jaw dropped and her eyes went round, he gave her a disbelieving look. *Really?* She thought he was capable of *that*? "You need some cash. I'm happy to give you some."

"Kat? I'm good. I got it, so I'm on my way." She started to lower the phone, but then jerked the phone back to her ear. "Wait, Kat? Listen. Stay in the bathroom until I get there. Promise me you'll lock yourself in a stall. Okay, see you." She took the money. "I don't know what to make of you, but I need this, so, thank you. I'll pay you back tomorrow."

Ryan shoved his wallet back in his pocket. "Not necessary." He stepped aside, letting her go through the doors. She breezed past, leaving him in a cloud of her sweet scent.

"Is your friend all right? I heard you talking."

"She went into town with some guy she met here." She glanced at him over her shoulder, as she headed across the wide-planked wood floor of the vast lobby. "He dumped her for someone else, and now she's stuck in a really scary bar. You know it's DJ week on the island, right? So the town's jammed with people, everyone partying like it's the end of the world, and she's scared to death."

"Is she in danger?"

"A bunch of drunken idiots had her backed against a wall. She managed to run into the bathroom, but she's afraid to come out. She can hear them outside the door."

"Do you need me to come with you?"

"I...what?"

Why did she still look like she couldn't trust him? *Him*, for Christ's sake.

*Right.* Because he'd touched her. Told her he wanted her. Had he really done that? He was more fucked up than he realized. "Do you have a plan for how you're going to help your friend against those guys?"

Her features fell. "I didn't really think about it, but no, I guess not."

"Then I'll go with you."

"I don't have time to argue, and I really could use the help of those nice muscles you've got there, so I'm not going to argue if you want to come." She strode forward, heading outside.

A slight chill in the air had her hugging her arms across her chest. He couldn't help but notice the way her breasts pushed together, creating a mound he found ridiculously distracting. "I'll grab a cab."

As he headed to the valet station, he thought about all those women in the bar down to party with him right then. He could be pounding babes and brews, just like his friends.

Instead, he was heading into town with the one woman at the resort who had no interest in him.

And, strangely, there was nowhere else he'd rather be.

Made in the USA
Lexington, KY
18 December 2016